The Sorcerer's RETURN

BROCK E. DESKINS

MYSTIQUE PRESS

"The outcome of any battle is largely based upon proper preparation," Azerick explained. "They will have the superiority of numbers and even raw power, particularly since I cannot bring my full power to bear without risking losing control. I also do not want to kill them."

"Why not? They'll kill you to get the codex back, won't they?" Ellyssa demanded.

"Probably, but they aren't convinced of the danger I warned them about. Humans are just too short-term thinking."

"You said we had to save the world. I thought you were joking."

Azerick smiled and shook his head. "No, I am not much for jokes these days. We are all in a great deal of danger."

"From what?"

"An ancient foe, banished by the gods, is returning. They will annihilate nearly every intelligent race on the planet if we do not stop them."

"Can't the gods destroy them, or at least banish them again?" Ellyssa asked.

"It will be a war between gods, and the old gods are stronger. Our gods will need our help to have a chance at victory, and that means I need every man, woman, and wizard to fight with me. That is why I cannot simply kill the inquisitors or the Academy wizards who will invariably resist what I tell them. I need to beat them soundly without killing them, at least not many of them, and hope it is enough of a deterrent to keep them from trying to take the codex by force. As the only ones able to use it to its fullest, it must remain with us so that we can prepare for the final battle."

To my wonderful children: Jenice, Josh, and Elissa.
I hope you know how much I love you all.

CHAPTER 1

When Raijaun was not clinging to Azerick's back with his arms clasped around his neck, he was scurrying along the ground and climbing the sparse trees chasing after small animals. When he caught one, he devoured it fur, bones, and all. It was fortunate Raijaun could not fly yet; Azerick doubted his ability to control him if he could.

Azerick chose to stick close to the Great Barrier Mountains. Not only was it nearly a straight line to Argoth, it was an out-of-the-way route that allowed him to avoid most human settlements. Few people made their homes near the imposing mountain range. The unnatural peaks were viewed with a significant amount of superstition, and the lands near them were rocky and provided few resources. Rains washed much of the soil farther down into the valleys where people erected small towns to eke out a living as farmers and ranchers.

He could have shifted back into Klaraxis's form and flown to Argoth in a fraction of the time, but his control over the demon lessened when he gave up his human body. Azerick also luxuriated being in his own body, especially here in his world where it almost made him feel normal. He knew it was a lie, but it was real enough to provide a measure of peace to his otherwise troubled soul.

He also needed to spend time with Raijaun before entering Argoth. His son's demonic nature was at the fore, and he needed to teach him to embrace his other parts. Lissandra said he would rise to great power, and Azerick needed to shape him into a rational and decent person or the results could be catastrophic.

Azerick spotted his son near the top of an aspen tree. "Raijaun, come down. It is getting dark, and it is time we made camp."

Raijaun glanced down at his father before turning his attention back to another tree nearby. He tensed his muscles in a crouch and leapt, using his wings to guide him toward his target. Raijaun landed atop the unwitting opossum. His short but sharp claws locked onto the creature and a swift bite to the back of its neck ended its struggles.

"Raijaun," Azerick shouted again, "come down now!"

Raijaun glared and growled a protest before obeying. His meal clamped in his teeth, Raijaun descended with the ease of a cat and cautiously approached his father. Azerick knelt and beckoned his son over.

Azerick reached toward the dead animal Raijaun held in his hands. "Give me that."

Raijaun pulled the opossum in tighter and hissed in response.

"Give it to me, now," Azerick ordered more forcefully.

Raijaun narrowed his reptilian, golden eyes but relented. He shuffled forward and set his kill in Azerick's outstretched hand. Azerick directed a small amount of his abyssal power at the unfortunate creature and peeled the skin and fur away. He then gestured to a firepit, and the logs combusted into a flickering orange glow. He proceeded to spit the carcass on a stick and roast it over the flames.

"This is how civilized people eat," Azerick patiently explained. "You must learn this. Your appearance is going to make it difficult for people to accept you, so it is important for you to act appropriately. Let people see your good character, and the important ones will accept you. Do you understand?"

Raijaun flicked his eyes at his father, but the crackling of dripping fat and the smell of roasting meat took them captive again. He shuffled his feet impatiently and reached for the cooking meat.

"No," Azerick said, "you need to wait until it is cooked."

Raijaun hissed his displeasure and made another grab.

"No."

His son began stamping and clawing the ground.

"Throw a tantrum all you want," Azerick said calmly. "You will not eat until it is done."

Raijaun growled and spit, then stared at the fire intently. Cocking his head to one side and furrowing his brow in concentration, he extended a clawed digit and drew a shape in the air. Azerick dropped the spitted meat and leapt back as the flames of his campfire erupted upward. Raijaun darted in, grabbed the charred stick holding his meal, and snatched it from the fire.

Azerick held out his hand. "Give it here. It's not done."

Raijaun worked his tongue around in his mouth and smiled. "No."

Azerick could not help but grin at his son's first word, regardless of his defiance. Taking his father's smile as a sign of approval, Raijaun began dancing around the fire with the carcass held over his head, gleefully repeating "No!" The meat was seared on the outside and raw in the middle, but Azerick decided it was good enough and let him have it. The demonic child then shoved it into his mouth and began savagely tearing at the meat.

This time Azerick did get up and take his food away. "We do not eat like that. Eat like this." Azerick began pulling off strips of meat with his fingers and popping them in his mouth to demonstrate before handing it back to his son.

Raijaun snatched the food from Azerick's hands and made to cram it in his mouth once more.

"No," Azerick said.

"No!" Raijaun countered.

"Yes."

"No!"

Azerick glared at his son. Raijaun let out a loud huff through his nose and began picking off strips of meat as he had been told. Seeing his son was going to behave, Azerick pulled a book and quill from his small satchel and started writing. Raijaun watched him intently as he consumed his meal, sidling over and peering past Azerick's shoulder as he wrote. Raijaun finished eating and drew in the air with his finger. He then reached over Azerick and tapped the page of his book.

"Those are letters," Azerick explained. "When put in order, they make words. These words are telling us about the Scions. I will need to tell a lot of people about them and the danger they represent. Writing it down is the best way to do so."

Raijaun drew in the air once more, so Azerick grabbed a small stick and scribbled in the dirt. "I'll show you the letters of the alphabet."

Azerick began scratching out the letters while Raijaun watched attentively. He used the claw of his index finger in an attempt to mimic his father's drawings in the dirt. He did well on the letters with straight lines, but curved shapes were a trial.

"Like this." Azerick drew the letter again with deliberate care.

Raijaun tried again, but the curve came out scraggly.

"Watch carefully," Azerick said as he drew the shape again.

Raijaun tried once more, but the shape vexed him. He clawed at the dirt, destroying the letter, and raced up a nearby tree, where he began tearing off the smaller limbs in a fit of pique.

"Tantrums will not solve your dilemma, only practice and rational thought," Azerick called up to his son.

Raijaun climbed back down the tree and gestured at the fire, causing the flames to erupt again. "Fire!"

"Yes, fire. Very good, but you still need to learn how to read and write. Still, at four days old, you are a very smart boy."

Angry, temperamental, and lashes out violently when vexed. So much like his father, Klaraxis said inside Azerick's head.

"Shut up, demon. You are not, nor will you ever be, his father."

I was referring to you.

"Hilarious, now go away and sulk some more. I have a lot to do without you distracting me."

Azerick went back to writing while Raijaun doodled in the dirt. He had so much to do and so many things to put in place, he wondered if it was remotely possible. It reminded him of the old joke, "How do you eat a dragon? One bite at a time." His first bite was writing down everything he knew about the Scions and developing an intense training regimen to fight the terrifying horde of creatures at their command.

At the same time, he needed to teach Raijaun everything. It would be one thing to teach him magic, but he had to teach him basic education and behavior, and that before he learned how to incinerate a city all on his own. From what Azerick had already observed, he did not have much time. Fortunately, it appeared as though Raijaun was a very fast learner. Of course, that meant Azerick had even less time to teach him.

Neither Azerick nor his son slept. Azerick had no need of such a thing, but Raijaun did occasionally sleep when he was bored or simply because he wanted to. When Azerick finally looked up from his writing, he saw Raijaun had scribbled letters throughout the entire clearing. He looked around for his son and spotted him hanging upside down from a low tree branch with a large rabbit clasped in his hands. Raijaun caught his father's visual cue and looked at the rabbit.

"Fire!" Raijaun said, then gestured with a free hand.

A small ball of fire hot enough to burn away every strand of fur and crisp the outer skin burst between his hands. Azerick nodded, conceding it was enough, and began packing away his things while his son ate his morning meal. His table manners still needed work, but he was getting better every day.

The morning was just dawning, casting the increasingly sparse forest in a blue twilight. Winter must be near at hand or on the way out. The air was crisp, and plumes of fog belched from their noses and mouths with every breath. The chill air was no more a problem than the wan light thanks to their monstrous physiology.

The walk to their destination was long, and Azerick spent the days writing and educating his son. He avoided teaching Raijaun any magic since he was still quick to react in anger. This did not prevent him from discovering some small spells on his own, spells which kept Azerick on his toes and with a quick admonishment on his lips. Raijaun was yet another thing in which time was determined to battle against him. One bite at a time, he kept reminding himself.

The farther south they traveled, the more barren the land became. The sparse trees dwindled into shrubs and continued to shrink until only an occasional thorny twig crawled out from under a boulder. The days were warm but the nights near freezing. Were either of them human, it would have been a treacherous journey. Azerick avoided the few small settlements and rare traveler. Despite its ruggedness, the rocky desert provided valuable minerals for those willing to brave the inhospitable land.

It was three weeks of unhurried travel before they reached the city of Argoth. The city was a sprawling affair of mostly two- and three-story sandstone structures. Argoth was the primary center of commerce for all eastern Valeria and Sumara. Throngs of people crowded the bustling streets, engaging in boisterous trading or just trying to navigate from one place to another as Azerick was doing.

Azerick held Raijaun close to his chest, concealing his features within a deeply hooded peasant's tunic and trousers. It did not take long for him to spot the castle located in the center of the city, as well as the less expansive but equally impressive Hall of Inquisition. He assumed Ellyssa and the codex were both secured inside the hall, but he needed to find someplace safe for his son. If he failed to intimidate the inquisitors into submission, things could get ugly, and he did not want his son caught in the middle.

He knew the perfect place, and it did not take long to find it. The brothel was only half a mile from the city center, and its staff was accustomed to unusual requests. They also understood the value of gold and the threat of harm. Azerick drew several looks as he entered, some of scorn for bringing a child in with him, but most simply sized him up to judge his wealth.

A woman in silk robes and wearing a thick layer of makeup to hide her middle-aged appearance sauntered toward him. "Hello there, handsome. What's your pleasure today?" she purred in a seductive voice.

"No pleasure, only duty, I am afraid," Azerick replied. "I have business to attend to that is best not conducted in front of my son, so I am leaving him in your care."

"Sweetie, this is a brothel, not a nanny service or boarding school. I have enough trouble with my girls bringing their little bastards into work."

"I understand, but my son is special."

"Honey, everyone thinks their kid is special. Half of them ain't, and the half who are, ain't special in a good way."

Azerick tilted Raijaun's head up so the madam could see his face. The woman gasped and took a step back as her hand flew to her painted lips. Even her liberal use of blush did not hide the paling of her face.

"Dear gods, what is that?"

"He is my son, and I shall pay you well to watch over him." Azerick pulled out a pouch and trickled several small but flawless gems into his hand. "These shall be yours for performing what should be a simple task. All you need to do is keep him safe until I return. Should I fail to return within twenty-four hours, you will follow the instructions on this note."

Azerick pulled a slip of paper from another pocket of his black clothes. "You will give this letter and my son to whoever is in charge of the next Tower Trading Company caravan to arrive in the city. When last I knew, they had one arriving every three months. I do not know when the last was here or when the next shall arrive, but it should be easy to find out."

The madam visibly swallowed and took several deep breaths. "I-I don't know if I can."

"My dear lady, it is not a request." Azerick cast an incantation upon the pouch of jewels and placed it into the trembling woman's hand. "In case you think to abandon your duty and disappear with your riches, know I have placed a spell upon them. Not only will I know where to find you, but your flesh will shrivel and your eyes shall melt from their sockets if you try. I killed the mushadan of one of Sumara's largest cities and slew almost a score of his wizards because he had purchased my apprentice to be his slave. Imagine what I would do for my son. Imagine it well, madam," he finished softly.

"W-what shall I do with him?" she asked, barely able to command her trembling legs to keep her upright.

"Take him to one of your rooms and make him comfortable. He has a voracious appetite and will want to eat frequently. Meat seared on the outside for the sake of civility. He also enjoys milk with an even mixture of blood."

"B-blood? Whose blood?"

Azerick could not suppress the smile tugging at his lips. "I recommend goat for both. I saw a multitude of them on my way across the city, so it should pose no problem to get either. Remember my instructions and follow them to the letter." Azerick knelt next to Raijaun. "Raijaun, I must go take care of some things, and it is too dangerous to bring you with me. I need you to stay here and behave yourself. Do you understand?"

Raijaun nodded solemnly and took a step toward the madam. To her credit, she did not run from the room screaming or even step away, despite what the terrified portion of her brain demanded. Her fear of the small creature next to her paled in comparison to what she felt for the young man.

I am impressed, Klaraxis said as Azerick pushed through the bustling streets toward the Hall of Inquisition. *You are finally acting the way you should, instead of with all the simpering please and thank you of a weakling.*

"Do not think I did not feel your influence on my emotions and action. In this case, I felt it expedient to give in to your manipulations. If you are as smart as you keep proclaiming, you will not continue this battle over my actions. If I fail, we all die, including you."

I know this, fool. Why do you think I am not fighting you for **control** *every waking moment? But I still think I am better suited to fight the Scions than you are, and I will take* control *when you slip. But I will not distract you with our petty squabbles. When I take back my body, it will be swift, and you will not even know the battle has begun until you are sitting in this prison, able to do nothing but look out between the bars, just as I do now, and watch as I destroy everything you have created.*

"Fine. You can start by shutting up. I need to think."

CHAPTER 2

Inquisitors Elias and Fennrick sat in plush chairs across from Duchess Paullina who reclined on a sedan sipping wine in her parlor.

"Fennrick, what progress on the girl and the codex have we made?" the duchess asked.

Both inquisitors shifted nervously in their chairs. "None, Your Grace," Fennrick replied.

Duchess Paullina set her glass on the low table separating her from her guests and sat up. "None? It has been over a year since you brought her here. How is this possible?"

"The girl is extremely resilient," Fennrick explained defensively. "She has been subjected to torture before, and there appears to be little we administer that she has not already undergone. Couple that with her madness, and we face a significant challenge. I did inform you this would take time."

"Yes, and in this time, I have been plagued with the company of nearly a hundred pilgrims from the Academy, a dozen requests, each more insistent than the last, to hand over the Codex Arcana, and another five hundred requests from every wizard and charlatan in the kingdom to view it to see if it will speak to them. Headmaster Florent has threatened to start sending journeymen wizards here by the wagonload if we do not gain access to it soon!"

"Perhaps Fennrick is being too gentle," Elias suggested. "If she has faced pain before, we simply need to apply more pain than those Sumaran barbarians did."

Fennrick shook his head. "It is not that easy. I have applied a great deal of pain. When it gets too much, she simply goes catatonic and becomes completely unreachable, for days sometimes. If we continue to push as we are, we risk sending her over the edge forever."

"Then what are we going to do?" the duchess demanded.

Elias stared at the ceiling and let out a slow breath. "I am at a loss, Your Grace."

"Of course you are! You always are because you are an idiot! Obviously, I was asking Fennrick."

"I have concluded that we will not find the solution through physical means, even those of discomfort as we have been using. Sleep deprivation, near drowning, excessive heat and cold, none are working," the inquisitor said. "I think the resistance her emotional condition gives her against physical coercion could hold the solution."

Paullina leaned forward interestedly. "Explain."

"I have been studying the girl and doing research on mental abnormalities, and I think that if we are ever going to break her or convince her to help us, we must focus on her mind with no other physical stressors. We know there is a weakness already present. We simply need to find the most effective way to exploit it."

"I assume you have some ideas."

"I do. I think it is time she had some visitors."

Ellyssa sat on her cot, held her knees, and gently rocked back and forth. It had been days since they last tortured her, and she knew they would be coming again soon. She used to fear their coming with each beat of her heart, but not anymore. When the pain and turmoil got too bad, she simply went away. It was getting easier to go away these days. The first time it happened, she thought she had died, but then reality slammed home once again and she found herself back in this room.

She looked forward to going away even though it took so much pain and fear to get there, but it was worth it. When she went away, she was back home using her magic. Ellyssa realized it was not the huge, flashy, destructive magic that brought her the most joy. It was the simple things like the time she had stalked Wolf through the forest while he was hunting. She created an illusion of a rabbit and watched as Wolf chased it for over an hour, cursing furiously every time he failed to hit it with one of his arrows. Ghost saw right through her magical camouflage and almost certainly knew the rabbit was a fake, but he never let on. That was one unusual wolf.

Thinking about her magic got her wondering about the spells used to keep her from reaching the Source within her cell. She had first thought the runes carved deeply into the walls made the entire interior a magic-free zone, but later realized the wizards here had no problem using magic to torture her.

It meant there had to be an associative spell in effect as well, one that either acted with the runes to prevent her from using magic or allowed the inquisitors to cast within her cell. She searched her body for any magical sigils but failed to locate any. There could be something on her back, but she had no mirror to check. More likely, those tasked with her torture wore an item, like a bracelet or pendant working in conjunction with the negation magic in her cell to give them access to the Source. If this was the case, all she needed to do was take it from one of them, and then she would bring this whole place down upon them all.

The problem would be getting it. Ellyssa needed to know precisely what it was and where they wore it. If she tried to relieve them of it and failed, she likely would never get another chance. So far, she had seen nothing that appeared to be what she was seeking, if it even existed. For this reason, she held on, waiting for the day one of them got careless and revealed it.

Ellyssa snapped out of her thoughts when she heard voices echoing through her door from the passageway beyond. She flinched and drew back on her cot at the sound of the heavy bolt being drawn back. A startled gasp escaped her mouth when she saw Allister and Miranda filling the doorway.

"Hello, dear," Allister said kindly. "How are you?"

Ellyssa looked down at her feet drawn up against the edge of the cot and remained as silent as Miranda.

Seeing he would get no response, Allister continued. "We wanted to come and tell you we did not abandon you. The Academy, particularly the Office of Inquisition, wanted to execute you for your crimes. I made a protest to the Academy and Miranda sent an official plea for leniency. Although we were able to achieve a stay of execution, we were unsuccessful in getting you a pardon or moving your incarceration to North Haven. We even beseeched the king, but the Academy has a significant amount of autonomy. We have exhausted our last resources to try and improve your situation despite the damage you have done to the school and those within it."

Ellyssa looked away and studied the runes on the far wall as tears cleaned away some of the accumulated grime on her face.

"Inquisitor Fennrick told me of his offer to move you to more comfortable accommodations if you helped them use the codex," Allister continued. "I know you feel responsible, and maybe some of your unwillingness to accept their offer is so you can continue being punished for killing Azerick. You do not have to do that, child. You have suffered enough. Help them, and help yourself, because none of us can help you anymore."

Ellyssa returned her gaze to her feet, refusing to meet the old wizard's eyes. "I can't."

"Why not? You are not just helping them or yourself, you are helping to advance magic as we know it for all wizards. Ellyssa, the Codex Arcana could save countless lives."

Ellyssa shuddered and shook her head. "You wouldn't understand."

Miranda finally broke her silence as her anger reached its limits. "I understand perfectly! You have always been a stubborn, selfish child!"

"Miranda, please," Allister begged.

"No! I am sick and tired of pretending I forgive her, that I still give a damn about her! Her selfishness killed my husband, and I hope she clings to that same stubbornness so she can live in the same pain I do every day for the rest of her miserable life. I cannot stand to look at her anymore," Miranda declared, storming away, wiping the tears from her face as she retreated.

Allister watched Miranda for a moment before turning back to Ellyssa. "I'm very disappointed in you, as would be Azerick." He turned and followed Miranda.

Ellyssa flopped down onto her bed as sobs wracked her body. She desperately willed herself to go away again, but it was the wrong kind of pain to pay the fare, so she had no choice but to lie there and endure it.

Allister caught up with Miranda near the stairs leading out of the dungeon. Both stopped before Inquisitor Fennrick as he stepped into the hallway.

"How did it go?" Fennrick asked.

The couple's faces shimmered and contorted as they dropped their illusions. "Perfectly," Inquisitor Tamara answered.

"She is sobbing uncontrollably. Her spirit is seriously compromised if not broken," Inquisitor Mills said. "A few more sessions like this and we will certainly have access to the Codex Arcana."

"And you will have your promotion to senior inquisitor," Tamara added.

Fennrick beamed under the successful report. "I have to admit, using illusions against her fills me with a certain amount of ironic pleasure all its own. Well, I had best go play my part."

Fennrick walked toward the sound of Ellyssa's sobbing and paused in the open door until she sat up and looked at him. He had watched the girl tortured, even inflicted a great deal of suffering himself, but her face showed more pain than he had seen from her before. He doubted she was broken yet, but they had certainly managed to create a flaw in her defenses. Now he just needed to exploit it.

"I could not help but overhear," the inquisitor said. "It sounds like you are truly on your own now. You don't have to be, you know. I have been thinking. You showed a great deal of strength and cleverness when we fought. You certainly humiliated those Academy weaklings. We could use those kinds of talents here. Our numbers are declining just as the Academy rolls are, and our mission is vital to the security of the kingdom."

Fennrick tapped his chin as if in thought. "I think my associates would support me in requesting that you be given the chance to become one of us. It would be on a probationary basis, and you would be guarded and limited in freedom for a time, but if you showed you were willing to act properly and worked with us, I am sure I could convince the Academy to give you a chance. Think about it."

Fennrick turned and walked away. Ellyssa was so lost in thought she did not even hear the door slam shut and the lock clank home. She wanted to ignore the inquisitor, wanted to spit in his face as she had at his previous offers, but this time she could not help but consider it. And for that, she hated herself.

***

Fennrick wearily strode down the hall toward the senior inquisitor's office where Elias and Duchess Paullina awaited his weekly report. Not only did he have to disclose yet another week of failure, but now a dead man demanded an audience with the Council of Inquisition. He paused to compose himself before entering Elias's office. Elias sat behind his desk, ready to leap to the duchess's commands, while Her Grace reclined on a sedan sipping wine. Fennrick thought it was far too early for such libations, but the repeated image no longer surprised him.

"Fennrick, right on time as usual," the duchess said as he entered. "How goes your progress?"

"It goes as always," he answered in frustration, "Nowhere but backward. The use of illusion magic and mental manipulations appeared to have had some effect early on and appeared promising, but of late, the girl is increasingly slipping away to wherever her mind takes her, even under moderate coercion. However, that is the least troubling thing I have to report."

Paullina quirked an eyebrow at the inquisitor. "What else occurs?"

Fennrick cleared his throat and stiffened his spine before speaking. "It appears Lord Azerick Giles has returned from the dead and is now demanding an audience."

Elias's normally laconic expression vanished as he stood and leaned against his desk. "Lord Giles? Are you certain it is him?"

"He looks exactly like the portrait I spied of him in North Haven, and I detected no illusion or enchantment of any kind."

"Did you read his aura?"

Fennrick sighed. "Yes, Elias, I have been doing this for more than a few days now. Strongly sorcerous, but there was a hint of something else as well."

"What else?"

"I do not know," Fennrick admitted. "I have never encountered it before. I got a feeling it was deeply suppressed but dark and still very strong despite his attempts to hide it."

Duchess Paullina sat up and set her glass upon the low table before her. "There were rumors Lord Giles had an encounter with some kind of demon. Could that be the cause?"

"It is plausible, Your Grace," Fennrick replied, "particularly if any sort of possession took place."

"I am certain his death was no ruse. Could he have truly died and yet returned?"

"It is possible for mages of sufficient power to escape the afterlife, especially if they have the assistance of powerful wizards and clerics here amongst the living. I do not know if anyone has ever taken it beyond the theory, however."

Paullina paused for thought. "He does have both of those available to him. Where is he now?"

"In the anteroom awaiting an audience with the council. Your Grace, he did inform me he had pressing issues and would wait no longer than thirty minutes before taking matters into his own hands."

"Well, he certainly sounds like Lord Giles. Lord Giles or no, I'll not jump to it for the dead husband of my rival's daughter," she declared emphatically.

Fennrick cleared his throat. "Technically, Your Grace, this is an Academy matter for the inquisition council to address."

"Technically, I do not care," the duchess snapped. "This is my city and I will decide any matters concerning it. Now go summon the council and have them await me."

Seeing his subordinate about to argue, Elias ordered, "Now, Inquisitor."

Fennrick's body went rigid. He bowed slightly at the waist, spun smartly, and stalked from the room with suppressed indignation.

Paullina drained the last vestiges of wine from her glass. "I do believe the strain of the interrogations is wearing on our dear Fennrick. Maybe it is time we found another. Perhaps then we can get some results."

"Your Grace, if it is indeed Lord Giles, I must presume he is here for his apprentice as well as the codex," Elias warned.

"So what if he is? I'll hand over neither of those things. The codex is mine, and the girl is a criminal."

Elias's eyes shifted nervously. "I am just reminded of our reports of his activity in Bakhtaran, Your Grace."

The duchess waved a hand dismissively. "He had an army with him. Does he have an army here?"

"I imagine Fennrick has tasked a detail to look for such a thing and would have reported anything unusual."

"Then I see no reason to worry myself. It is not as though he can challenge the entire Hall of Inquisition. Come, let us make our way to the council chamber and greet our young, dead lord."

Elias and the duchess found the senior council already in attendance as well as several inquisitors seated in the gallery. The duchess took her seat in the center chair normally reserved for the senior inquisitor, while Elias sat dutifully to her right amongst the council. Fennrick stood below the elevated council upon the chamber floor, agitation etched clearly upon his face. His eyes continually shifted from the duchess to the main doors behind which Lord Giles impatiently waited.

"Your Grace, Lord Giles did express his urgency in meeting with the council, and I believe the time is near at hand," Fennrick murmured.

Paullina glared down at the inquisitor. "Lord Giles has always been an arrogant little upstart, and it will do him well to learn patience, particularly when dealing with his betters," she sniffed, then turned her head to Elias. "I assume those doors are sufficiently warded to prevent even him from foolishly barging in?"

Elias inclined his head. "They are indeed, Your Grace. It would take several archmages to unravel or bash down those wards."

"Good. Let the pompous little man wait."

The duchess still wore her condescending smirk when the doors exploded inward with a deafening boom. Only the secondary wards and quick actions of the experienced inquisitors prevented the wood, bronze, and stone fragments from becoming lethal projectiles. Hastily erected wards flared amongst the gathering even as several of those closest were blasted from their seats and sent sprawling. From the cloud of dust and destruction, Azerick strode into the chamber without a hint of fear or hesitation.

Duchess Paullina quickly regained her composure and raised a hand to prevent the astonished wizards from striking out. "Lord Giles, I had heard you died. Was I misinformed?"

"You were not, Your Grace. But like a bad meal, the abyss found me distasteful and spat me back out."

"I see death has done nothing to change your abrasive disposition."

"On the contrary, I have far less patience and sufferance for fools than I once had."

"Are you calling me a fool?" Paullina demanded.

Azerick shrugged. "It would be the height of foolishness to try and prevent me from retrieving what is mine."

"Lord Giles, your re-emergence intrigues me, and for that reason alone I allow you a certain amount of leave. Do not test my tolerance. What is it you want?"

"It is my understanding this place holds something belonging to me as well as my apprentice. I will have both of them returned."

"Your apprentice is a criminal and has refused offers of parole. As to your property, I presume you refer to the Codex Arcana. The codex is the property of the Academy by law, and it is illegal for an individual to possess it," Duchess Paullina declared.

"It is interesting you would bring Academy law into this," Azerick responded dryly. "Academy and king's law also require a significant separation of Academy and governmental jurisdictions. This is purely an Academy situation, so why am I discussing it with you?"

Paullina shifted in her seat and set her chin. "The Office of Inquisition and I share a close relationship, given our mutual requirements for protecting the border."

"Perhaps too close," Azerick responded darkly. "Ulric also shared a close relationship with certain members of the Academy, a relationship I severed."

Duchess Paullina pushed herself up in her seat and leaned down toward the upstart sorcerer. "You dare threaten me?" she shouted.

"I merely voice the reality of what will occur for anyone choosing to be my enemy. Do not put yourself or these wizards in that position, Your Grace," Azerick said without emotion.

The powerful duchess of Argoth shook with indignation, her rage blazing from her face like the searing heat of the desert sun. "Let me warn you, boy; only the political stability of my duchy prevents me from sending you right back to the abyss where you belong! Test my patience further, and I will have my wizards do exactly that, consequences be damned!"

Azerick turned his stony gaze upon Elias. "Senior Inquisitor, I assume you, and probably everyone else in this hall, took in my aura when I entered. Before anyone does something foolish, I recommend you do so again and advise your duchess accordingly."

With a curious look, Elias, along with every other wizard in the chamber, did exactly that. Slipping into a light meditation, the wizards looked beyond simple visual sight to glimpse the invisible energies surrounding all living things. Azerick stood as before with his golden, sorcerous aura brilliantly limning his body, but he no longer suppressed Klaraxis's terrifying power.

Encasing the golden glow, a black cloud of malevolent energy nearly filled the entire room. Klaraxis's aura washed over everyone in the chamber with so much vile power, wizards scrambled away from him, pressed themselves against the walls, and tried to flee the room. Several fell from their seats and knelt on the floor, gasping. Even the duchess felt the deathly wave wash over her and sat back heavily upon her seat, her face paling with a fear she could not comprehend.

"Elias, w-what is this?" she rasped out.

"It is our death, Your Grace. We must capitulate," the inquisitor whispered hoarsely.

"What you have seen and felt is the demon lord, Klaraxis," Azerick declared as he suppressed the aura once more. "I control his body and power, but only nominally. If you force me to fight, I will likely lose that control and the demon will wreak havoc upon this city and beyond until the Academy and Church can work together to banish him back to the abyss. He would eventually fall, but not before reducing this city and likely several others to ruins."

Paullina leaned over and whispered, "Elias, can your people not defeat him?"

"Perhaps, if we were prepared, but even then, the battle would be devastating to the city. If we were ready and had a contingent of Solarian's Light, we could force him to return to the abyss at the least. But at this moment, it would mean our destruction."

She could not care less about the girl other than her connection to the codex, which thus far had proved useless, but she despised the idea of giving up the book. However, she was not foolish enough to press forward in a battle she knew she was destined to lose. It was why she was still alive and Ulric and his conspirators were not.

Duchess Paullina straightened in her seat and did her best to regain her composure. "Very well, Lord Giles, I will have someone bring you the codex. It is heavily secured and will take a bit of time to remove it."

"You have already wasted enough of my time. I will get it myself."

Azerick pointed his staff at the high ceiling and made a circling motion. The hall shuddered as a round section of the ceiling the size of a small dinner table broke free and descended through the floor. Story after story of the tower above sank through the floor as loud, crackling explosions resounded through the Hall of Inquisition from the multiple wards protesting their destruction.

The wards protecting the codex were the most formidable possible and would have withstood Azerick's sorcery even with the additional power of his staff, but they were not designed to stand against the demonic power lacing his magic. When the rumbling destruction stopped and the dust cleared, the Codex Arcana sat before Azerick on its stone pedestal.

Azerick reached out and casually tucked the tome under his left arm. "My coming here and asking for what is mine was mere courtesy. I would have forgone even that had I not a dire message to convey as well, and I hope my ridiculous display has convinced you to take me seriously. The greatest threat of our existence is dawning, and we all need to stand together to defeat it. You all have a passing knowledge of The Great Revolution?" he inquired.

Several heads nodded numbly but only Paullina spoke. "We defeated the dragons and gained our freedom."

"The dragons were merely our part in that great conflict. The true battle lay with the elves and their magic. They took the battle to the beings controlling the dragons. These Scions are the original gods of this world, and they are returning to take back what they feel is theirs. Our gods and elven magic banished them, so they hate magic users like no others. They will destroy all who possess the ability to wield magic along with the vast majority of the races.

"You see the power I possess. The Scions and their legions will crush me like an insect if I stand alone. I plan to petition the Academy, the Church, and King Jarvin to prepare for their invasion. You inquisitors are already battle trained, but it is not enough. You must train with a rigor like no other, every day, and as hard as you can stand. You must be prepared to battle against hundreds of thousands of evil creatures who have no fear of death. To fail means the destruction of all we are, with no future but one of primitive subservience for the few who are allowed to live. Now, someone take me to my apprentice. I have much to do," he finished darkly.

It took a moment for the duchess to respond as she tried desperately to make sense of what the sorcerer had said. "Fennrick, please escort Lord Giles to the girl."

The hall was quiet and all eyes followed Azerick as Fennrick led him from the room. They all sat in stunned silence as they tried to process the enormity of what he had told them. Could it be true? Could they believe the word of a demon?

Fennrick fought to collect his thoughts as he led Lord Giles down the hall toward the prison cells. "I was impressed when you destroyed the doors," he said tentatively, "but to take down the wards surrounding the codex with such apparent ease was particularly disconcerting."

Azerick grinned. "Blowing apart doors is kind of becoming my thing."

"I have never heard of the Scions. How do you know of them?"

"Sharrellan told me, and the last remaining creature to have fought them showed me their prison. You are wondering if you can believe me."

Fennrick took a breath and nodded.

"It is imperative that you do. There must be something about them located within the Academy archives, no matter how passing the reference or how deeply buried it may be. We all need to be ready for their return, and that means honing our power to its highest level. What would I gain by enticing my enemies to greater power if I am lying?"

"Nothing I can think of, but you proclaim yourself to be a demon lord, and they are devious beyond the imaginations of most."

Azerick grunted in agreement. "You need to heed my warning, Fennrick, and convince the others. Many will doubt me. Probably most, but you must convince them. You must drive your people to train with fervor, for their lives, the lives of their families, and almost every intelligent creature on this world depend on it."

The inquisitor ran his tongue across his teeth in thought and nodded. "Lord Giles, I must tell you that our efforts to induce your apprentice to cooperate with us have taken their toll. She is likely not the same person you remember."

"I think many of us are not the people we remember. For good or ill, the events in our lives shape who we are. Some events are by circumstance, others by design. You are worried about retribution?"

"I did my duty, but I took no pleasure in it."

"I imagine I would have once considered punishing those who hurt my family regardless of their reasons, but so much has happened to me." Azerick sighed. "I have come to learn that even unpleasant things transpire for a reason. It may be that what she has endured was necessary to shape her, to make her stronger and wiser. It could also be I simply have too much to do to waste my time on revenge."

Fennrick stopped in front of a stout door and inserted a key into the lock. "She is in here."

He opened the door and stepped back. Azerick looked into the room and barely recognized the wretch sitting limply on a pallet and staring vacantly at the floor. Ellyssa's hair was matted and filthy, as was the rest of her. Her eyes were sunken and ringed with dark circles, and her whole body looked frail and emaciated. Her once fiery and defiant spirit now looked to have been shattered; Azerick hoped not irreparably. She needed that spirit to perform the duty he was going to lay upon her.

Ellyssa looked up and her entire countenance changed in an instant. Rage suffused her body when she spied Azerick's image in the doorway. Fennrick and his cronies had long been using illusions to manipulate and break her spirit. She had fallen for their lies in the beginning, but as more people she knew visited, she finally saw through the veils and understood their intent. But this was the first time they had used Azerick against her, and it was more than she could bear.

Ellyssa leapt from her meager bed with her hands twisted into claws. Tiny sparks of electricity arced between her fingers despite the wards against magic placed upon the room. "How dare you! You have no right!" Ellyssa shrieked as she tried to physically rip Azerick's image off the imposter's face.

Azerick grasped her wrists and held her as easily as a small child. "Ellyssa, it's me. I am back. It is time to go home."

Ellyssa looked at Fennrick standing sheepishly behind Azerick. She stepped back when Azerick let go of her. Her gaze was drawn to the codex and his staff tucked beneath his arm. She knew the codex was real. Not only could she see it, but she could hear the book whispering to her even now.

"H-how is this possible? I killed you," she declared as tears sprang to her eyes.

Azerick smiled down at his ward. "You were always good, kid, but you were never that good. My death was the result of my own choices and the designs of the gods. Had I not come for you in Bakhtaran, I am certain Sharrellan would have orchestrated another method for my demise."

Ellyssa took a tentative step forward. "It's really you?"

"It is. We need to go now. We have much to do."

Ellyssa rushed forward, wrapped her arms around Azerick, and wept loudly into his shirt. "I'm so sorry!"

"For what, soaking this shirt? It will dry."

Ellyssa coughed out a laugh as Azerick led her away. "Are we going home?"

"Soon, but first we must go get my son before we leave."

Ellyssa looked up at Azerick in surprise. "Daebian is here?"

Azerick shook his head. "No, my other son."

Ellyssa stopped to consider this next shocking revelation. "What have you been doing while you were gone? Or should I ask, *who* have you been doing?"

Azerick laughed loudly. "It's a long story, and I do not have time to explain it now. We need to be away from here. There is much to do, and I need your help to do it."

"Help to do what?"

"Not much," he replied as he strode down the corridor. "Just save the world."

CHAPTER 3

"Your son is in a brothel?" Ellyssa asked incredulously as they approached the house of disrepute.

"In these times, it was the most reliable place I could think of."

A shrill cry split the air from somewhere within. Azerick bolted through the doors and up the stairs, following the source of distress with Ellyssa chasing hastily behind. Azerick burst through the door and found Raijaun clinging to the ceiling in the corner of the room. The brothel madam cowered against the far wall of the room covered in the spilled contents of the empty skin lying in front of her.

"You failed to add blood to the milk," Azerick said.

"I-I'm sorry!" the woman wailed. "I couldn't bring myself to do it!"

Azerick faced his angry son. "Raijaun, come down this instant, and stop your tantrum. That is no way to behave. You have terrified this woman who only wanted to take care of you. Come apologize," he said firmly.

Raijaun dropped to the floor and looked at his feet. Ellyssa stared at the creature and said nothing, but she had plenty of questions for later. Azerick turned back to the frightened woman.

"You already have your payment. We will be leaving shortly. You may go."

"W-what of the spell upon the bag?"

"Other than the locational, there was no spell."

The woman looked unconvinced but fled the room. Getting away from the terrifying man and his pet demon was far more important than wealth at the moment.

Azerick faced Ellyssa. "We both have many questions, but they must wait for now. We need to be away from this place immediately."

Azerick slashed the air with his staff, slicing open a portal to somewhere outside. He pulled Ellyssa and his son through the rift and stepped into the rocky, open terrain of the desert. Ellyssa swooned heavily and her knees nearly buckled from the disorientation. When she caught her balance, she looked behind her and saw the city lying at least a mile away.

"So far," she whispered.

"Steady yourself," Azerick advised. "We must gate several more times to put as much distance between us and the city as we can."

Before Ellyssa could ask why, Azerick ripped open another portal and pulled them through. When Ellyssa was able to focus her eyes once more, she could barely make out the tallest towers in Argoth. Azerick's gate spells easily took them five times farther than anything she had ever made or even heard was possible. He was already opening a third gate and pushing them through.

"Azerick, please..." Ellyssa tried to protest before being shoved through.

This time, Ellyssa did fall as she stumbled through the gate. She braced herself on her hands and knees as she tried vainly to heave out a nonexistent meal.

"Azerick, please, no more. I can't take another one," she pleaded.

Azerick looked back in the direction of Argoth and sat on a boulder while Raijaun turned in circles with his arms outstretched, enjoying the dizziness caused by the gate travel.

"All right, we can wait here for a bit, but we need to move away soon."

Ellyssa rolled over and propped her back against another boulder. "Why? I thought Duchess Paullina let me go?"

"She gave me what I demanded because she had no reasonable options at the time. She is as ambitious and covetous a woman as they come. Now that she has had time to think and prepare, she will foolishly begin to reassess her options and will act to recover the codex."

"Can we beat them if they come after us?"

"The outcome of any battle is largely based upon proper preparation," Azerick explained. "They will have the superiority of numbers and even raw power, particularly since I cannot bring my full power to bear without risking losing control. I also do not want to kill them."

"Why not? They'll kill you to get the codex back, won't they?" Ellyssa demanded.

"Probably, but they aren't convinced of the danger I warned them about. Humans are just too short-term thinking."

"You said we had to save the world. I thought you were joking."

Azerick smiled and shook his head. "No, I am not much for jokes these days. We are all in a great deal of danger."

"From what?"

"An ancient foe, banished by the gods, is returning. They will annihilate nearly every intelligent race on the planet if we do not stop them."

"Can't the gods destroy them, or at least banish them again?" Ellyssa asked.

"It will be a war between gods, and the old gods are stronger. Our gods will need our help to have a chance at victory, and that means I need every man, woman, and wizard to fight with me. That is why I cannot simply kill the inquisitors or the Academy wizards who will invariably resist what I tell them. I need to beat them soundly without killing them, at least not many of them, and hope it is enough of a deterrent to keep them from trying to take the codex by force. As the only ones able to use it to its fullest, it must remain with us so that we can prepare for the final battle."

Talk of a war between gods made Ellyssa feel very small and insignificant. "How could I possibly help with that?"

"First, I need you to keep Raijaun out of trouble and teach him some basics, like manners, reading, and writing. I'm not ready to return home right away. I need to write a training doctrine for my students to follow. Once that is complete, you will use it to take over the training of the school."

If Ellyssa had not been sitting, she certainly would have fallen over. "What? I can't take over the school! I'm not even a full wizard!"

"Tell me how you ended up branded a criminal and stuck in the inquisitors' prison."

Ellyssa sighed and looked shamefully at her feet. "I don't know. I blamed myself for your dying, like everyone else. At least that's what I thought. I started having nightmares when I went to sleep, and then they were even coming when I was awake. Sandy said it was because the man who took me captive was still alive and I couldn't feel safe again until he was dead."

"It sounds like Sandy has gotten wise while I was gone."

"Yeah, and as big as a house," Ellyssa said with a smile.

"So what did you do?"

"I started looking for him, for Captain Jake, and killing slavers when I found them. I made a real mess. The Academy sent some idiots to bring me in. They failed."

"Quite a feat for someone of your inexperience."

"They knew I had the codex and that it spoke to me, so they couldn't risk killing me," she explained grimly.

"All the same, it takes some strength and very clever use of magic to defeat even wizards who aren't battle trained. So they failed and sent the inquisitors after you."

"Right, but I trounced them the first time we met too. They got me after your friend Andrill betrayed me in Southport."

"I see. Would you like to make a stop in Southport and deal with Andrill?" Azerick asked.

Ellyssa sighed and shook her head. "No. Andrill did what he thought he had to do. Chasing revenge only made everything worse. The Academy is now running the school, and I got thrown into prison where I would still be if you had not rescued me…again. It's not worth it."

"It sounds like Sandy is not the only one who has grown in both size and wisdom."

"Well, five years of absolute torment will do that."

Azerick stared into the distance and whispered, "Five years." He brought his attention back to his apprentice. "All those things are why you are the best qualified to take over the teaching of my new curriculum. Rusty is good, but he is purely Academy trained. Allister and Aggie are both powerful beyond measure, but I don't think either of them is willing to push the students the way they must. Josh and the other former Black Tower students are probably as close to being familiar with what needs to be done as anyone can be, but they have not had the real world combat experience you have had. I know you have suffered a great deal these last few years, but I need you to be strong for me. Can you do it?"

Ellyssa desperately wanted to deny it as she fought to control her fear and sense of unworthiness. She knew she could do this. She knew what it was like to fight for her life, and that was what Azerick needed her to teach the others.

"I can do it."

"Don't look so fatalistic. You have the easy job."

"If taking over the school is the easy job, I'm afraid to ask what would be a hard one."

"I have to convince the Academy to accept it also. Now, tell me about these Academy wizards in my school."

"I don't know much except what Wolf told me. Some man named Harvey is in charge now. They didn't shut it down, even though Harvey would love to do just that. Several wizards from the Academy came with him and took over teaching. Wolf thought there was going to be a battle. The Academy brought a lot of wizards and soldiers with them, and Duchess Mellina was furious. She sent her soldiers in behind them, but they all decided not to fight."

"So, Allister had a defensible position with the enemy between two strong forces. What would you have done?"

Ellyssa studied the ground as she thought. "I would not have given up the school. I would have tried to convince them to leave. If they had not, I would have fought them."

"People would have died. Probably a lot of people."

"Better to die than let someone walk all over you, telling you that you are unworthy or inferior. That's what the Academy thinks of us, that we aren't good enough to be wizards."

Azerick nodded and smiled. "That is why you are the one to take over training. Allister and the others believe in peace at all costs when we are at a time where we must believe in freedom and survival at any cost. We are facing a battle like no other. Even the Great Revolution cannot compare to the number of people who will fight and die for their right not just to exist, but exist as a free people able to choose their own destinies. Come, we need to move again," he said as he rose to his feet.

Ellyssa stood with a sigh. "I wish we would have had the time to get something to eat before we left the city. I'm starving."

"I wish we would have had the time for you to take a bath. You reek," Azerick quipped as he wrenched open another gate.

Duchess Paullina gulped down the last of her wine and hurled the empty glass against the wall. She grabbed the bottle from the table and, upon finding it empty as well, sent it flying after the glass. Fennrick ducked to avoid the flying shards as he stepped into Elias's office.

"This is beyond intolerable!" the duchess railed once more.

Elias jumped up from his chair and began searching a cabinet. "I am certain I have more wine somewhere, Your Grace."

Paullina grabbed a stylus case from his desk and began beating him on the head with it. "Not the wine, you simpleton! How can a man walk in here, destroy my hall, free a prisoner condemned to death, and walk out with the most important artifact in the kingdom?"

"He was not exactly a man, Your Grace!" Elias cried out from beneath the protection of his arms.

"I don't care if he was Solarian himself! A score of inquisitors filled that hall, and all they could do was cower and wet themselves!"

"Your Grace, we were not prepared!"

"Then you had best get prepared!" The duchess spun toward Fennrick. "Fennrick, ready as many inquisitors as you can, and go get my book. I no longer care about the girl. She has proven less than useless."

"I think not, Your Grace," Fennrick replied.

"Excuse me?" Paullina exclaimed incredulously.

"You have no idea what we face, none of us do, and I will not throw away the lives of my people for your selfish desires. Lord Giles was correct, you truly are a fool."

"You forget yourself, Inquisitor!" the duchess raged.

"No, Your Grace, we have all forgotten ourselves, and I think it is time I remind the Hall of who we are," Fennrick replied forcefully. "We have forgotten our real mission to protect the realm and now bow to your desires, defy the Academy by hoarding artifacts, and torture children."

Shaking with outrage, the duchess spun on Elias. "Elias, order your man to obey me this instant!"

"Fennrick, have you lost your mind? Prepare a full company of inquisitors to recover the codex!"

"Elias, the only thing I will recover for you is a rough-hewn staff. If you are unsure of what to do with it, I was given a detailed set of instructions that I am more than happy to share with you."

"You are insubordinate, Inquisitor! I will have you expelled from the order!"

"And you are the moron your precious duchess continually proclaims you to be. I think we both know the only reason I do not have your job is that after seeing how it has pushed you to twist and corrupt our order, I no longer want it. Now, if you will excuse me, I have better things to do than waste my time with fools."

"Where are you going, Fennrick?" Elias demanded.

"I am going to go prepare my people for the end of the world."

"Do you honestly believe the words of a self-proclaimed demon?" Paullina asked heatedly.

Fennrick gestured irritably. "Whether I do or not is irrelevant. We have gotten lax in our training and duty since Jarvin ended the war, and I will ensure my troops are prepared for whatever arises, be they Sumarans or gods."

"It appears Fennrick has lost his stomach for this business and replaced it with a very annoying conscience," Paullina said when Fennrick left the room. "I hope you are not turning on me as well."

"Of course not, Your Grace," Elias answered sycophantically.

"Good. Now, I want you to rouse every wizard in your command. You are to kill Lord Giles, his petulant apprentice, and get back my book. He was killed before and he can be killed again."

"At once, Your Grace. It will take a few days for us to prepare."

"See to it, Elias. Is there no more damn wine in this place?" the duchess shouted.

Azerick finally relented and allowed them to camp after four more gut-wrenching gate spells. While Ellyssa lay on the rocky ground willing the world to cease its spinning, Azerick magically excavated a depression in the rock and drew up the water hidden beneath the surface. He stuck the silvery end of his staff into the water and heated it to the point it was just bearable to soak in.

He pulled a few articles of clothing out of his travel pack and set them by the steaming pool. "I liberated these from the brothel. They aren't exactly travel clothes, but they will serve better than the rags you are wearing."

"I don't suppose you liberated any food as well?"

"I'm sorry, it's been so long since I had to worry about that I forgot," he replied abashedly. "Raijaun is a good hunter. We'll scare up something while you clean up."

Ellyssa gasped in pain and pleasure as she slipped beneath the hot water. She groaned as the heat pulled the filth away from her skin and a great deal of tension from her muscles. It sure beat the prison's weekly washrag and bucket of cold water.

The smell of cooking meat eventually coaxed her from her bath. Azerick was right; the clothes were too thin to withstand the weather and rigors of travel, but they would suffice. Her magic would keep the worst of the weather from reaching her, and they only had to last until they got home.

Ellyssa descended the low hill to where Azerick had made camp and was cooking a large lizard and desert hare over a fire. Raijaun sat on a boulder, eagerly devouring the remnants of a thick lizard tail or a snake.

"I hope you like lizard," Azerick said as she took a seat.

"I would eat a buzzard right now and swear it was chicken."

Ellyssa finished off the lizard and started in on the hare. It was stringy and would have been bland had Azerick not found some desert sage to rub into the meat.

"So tell me about Raijaun," Ellyssa said between bites.

Azerick set his gaze upon his son, who looked up at the mention of his name. "The elves created a creature they called a Guardian by combining the physical and spiritual essence of a dragon and an elf. The last of the Guardians freed me from the abyss and combined my essence and hers to create Raijaun. Right now, his demonic nature is dominant, but I believe I can bring out his other heritages. It is why I am not rushing back home. I need him to behave properly before we get there. Once we are back, a lot of things need to happen, and I cannot afford to be distracted."

"You think that will be enough time?" Ellyssa asked dubiously.

"He grows very fast, both physically and mentally," Azerick assured her. "From what I understand, their toddler phase passes very quickly. He was nearly animalistic just a few weeks ago and has already grown into a petulant child. I expect us to take about a month to reach North Haven. I hope that with your help and example, he will come into something nearing middle human childhood."

"What exactly do you want me to do?"

"Teach him to read, write, and act like a human. I do not know how quickly he will come into his magic, but help me contain it as best you can. It resembles sorcery far more than wizard magic, so I will have to do his actual training. For now, I just need you to help me keep him from setting everything on fire when he gets mad," Azerick admitted with a grin.

Ellyssa's face dropped and she looked at the ground. "I lost your ring and bracelet. I'm sorry. I needed them, but the inquisitors took them when they caught me."

"You mean these?" Azerick opened his hand, and glittering in the late sun were the ring and bracelet. He handed them to Ellyssa. "Here, you will need these more than I will."

Ellyssa took them and looked at him in wonder. "How did you get them back? When?"

"The same time and the same way I got my book. I am not easy to steal from," he chuckled.

"Do you still think they are coming after us?"

"I would be very surprised if they did not. The inquisitors have been one of the most powerful forces in Valeria for a long time. They know I caught them unaware and will be certain they can defeat me if they are prepared. The duchess has far too much influence in their order, and she will demand they recover the codex."

Ellyssa gnawed her lip worriedly before asking, "Can we beat them if they come prepared?"

"There is only so much one can prepare for. Even the best-laid plans often fail upon meeting the enemy, because the enemy has plans of their own. It all rests upon who has the best plan, and the plan most able to withstand the engagement," he said somberly.

"You have a plan?"

Azerick smiled. "I always have a plan. Moreover, I have the codex."

Azerick spent the entire night deeply immersed within the pages of the codex while Ellyssa taught and entertained Raijaun until the need for sleep won out. Until exhaustion finally overtook her, Ellyssa worked with Raijaun on his letters and even improved his speech beyond a few single word demands. Azerick was right; he learned very quickly.

The next morning, after a quick breakfast, Azerick dragged them through another series of magical gates until Ellyssa was certain her head would split in half and her stomach would leap out of her mouth and make a run for independence.

There was little conversation as they trudged on. Azerick always seemed lost in thought, and Raijaun scurried to and fro chasing and devouring almost anything he could catch. He and Azerick were both tireless, and Ellyssa had to use her magic to ward off much of her fatigue to keep pace with them. Her sedentary imprisonment had definitely taken its toll on her strength, but she was recovering quickly.

"How long do you think it will take them to catch us? I don't see how they can if we keep using your portals," Ellyssa said.

"It will likely take a couple days before they are prepared to leave Argoth. They won't know how fast we are traveling until they find the residual energy of my gates. They can use the same network of horses as the king's Blackguard and cover a great deal of ground in a short amount of time. We will keep using the gates until we reach Sandusk where we can rest properly and prepare. You will need to be ready. They will find us two days out of Sandusk," Azerick replied absently.

"How can you be so sure?"

"Because that is my plan. We will wait for them in an area I passed through years ago. My gates leave a prominent amount of residual energy, and they will have little trouble finding them to ascertain our direction and speed of travel. If you have not noticed, I cast the same number of gates and we walk for the same amount of time each day. Nothing short of leaving a note for them will give them a better clue of our whereabouts."

Ellyssa scrunched her face in worry. "Shouldn't we just keep running until we are back at the school? Then we would have help with a lot less risk of losing. I don't know how powerful you are, but these are inquisitors, and there will be a lot of them."

"Sometimes, you can achieve more with a bluff than with a strong hand. We have a strong hand, but it is not unbeatable by any means. If we dig in at the school, the inquisitors will likely call upon the Academy for support and our odds will actually decline. It also creates a political element we do not have to contend with out here. You saw how Allister caved in to Academy pressure before. I love him and Rusty dearly, but our ideals do not always coincide. It is not enough to just beat the inquisitors and the Academy. I have to convince them the threat of the Scions is real and more important than taking back the codex. They must see that the codex needs to be in my hands if we are going to have any hope of victory."

Ellyssa rolled her eyes and curled her lip in a sneer. "Good luck with that. The Academy is nothing but a bunch of arrogant, hardheaded fools."

"Which is why I have to be even more hardheaded," Azerick replied grimly.

Partway through another stomach-churning day of gating, Ellyssa noticed Azerick scratching runes in the dirt or on a rock and hiding it from view.

"What are you making?" she asked, curious.

Azerick set the rock he was carving on rune side down and looked over. "I need to know when the inquisitors find my gate locations so I can watch them. The runes inform me when someone comes near it and gives me a way to scry the location quickly and easily."

Ellyssa nodded her understanding. Scrying was only possible if the person performing the spell was familiar with the target, whether the target was a person or a location. A good spellcaster could blind scry, but it was like trying to find a small object in a big house in pitch blackness. It was also easy for another magic user to detect such stumbling attempts.

Ellyssa looked around at the vast, rocky terrain. "Do you think they will even find these spots? This place is huge, and we're not exactly taking the trade roads."

"They should. I am leaving a pretty big magical stink for them to sniff out."

"I wish I was as confident about facing them as you are," she sighed.

"Make no mistake; we are luring fleshreavers into a trap with nothing more than sticks for weapons. We just need to make sure our sticks are sharp."

By the time they reached Sandusk, Raijaun was almost speaking in complete sentences. His behavior was near that of a normal human child, and Ellyssa had no trouble overlooking his peculiar appearance. Ellyssa also felt more like her normal self, at least physically. Azerick's return even made her feel better emotionally than she had in a very long time, despite everything else she had endured. Maybe it was because she found it hard to think of anything except a night's sleep in a real bed.

Several people on the streets of Sandusk stopped and stared, and a few ran off with looks of fright evident on their faces. It was apparent some of the citizens recognized Azerick from his visit several years previously.

Azerick led Ellyssa and his son to a quaint boarding house. It was one of the few buildings in this harsh environment where the owner had taken the time and expense to maintain it. It was obvious from the look of shock and displeasure on the face of the prim, older woman sitting behind the reception desk that she also recognized Azerick.

"Can I help you, My Lord?" she asked, suppressing her unease.

"We require a room. A large one with three beds, if possible," Azerick replied.

The woman folded her hands on her desk, likely to control their shaking. "I am afraid we are booked up. Perhaps you can find a room at the inn down the street."

Azerick smiled. "I think you have a room. Sandusk is not exactly on a major trade route, or known as a prime vacation spot."

"I'm sorry, but I just cannot go through what occurred the last time you were here!" she exclaimed.

"I do not expect anything like that to happen again," Azerick assured her.

"Were you expecting it last time?" she challenged.

"A fair point. I was not. However, you were well compensated."

"Sir, there is not enough gold to adequately compensate or enough soap to scrub the image from my mind in the entire world!"

Azerick dropped enough raw gold on the counter to pay for a month. "I do not expect to be here for more than a few days. We will find the room ourselves."

Azerick found a large room at the end of the hall. It had two beds and a sofa, as well as a desk and several comfortable chairs. The sofa would suffice as a bed for Raijaun.

"Azerick, she did not exactly agree to let us stay," Ellyssa said uncomfortably as Azerick dropped his travel pack.

Azerick harrumphed irritably. "A great many people are not going to agree with me and challenge what I have to do. I do not have the time or patience to argue with them all. I need to wash the dust out of my mouth with something more than water. Stay here, watch Raijaun, and study."

Ellyssa stared at the door for several moments after Azerick left. She was not accustomed to Azerick's cold and compassionless tone, and it definitely unnerved her. He had always been moody and quick to do what needed to be done, but he had never been so dismissive and bullish, particularly toward the common people.

Ellyssa sighed as she realized that another person she loved had changed irrevocably. She looked at the codex resting on the table and decided there was little to be done other than accept the changes and prepare for what could be the biggest fight of her life. She shuddered as she sat down, felt the power of the Codex Arcana thrumming beneath her fingertips, and sighed when the soft voice whispered in her mind once more. Ellyssa had been in a state of great anxiety, fearful the codex would no longer speak to her since Azerick was back.

Azerick strode through town without fear despite the numerous eyes watching him. When he stepped into the same bar in which he had a run-in with a local a few years ago, the conversations ceased except for a few patrons leaning over and whispering to someone next to them. Azerick shrugged dismissively; they were probably relating a grossly exaggerated version of his previous visit. Azerick approached the bar and the nervous bartender.

"Louis, isn't it?"

"Yessir," the barkeep answered.

"Louis, get me a mug of your best beer."

"Yessir," Louis answered before darting down the steps leading to the cellar.

Louis only had the one keg of special brew he normally saved for the holiday, but if the wizard wanted his best, he would get it. Even though he killed some folks the last time he was here, he did pay well.

Azerick dropped a chunk of gold ore on the bar and scooped up the glass as soon as Louis plunked it down in front of him. He gave a satisfying sigh and smacked his lips after draining half the glass in one pull. He then set a polished topaz on the counter.

"Louis, in a few days, there may be a large number of inquisitors passing through town looking for me."

"Inquisitors?" he replied quizzically.

"Wizards who specialize in fighting and arresting other wizards and sorcerers," Azerick explained.

"They after you?"

"They're after something I have, something that belongs to me by every right and law except theirs."

Louis nodded his head sagely. "I see. You want me to point them in the wrong direction if they ask if I seen you."

"No, I want you to let them know exactly in what direction I was headed. Northwest almost as the crow flies. I'm sure you and the rest of the town will know when I leave and can pass that on to them as well."

Louis looked at the dangerous young man in confusion. "Most folks don't want people who are chasing them to know where they are."

"I think you can agree I am not most people," Azerick answered with a smile.

Azerick enjoyed one more beer and walked about a mile out of town where he made a shallow pool in a natural rock bowl. Bending his magic into the reflective surface, he willed up an image of the first place he laid down a marker. The area was empty, but bringing the image closer showed the ground churned by an innumerable number of horse hooves. He shifted the image to that of the next gate and found what he was searching for.

Nearly two score of men and women were setting up camp for the night. Azerick could tell they were all wizards even without their uniforms or expending the concentration to read their auras. Besides, attempting an aura read would almost certainly gain their attention. Azerick dispelled the image and sighed. Forty experienced mages against him and a girl. He needed to better his odds. Turning his attention back to the puddle, he willed up another image.

CHAPTER 4

Azerick returned to the boarding house and paused outside the door when he heard a heated conversation issuing from inside. He recognized the complaints of the house marm directed toward an unknown man.

"What exactly do you expect me to do about it?" the man demanded.

"You are supposed to be the law in this town. I expect you to do your job!"

"Did he pay you? Has he caused trouble or killed anyone?"

"Not yet! Paying or not, I do not want him in my house," she said in exasperation.

"And I don't want him in my town, but I can't go about tossing out everyone who makes me uncomfortable. We have an open town, and you run a boarding house. Getting uninvited guests is part of the risk of doing business."

"You are worthless and a disgrace to your profession! Captain Cruthers would never display such wanton cowardice!" the woman shrieked.

The beleaguered watchman sighed. "Fine, I will do what I can." Both sets of eyes snapped onto Azerick as he entered. "Milord, would you be willing to find another place to stay during your visit?"

"No," Azerick replied.

The watchman turned his palms up. "Well, I did what I could."

"I hope there is not going to be any trouble. I will be leaving the day after tomorrow," Azerick assured them.

"Wonderful, problem solved! I'll be at the Sandy Bottom doing my job if anyone needs me."

The house marm glared hatefully at the man as he left. Azerick ignored her and returned to his room. He stopped and stared as he entered. Raijaun sat in the middle of the floor, directing a luminous red orb around the room.

"Azerick, do you see what Raijaun did?" Ellyssa asked excitedly. "He was watching me study and practice my weaves, so I showed him the same spell I taught the other kids when I was young. I don't know how he did it, but he made the light!"

"You are supposed to be studying."

"I was. It's just that Raijaun was really interested in what I was doing, so I showed him the spell. I thought you would be happy," Ellyssa said dejectedly.

Azerick gave her and Raijaun a smile. "I am. I found the inquisitors, so there is no more question of whether they will come. They will reach Sandusk in about three days. We will leave the day after tomorrow, so you must be ready."

"I will be, as best I can."

The orb streaked past Azerick's head and circled him several times. "I did good?" Raijaun asked timidly.

Azerick squatted next to his son and hugged him. "You did very well. Perhaps it is time I started teaching you how to use your magic."

Raijaun beamed under his father's praise and the promise of learning magic. Azerick began Raijaun's instruction just as Devlin had started with him. He explained how to concentrate, feel the Source, and discover how best to shape it to his will. Raijaun was a natural study, adept at wielding magic through the innate abilities of his demonic heritage and the dragon memories of his mother.

Not being a dragon or a demon, Raijaun needed to learn how to shape his magic to suit his unique form. It was something with which Azerick could do little in the way of teaching him; he could merely guide him through a process of trial and error.

Azerick left the Codex Arcana with Ellyssa so she could study and prepare while he took Raijaun outside of Sandusk. He found a suitable area about a mile from the town, and began talking Raijaun through channeling the Source.

"Reach out with your mind and find the power with all of your senses. See, feel, hear, taste, and smell the energy all around you. Gather it with your mind, and shape it to your desire," Azerick said soothingly.

Raijaun's face took on a look of intense concentration as he closed his eyes and began pulling in arcane energy. His ability to grasp and hold the power was remarkable. It often took months, or even a year or more, for a student to learn how to tap the Source and hold it with such ease.

"Excellent job. Now stop gathering energy and start shaping what you have into a spell. Raijaun, stop pulling in the power," Azerick repeated as the energy continued to build at an alarming rate.

Raijaun looked at his father, concern etched in every crease of his furrowed brow, not understanding what to do as the power flowed into him faster than he could manage and raged out of control.

"Release it, Raijaun! Release the power!" Azerick urgently ordered.

Azerick reached out with his mind and grabbed hold of the mass of arcane energy his son barely held in check and gave it a push. Raijaun understood what Azerick was trying to do and followed suit, hurling the magic away from him in a bright, sparking mass of raw energy. The wild power streaked away and slammed into a wall of stone several yards away, the impact shattering a large section of a small cliff face. Shards of stone rained down around them as the wind slowly blew the resulting dust cloud away.

"Okay, gathering power is no problem for you, but we really need to work on your ability to stop," Azerick chuckled.

"Sorry, Father," Raijaun said as he looked at his feet and drew in the sand with his toe.

"It's all right; that is why we are out here," Azerick reassured him. "Try again, slowly."

Raijaun drew in a trickle of power. It took several seconds for him to gather enough energy, but he was able to cut off the flow when Azerick told him to.

"Use your mind's eye to grab at the threads of magic within the mass of energy, and shape them into a recognizable form. Watch as I do it," Azerick instructed.

Azerick pulled at the Source and slowly wove a simple light spell. Raijaun watched attentively and mimicked his father's actions. A ball of light materialized in his small hands, flickering but maintaining its form.

"Good, now I want you to..." Azerick began to say.

Raijaun plucked at different strands of energy and twisted them about, changing the color and intensity of the light as he did so. He made more complex changes in the weave and formed the light into shapes. The shapes were simple at first, but Raijaun began creating more sophisticated forms like animals and people.

"Okay, I think you have that down," Azerick said, amazed at his son's adeptness.

Azerick continued to practice with Raijaun during their short stay in Sandusk, and his growth in drawing and shaping magic was nothing short of astounding. By the time they packed up and departed Sandusk, Raijaun was easily as skilled as a second-year novice, and a good deal more powerful.

Inquisitor Harrison led his two score of inquisitors in pursuit of the renegade sorcerer. He would have had half again as many if Fennrick and his people had not suddenly developed a stomach illness. Their obvious refusal to obey orders infuriated him.

Following the sorcerer proved to be a simple matter. He had used a magical gate to flee the city, which left a magical signature so strong even a blind charlatan could have found it. The distance he was able to travel using the gates astounded him and his companions, making him wish for Fennrick's mages every time he found the residual energy left behind.

Lord Giles was able to conjure enough of the portals to make catching up to him a chore. It did not appear he and his apprentice had horses as of yet, and was the only reason he was able to gain on them. Once he realized the sorcerer was headed straight for Sandusk, it became much easier to close the distance. It allowed him and his people to use the way stations to trade their horses for fresh mounts.

They had discovered a third set of footprints, small like a child's. None of them could fathom to whom they might belong. If the sorcerer was foolish enough to bring a child with him, it could make this task distasteful, but it would not stop him from doing his duty. This was their third day out, which put the sorcerer and his apprentice two days ahead of them. Tomorrow would cut the distance in half, and they should be able to strike in the next two or three days, assuming they maintained a similar pace.

The large party of wizards drew curious and frightened stares from Sandusk's citizens when they rode through the middle of town midway through the next day. Inquisitor Harrison could tell by his previous scrying of the now familiar energy signature that the sorcerer had already fled town.

Harrison took four of his fellow inquisitors with him to ask some questions while the others watered and fed the horses. The best place to find information about a traveler was the inn. Sandusk had only one, so his inquiries should be blessedly short. He and his associates captured the attention of the room when they entered, as expected. Harrison ignored the stares and whispers and approached the bar.

"I am looking for a man," Inquisitor Harrison told the innkeeper.

"Funny, most folks around here are looking for a woman," Louis replied with a nervous smile.

"I am Inquisitor Harrison. I am looking for a very dangerous man, and I am not in the mood for jocularity. He is on foot, traveling with a young woman. There may also be a third person with them. Someone small, perhaps a child."

Louis grunted. "Didn't see no woman or child, but I know the man you're asking about. He came in three days ago and left just yesterday. He stayed over at the boarding house, so if someone else was with him they must have stayed there as well."

"Did you note their direction of travel?"

"Not personally, but I heard someone mention they saw him headed northwest," Louis replied reluctantly.

"Excellent. I imagine my people will want to wash down the trail dust before we leave." Harrison set a stack of silver coins on the counter. "This should cover their expenses."

It did not take long for him to find the boarding house. The woman sitting behind the counter gave him an unfriendly look as he and his entourage entered.

"Good day, madam. I am looking for a man who was traveling with a young woman and perhaps a child. I understand they stayed here," Inquisitor Harrison said.

"They did, against my wishes," the woman snapped. "Useless town watch wouldn't even throw them out! Well, they're gone now and good riddance to them. The last time that man stayed here he killed his twin and left an ungodly mess!"

"Killed his twin, you say?"

"Was a spitting image of him, what was left of him."

One of the inquisitors offered, "It could have been a changeling or someone under a transmogrification spell."

Harrison nodded his agreement. "Tell me of the others who were with him. Did you see them?"

"I did. A young woman and a child. The girl looked too young to be the mother, but anything is possible. I can't really say how old the child was or even if it was a boy or a girl. They had it wrapped head to foot and it kept behind the girl. Could have been a goblin for all I know," she replied.

"I see. And they left yesterday?"

"That's right, first thing in the morning."

"Thank you." He turned to one of his men. "Round up the others. We will not be able to use the way stations, and I do not want them to get too much of a lead. Meet me on the road at the west end of town. I will try and find the sorcerer's most recent gates."

Ten minutes later, the contingent rode up behind Harrison. "He tore open a portal about two miles northwest of here. Given his previous rate of travel, I expect to catch him in a little over a day if we ride swiftly."

Inquisitor Harrison called them to a halt late the following night. They had pushed on, getting only minimal rest to ensure they were prepared to face two formidable foes. Just two miles from where he was able to scry their target's location, he ordered his people to dismount. They would walk from here, using their magic to hide their approach.

Tensions were high as they stalked toward their prey. Inquisitor Harrison and over a dozen others were present when the sorcerer came to the Hall. His power was unlike anything any of them had experienced before. No one knew the full potential of his power or his limits, so surprise with overwhelming force was vital.

The faint glow of a small fire cast just enough light to pinpoint the sorcerer and the girl's location. They were camped in a deep gulley perhaps a hundred yards wide. The trio was easily visible from Harrison's position, perhaps a hundred fifty feet distant and fifty feet above them. The sorcerer appeared to be conversing with a child while the girl read from a large book near the fire. The inquisitor had to assume it was the Codex Arcana.

He considered surrounding them but discarded the idea. More movement this close could result in detection and take too much time. He also needed his people near enough to assist each other should their opening strikes fail to kill the sorcerer. They would concentrate their attack on Lord Giles. The girl was little danger by herself, and they could not risk damaging the codex. They would execute the girl after getting the book. The child would likely be collateral damage.

Harrison gave a silent signal with his hand and all forty wizards unleashed more concentrated arcane power in that moment than in any single engagement in their decades-long war with Sumara. Brilliant beams of intense light and power lanced out and lit up the gulley more brightly than the noonday sun. Massive waves of thunder echoed across the land, as the eldritch power caused the air to explode from the intense heat.

Twenty-five inquisitors struck the sorcerer while the remaining wizards wove chains of magic to pin the sorcerer in place. Azerick's wards flared as brightly as the powerful rays striking them as he writhed beneath the onslaught. His body contorted as the intense struggle and pain forced him to shift into Klaraxis's form. Seeing the terrifying image, the inquisitors unleashed a second salvo.

"Raijaun, run!" Ellyssa shrieked.

Raijaun rolled away from the attack, the power of it blistering his skin despite his quickness, and fled into the night. Ellyssa darted in the opposite direction, raised a protective ward around her, and prepared to strike back, but the inquisitors' second attack broke through Azerick's defenses. The contest between the two powerful magical forces created a deafening explosion that hurled Ellyssa several yards and left her stunned. Only her wards prevented the detonation from blasting her to pieces.

Ellyssa struggled to get to her feet and fell back when she looked at Azerick's destroyed body. Once the rays penetrated his wards, they had cut through his body and left him riddled with gaping, charred holes.

"Azerick, no!" Ellyssa shouted hysterically.

The assault was as brief as it was furious. Inquisitor Harrison looked down at the destruction below. He shuddered upon seeing the ruined demonic body. The ground around the demon glittered from the glass created by the intense beams that melted the sand and rock. Smoke curled lazily into the air from the charred corpse.

"Half of you follow me. The rest of you watch for any sign of treachery. Destroy the girl if she so much as moves," Harrison ordered.

The inquisitors made a sliding descent to the base of the gulley, keeping a wary eye on the hideous form still lying unmoving a short distance away. The girl barely acknowledged their approach as she sat on the ground weeping. Ellyssa's eyes darted to the codex lying a few feet away as the inquisitor stalked closer.

"Do not do anything foolish, child," Harrison warned, "I will have what I came for."

Her tears vanished and a smile spread across her face. "Then you must have come for your death, for you will not get what you want, only what you deserve."

The young woman and the codex crumbled into the same rough sand and grit of the surrounding terrain. Inquisitor Harrison spun and watched the demon's corpse likewise change into a pile of dirt and gravel.

"Dear gods above," the inquisitor managed to whisper before his world was literally torn apart.

Six runes the size of bar tables briefly flared around the camp before sending massive beams shooting into the night sky as if to stab out the stars themselves. The intensity dwarfed that of the wizards' assault, leaving them all blinded and desperately trying to blink away the miniature suns now floating across their vision.

The world shrieked in protested agony as Azerick ripped open a huge wound in their reality. High above the gulley, a great black gash opened in the night sky, sucking up everything below it in a powerful vortex. Wizards cried out as they flew upward into the black maw, along with tons of dirt, sand, and stone. The gulley was scoured clean all the way down to the bedrock. The rift slammed closed seconds later and instantly cast the area into a dark and eerie silence.

The closing of the rift did not signal an end to the fight, but was just the opening gambit of a battle no one could have expected. The remaining inquisitors were already raising wards and hastily backing away from the edge of the gulch when a massive wave of force struck them on their left flank, sending them flying dozens of feet and tumbling a score more. Numerous arms made of sand and rock rose from the ground and began pummeling the wizards with fists of stone the size of wagon wheels.

The inquisitors were experts in magical combat and recovered quickly. Several erected wards, while most lashed out against the earthen fists, trusting their brothers and sisters in magic to shield them. Lightning and searing rays of arcane power lashed out and destroyed the constructs. The wizards spotted their foes in the flashing illuminations of their spells and turned their power onto the sorcerer and his apprentice.

With their trap sprung and the element of surprise lost, Azerick and Ellyssa joined the inquisitors in direct combat. Although their odds were greatly improved by the removal of half their enemy, the rift trap was magic beyond the capability of even the most powerful human wizard, and it left Azerick exhausted. The fatigue and amount of power it took to withstand the inquisitors' magic severely limited his ability to fight back. To draw more arcane energy meant tapping into even more intense emotions, both of which would empower Klaraxis. Too much, and the demon could take control.

As the two sides hurled earth-shattering magic at each other, Azerick felt himself faltering. He had to put more power into shielding himself and Ellyssa and was soon on the defensive. Her wards next to useless, Ellyssa let Azerick protect her from the wizards while she put all her strength into offensive spells. One scarlet beam shattered the ward of an inquisitor, striking her in the chest and throwing her back. She did not rise again.

With few of her spells powerful enough to pierce the inquisitors' magical shields, Ellyssa used subtler magic on the ground around them, opening deep crevasses and raising pillars of stone to either swallow or hurl wizards skyward, as such spells made their wards far less effective. Ellyssa noticed Azerick's strength failing and the slow retreat they were making. If something did not happen soon, they would need to make some kind of escape.

As if reading her thoughts, she heard Azerick mumble, "I need your help."

Ellyssa spared Azerick a brief look. "I'm sorry. I'm doing everything I can."

Azerick's lip twitched in a grin. "I wasn't talking to you."

Blackness filled the sky, and a huge swath of bright stars vanished. Ellyssa could feel a wind picking up at her back and growing stronger. A sound like someone shaking out a rug, only a thousand times more intense, echoed out over the sounds of battle. Ellyssa's eyes followed those of the inquisitors as they stared in terrified amazement at the dragon dropping from the sky.

As big as a castle, Sandy struck the ground with enough force to create a tremor so powerful it knocked several wizards from their feet. She let out a deafening roar that made bones tremor and bowels loosen. Sandy inhaled deeply before blanketing a massive tract of land in hellish fire. Every shrub and scrawny, dry tree dotting the land burst into flames. Sand melted into glass, and rock cracked and turned to slag under her inferno. Hissing out in the ancient language of the dragons, she reared up and crashed her forelegs onto the ground. The earth buckled and sent a rolling wave hundreds of yards wide undulating out toward the inquisitors.

Wizards not incinerated by her fiery breath uselessly poured magic into their wards. When the wave rolled beneath their feet, the ground turned no more solid than mud. They sank into the ground, some up to their necks, before the rock resolidified and trapped them in its tight grip. A few wizards, their hands free enough to resist, tried to turn their magic against the rock, but Azerick slammed them senseless with invisible strikes of force.

"If any of you wish to live beyond the next few moments, I suggest you cease resisting and surrender," Azerick called out as he stalked forward. He gave Sandy a pat on her house-sized flank as he passed.

"What will you do with us, demon?" a wizard demanded to know.

"I will leave you here with a warning for your hall, your duchess, and the Academy. The codex is mine. I retrieved it from creatures of unparalleled evil. I fought a dragon for it when I was little more than a journeyman. It speaks to me, and it speaks to my apprentice. Never in our recorded history has it spoken to more than one person at a time. It is a tool created by our gods to aid in a battle against a common enemy more terrifying than you can imagine. Tell your duchess and your Academy, I do not want to fight you. Our world will need everyone, especially wizards, to fight these creatures who strike fear into the hearts of our gods. But if you fight against me, you are worse than useless; you are a detriment, and I will end you," Azerick promised.

"You killed several of us here tonight!" the inquisitor accused him.

"You forced this battle."

The speaker looked at his trapped and fallen fellows and shifted his eyes to the sorcerer and the awe-inspiring dragon. Such a thing was a creature of legend and nightmare. How this man came to befriend one, he could not fathom. What he did know was that he was beaten.

"Where are the others, the ones lost to the rift?"

Azerick shrugged. "Somewhere in Sumara. Transdimensional magic is not my specialty. Most of them should have survived their journey, assuming it took them where I intended. Fight me again, and

I will rip open a gate straight to the deepest pits of the abyss and throw you all in, where my demons will devour your flesh and drink your souls."

Azerick turned and walked briskly away. Ellyssa and Sandy followed him into the darkness. Behind another rise, Raijaun hid in a deep cleft between boulders, using his demonic magic to wrap himself in impenetrable darkness. He rushed out of his hiding spot and hugged Azerick tightly.

Out of earshot of the inquisitors, Ellyssa finally asked the question she had been dying to since Sandy appeared. "Sandy, how did you get here, and when did you get so damn big?" she exclaimed.

Sandy's scaly face could not hide her grin as Azerick spoke a word and made a gesture. Her image wavered and shrank before their eyes until she was her normal, but still formidable size.

"It was all an illusion?"

"Like I said, sometimes a bluff is better than a good hand," Azerick responded with a smirk.

"But her roar and the fire and the shaking ground?"

"All augmented by me. When her appearance caused the inquisitors to balk their attack on me, I was able to lend my power to her breath and the effects of her magic."

"But how did she find us?" Ellyssa asked.

"I was able to contact her when we were in Sandusk."

Sandy said, "Imagine my surprise when I went to get a drink from my spring and saw Azerick's face staring at me from the water!" She craned her neck down and studied Azerick. "So it really is you. You smell funny."

"I'm not quite myself," Azerick replied. "Come, we need to put some distance between us and these idiots in case they get free and suddenly develop another acute case of stupidity. Sandy, you know where to meet us?"

The young dragon nodded, trotted a short distance away, and took to the air. Ellyssa shielded her eyes as the wind from Sandy's beating wings kicked up dust, sand, and gravel. Once free of the ground, Sandy vanished into the darkness of the night.

Azerick slashed at the air with his staff and a portal opened in the space before him. Ellyssa watched him pause to steady himself, giving evidence to his exhaustion and the strain of the night's battle. Azerick spied the look of concern on his apprentice's face, smiled, and nodded at the portal.

Ellyssa took Raijaun by the hand and stepped through, reeling and stumbling as she exited more than a mile from where Azerick stood on the other side. Azerick crossed over a moment later, and Ellyssa watched him stagger just a bit. This was the first time Azerick had shown how exhausted he was. She was concerned to see he was reaching his limitations, but at the same time relieved to know he had them.

"Do you want to stop and rest?" she asked worriedly.

Azerick took several deep breaths and shook his head. "We need to keep moving. I do not want to encourage the inquisitors to follow us. It is unlikely we would survive a second encounter. I just hope they continue to believe my bluff and do not recognize it for what it was."

He steadied himself, opened a rift once more, and took them another mile away. Azerick did not falter as he stepped through, but Ellyssa saw the effort it took firmly set in his face. He obviously did not want her to see how weak and tired he was. Two more gates took them almost five miles from the battle before Azerick called them to a stop.

"We will camp here," Azerick said as he slumped against a boulder.

"Do you think they will follow us?"

"I do not know. I took us in a more westerly direction this time and left a much smaller magical signature behind. Sandy is contaminating our trail as much as possible with her magic, which should make it much more difficult for them to follow us if they do decide to give chase. I need you to place some wards around our camp, at least two hundred yards out. Can you manage it?" he asked, his voice heavy with fatigue.

Ellyssa nodded. "I can set some detection wards. I'm too tired to set much in the way of anything offensive."

"That will be fine. Raijaun can find us some food, can't you, Raijaun?"

Raijaun showed his double row of needle-like teeth and bobbed his head excitedly. He darted off into the night in search of anything edible and too slow to avoid him. Ellyssa walked out into the night and set several wards she hoped were sufficient enough to alert them to any intruders, yet subtle enough to avoid detection if any wizards chose to give chase.

It was a large perimeter, and it was nearly an hour before she completed her task and returned to the camp. Azerick was still fetched up against his rock and did not respond to her approach. She did not know if he was sleeping or was just too tired to acknowledge her. Raijaun returned a half-hour later, looking depressed over his meager catch of a single hare.

"It's all right, Raijaun, we'll find something more in the morning," Ellyssa said encouragingly.

"You eat," Raijaun said.

She smiled warmly. "No, we can share. You are growing and need it more than me."

It was something of a lie. Her use of magic had left her famished, and she knew she could easily devour the scrawny rabbit by herself. Ellyssa gathered up a pile of dry shrubs and small sticks for a fire. She was just about to light it when something heavy dropped from the sky and thudded heavily onto the ground, raising a cloud of dust. Ellyssa jumped and let out a startled gasp. The sound of Sandy's wingbeats preceded her as she set down near the body of the small desert antelope she had just dropped.

"I thought you might be hungry after your battle," Sandy said as she touched down.

"You scared me to death!"

"I also thought it might be funny to almost hit you with a dead deer."

Ellyssa glared at the dragon. "Your humor has gotten really perverse lately. I think maybe you spend too much time with Wolf."

"I won't argue your point. He certainly has a way of instilling bad habits."

Ellyssa looked at the antelope and to her tiny firepit. "I don't think I can cook that even if I knew how to skin it."

Raijaun jumped up, pointed a finger at the corpse, and shouted, "Fire!"

Flame leapt from his outstretched hand, singed away all the hair, and charred the skin black. He danced around the smoking body, crowing at his accomplishment.

"I hope you like your antelope well done," Sandy remarked.

Azerick stirred from his rest and said, "Sandy, what are our inquisitor friends up to?"

"They had just gotten themselves unstuck and were chasing after the horses I found and spooked back toward Argoth. It will probably take them the rest of the night just to catch them."

"Excellent. Can you fly overhead and keep an eye on them while we rest? I want to make sure they keep heading southeast after they find their mounts. If you stay high enough, they will not be able to gauge your true size and call my bluff. Assuming, of course, they have not already deduced our little ruse."

"I will."

"Sandy, do you want to eat before you fly off?" Ellyssa asked.

"No, you can have it all. I can catch something while I'm watching those stupid wizards. I can also try out some of my new weather spells and make their ride home properly miserable," Sandy replied, grinning.

"Just be careful. They may be idiots, but they are dangerous idiots."

"She is right," Azerick agreed. "You are big and you are strong, but you are far from your full potential. Even fully grown, that many wizards would be dangerous, and if you fly within range of their claws, they could snatch you up and pull you into their maw."

"I'll be careful," Sandy promised before beating her wings and launching herself into the air.

"Do you want any of this?" Ellyssa asked, indicating the meat Raijaun was currently tearing into strips and devouring.

Azerick's stomach grumbled, apparently not completely free of the need, or at least the desire, for food in this world. "Save me a bit. I will eat it in the morning. For now, I just need rest. The inquisitors were not the only ones I was battling."

"The demon?"

Azerick nodded wearily. "Yes. Active combat taps into some strong emotions. Emotions are the playground of demons like Klaraxis, and it gives him strength. That is another reason I do not wish a second fight with the inquisitors."

Ellyssa was beginning to feel the full effects of her own exhaustion as well, but hunger won the immediate war for attention. She scooted over to the charred antelope and peeled away the pieces lying between the burnt and raw layers.

Even with the knowledge of Sandy flying overhead keeping watch and the wards she placed around camp, sleep did not come easy despite her fatigue. Every time the weight of her eyelids dragged them closed, fear snapped them wide open and made her scan the shadows for enemies.

Azerick sensed her restlessness. "Go ahead and sleep. Nothing will come near us without me or Sandy knowing it."

Her nerves at least partially placated, Ellyssa was able to allow sleep to pull her into its embrace. She slept soundly despite the battles her dream world brought. She did not fight inquisitors but horrific creatures that moved with the speed and ferocity of a Habberback hunting cat. But Azerick was there by her side as well as Sandy, Roger, and the other students from the school. Wave after wave of creatures leapt at them, snarling their hatred and slashing with short blades. The bodies piled up until they created a wall too high for her to see over, but still they came on. She did not wake until the whumping sound of Sandy's beating wings pulled her from her nightmare.

Azerick was already up and eating, morosely picking over a haunch of meat. Sandy kicked up a cloud of dust as she set down. Raijaun hopped up and down, clapping his hands at Sandy's arrival. He ran over as soon as she landed and scratched at her scales.

"What are our friends up to?" Azerick asked once the dust settled.

"They buried six of their members last night. Half again as many wounded needed assistance walking. They did manage to find their horses and continued heading toward Argoth for as long as I watched them."

"Good. It sounds like they chose a wiser course, although they may have second thoughts about it when they report their failure."

"I spent the whole night pelting them with sleet to encourage them to keep moving. Their wards kept them dry, but it didn't do anything for the road," Sandy smirked.

"Thank you, Sandy. You did very well. You can probably go home now if you like," Azerick said.

"I can probably fly everyone back. It would be a lot faster," Sandy offered.

Azerick shook his head. "I am a lot heavier than I look, and I have some things I need to prepare before I return home. Sandy, I am not ready for anyone to know I have come back yet, especially since the Academy is entrenched in my school. Please keep this a secret. I can only hope we beat home any word coming out of Argoth of my return."

"I won't say anything," Sandy promised. "I will probably fly around for a couple days and make sure those wizards don't turn back."

"I would appreciate it."

Sandy took wing, kicking up another cloud of dust and grit, and disappeared over the southern horizon. Azerick appeared lost in thought as he picked at his food.

"Are you feeling better?" Ellyssa asked.

"Much. We will keep heading northwest. I expect to reach a town called Bruneford's Mill near the northern region of the Habberback Plains in about four days. We will spend a couple days there to rest and give Raijaun some more experience being around people."

"He really has calmed down a lot," Ellyssa said as she looked over at Raijaun, who smiled at the attention.

"He has come further and far faster than I had hoped possible. His progression is truly astounding," Azerick agreed as he continued to pick halfheartedly at his food.

"Is the meat not cooked to your liking?" Ellyssa asked.

"It is not what my body desires."

"What does it want?"

Azerick's lip twitched in response. "You do not want to know."

CHAPTER 5

A million Scion minions clawed at the invisible wall of their prison, some taking out their pent-up savagery and frustration on those weaker and close to them. High overhead, dozens of ships, not unlike regular seagoing vessels only sleeker and more angular, sat statically. Their crews paced the decks, anxiously awaiting the inevitable destruction of their prison walls.

In the center of the chaotic mass, floating amidst the ships and shining like a star, a crystal palace cast its radiance down upon the throngs. Tall and sleek like the surrounding ships, its minarets stabbed at the black, starless sky like a many-pointed crystal dagger.

Five figures, tall, impossibly thin, and dressed in tight-fitting, broad-shouldered, hooded robes occupied the vast central chamber of the crystal fortress. Here dwelled the Scions, also called the faceless ones due to their lack of facial features. Only their large eyes broke the featureless plain of their faces, which looked like two small galaxies replete with shining stars. They were the original gods of the world from which they were banished. The Scions gazed out across a landscape as featureless as their faces. Hundreds of feet below, their vast army waited for the day the wall was destroyed, releasing them from their prison to wreak havoc upon the cursed races that turned against them. That day was fast approaching.

Doaz hovered over a flat-topped pillar ten feet across. *"Brethren, something transpires."*

The other four Scions glided near and looked upon the image brilliantly displayed within the crystal surface.

"What is it?" Xar asked.

"I detect a weakness in the barrier."

"Can we breach it?"

"For a moment. I sensed a curious use of magic not far from the flaw. It was powerful, by mortal standards, and may have contributed to the weakening. Do you feel it?"

"We do," Zyn replied. *"It feels like the unusual creature Lissandra flaunted before us, does it not?"*

"It does," Kaz and Arhal both answered. *"Is he still near?"*

"I believe so, and two others who dare touch the power of the gods."

"This should prove interesting. Let us test the mettle of Lissandra's replacement and see if he is worthy of the title Guardian."

All five Scions laid their long, three-fingered hands upon the plinth and focused their energy into the crystal of their fortress. A white ray of light with the power to destroy a mountain lanced out from the center spire, disintegrating over a hundred creatures crowded around the point of impact. The beam struck the shimmering barrier with the force of a comet. Excess energy exploded into the ranks of fleeing creatures, destroying hundreds more. The barrier trembled under the onslaught and began to waver where the beam continued to punish it.

With a final groan and massive clap of thunder, the ray punched through. The Scions created a portal within the breach and ordered their minions through. Ravagers, the most plentiful of their troops, sprinted toward the fissure and hurled themselves into the rift before it sealed shut once again. The rift was open only a few seconds, but ravagers were frighteningly swift and nearly two hundred of the creatures darted through before the breach snapped shut, locking out the ones too slow to reach it and cutting the slightly faster ones in half.

The ravagers tore across the tall grass blanketing much of the Habberback Plains, using their long arms to hurtle themselves forward like an ape with the speed and ferocity of a plains lion. However, they were not animals; at least, not in the classic sense. They looked like men with dark red skin, bald or bristly black hair, and carried short blades in each hand to slash their enemies to ribbons. Taut, corded muscles flexed and rippled across bodies covered with little more than a weapons belt and a loin cloth, if they wore even that much.

They were locusts of unparalleled terror, killing and devouring every living thing in their path. A herd of antelope sensed the approaching predators before they ever saw them and bolted. Fleet of foot, the herd put some distance between them and the fearsome new creatures, but unlike the ravagers, they eventually tired. The ravagers tore into the exhausted animals and slaughtered them en masse.

Their bellies full and their bloodlust only heightened, the ravagers continued racing for the town the humans called Bruneford's Mill.

The caravan continued to travel after sunset in hopes of reaching Bruneford's Mill before noon the next day. They carried a large load of iron, copper, and timber they would sell for coin and trade for the grains the plains were famous for producing. The road was good but not great, and the wagon master finally called them to a stop.

It took nearly an hour to move the huge wagon train off the road and to form a circle to provide a meager form of protection. In this case, the only protection they needed was from the frequent winds that often howled across the prairie, carrying mouthfuls of dust with every breath. One favorable thing about the plains was there was ample space to move the wagons and horses off the road and make camp.

"Aaron, picket your horses on the north side away from the road. Let's get those cook stoves going. Set some greenhorns to chocking the wagons. Last thing we need is some plains cat to spook the oxen," Wagon Master Owen barked needlessly.

He had an experienced crew, and everyone knew their job, but he had a job to do as well, and he was certainly going to make sure everyone saw him do it. They would reach Bruneford's Mill just before noon the following day if they left before sunrise. His job was almost halfway over and he looked forward to completing it. It was the largest caravan he had commanded during the year. His commission from this venture would pay for the addition to his home, which he desperately needed with the new baby on the way. Owen sighed, feeling too old to be a father again, but he had married a young woman and was still healthy despite cresting the hill of forty years.

He watched his people efficiently carry out their duties, barking out a few orders every so often just to ensure they knew he was playing his part. Owen liked working with people he knew and who knew their job, because it made his a lot easier. Some seasons, he had a green crew and had to play both wagon master and nanny to ensure everything was done properly. It had been less of an issue these last few years since most people who hired on at the Tower Trading Company stuck around. They paid the best and treated everyone properly, and only a fool went looking for better when you had a good employer.

Aaron, his guard captain, approached him from out of the darkness, which was just now being broken by several campfires. Owen recognized him even before he could make out his face due to his peculiar gait. It was the walk of a man more accustomed to sitting in a saddle than walking on his own legs.

"The horses are picketed and a quarter of my men posted around the camp, Owen," Aaron informed the wagon master.

A quarter of the guards made for a light watch, but it was sufficient. The plains were a mostly peaceful place. The scattered tribes of plains barbarians were honest folk and traded fairly. Owen actually looked forward to dealing with the ones who always intercepted his caravan en route to Bruneford's Mill. They brought unusual trinkets, pelts, and carvings not found anywhere else in exchange for steel. Folks called them barbarians, but despite their crude living, they were more pleasant to deal with than many of his "civilized" countrymen.

"Excellent work as always, Aaron. The cooks should have them fed within the hour." Owen Cocked an ear toward a rhythmic thrumming sound in the distance. "Do you hear that? What is that, horses?"

The guard captain turned and listened. "The gait is wrong and too light to be horses. It's short and soft, like wolves."

"There ain't no wolves on the plains, and the cats don't move in a pack. Aaron, put your men on alert. I got a chill running up my spine cold enough to make my bones brittle." Others in the camp had heard the noise by now and were pausing in their duties to listen. "Don't stand around gawking, people; put something in your hands and watch yourselves until we know what's coming!"

Aaron returned with his helm firmly strapped in place and his sword in his hand. "The men are ready and using the wagons for cover. Whatever is coming sounds fast and outnumbers my horses. Best to fight on the defensive if it comes to that."

"You know best, Aaron. Whatever it is, it doesn't sound like it's slowing. Maybe it is just an animal herd and will run past."

Barely two seconds passed between the first warning shouts and the ravagers leaping over the wagons and proceeding to slaughter the humans just beyond their feeble barriers. Crossbows thrummed, but only a few bolts found their marks before the terrifying creatures were amongst them.

"What in the abyss are these things?" Aaron shouted.

"I think you got it right. Only the abyss could spawn this," Owen cursed.

Aaron was as capable as any man Owen had ever seen, but the ravager cut him down with little effort. He had almost no time to process the death occurring around him before the creatures leapt upon him and ended his life. The battle was brief, and in just a few short minutes, a hundred fifty men and women met a brutal end. The ravagers destroyed the wagons and killed any animal unable to flee, before turning eastward toward Bruneford's Mill.

Azerick, Ellyssa, and Raijaun were spending their fourth night in Bruneford's Mill. Ellyssa was asleep and Azerick was writing in his book, as he always did, and would continue to do so until morning. Raijaun, like Azerick, needed little rest and was drawing letters and sigils on a piece of parchment.

It had been several days of travel to reach Bruneford's Mill, and they all enjoyed the decent rest and good food; Ellyssa did, at the very least. Azerick merely preferred being out of the elements, and Raijaun seemed immune to the hardships of travel.

Their journey was nearly halfway through, and Azerick decided he would soon need to split his time between writing out his training manual and teaching Raijaun how to work magic. He was already working some small castings on his own. He had set a swath of plains grass on fire with a localized lightning storm, but Azerick and Ellyssa were able to put it out. His son's inherent knowledge and ability to call upon and weave multiple sources of magic amazed him. Azerick was eager to take the time to sit down with him and shape his raw talent into something more controlled.

Azerick put down his quill and listened. He thought he heard the faint sounds of distressed voices but was unsure. However, as he sent his senses out into the town, he found an undeniable tension in the air. There was violence being enacted and on a large scale. It called to his demonic nature like the insistent allure of an ardent lover.

"Ellyssa, get up," Azerick called out hurriedly.

Ellyssa stirred and sat up. "What is it?" she asked groggily.

"Trouble. Quick, throw something warmer on, and grab your pack. We may have to leave town quickly. Raijaun, stay close to me no matter what."

Azerick packed up their meager belongings and the codex while Ellyssa threw a sturdy cloak over her shoulders before following him out of the room. The cries throughout the town were now clearly distinct, and other patrons of the inn began shuffling out of their rooms, their nervousness evident on their faces and in their voices.

"What's happening?" a serving maid who lived at the inn asked.

"I'm not sure, but I suggest you all stay in your rooms and lock the doors," Azerick advised before he stepped out into the night.

Screams of sheer panic and the smell of smoke assaulted them the moment Azerick opened the door of the inn. Far more people than would normally be out at this hour ran wildly through the streets. Men raced through town with weapons in their hands while women fled in the other direction holding babes.

"Azerick, what is happening?" Ellyssa asked as she cast her gaze up and down the street, taking in the pandemonium around them.

"Something is violently attacking the town. I can feel the people's terror and death. Whatever it is, it is awful."

"Are we going to help them?" Ellyssa asked.

The internal conflict so evident on Azerick's face and posture shocked her. She remembered the Azerick who would have leapt to the defense of these people without hesitation. This new Azerick was cold and dispassionate, and he scared her.

Ellyssa breathed a sigh of relief when he answered, "Yes. Keep Raijaun close. I do not know what is attacking the town, but I feel the Scions' hand in it, and I doubt he can protect himself from whatever they are."

The three pushed toward the west side of town, struggling to avoid those who fled eastward away from the source of the destruction. Howls, snarls, and maniacal laughter joined the chorus of screams and death knells as they drew closer.

It took only minutes for them to spot the first ravagers. Bruneford's Mill was far from any hostile lands or people and sported no defensive walls, which allowed the ravagers to push deep into the town. Only the time it took to tear through doors and slaughter the inhabitants slowed their progress.

Several ravagers struck from out of the darkness, the blood painting their bodies almost indistinguishable from their own skin in both color and coverage. Two of the creatures leapt into the air with their strange punch daggers cocked back and ready to slash their foes to pieces. Azerick lashed his hand forward and across, cleanly bisecting both of them with a whip of arcane energy.

Ellyssa conjured a shard of stone from the street, sent it hurling toward the third ravager, and pinned it to the wall of a building. A keening howl erupted across the town as the ravagers sensed the use of magic. Wizards and sorcerers were their masters' most hated enemies, and they would stop at nothing to destroy them. The ravagers ceased their chaotic, wanton destruction and converged upon the source of magic.

Azerick and Ellyssa found themselves in the heart of a maelstrom of death as the ravagers leapt from rooftops and raced at them from all directions, heedless of their own lives. Arcane energy split the night air with fire, lightning, and bolts of power as the pair fought furiously to keep the monsters at bay.

Azerick could not know if there were still people around and avoided unleashing his most destructive magic. It would be easy for him to scour clean several blocks of the town and destroy the bulk of the invaders—too easy. He felt Klaraxis's constant but subtle urgings and refused to give in to them, but that could change soon if the ravagers kept coming. In the coming battle, the death toll would be measured in the hundreds of thousands. The few thousand lives of Bruneford's Mill were expendable in the greater scheme of things.

The ravagers continued to press their attack, hurling stones, timber, and even human bodies at the two magic users who were devastating their numbers. Several climbed to the roofs of nearby buildings, took a running leap, and dropped down upon the defenders. Neither Azerick nor Ellyssa were taken completely by surprise, having beaten back this tactic before, but there were several of them and a few broke through their defenses.

Azerick and Ellyssa instantly turned their attack onto the ravagers in their ranks, but before either of them could respond, one of the creatures grabbed up Raijaun and leapt away, disappearing into a dark alleyway.

"Raijaun!" Azerick shouted.

Fear and rage suffused Azerick's soul and he lashed out, heedless of the damage he caused. His fear turned to terror when Raijaun's shrill screams emanated from out of the alley. Pure terror fueled his spells as Azerick blasted a hole through the ravagers' ranks in an effort to get to his son.

As Azerick fought his way to Raijaun, he sensed an immense buildup of power. It took a moment for him to comprehend what was happening. Mingling with the familiar arcane energy was a strange magic very similar to that used by Lissandra. Azerick grabbed Ellyssa, pulled her down, and covered them with the most powerful ward he could conjure in an instant.

The world seemed to explode around them as fire washed over his ward like a tidal wave. Buildings burst into flame and crumbled under the intense heat, but the destruction did not end. The ground buckled and split open, spewing molten rock into the air, which came down like a meteor storm. Azerick could not hear Raijaun's terrified screams, but he could feel his son's fear and panic. Lissandra said Raijaun would be the most formidable weapon he had, but Azerick could not have imagined this. Not yet.

Driven by fear, Raijaun would destroy the entire town and its inhabitants if he did not destroy himself first. He was a frightened child, lashing out with everything he had without thought of the consequences. He was channeling far more power than his body could safely manage and was probably moments away from being consumed by it.

"Ellyssa, I have to get to Raijaun and try to calm him down!" Azerick shouted to be heard over the chaos. "Keep those things away from me as best you can; I have to keep my focus on this ward."

Despite the rampant destruction, ravagers continued bounding out of the shadows, leaping the flaming fissures, and dodging the falling molten rock. Azerick and Ellyssa both fought their way to the remains of the alley now made up of little more than piles of stone and charred timber. Ellyssa sent her magic into the ground and raised four enormous constructs from the cobblestones. They were not true golems; these had very little autonomy, and it took almost all of Ellyssa's concentration to direct their attacks toward the ravagers.

She used them to block the opening to their tiny oasis within the hellish destruction, lashing out with huge stone fists to crush any ravager trying to fight its way past. Several tried to leap over the constructs, only to be plucked from the air and pulped against the ground or hurled into a nearby fissure.

Azerick pressed into the remains of the alley and spotted Raijaun, seemingly lost in his terror and caught up in the grip of the magic he wielded. Like a fire, the magic had taken on a life of its own and raged out of control. The fact Raijaun was able to keep it from destroying him for this long was amazing. Azerick looked into the ether where normal eyes could not see, and watched his boy wrestling with forces that would have already consumed an experienced wizard.

Azerick reached into that invisible, arcane maelstrom and began gathering up the threads of magic in an attempt to control and safely release it back into the Source. Grabbing those strands was like trying to snatch loose lines on a sail flailing around in gale-force winds. The strands lashed out at him, fighting his attempts at control. The magic was like a living creature now, and it did not want to be vanquished.

"Raijaun," Azerick called out loudly but gently. "Raijaun, I have it now. You can let go."

Raijaun finally opened his eyes, and Azerick could see the tears streaming down his face, glinting on the light of the surrounding inferno. "Father? Father, help me!"

"It's okay, son, I am here. I have the magic. Let it go."

Reluctantly, Raijaun loosened his hold and allowed the magic to slip from his grasp. He looked once more at Azerick and crumpled to the ground. Azerick released the pent-up energy into the sky in a massive column of searing white power, illuminating the countryside for miles around. He scooped Raijaun into his arms and tore open a portal.

"Ellyssa, time to get out of here!"

Ellyssa glanced over her shoulder, spotted the gate, and ran through. Her constructs fought on for perhaps a score of seconds before crumbling back into piles of useless stone. Azerick carried Raijaun's limp body in his arms and followed after, snapping the portal shut the instant he stepped through.

"Azerick, what about the people in town and those creatures?" Ellyssa asked desperately, looking at the orange glow of the burning town in the distance.

"I do not believe there were many left. The townspeople will have to deal with them the best they can."

Azerick opened another gate and stepped through, giving Ellyssa no time to voice any further concerns or protests. Twice more Azerick hurried them through his gates before stopping.

"If we do not use our magic, I do not think those creatures can find us, if any still live."

"What were they? Where did they come from?"

Azerick pulled the Codex Arcana from his shoulder satchel. "Show me." The book fanned open. "Ravagers, the footmen of the Scions. They are fast, strong, and savage."

"I thought the Scions were still locked away?"

"They are, otherwise the entire kingdom would be like Bruneford's Mill right now. My guess is there was a flaw, a minor breach the Scions were able to exploit. It has happened in the past. I do not think we have as much time to get home as I had hoped. I need to get back to my tower and establish a base from where I can better watch the Scions' prison. If there are more of these flaws, it could prove disastrous. I do not have the time to go stamp out small fires like this all over the kingdom," he said impatiently.

Ellyssa was taken aback by his callousness. "A lot of people are dead. I think the entire town will burn to the ground, and you call it a small fire?"

"In the larger scheme of things, that is exactly what it is. Ellyssa, I am glad to see you still care about the lives of people, even strangers, but this is going to be a war like no other, with death on an unimaginable scale. If we allow our sentimentality to guide us away from what we must do, we will lose not just our homes or even our kingdom; we will lose our existence as a species."

Ellyssa's mind simply could not process horror on such a scale, so she turned it toward more local and immediate concerns. "How is Raijaun?"

"Exhausted. The amount of power he had coursing through him was something that would make even me pause for concern. It is either a miracle he survived, or he is far more powerful than any of us can imagine."

Ellyssa shivered. "What was that? I felt magic like none I have felt before."

"It was the magic of the Guardians, which is an amalgamation of elvish and dragon magic. That is why it is so elemental in nature. Both elf and dragon magic are powerfully elemental, but unique to each of the races. Because elves use the Source just as human wizards and sorcerers do, they can shape it into spells, only with far greater effect, when directing the power of nature."

Ellyssa looked at Raijaun lying unconscious upon Azerick's lap. "Will you call Sandy back to take us home then?"

"No. It is now more important than ever to teach Raijaun control before we return, but I cannot afford to dawdle like I was. I am nearly finished with what I need to write and, to be honest, I was delaying our return."

"Why?"

Azerick bowed his head. "Miranda and Daebian. I am not who I was, and I am afraid. I fear their reaction, what they think of me, and how I think of them. I am not coming home to be a loving husband and father, but a general who must prepare a nation for war. I have no time for familial sentiments, and I am ashamed of it."

Ellyssa could not control the tears that came unbidden to her eyes. It was the first spark of humanity, of the old Azerick, he had allowed to slip through the iron façade since his return. She sidled over and put her arms around him.

"They'll understand."

Azerick smiled at the top of her head. "I wish I could be so young and naïve again. But we can wish, can't we?"

CHAPTER 6

Raijaun awoke the next morning. Azerick chose not to sleep, instead staying awake and watching over his son and apprentice. He hurried to his son's side as he sat up and looked around.

"How do you feel?" Azerick asked.

"Hungry," Raijaun answered.

"I'm sorry, but I did not think to grab any food before we left. How are you?"

"My body hurts really bad. What happened?"

"You panicked and channeled too much power." Azerick gripped Raijaun's shoulder firmly. "Raijaun, you lost control last night. You let fear take over, and it cost some people their lives, and more importantly, almost your own. You cannot ever lose control like that again."

Raijaun looked at the ground and his shoulders slumped. "I'm sorry, Father. I was scared."

"I know, but you must not let your emotions control you. You are very powerful and very important. Everything and everyone is counting on your ability to control your power and use it wisely. I will need you in the coming days, and I must be able to rely on you and your judgment. You must never lose control again."

"I understand, Father. I won't."

Azerick smiled at his son. "Don't feel too bad. I did the same thing—twice—just on a smaller scale. I will start working with you more so you can learn more control and focus."

"Okay, Father, but not today please," Raijaun begged, his pain and exhaustion evident in his eyes.

"Are you sure you are all right?"

"It hurts. It feels like my blood is hot and burning me."

Azerick squeezed Raijaun's shoulder. "I am sure you will be fine. You just pulled in too much power and your body is protesting its abuse."

Ellyssa sidled over and sat next to Azerick as Raijaun lay back down and went to sleep. "How is he?"

"He is afraid, and in a lot of pain."

"He channeled a lot of power, more than I ever could, and I almost died when I overreached myself."

Azerick shook his head. "I think it is more than that. Did it ever feel as though your blood was burning in your veins?"

"No, more like someone had beaten me with a stick for the better part of the day," Ellyssa commented wryly.

"I would use a similar analogy for what I felt. It was more exhaustion and muscle pain. I will need to consult the codex, but I think he may be experiencing some sort of conflict between his differing magics."

"You wield different magic, don't you? Does it hurt you?"

Azerick thought a moment. "It conflicts, but I can force it to work together. I think that conflict is what makes the combination so powerful. It is uncomfortable but bearable. Raijaun also controls whatever magic the Guardians possessed. It is similar to dragon magic, which is natural and elemental as I said. Abyssal magic is nearly its opposite, and is wholly unnatural. Wizard and sorcerous magic lies somewhere in between."

"How bad could using his magic hurt him? If it does hurt him, how is he going to be able to fight the Scions?"

"I do not know. It may be something he will have to avoid unless absolutely necessary, and simply suffer through it when he does. For now, we must teach him control."

Azerick allowed Raijaun to rest another day before guiding them onto the path home. Raijaun still hurt, but he kept up and never complained. His sullen expression and body language spoke of his shame for losing control and hurting people in Bruneford's Mill. Azerick was relieved at his son's ability to empathize. It meant his heart was much more human than demon.

Azerick searched the codex for answers regarding his son's affliction, but nothing like Raijaun had ever existed. He studied abyssal magic and gained some knowledge of Guardian and dragon magic, but no one had ever combined them before. Azerick eventually decided that his theory regarding the conflicting magic was sound. There was simply too much divergence between abyssal and Guardian magic. Forcing the two to form a magical weave, although extremely powerful, was also painful if not dangerous to the wielder.

"Are you ready to practice?" Azerick asked Raijaun after they finished their supper.

Raijaun was hesitant but nodded. "Yes, Father."

"First, I want you reach for the Source. Pull in as much as you feel comfortable doing." Raijaun nodded and began gathering the Source to him. "Keep going, I know you can do more than that."

Raijaun's eyes darted nervously as he gathered a little more power into him. Azerick knew he was not coming close to his potential but decided to let Raijaun set the pace for now.

"Shape your spell." Raijaun plucked at the individual strands of summoned energy and shaped them into a spell. "Good, now reach for the other magic. Let us do the Guardian magic."

"Father, I would rather not. I am afraid it will hurt me again."

"You do not need to fear it, Son. It is the black abyssal magic that conflicts with your Guardian magic. This will not hurt you."

Raijaun looked uncertain, but he trusted his father and obeyed. Plucking at the strands of golden power surrounding all things in nature, he threaded them into his sorcerous weave. Visible only to those able to see beyond the physical and into the ether, his spell form glowed with an almost blindingly silver and golden radiance.

Azerick examined the spell his son held in stasis. Still just a child, he easily controlled as much power as a competent wizard and was not close to stressing himself. Raijaun's weave began to tremble and errant arcs of energy began sparking chaotically as his nerves began to fray.

Azerick pointed to a scrubby bush. "Release it over there."

Raijaun unleashed his spell in a powerful ray of gold and silver light, incinerating the bush and setting fire to the surrounding foliage. He looked to his father worriedly.

"It is all right. Use your magic to put the fire out."

Raijaun grabbed at his Guardian magic like a miser scrambling after a fistful of dropped coins. He clawed the magic, forced it into a weave, and released it. Clouds rolled in, black and angry, thundering their displeasure. Ellyssa shrieked as a torrent of rain washed down from the sky, inundating the land. The rain instantly extinguished the small fires, but now their camp was awash with several inches of water.

"Raijaun, please stop the rain before we drown," Azerick said dryly.

"I'm sorry!" Raijaun exclaimed, then plucked apart the strands of magic holding the unnatural storm together.

Despite no longer being magically driven, it took several minutes for the rain to stop and almost an hour for the clouds to disperse. The camp was a mess. Their fire was snuffed out and washed away, and everything was soaked. Fortunately, being wielders of magic meant their discomfort was only temporary. It was a simple matter for Azerick and Ellyssa to dry out both themselves and their things. The sodden ground all around was a much greater problem, as water seemed to trickle in from everywhere.

"Sorry," Raijaun said again.

"We will have more time to practice. Keep working on drawing, forming, and holding your magic. Just remember not to work the conflicting sources just yet."

Raijaun shook his head vehemently. "I will not forget, ever."

"So Harvey walks into his office and finds a wolverine tearing the room apart," James said, regaling his friend as they shared a guard shift atop the wall. "And the smell! That thing sprayed everything! It was hilarious until they found wolf prints around the sally port I was guarding. They blamed me for letting Wolf in despite my protests of innocence. Now I'm pulling double duty for a month."

"Did you do it?" Dustin asked.

"Of course I did! Harvey's an ass. Several of us old-timers have been letting Wolf in to harass those Academy jerks since they showed up. They never did figure out who disabled the wards on Harvey's door. My guess is Roger."

"I'm just glad they pretty much leave us martial students alone. I feel bad for the wizards though." Dustin squinted at the road in the distance and brought a brass spyglass to his eye. "Looks like three people approaching on foot. One woman, a man, and a kid. The woman kind of looks like Ellyssa."

James peered through the spyglass when Dustin passed it to him. "That's definitely Ellyssa. Who's the man?" James watched the small group approach and nearly dropped the glass over the wall. "Holy crap! Kimberly, come over here, now!"

A young woman posted at the northwest corner stalked briskly over. "James, you better not be screwing around again."

James thrust the spyglass into her hands. "Look at who's coming up the road and tell me who it is."

Kimberly studied the trio intently. "The girl is definitely Ellyssa. The man...no freaking way!"

"Is it Azerick, or am I completely insane?"

Dustin looked at his two comrades. "Are you talking about Azerick who used to run this place and died like five years ago?"

The two older soldiers ignored the younger. "I would say it was someone who looked a lot like him, but that is his staff. That would explain how it came up missing a few months ago! If he came back, he could have magicked it to him."

"Wait," Dustin exclaimed, "people don't just come back from the dead."

James looked at his friend and smiled. "You don't know Azerick. Kim, watch the wall. I'm going to go tell the tower."

James sprinted down the steps two at a time, raced across the grounds, and ran up the steps to the new tower. He wrenched open the doors and burst into the dining hall a moment later. As he had expected given the time of day, he found Lady Miranda and most of the original school staff sitting down for lunch.

Alex looked at the intruder sharply. "James, I hope there is a good reason for leaving your post and barging in here like a madman."

James braced his hands on his knees and took several deep breaths. "Coming up the road...Ellyssa..." he gasped out, pointing behind him.

"Ellyssa? Could they have let her go?" Miranda asked.

"It is highly unlikely," Allister replied.

James shook his head vigorously. "Azerick is with her!"

Allister's face reddened and his brow grew even more furrowed. "James, if this is one of your jests, it is in extremely poor taste."

"No, I swear! I asked Kimberly, and I saw the staff!"

Miranda clutched her chest. "Is this possible?"

All eyes turned to Aggie, the resident expert on transdimensional magic. "I thought it might be, especially after Azerick's staff vanished. But I have no idea how it could be done, and I did not want to raise any false hopes with speculation."

"Imposter or not, we had best see to it," Allister said.

By the time the assembly moved outside, people were already speaking excitedly as word spread. Headmaster Harvey was observing the applied magic class when a student burst in.

"Azerick is back!"

The younger students looked at each other quizzically, but the older students jumped from their desks and pushed for the doors, speaking animatedly.

"You students get back to your seats if you do not wish to be expelled!" Headmaster Harvey shouted. "If you know what's good for you, you will sit down this instant!"

"Go kiss a troll, Harvey!" someone shouted from the mass pressing through the door. "If it really is Azerick, you will have your things packed and be on your way if you know what's good for you!"

Harvey was forced to wait for the students to clear the door before exiting the room. He cursed them all for crude, low-born riffraff as he hurried to his office. He swore once again to bring that accursed wildling to heel when the still pervasive odor of wolverine spray assaulted him. Thus far, his attempts to capture the half-elf had resulted in humiliating failure. His people were not experienced woodsmen, and that lack of skill resulted in defeats every bit as painful and embarrassing as his attempt to bring in the girl. Once again, he wished the Academy had given him leave to shut down this school. It was nothing but a warren of vagabonds and criminals, in his opinion.

Wolf and Ghost had been watching the three travelers almost since they left the major trade road. The pair kept their distance from the school since Wolf had snuck a wolverine into the headmaster's office. Wolf mentally reminded himself to check his badger traps later. He also had a good plan for a huge fire wasp nest he found. It would have to wait until the weather cooled and the wasps went dormant before he could move it into the headmaster's office, where the warm room would make the hibernating insects very active. He hated waiting. Maybe Sandy could help him again with her magic. She was getting very good at controlling the weather around her.

Wolf could barely believe his eyes when he recognized Azerick. When Ghost sniffed the air and let out a low rumble, he did not believe them at all. He pulled an arrow from his quiver, set it to the string, and took careful aim.

"Stop right there," Wolf called out from the shadows of the nearby trees.

"Wolf, it's Azerick!" Ellyssa shouted into the trees.

"Ghost says he doesn't smell like Azerick."

"Sandy said the same thing."

"I'm starting to get a little offended by everyone commenting on my smell," Azerick said.

"I thought you were locked up or killed by those wizards," Wolf said suspiciously.

"I was, but Azerick came and busted me out," Ellyssa explained.

"Sounds like something stupid Azerick would do." Wolf and Ghost stepped warily from the trees. Wolf pointed his bow down but kept the arrow nocked. Ghost walked in a crouch, ready to leap, his ears flattened against his head. "Sandy saw him?"

"Yes. She flew south a few weeks ago to help us with the inquisitors who wanted to take back Azerick's book."

Wolf tallied the time in his head. Sandy had disappeared for a few days around the time Ellyssa mentioned. He did not know much about magic, however elves believed death was not an end to one's existence, but merely a transition to another life. If so, he supposed it was possible to transition back, especially since they were talking about Azerick.

"Azerick?"

"Yes, Wolf."

"What was the first thing you gave me?"

Azerick smiled. "A bath, because you stunk too bad to eat next to. Then I fed you and Ghost. You might say I gave you a blanket, even though I'd say you stole it."

"I guess it is you." Wolf's face broke out in a devilish grin. "Are you going to throw out those Academy idiots?"

"Absolutely," Azerick answered, matching Wolf's eager expression.

"Oh, man, I gotta see this!" Wolf looked at Raijaun as if noticing him for the first time. "Who's the kid?"

"That's Raijaun, Azerick's son," Ellyssa supplied.

Wolf peered into the deep hood, studied Raijaun's face, and looked questioningly at Azerick. "And his mother is…?"

"Gone," Azerick answered shortly.

"Okay, well, nice to meet you, Raij. I'm Wolf and this is Ghost."

"Hello," Raijaun replied shyly. He reached out slowly toward Ghost when he came near, but the wolf put his ears back and slinked away.

"Don't mind him. He lacks my excellent social graces."

"Speaking of your excellent social graces, how have you been getting on with the new headmaster and his teachers?" Ellyssa asked.

"I fed a wolverine a bunch of pickled cabbage and locked him in Harvey's office the other day. Last week I rubbed goblin wart nectar all over their robes while they hung out to dry. They never did figure out why the flies wouldn't leave them alone. I once rubbed poison ivy on the inside of their robes while they hung on the drying line."

"You would think they would post a guard after the first time," Ellyssa said.

"They did."

"Who?"

"James."

Ellyssa laughed. "That's like hiring a thief to guard your gold!"

Azerick searched his memory and recalled the boy's face. Young man by now, he corrected himself. He was the lad who gave Ellyssa so much grief when it came to coming and going through the gates. He had made a bet with another young guardsman that Azerick would cheat before saying the passphrase "steel is real but magic is tragic" to be let through the gate.

Someone must have recognized him as they made their way toward the school. There was a significant amount of activity atop the wall as they approached, far more than they would show for a typical visitor, even a stranger. Azerick was near enough now he could hear his name being spoken amongst the press of people on the walls.

The main gates swung wide and a mass of people pushed through. Miranda held her hands clenched to her chest, scarcely believing what she saw as their eyes locked. Azerick finally looked down at Daebian and shuddered. He had hoped Daebian would look different from the boy he saw in the Valley of Lies, but it was the same face if a little older. Apparently not everything in the valley had been a lie.

Miranda had started to step forward when a voice boomed, "Miranda, stay back!"

It felt as though a giant had punched Azerick in the chest and then sat on him. Bands of magical energy wrapped around his body, pinning his arms in place and anchoring him to the ground.

"Allister, what are you doing?" Miranda cried out.

"That is not Azerick!" the archmage grunted out as he struggled to hold the demon in place. "Brother Thomas, help me!"

Brother Thomas said a quick prayer and saw what Allister saw. The Chosen of Solarian called upon his god for power and began a ritual of banishing. Azerick struggled to control his anger despite the rage demanding he crush these insects. He could feel Klaraxis fueling the fires of his anger and pride and refused to let the demon influence him. It was not until Brother Thomas was deep into his ritual banishing that Azerick felt true pain.

"Allister, stop!" Ellyssa shouted.

Azerick raised his head from the ground and looked at his old friend and mentor. "Allister, it is me. If I were truly the thing I appear to be, I would tear your restraints apart and destroy you and everyone else here."

"If you are truly Azerick, how did you return here, and why in this form?" he demanded.

"How I got here is a long story. As to my body, do you remember the little problem I had with the demon? Our roles have undergone a slight paradigm shift."

Allister looked to Brother Thomas, still unconvinced and very much afraid. The Chosen shifted into a slight trance and studied the creature Allister struggled to keep pinned to the ground, only succeeding because it did not appear to be resisting much.

"Azerick's soul does exist within the demon's body," he confirmed.

"Can you tell which is dominant?"

"It appears Azerick is at the core, but there is no way I can say with certainty. We did discuss this very possibility." Thomas thought a moment. "There is something I can try, but it carries a measure of risk."

"What is it?"

"I can bring the demon forth and question it directly. It cannot lie to me."

"Thomas, no!" Azerick exclaimed. "He must be suppressed. If he takes control everything is lost!"

"The risk is not great. I will bring him forward just enough to allow him to speak with his own voice. It is the only way I can be certain he is not using your spirit to shield himself from my power. Please do not resist."

Brother Thomas recited a complex incantation and Azerick could feel Klaraxis slipping through his grasp. He felt a moment of panic and fought to maintain control. At Thomas's urging, Azerick relaxed once more as he felt the Chosen's grip on Klaraxis next to his own.

"Tell me your name, demon," Thomas commanded.

"To the abyss with you, priest!" Azerick shouted with Klaraxis's deep, gravelly voice. "I will enjoy devouring your soul when I am free of this wretched prison!"

"Tell me your name, demon!" Thomas shouted again, holding forth his brightly glowing sun symbol.

Klaraxis screamed in pain and rage. "You know me as Klaraxis, master of the Fifth Circle, but you will never get my soul name!"

Brother Thomas knew better than to try. Extracting a demon's soul name was a monumental task and a battle he was not prepared to wage.

"Is the sorcerer, Azerick Giles, in control of you and this form?" Klaraxis snarled and curled his lip in disgust. "Is the sorcerer, Azerick Giles, in control of you and this form?" Thomas demanded, shoving his holy symbol at the demon.

"Yes, but I swear his time is limited, and when I break free, I will destroy him and everything he values! I will tear his soul to shreds and consume it bit by bit, savoring every piece for a thousand years until he is no more!"

Brother Thomas stared into Azerick's eyes and commanded, "Back to your cage, demon."

Azerick felt Klaraxis being shoved back into his mental and spiritual prison. He breathed a sigh of relief when the demon lord was firmly under his control once more.

"Let him up, Allister. It is Azerick," Thomas said.

Allister looked to Brother Thomas who nodded. Azerick felt the invisible bands slacken and then vanish. Azerick stood and dusted himself off. He spared Raijaun a smile to tell him everything was all right as he hid behind Ellyssa, clinging to her traveling cloak.

"You still pack a punch for an old man," Azerick said glibly.

"I think we both know you took a fall, and I thank the gods for it."

"Azerick?" Miranda called out hesitantly.

Azerick smiled and extended his hand. Miranda rushed forward and into his arms, holding him as tightly as she could as if he might turn into smoke and disappear at any moment.

"Oh, my love, I knew you would return to me! I knew not even death would keep you from me!" she sobbed into his chest.

Azerick did not respond, could not respond, as he held her just as tightly. In his heart, he knew he did not return for her but to save the world. He felt like a fraud and a liar. Love was an illusion created by selfish want, guilt, and a sense of duty. Images of his journey through the Valley of Lies flashed before his eyes as Krade's taunting laughter echoed through his mind.

Deep within Azerick's subconscious, Klaraxis rejoiced. The demon relished in his small victory, landing the first of many strikes yet to come against the sorcerer. His doubts, fears, and guilt made it easy for Klaraxis to slip in and tweak those sensitive emotions ever so slightly and heighten their reality. Despite the sorcerer's incredible will and strength, he was still human with all their inherent emotional weaknesses. Klaraxis gave up on trying to win the battle for his body and focused on the war. His body was his kingdom, and he would win it back inch by inch.

Miranda forced herself to turn away and beckoned for Daebian to come to them. "Azerick, this is our son, Daebian."

Daebian took a few steps forward. "Hello, Father."

Azerick felt the weight of Daebian's dark, almost black eyes upon him, studying him, judging him down to his soul. He took in the slight smile on the boy's face, a smile hinting at knowledge and secrets untold. Could Daebian have truly experienced what Azerick had done in the Valley of Lies? Had part of him really been there? No, it was all a construct of Krade and the valley. He was just a boy, unsure of this sudden change in his life.

"Hello, Daebian. I am very glad to meet you." Azerick turned to Ellyssa and Raijaun. "Miranda, this is also my son, Raijaun."

With some coaxing from Azerick, Raijaun peeked around Ellyssa's waist and gave Miranda a shy wave. Miranda touched her lips and gasped, but she composed herself. She walked over, smiled a greeting to Ellyssa, and knelt.

"Hello, Raijaun, my name is Miranda. It is nice to meet you," she said, extending her hand palm up.

Raijaun slowly reached out as if trying to stroke a butterfly's wings and touched the tips of his fingers to hers. "H-hello."

Miranda stood and took him by the hand. "Welcome to your new home."

"We should get inside," Azerick said. "There is much to discuss and even more to do. Our greatest opponent right now is time."

Azerick led the way back through the gates as Rusty and Allister flanked him on both sides and everyone else filed in behind them. Azerick passed through the gates amongst a chorus of cheers and welcomes.

"Azerick, there have been some changes," Rusty began explaining as they entered the inner courtyard.

Azerick nodded. "I know. Ellyssa filled me in."

Azerick had barely made it through the gates when he saw a man wearing the robes of a headmaster rapidly approaching and trailing nearly a dozen wizards whom he did not recognize. A few he thought he may have seen during his brief stay at the Academy, but none were his regular instructors.

"Lord Giles, welcome back," Headmaster Harvey said with an obviously forced smile. "I see not even death is able to thwart your reputation. My name is Headmaster Robert Harvey."

Azerick stared stone-faced at the man. "Get out."

Harvey's smile fell as if slapped from his face. "I am afraid that is not possible. There have been some changes since you…left, and I am now headmaster of the school." Harvey extended a writ at arm's length. "As you can see, Duchess Mellina and your wife have both signed this accord under the jurisdiction of the Academy, placing me in charge. Of course, the tower and grounds are still technically your property for use as a personal dwelling, but any instruction in magic is entirely under my control."

"Miranda, did the duchess revoke any property, titles, or rights upon my death?" Azerick asked.

"No, she did not."

Azerick looked back at Harvey who still held the piece of paper in front of him like a shield. "Since I am not dead and retain all rights of title and property, any agreement made regarding the disposition of this school or its students is invalid."

Harvey thrust the paper at Azerick again. "But this writ…"

The paper burned to ash in an instant with nothing more than a look from Azerick. Harvey took a step back and the wizards behind him flinched defensively.

"The first one of you who reaches for the Source will die before you take another breath," Azerick warned.

Grounds that were a moment ago filled with the joyous calls of Azerick's return were now silent beneath a pall of violent tension. Azerick had been gone for years and, in his place, Harvey had supplanted him as the school's master. Many were unsure of what to do. The oldest amongst them, those who were the first students, readied themselves in Azerick's defense. Others prepared to leap to the aid of the people they knew to be in charge, but most simply stood silent, not knowing what to do.

Magus Harvey steadied himself and glared back. "I had heard of your contrariness, Lord Giles, but do not think to come into my school and bully me or my fellows about!"

Azerick pulled the book he had been writing from his satchel. "The Academy should have received a full report by now detailing the inevitable outcome of any person or body attempting to take something belonging to me. I recommend you read it in full after you take this back with you."

Harvey looked at the book Azerick held out but did not take it. "What is that?"

"It is a journal detailing the fall and return of the Scions. It also contains explicit instructions on how to best train your wizards and students to battle them."

"What exactly is it you expect me to do with it?"

"You will take it to the Academy and ensure its instructions become the primary focus of your curriculum. You will need to make copies for everyone at the Academy and should probably forward some to the Hall of Inquisition as well."

"You are completely mad if you think to come in here and order me about like a servant! I am here under the full authority of the Academy and will not bow to your ridiculous demands, regardless of your return from the dead!"

"Magus Harvey, I apologize if you mistook me."

The wizard smiled, feeling certain Azerick was giving up his attempt to dominate the situation. Once again, Azerick verbally slapped the smile from his face as he continued.

"Nothing I have said here was in any way a request."

Azerick grabbed the front of Harvey's robe, pulled him close, and thrust the book inside the folds. Before the wizard could protest his manhandling, Azerick twisted the loose fabric into a wad and hurled him up and over the wall with no more effort than pitching a stone. Magus Harvey's shrill scream ended abruptly with a dull thud as he struck the ground several yards from the outside base of the wall.

Azerick turned to the other Academy wizards who stood dumbstruck. "The rest of you may leave through the gates or likewise be hurled over them. That choice is yours alone to make. If any of you have a healing potion in your possession, I suggest you take it to Magus Harvey as he is certainly in dire need of one." The wizards looked at each other, unsure what to do. "You need to leave now. I will order one of my ships take you to Southport. I will have your belongings packed and sent to you."

Most of the wizards hastened out of the gate without a backward glance, tended to Magus Harvey, and carried him away. Five Academy wizards still stood their ground looking nervously at one another.

"Did I fail to make myself clear?" Azerick asked ominously.

A young woman stepped forward of the group and bowed slightly. "Lord Giles, if we may, we would like to stay on here. You have many talented students, too many for just your original staff to provide the education they deserve."

Azerick studied the young woman and the other wizards in her group. They were all young, likely recently promoted to full wizard, and could expect little in the way of promotion or real purpose at the Academy.

"What is your name?"

"Amy, My Lord."

"Do you speak for your group?"

Amy looked at her group and received nods from each of them. "I do."

"You will each pledge your loyalty to me. I will hear any suggestions you may have for improving our training, but I will not tolerate argument or dissension. Do you understand?"

"We do, My Lord."

"I certainly hope so, because your lives depend on it. Follow us to the tower. You will all need to hear what I have to say."

No one spoke as Azerick led them to the new tower's large dining room. Those who knew him remembered him as a determined young man who would protect his people and home at any cost. This Azerick was lethal and emotionless in the face of inflicting violence. The old Azerick would have used whatever force was necessary to cast out Harvey, but this new one went beyond the necessary. This Azerick felt he needed to send a message, and he had no qualms about doing so.

"Miranda, Daebian does not need to be part of this," Azerick said as they filed into the tower.

"Of course. Perhaps he can show Raijaun around the grounds?"

"No, Raijaun can stay. He will be deeply involved in what is to come."

"He is just a child."

"He is no ordinary child, even beyond his appearance."

"Daebian is far from ordinary as well, and if Raijaun can hear what you have to say then I see no reason why Daebian cannot," Miranda said, irritated at Azerick's easy dismissal of Daebian.

"I am sure he is special, but Raijaun is capable of wielding powerful magic, which will be instrumental in what is coming. I would rather the students hear what I have to say from their instructors after I have laid out my plans, not through a child-driven grapevine. Such a thing would cause unnecessary fear."

"It is all right, Father," Raijaun said before Miranda could interject. "I know much of what I need to already. I would like to look around."

"I suppose you are right." Azerick turned to Daebian. "Daebian, would you show Raijaun around?"

Daebian smiled pleasantly. "I would love to, Father. It does not look as though I am wanted here."

"Daebian," Miranda said sharply.

"What, Mother?" Daebian asked, still smiling. "Come, little brother, I will give you the grand tour."

Daebian led Raijaun out of the main hall and into the kitchens. Unlike almost everyone Raijaun had ever met, Daebian did not seem the least bit disturbed by his appearance, taking him by the hand and showing him around.

"This is where they make the food for the people who eat in the tower. There are bigger kitchens out on the grounds where they prepare meals for everyone else. You can come in here and get something to eat whenever you're hungry, assuming you eat people food. If you don't, there are a few people around here I wouldn't miss much."

"I do not eat people," Raijaun said softly.

Daebian shrugged, acting as if it would not have bothered him if he did. "Whatever. How old are you?"

"I lived six months in my egg and almost three months out of it."

"Interesting. I'm glad you are here."

"Really?"

"Yes. Next to you, I am no longer even close to being the biggest freak here. Come on, I'll show you my room. I have the whole top floor to myself. Mother will probably put you in one of the extra rooms, so we best pick you out a spot."

Raijaun winced at Daebian calling him a freak, but the guileless way he said it made it feel less like an intentional insult. Raijaun found his big brother very confusing.

CHAPTER 7

Ellyssa sat on her bed and stroked the soft blanket beneath her as she slowly looked around the room as if to assure herself she was indeed finally home and not trapped in some elaborate illusion crafted by the inquisitors to torture her. It would not have been the first time they had used such a tactic. Her eyes shot to the door when she heard a knock.

"Enter," Ellyssa called out in a soft and trembling voice.

She released the tension constricting her entire body when she saw it was Azerick and not Fennrick.

"How are you feeling?" Azerick asked.

"Uh, okay I guess. Well, maybe a little less than okay," she amended when Azerick arched his eyebrows.

He held out a small box wrapped in colorful paper and tied with a bow. "Maybe this will make you feel a little better."

Ellyssa reached out with a tentative hand and took the present. "What is it?"

Azerick shrugged. "I don't know for sure. It just arrived, which is a surprise considering we only just got here less than an hour ago, but given who it from, I think you will like it."

Ellyssa pulled at the dangling end of the bow, gently unwrapped the delicate paper, and opened the box. She could do nothing for a full minute other than stare at the shiny gold eyetooth laying atop a tiny velvet pillow. Taking a deep breath, she plucked out the folded piece of paper tucked between the velvet padding and the box and read the note.

Dearest Ellyssa,

Through no small effort, I was able to keep my promise to you. While I am sure you would have preferred to deliver your own retribution unto the scoundrel, I decided to enact it on your behalf as I did not wish to lose my quarry and was unsure when you might be able punish him yourself.

I know this small token is insufficient to make up for my betrayal and the awfulness you surely endured at the hands of the inquisitors, but I hope it brings you a measure of solace. While such a small gift is unlikely to make us friends, I do hope is enough to prevent us from being enemies.

Forever in your debt,
Andrill

"I'll give you moment to yourself," Azerick said. "Please meet us downstairs when you're ready."

Ellyssa simply nodded in response as she continued to stare at what remained of Captain Jake. Knowing she had more important matters to attend to, she used a sliver of magic to drill a hole in the somewhat macabre ornament, attached it to a gold necklace she retrieved from a jewelry box, and affixed it around her neck. With a nod and almost imperceptible smile, she made her way downstairs.

Azerick gathered his core instructors and staff within the dining hall of the new tower. A million questions burned on the tongues of nearly everyone there, but they all chose to stay silent and wait for Azerick to speak.

"I know my return is a shock to you all, and you must have a lot of questions. I hardly know where to begin, so I will get straight to the point. I spent the last..." Azerick looked to Ellyssa.

"Five years," she answered.

"I have spent the majority of the last five years trapped in the abyss. The soul of the demon lord, Klaraxis, and mine are fused and inseparable. When I died, he carried my soul with him back to his body, hence my current situation. I am able to use his ability to assume human form to look much as I once did."

Miranda squeezed his hand, partly in reassurance and partly to assure herself he was not an illusion.

"We had discussed such a possibility, and our conclusion was near that," Allister said, "especially when your staff up and vanished a couple months ago."

"The state of my death is not nearly as great a concern as the reason for my return. My return was not of my own devising. Do any of you know anything about the Scions?" Everyone exchanged puzzled looks and shook their heads. "It is not surprising. The Scions have gone to great lengths to purge the memory of their existence from human history. I do not know how successful they were at doing so with the other races, but it appears their agents throughout the millennia have done an excellent job with us."

Azerick explained what he knew of the gods before their gods and the true battle for freedom during the Great Revolution. "The gods and the last Guardian helped free me from the abyss. The Guardian took part of me and combined it with part of herself to create Raijaun in the same manner as the elves created her and her kind long ago."

Miranda asked, "But why?"

Azerick held the entire gathering with his steely gaze. "The Scions are returning to destroy us all. Due to the plurality of our nature, Raijaun and I are not susceptible to their awesome mental domination. Our nature allows us to guard the barrier holding them in check and to face them directly just as the Guardians did."

Worried conversation broke out around the table. It continued for several minutes until Aggie interjected and willed everyone to quiet down.

"Azerick, I cannot imagine what you have been through, but how certain are you of the reality of all this? The abyss is a world of lies and cruelty. Is it possible this is all a cruel joke of Sharrellan to sow discord and fear?"

"No. I know we have all been taught that Sharrellan's sole purpose is to cause pain and torment, but she does nothing without good reason. She is the mistress of the abyss, a place just as you described, but I do not believe her to be any more evil than the warden of a prison. She has a duty to fulfill, and she does it as it needs to be done. I have seen the Scions and their army with my own eyes. I have seen the wall holding them in their prison world and the flaws within it.

"One such flaw allowed little more than a couple hundred of the Scions' shock troops through. Two or three hundred ravagers nearly destroyed Bruneford's Mill and would likely have succeeded in its total annihilation had Ellyssa and I not been there."

"Mother received the report from Bruneford's Mill," Miranda said. "It blamed the attack on demons."

Azerick nodded. "I am not surprised. Ravagers are horrible creatures. They are tall, lean, and extremely fast. They look very much like abyssal creatures. They are goblinoid in appearance, with dark red skin stretched tightly over muscles that are able to move them with great speed and strength. These are by far the most numerous of their horde, and their primary shock troops."

"How many are we talking about?" Alex asked.

"More than I could count. Possibly a million, maybe more."

"A million; and a couple hundred of them nearly destroyed a town of close to ten thousand? Granted, that's only about three thousand of fighting age, but still. How could we defend ourselves from that?"

"By preparing and uniting the races against them," Azerick said with sureness. "I have created a plan to prepare for their invasion. I will make copies from the codex and distribute them to every military organization in the kingdom. It is up to the leaders to ensure it is followed. Failure to break from established routines will ensure our defeat."

"I think we understand," Rusty said. "We have had to prepare for an attack before and used your training curriculum."

Azerick shook his head. "No, Rusty, not like this you have not. This will require an altogether new and extremely intensive program. Not only will the magus and martial students learn to fight together and use their abilities to create the most powerful offense and defense possible, it will push each of us to the highest limits of our ability and beyond. That is why I am putting Ellyssa in charge of the overall training."

"Ellyssa is not even a certified wizard!" Rusty shouted above the spontaneous verbal tumult.

Azerick's eyes bored into Rusty's. "How long did you hold out against the Academy's incursion on this school?"

Rusty practically wilted beneath the power of his best friend's gaze. "We, uh…"

"Azerick," Allister interrupted, coming to Rusty's aid, "we thought it more prudent to set terms to avoid loss of life and ensure the continuance of the school. Perhaps we could have provided enough resistance to convince the Academy to leave us be, but at the cost of how many lives?"

"And that is precisely why Ellyssa is going to be in charge. She may be inexperienced, but she is strong and her ordeals have given her insight on how to wield magic in true battle. Rusty, Allister, you are my dearest friends, but your hearts are too soft and too kind to do what must be done. You will agree with me today, resist when you read my requirements, and hate me when you see it in action, but it will be done. This is not about the lives of a few, but the lives of us all. There will be no terms given. There will be no opportunity for surrender or treaty. There will be no way to spare the lives of our race except by killing our enemy in its totality."

"All right, Azerick. What would you have us do?" Allister asked in defeat.

"Much of the immediate preparation is on my shoulders. I must meet with the heads of the kingdom, Academy, and even the other races. We cannot stand alone on this, and their existence is in as much peril as ours. Miranda, I must speak with your mother as soon as possible, and I will need you to urge her to support what I propose."

"Of course."

"Simon."

The nervous little steward visibly jumped. "Yes, uh, Lord Giles?"

"You are going to hate this, but I must open my treasury. I will need to hire every man or woman capable of forging metal or shaping timbers. We are going to need weapons and armor on a scale you cannot imagine. The mountains behind us are full of iron. Anyone not conscripted into military service will be supporting the war effort. That means blacksmiths, wainwrights, leatherworkers, miners, cooks, carpenters, coopers, and every profession you think an army needs to survive."

Azerick scanned the assembled crowd. "Peck, I need you to establish a communication line between the four primary cities of the kingdom. I have an idea for quick travel between the cities, but it will be up to you and your team to warn the towns in between. Argoth is too far for horses, and I am counting on the Academy to communicate with the Hall of Inquisition to warn of the invasion. The first thing I need is for you to carry a letter to King Jarvin. Miranda, can the duchess issue Peck an order giving him permission to use the Blackguards' way stations?"

Miranda nodded. "For matters of urgent concern, regional rulers can issue such writs."

"Peck will need that today. Peck, I want you to pick your own team. Find a dozen of the best riders we have. I will give you a more detailed explanation of your duties later."

Peck saluted smartly. "Yes, sir!"

"I will have the new training guidelines to the rest of you tomorrow. I cannot express enough the importance of working together. Many of you are going to think my training barbaric and unnecessarily brutal, but you must all understand why it must be so. Our enemy is going to be twice as intense and brutal as anything we can physically and mentally prepare for. We must push ourselves to our limits to have any chance at victory."

"All right, son. We're with you," Allister assured him.

Azerick smiled and shook his head ruefully. "You are today. Let us see what tomorrow brings. I must go and prepare a great many things. It is wonderful to see you all again."

"Azerick," Allister butted in, "you just returned. Take a day for your wife and son."

"Allister, as much as I want to, I have a hundred things to do today and just as many tomorrow."

"Then do two hundred things tomorrow. Today you have but one thing that must be done. See to your family."

Azerick looked into Miranda's pleading eyes and smiled. "You are right, Allister. Thank you."

"And thank you for not making me put you over my knee."

Everyone appreciated the break in the tension and chuckled as they dispersed. It took only a few moments of scraping chair legs and the stomping of retreating feet before Azerick found himself alone with Miranda. He felt like a boy again, nervous and unsure of what to do. The rare instance of not being totally certain of what he was doing and in control of the situation was so unnerving he almost felt normal.

Miranda broke the awkward silence. "I never stopped thinking of you. I missed you so much, but I went on knowing that somehow we were not done. Not yet and not you. In my heart I knew you would return. Did you think of me?"

"I tried not to," Azerick answered honestly. "I spent every moment trying to find a way out to get back to you. I could not afford the grief thinking about you and Daebian caused me. When I was unable to distract myself from your memory, it was devastating."

Miranda held Azerick tightly. "You are back now, and we are together. That is all that matters."

Azerick gently pushed Miranda to arm's length. "Miranda, I need you to understand the gravity of what we are facing and my role in it. I must have your total support. Many people are going to resist me, deny what is coming. Denial will doom us before the first enemy reaches our shores. Can I count on you?"

"You have to ask? Of course you can count on me. You can always count on me no matter what."

Azerick smiled, but his eyes left her face and stared into the distance. He knew Miranda meant what she said, but her answer was based on things she could not understand, and he knew those things would stretch her love and understanding to breaking point. He just prayed not beyond.

"We should check on the boys."

Miranda and Azerick spent much of the day turning one of Daebian's rooms into a bedroom for Raijaun. Azerick expected some resistance, as any child would object to someone encroaching on their territory, but Daebian surprised them both. The boys spent most of the day moving things out of the playroom to make room for Raijaun.

The dinner meal was served with a heavy amount of questions, most of which Azerick evaded. There would be answers and more questions, along with objections, when he gave them his training guide. His friends obliged him his reluctance and let him steer the conversation to the more mundane.

After dinner, Miranda and his closest friends spent the evening telling him about everything that had happened while he was gone. The school had continued to flourish until the Academy practically halted magical training. His trading company had continued to grow, absorbing several smaller outfits until it dwarfed its nearest rival. North Haven's economy was the best it had been in generations, thanks to the tax revenues generated by Azerick's company and the employment it provided.

The evening seemed to drag on for an eternity. Azerick felt as if he might jump out of his skin if he did not get to his lab. He had so much to do and scarcely knew where to begin, much less how he would get it done. He felt a surge of relief when everyone began retiring to their rooms.

"I suppose we should seek our bed as well," Miranda said once they were alone.

"Miranda, I have so much to do. I have lost so much time today already." Azerick inwardly winced when his brain shouted 'wasted.'

"Azerick, please, give me this night," Miranda begged. "You said you would give us a day. Please, start your day on the morrow."

Azerick smiled at his wife. "Of course. Forgive me. I am preoccupied with a thousand things."

Azerick lay next to Miranda, staring up at the ceiling darkness could not hide from his demonic eyes. He listened to Miranda's soft breathing as his emotions waged a pitched battle within his heart. He knew he was not the man Miranda needed. He felt like a liar every time he held her. Azerick slipped his legs over the side of the bed and stealthily made his way down to his laboratory.

Unable to sleep, Miranda felt Azerick leave. He looked and sounded like her husband, but there was something missing in the way he touched her. It felt strained, almost like a stranger. The love was still there in his touch, but the passion it once conveyed was gone. She had promised to support him and she would. She would do her duty as a proper wife. Duty, like she felt in Azerick's touch. She flipped her pillow over to the side not sodden with her silent tears and willed herself to sleep.

It was an easy task for Azerick to use the Codex Arcana and a stack of blank books to create copies of his training manual. In less than an hour, he had two dozen books detailing what he knew of the Scions and their forces, and the grueling training he hoped would allow them to battle such a terrifying enemy.

His next task was far more complicated. Azerick stood in front of a polished silver mirror hanging on the wall. As he drew in the Source, he pictured a face in his mind, imagining every strand of hair, wrinkle, and pore. He imagined his voice and the particulars of his individual spirit.

The mirror remained dark for several minutes. A yellow glow began to shine from within and grew brighter. A face appeared in the mirror, illuminated by a floating orb of soft yellow. Although Azerick stared into a mirror, the face looking back was not his own.

"Azerick, is that you, boy?" the elder sorcerer asked in astonishment.

"Yes, Master Devlin."

Devlin grinned at his former apprentice. "I told you before, you've no business calling me master, now more than ever. Interesting spell you have here. Is it from the codex?"

"It is," Azerick replied. "I have had need to use a great deal of information from the book."

"I am glad to see you back. I heard of your return, and of your attacking the Hall of Inquisition."

"It was hardly an attack. They had things belonging to me. I merely asked for them back."

"Your wayward apprentice and the Codex Arcana," Devlin said with a nod. "Still, I hear there was a battle."

"There was some foolishness," Azerick admitted ruefully. "I hope I have resolved the disagreement well enough to prevent any more such hostilities. Our kingdom, yours and mine, can ill afford it."

"What do you mean?"

"Have you heard of the Scions?"

Devlin mentally tore through the pages of his impressive store of knowledge. "I am afraid I do not recall any such beings."

Azerick explained what he knew of the Scions and their hatred of the races. "They have gone to great length to make us forget they ever existed, but that is soon to change. When they break free, they will eradicate anyone capable of wielding magic and their entire bloodline. I am speaking of a purge of the races beyond imagining."

"This is very difficult to digest. What is it you wish of me?"

"Are you in Sumara now?"

"I am," Devlin affirmed. "I am afraid I wore out my welcome a while back, and the Academy made a formal request to my brother to recall his ambassador. I am not terribly upset. Your Valerian cuisine leaves much to be desired."

"I am glad you are home. I will send you a copy of a book I wrote detailing everything I know of the Scions and the tactics I am ordering adopted to fight them."

"I see. What would you have of me?"

"I need you to convince your brother to begin conscripting the largest army he can. I am going to persuade King Jarvin to assist you by sending additional food south. My standards are going to seem excessive and many will resist employing them, but you must follow them. The old ways of doing battle will not suffice, especially concerning the wizards."

Devlin looked serious as he thought. "I think I understand. I will do what I can."

"There is one more thing, and you are not going to like it. In fact, everyone other than me is going to hate it."

"What is it?" the Sumaran asked.

"When the Scions come, your army must ride with all haste to Valeria and fight alongside us."

"Azerick, you are powerful and you have faced challenges I cannot imagine, but you know nothing of politics. Even if we could ride to your aid, it would be impossible to do so without it looking like an invasion. Even if we were able to enter into some sort of treaty, your nobles would suspect treachery and underhandedness and never agree to such a thing. Beyond that, you would ask us to abandon our homeland to save yours in the face of the most terrible enemy imaginable, if you are correct in your assessment. Such a request is beyond ridiculous."

"If it were any other enemy, I would agree, Devlin. You must understand your kingdom is not in immediate peril."

"Why is that?"

"Because they are all coming for me. I replaced the Guardian and am now the one slowing their escape. I also annihilated the closest thing they had to children. Devlin, I committed genocide upon their favored creations, and they will stop at nothing to make me pay for it. If Valeria falls, and without you it will, they will then turn south and destroy you just as easily."

"It is lucky for you my brother is the king, and I am such a skilled orator."

"Nothing leading up to this has been luck or chance. Our gods have carefully crafted every event that put us together. Will you try to do everything I have asked, or do I need to come down there and make the request in person?"

Devlin chuckled. "I would rather face these Scions and their minions in battle than face your *request*." Devlin released a deep sigh. "I cannot imagine leaving our homeland with an enemy invading our neighbors."

"May I make a suggestion?"

"Of course. This appears to be the night for suggestions."

"Part of my plan calls for putting weapons in the hands of every man, woman, and child able to wield them. Obviously, not everyone will be able to travel to Valeria. Pull all your villages and tribes into your major cities. This will provide a large garrison behind fortified walls to deal with any minor incursions the Scions may send. It would not be unreasonable for them to teleport some of their army into your lands to sow fear and draw your people home. Whatever happens, we must not let them divide us or we will all perish. Devlin, you must believe me in this, and you must make your brother believe it as well."

"I believe you, and if it takes my dying breath, I will make my brother believe as well."

"If he has doubts, take him to Bruneford's Mill. Little more than two hundred of the Scions' basic troops slaughtered nearly fifteen times their own number, and I was there to help fight them."

Devlin visibly blanched. "I read the report my people intercepted. I had thought it a gross exaggeration of events, or the panicked tales of peasants."

"It was little more than a scouting party, and it would have destroyed the town had my apprentice and I not been there."

"I give you my word; I will not fail in my task."

"Thank you, Devlin. I wish I was foolish enough to hope my own people will be so cooperative."

Azerick ended the spell, and the mirror showed him his own face once again. Convincing Devlin was one of his most important tasks, but the one which he felt the most confident of gaining support. He needed to make several more contacts in hopes of gaining the alliances to fight the Scions, but how those would go, he could not begin to speculate.

He decided to contact the least likely of his potential allies next, or attempt to anyway. He had met her only once, but she nearly killed him, and such a thing tended to leave a rather indelible mark on one's psyche. Azerick pictured Teraneshala's perfect alabaster face and hair so silver it looked as though the Source was cascading down her head. He recalled the flow of her magic and its unique signature.

Staring into the mirror, he called out her name. "Teraneshala. Teraneshala."

The abyssal elf's face filled the mirror with its haunting, ethereal beauty. "Little sorcerer, what an amazing surprise. Have you sought me out for a rematch?"

Azerick smiled at her and shook his head. "I have not."

"That is good to hear. I have a feeling it would not go well for me a second time," she said as she let the gathered Source slip away. "I sense you have grown a great deal since we last met, though into what I cannot say."

"It is a long story, and I have little time. None of us have much time, I am afraid."

"You sound so ominous. What has you so worried you would contact the likes of me?"

"I am contacting many people. Do you know of the Scions?"

The elf's face lost its amused look and turned serious. "My people will never forget those creatures. They are what forced us to abandon our surface homes and cousins and seek the solitude of the deep. What do you know of them?"

"The Guardians are all dead, and my son and I stand in their stead. The Scions are coming, and I cannot prevent their escape. I am certain they will concentrate most of their power on destroying me before subjugating the few they allow to live."

"Why should they focus on you when they could divide their power between the major races and conquer them all at once?"

"Several reasons. Our knowledge of magic has spread far beyond what it was during the Great Revolution as has our populations. I am the last to be named Guardian, and they have a particular hatred of me. Do you know of the destruction I wrought in the psyling city?"

"I sensed your hand in it. Whatever calamity you invoked was the reason I was able to escape in the split-second their control slipped."

"The destruction I caused was total. It destroyed the city and every living creature within it. The psylings were the favored creations of the Scions, their children almost. The Scions are rather angry about a mere human destroying something they spent a lot of time and effort creating."

Teraneshala thought back to her captivity. "Yes, I see the connection. It is so obvious in retrospect. What is it you wish of me?"

"Given your power, I assume you have some standing amongst your people." The abyssal elf nodded. "I need you to convince them to arm for war and join the surface races to fight the Scions."

"Why would my people do that? Many will argue to stay hidden or dig even deeper into the heart of our world."

"You know there is no hole deep enough in which to hide that the Scions will not dig you out from. They have not forgotten your part in their defeat and will not rest until they crush everyone beneath their boot."

"What you say is true, human, but some will still argue. Have you received the pledge of our surface cousins?"

"It is on my to-do list. How likely do you think they are to join us against the Scions?"

"Just mentioning those horrible creatures will have them swarming like bees. They will prepare, but whether or not they will shelve their arrogance and deign to fight with you is another question."

"I will cross that bridge when I come to it. What of you? Will you argue my case to your people?"

"I will, if for no other reason than to see you in true battle. When the time comes, we will be there."

"Thank you, Teraneshala."

"Thank you for freeing me from those vile creatures. Fortunately for you, I think so highly of myself that I consider helping you save the world nearly an even payment for my life."

The abyssal elf severed Azerick's modified scrying spell and vanished from view. Azerick breathed an enormous sigh of relief. He had been unsure if he would be able to speak to Teraneshala, much less convince her of helping him. The gods must truly be on his side. This type of two-way scrying was complicated and fatiguing, but he had one more person he desperately needed to contact before resting.

Azerick pictured his face in his mind and followed the insubstantial strand of magic through the foggy, ethereal dimension between realities. The energy slowly grew stronger, and he knew he was on the right path. The sorcerer sensed he was as close as he could get and searched for any change within the vapors. A little way off to his left he spotted a faint light glowing like a tiny candle. He willed his consciousness toward it and called out.

"Duncan."

The dwarven runecarver looked up at the polished steel plate propped between his workbench and wall and nearly fell off his stool.

He narrowed his eyes and slowly lowered the small hammer gripped tightly in his meaty fist as he recognized the face within the metal.

"Azerick, is that you?"

"It is. Nice to see you again."

"Nice to see you too. That's a nifty little trick you got there. How do you fare?"

"Until recently, I was dead," Azerick answered.

Duncan arched his thick salt and pepper brows. "Dead, you say?"

"It is a long story. The short version is I got taken by wizards and used as a vessel for a demon lord, killed the man responsible for murdering my father, opened a school for orphans, got married to nobility, got killed rescuing my apprentice, and pulled into service by the gods to save them and our world. So now I am here to enlist your aid in that endeavor."

"I see. Were it coming from anyone else, I would be surprised. I always felt the fates had you wrapped up tighter than a babe in a blanket. So what do you need from an old runecarver?"

"Ancient gods called the Scions are going to attack our world and seek to destroy us all. Do you know of them? They were the architects behind the Great Revolution."

Duncan worked his heavy jaw as he seemed to literally chew on his memory. "I can't say that I do, but if we ever did, it's written in the archives. We dwarves don't read a lot, but we write down anything of importance and keep it forever."

"I need you to find that lost history, Duncan. When you do, you must take it to your people and convince them to fight beside us. The Scions' hatred for your people is as great as the enmity they hold for mine and the elves. We were all instrumental in banishing them, and they want to punish us severely for it."

"Son, the dwarves haven't left these mountains in two thousand years. What you're asking is akin to telling a fish to jump out of the water and walk on land."

"I know, Duncan, but the Scions will crush you beneath your mountain after they destroy the rest of us. Would you rather fight them on the surface in joined forces or alone within your halls?"

"Put that way, it ain't a hard choice, but my folks' heads and hearts can be as hard as the stone around us. Let me search our archives. It'll be a waste of breath to say anything without getting something to back up what you claim. Even then…" Duncan wagged his bushy head. "I just don't know. It's one thing to prove they exist, another thing altogether to prove they're coming. Don't get me wrong, son, you say they're coming and I believe you. But dwarves can argue and dicker until the mountains crumble to dust."

"I have faith in you, my friend. I know you will do your best. The Guardians are all dead, Duncan. I am all there is holding the gates to the Scions' prison, and I am not up to the task. We do not have long."

The dwarf nodded. "All right, son. I'll get these boulders rolling. It's hard work, but once they start turning, not even the gods can stop 'em."

"Thank you, Duncan."

Azerick slumped down into a simple chair next to a workbench and sighed. He was amazed everything had gone so well, but he expected that to change. Tomorrow would surely be a test of his patience and courage. Tomorrow, he had to face his mother-in-law.

CHAPTER 8

Azerick stood at the foot of the high dais upon which sat Duchess Mellina, ruler of North Haven. An audience of key nobles and influential subjects sat in rows of chairs along the two opposing walls to his right and left. General Brague stood to Mellina's right, looking as though he wished to demand why the gods hated him so much as to return Azerick to the world of the living.

"Lord Giles, the court wishes to relay its heartfelt joy at your miraculous return." The duchess spared her general an icy look when he snorted a bit too loudly. "Had you not surprised us with your urgent request for a formal audience, we would have prepared a proper celebration."

Azerick inclined his head. "My apologies, Your Grace, but once I inform you of what we face, you will understand my urgency."

"Very well, Lord Giles. We will hear you now."

"Your Grace, esteemed audience, I have been dead and residing within the abyss for the better part of the last five years." Azerick waited for the hushed mutterings of the crowd to subside before continuing. "While there, I had an audience with the goddess Sharrellan and later a creature known as a Guardian. I was told of and shown beings of enormous power and with great armies of creatures. These beings are known as the Scions. They were the gods before our gods and the true masters behind the Great Revolution."

"The Great Revolution was against the dragons! Everyone knows that," someone shouted from amongst the assembly.

Azerick turned and faced the direction of the speaker. "That is what we remember and what the Scions wish us to believe. The dragons were merely guard dogs and slaves of the Scions. The elves, who brought us the gift of magic, created the Guardians. They and the Guardians fought alongside the new gods against the Scions while we, the dwarves, and the other races battled the dragons and their legions. The last of the Guardians gave her life to free me from the abyss. The walls holding the Scions imprisoned are crumbling, and soon they will return."

"Then we will beat them once more," General Brague announced. "We are stronger, more numerous, and have more wizards than before."

"We are scattered, General. The dwarves live inside their mountain homes within the Witchcrag and Great Barrier Mountains. The elves hide secluded far to the north, and the abyssal elves have buried themselves even deeper than the dwarves. The orcs, goblins, ogres, and other races are scattered in a thousand different tribes all across the continent. Most importantly, we no longer have the Guardians, beings whose duality in spirit allowed them to fight the Scions face to face. My son Raijaun and I are now two to replace a dozen of the most powerful wielders of magic ever to walk this world."

"You sound apocalyptic, Lord Giles," Duchess Mellina said flatly.

"An apocalypse is coming, but as your general said, we are not defenseless. However, we are at the moment greatly unprepared. Have you heard of the happenings at Bruneford's Mill?"

The duchess nodded. "I have received the report. It was a tragedy. I also received a report of someone claiming to be you attacking the Hall of Inquisition and threatening Duchess Paullina. She is demanding I have you executed on the spot."

"I did not attack the Hall nor threaten the duchess. I did request the return of my property and apprentice. My insistence could have been construed as a threat, I suppose. The Hall attacked me later. We were victorious because we were both prepared to meet a more powerful force. This lesson is what I desperately wish to convey here today. The fact is the Scions are more powerful than our wizards, and their army stronger, faster, and greater in size than our own. However, that does not mean defeat is inevitable."

The duchess asked, "What would you have of us, Lord Giles?"

"I have already spoken to the crown prince of Sumara and representatives of the abyssal elves and dwarves. I intend to speak with King Jarvin and a representative of the elves within the week. As I have told the others and will relay to our king, we must turn our minds and spears toward war. It is time to beat our plowshares into swords, conscript and train every available citizen, and adopt a strict military training regimen for our front-line soldiers."

"My soldiers are the best trained in the kingdom!" Brague shouted indignantly at what he felt was a slight against his proficiency. "I do not need some wizard telling me how to fight or train my men!"

"Calm yourself, General. I am sure Lord Giles meant nothing of the sort."

"I did not, Your Grace. General Brague, I have twice fought beside you and your men and know you to be an excellent commander with top-notch soldiers, but you do not understand the enemy we face. You can be the greatest antelope hunter in the world, but your skills will be inadequate when hunting plains lions or fleshreavers. You and your men are the best fighters I have ever known, but your methods of combat are ill-suited to the enemy we face. I have spent the past several months studying the Codex Arcana in order to learn as much as I can about the Scions and their minions. I have taken that knowledge and written a detailed training manual for both arcane and martial combat, particularly in combining those two forces into a cohesive force to maximize their ability to kill our enemies and survive."

Another nobleman stood. "Are you suggesting we arm and train every citizen in the city?"

"I am telling you we *must* arm and train every citizen in the kingdom."

"And who will pay for all of this?"

"You will. We all will. I have ordered my treasury opened to support this effort, but I am not foolish enough to think I can fund it on my own."

"That is preposterous! Maintaining an army is why we pay taxes!"

"And now you must pay more."

"We already paid a levy for the commissioning of the city's ships!"

"For which you enjoy increased security and trade. Both these things have increased your wealth even more than it was before the tax increase. Your trade vessels are no longer being plundered by pirates, and import and exports have nearly tripled. Now is the time to invest again, and this time it is not for useless bits of metal but for your continued existence. I would think such a thing would encourage you more than the prospect of increased income, since a rich dead man is still a dead man."

The assembly was abuzz with words of support for the nobleman and scoffed at the sorcerer's pronouncement until Duchess Mellina stood. "Quiet! Lord Giles has saved this city from invaders and kept our beloved Jarvin on his throne, both of which would have been lost without his intervention and foresight. I will hear any words of evidence refuting his claims, but I will not risk my city and its people for petty bickering and greed. Until I see evidence proving he is mistaken, I will trust in his judgment and act accordingly. I hereby order a state of martial law. Conscription will begin immediately. All tradesmen will receive instructions detailing their support of the war effort. None of you are to travel far, for I am assigning many of you to oversee much of our preparations."

"But, Your Grace, the Council of Lords..." the vocal nobleman sputtered.

"Exists as a courtesy, and one which I am revoking until the danger to our kingdom is at an end. This audience is over. Lord Giles, you and my daughter will join me and General Brague in the parlor for further discussion."

The court stood and bowed as General Brague escorted the duchess from the dais by way of the door hidden behind the thick curtains covering the wall. Azerick and Miranda made their way to the parlor through another hall. Duchess Mellina crossed the parlor floor the moment the couple walked in and slapped Azerick soundly across the cheek.

"How dare you return from the dead and make your first visit one of formality?"

"Forgive me, Your Grace, things have been happening rather quickly."

The room echoed with the sound of the duchess's second slap. "In court you refer to me as Your Grace. In private you will call me Mother."

Azerick could not suppress his smile. "Yes, Mother."

"And wipe that smirk off your face. It makes you look like a simpleton."

Azerick did as he was told but still received another slap. "What was that one for?"

"That one was for General Brague. He said you deserved it, and I trust in his judgment." Mellina left Azerick standing as she reclined on a sofa. "Do you have any idea what you put my daughter through by running off and dying?"

"Again, forgive me, Mother."

"It was damn selfish of you. Next time you die, you had best stay dead or incur my wrath. Now, tell me and the general more of these failed gods set on destroying us. I do not give a whit about why. I need to know what we are looking at from a tactical standpoint."

Azerick nodded as he gathered his thoughts. "There are five Scions, each of whom lorded over their own realm: what we call Valeria and Sumara, Lazuul, the land beyond the Great Barrier Mountains, and two that must lie far beyond wherever we have sailed."

"Why are they so set on coming here if there are four other kingdoms from which to choose? Will they be dividing their forces?"

"They will not, and the reason is twofold."

"Why divide and weaken your army when the kingdoms are separated by impassable mountains and unexplored seas," General Brague stated as he handed Mellina a glass of wine.

"Precisely. The reason they will destroy us first is due to a particular hatred of me."

General Brague poured himself a glass of brandy. "I can certainly understand that. Never one to rest on his accomplishments, Lord Giles has traveled to other worlds and found an entirely new host of people to infuriate."

"Darling, be civil. What are we looking at in the way of their army and ability?"

"The Scions themselves were the gods before our gods. They wield all the power of our gods, without the restrictions put on them by the All Mother."

"What kind of restrictions? How can anything put restrictions on a god?"

"To be honest, it goes into some huge cosmic thing I will not pretend to fully understand. Suffice it to say, there is a power greater than the gods with a consciousness far beyond our understanding. It is the force guiding the universe and does not exist on the same level we, or the gods, do. Our gods must work through us, which is why we will face the brunt of this invasion. The Scions also have an army of creatures they have spent the past two millennia creating, which numbers probably a million or more. It was impossible for me to count. They are bigger, stronger, and faster than humans."

"All right, five gods and a massive army of creatures better suited to killing than we are. What else are we facing?" the duchess asked.

"They have several ships that can fly through the air like ours sail on water. I expect them to call the dragons to their aid as well."

"You are just full of optimistic tidings."

"There is one thing we have in our favor. Scions abhor magic users like nothing else. Other than their own magic, I expect them to attack us with nothing more than brute strength and whatever dragons may still exist in the world. That is why having our wizards train amongst the soldiers is so important. Neither wizard nor soldier can hope to stand alone, but together, they can become highly formidable."

"What good does that do us if these Scions can simply obliterate us on a whim?" Brague asked.

"Because they cannot. We may be insects to them, but we can sting. Enough stings can bring down the largest of animals. Moreover, the Scions disdain us and will not seek to lower themselves to engage the rabble directly. Such a thing is left to their underlings. Also, they will not want to weaken themselves before they face our gods. Our gods may be limited upon our plane, but they are still gods and pose a threat, particularly when backed up by a couple thousand wizards."

Duchess Mellina set her glass down and scrubbed the fatigue from her face. "You say we are not alone, that you have contacted Sumara and other races. Can we reinforce the walls to withstand a siege long enough for them and the rest of the kingdom to come to our aid?"

Azerick shook his head somberly. "You do not understand. No walls can save us from this kind of attack. I have a plan to create stable gateways that will allow us to evacuate our populace to Brelland."

The duchess sat up straight. "You do not think we can hold North Haven?"

"I know we cannot hold it. I will create a similar gateway in Southport that will transport them to Brightridge. From Brelland and Brightridge, we will retreat into a valley I know of near the Witchcrag Mountains, where we will combine the might of all our forces in a final battle for survival. This will be a war of attrition with neither side willing nor able to offer or accept terms. Our only hope is to bleed them so severely that, by the time they reach our final field of battle, we can crush them decidedly. Have no illusions; we will lose our cities, and our people are going to be brutalized. What I am trying to do is create an army that will be more brutal than our enemy and crawl from whatever wreckage in which our kingdom may lie. This is not about glorious victory, but bloody and horrible survival."

Duchess Mellina grimaced. "Well, I am glad you saved that part of your speech for closed doors. Should the people hear it, they would likely flee in terror."

"And they would get to witness the death of our species before they too were found and crushed." Azerick pulled a book from his satchel. "This is the training plan I devised. It details what I want and what I hope to accomplish by doing so. General, I meant what I said about my opinion of your battle prowess. If you see ways to improve upon what I have written, I will certainly welcome your input. I will warn you now; it is brutal in training and execution, but that is what is necessary."

"We will do what we must. When will you speak with Jarvin?"

"I sent a courier yesterday. You should have issued him a license to use the Blackguard's relay stations."

"Yes, the short young man."

"He should reach the capital the day after tomorrow. Allow four days for a reply, and I expect to engage him and his council within the week."

"Good luck with that lot. They are twice as arrogant and prickly as mine are." Mellina stood and approached her daughter and son-in-law. "I had best get busy then, and I am sure you have plenty to do as well." The duchess hugged Miranda and then Azerick. "Do not go off and get yourself killed again. After all this, I cannot afford another state funeral."

"I will do my best," Azerick replied as he returned Mellina's embrace.

Miranda turned and looked to Azerick as they walked the halls on their way out. "Darling?"

"It would seem your mother and our esteemed general have become close."

"Can you imagine if they marry? That will make for some very interesting dinner conversations."

"I expect so, but I will return to the abyss before I ever call him Father."

CHAPTER 9

Azerick checked the arcanum-inlaid runes carved in his laboratory floor against those written in the Codex Arcana for perhaps the tenth time. Finally confident he had everything correct, he fed power into the design. The sigils flared brightly and the floor began to vibrate. The entire room began to thrum with the pulse of a giant beating heart.

A crack appeared in the floor and spiderwebbed out from its center. A small section of the floor buckled upward as if something were burrowing out of the ground and into the room. A round object breached through the stone floor like a creature being birthed, rising as the ground expelled it from its earthen womb.

The head-sized crystal sprouted from the floor on a stock of polished stone, waiting for its master to command it. Azerick placed his hands upon its glassy surface, closed his eyes in concentration, and fed power into the stone. Even through his closed eyelids, Azerick sensed the change in the light around him. The smells of his lab vanished and the moist seaside air became dry and sterile.

"The false Guardian returns. Have you come to plead for mercy?"

Azerick ignored the Scions' projected thoughts as he pressed his hands against the unending magical barrier in search of weaknesses. It did not take long to find the first one. He channeled power into the weave, fusing the many broken strands of magic like a fisherman mending a net.

"It does not want to talk to us. How rude."

"It does not want its voice to betray its fear."

"How incredibly pointless. Its mind is awash with fear."

"At least it has the intelligence to be afraid."

Azerick continued to repair weaknesses in the barrier even as the Scions bombarded his mind with images of the horrors they were going to inflict upon the races. Despite his mental defenses, the gods extracted bits of his memories and used them in a collage of nightmares. Azerick finally finished his work and broke the connection to the Scions' prison. He slumped down into his chair, physically and emotionally exhausted.

Daebian sat on the floor of his room carefully arranging his tin soldiers into battle formation. He played alone, like usual, since his new brother was off with Father or practicing with Ellyssa, and he could not stand the banality of children his own apparent age. Most people would see a boy playing with toys, but anyone with respectable military training would see the perfect arrangement of soldiers.

The smaller force stood poised behind barriers of wooden blocks and trenches drawn with chalk. Spearman, cavalry, and archers were all arrayed in perfect formation against the horde of beads and tokens used to identify the vastly superior enemy army. Five dolls towered over the battlefield: the five great generals of the enemy.

Daebian commanded the two armies to clash but did not touch a single piece. In his head, a dozen different battles played out in a dozen different ways but all with the same conclusion. Even with the tactical advantage of the smaller army, the power of the five generals and their much larger army resulted in an enemy victory every time.

You have an incredibly keen mind for battle.

Daebian looked up from the floor and stared into the shadowy corner of his room. "Who is there?"

Someone who cares about you.

Daebian looked back at his soldiers. "Only my mother cares about me."

Your father cares about you.

"No he doesn't. He only cares about Raijaun and magic. He probably would not care about him either if he did not have magic."

What you say is true, but I meant your other father.

"You mean the demon. He is not my father."

He is much more your father than Azerick. I am here while he avoids you in his laboratory, teaching and bonding with your brother.

"You are not here either. Neither am I for that matter. I know the difference between a dream and reality."

What you say is true; you are dreaming, but we are both here all the same.

"Why are you here? What do you want from me?"

I want to help you. I want to make you stronger as befits the son of a prince.

"You are a demon and a liar."

I am, but I will not lie to you.

Daebian's lip quirked in amusement. "Yes, you will, but you will not fool me. What do you want, and what is in it for me?"

I want to make you powerful. Having a properly powerful son is my reward.

"What can you do?"

As I am, very little beyond talking to you in your dreams. I am completely imprisoned within your father, but there is a way for a small part of me to escape. Within your father's vault is a black gem called a soul stone. A soul stone is able to trap the soul of a living creature within it. You can trap a small part of my essence within the stone. I will then be able to share some of my power with you.

"What is to keep you from invading my mind and taking my body?"

I will not be in your mind. I will be trapped within the stone and only a shadow copy at that. My true soul will still be trapped within your father.

"Then why go through the trouble? Demons do nothing without personal gain."

It allows me to help you become as great as you deserve to be. It also provides something of a window to my otherwise boring prison. At least then I could look out and experience things beyond the inside of your father's head.

"I will think on it, demon. Now leave my dreams."

As you wish, my son.

Azerick started awake, surprised more by the fact he had fallen asleep than the echoing of Klaraxis's laughter inside his head.

"What is so funny, demon?"

Nothing you would appreciate.

Azerick refused to engage the demon. There was too much to do to entertain him with dialog, certainly too much to do to waste time sleeping. He forced his weary body from the chair and opened the codex. He thought back to the huge rune-inscribed pillars that transported the psyling slave ship to their city.

"Show me."

The pages of the Codex Arcana fluttered as if caught in a strong draft and displayed the thing Azerick sought. The sorcerer read page after page of the complex spell and physical construction of the gateways.

"This is certainly going to take some work," he muttered aloud.

Daebian picked at his breakfast and tuned out the droning of the adults sitting at the table. As usual, his father was not present and neither was Raijaun. That could only mean his brother was in the lab with Father. Daebian was just finishing his breakfast when Raijaun entered from the kitchen. His meals were almost entirely meat barely cooked, and he preferred to eat them away from the eyes of the others.

"Ah, look who crawled out of his dungeon," Daebian said as Raijaun entered.

"Daebian, be nice," Miranda said.

Daebian ignored his mother. "What new and exciting things have you and Father been doing these past few nights?"

"Father is teaching me about using my magic, the barrier, the Scions, and how to resist them when he takes me to their prison world."

"Wonderful, there's a regular convention of monsters going on just below our feet."

"Daebian, enough!" Miranda ordered.

Daebian smiled. "My little brother knows I am just playing. Don't you, Raijaun?"

"I should go see if Father needs me."

Miranda stopped Raijaun before he could escape out the door. "Raijaun, I was going into the city today. I thought perhaps you would like to come with me."

"What a wonderful idea, Mother. If we are entertaining Ugly, perhaps I can take one of Peck's horses to the Winterfest ball."

"Daebian, that is enough! Apologize to your brother this instant!"

Raijaun had already fled through the door when Daebian shouted after him. "Raijaun, I'm sorry you're ugly!"

Miranda slammed her palm down on the tabletop. "What is wrong with you? Go to your room. You can spend the rest of the day there thinking of how you can apologize to Raijaun and treat him better."

Daebian left the room singing:

"There once were two brothers,

One more handsome than the other.

The gorgeous one has smarts,

While the ugly one smellsof farts.

Oh, how Mother hates the smart one's sass,

But better than looking like a warty troll's ass."

Daebian ignored Miranda's shouted rebuke as he darted out of the tower and crossed the grounds.

"What is wrong with that boy?" Miranda asked.

"A bit of sibling rivalry, I'd wager," Allister replied. "Azerick has been preoccupied with his work, and Daebian feels excluded since he cannot help like Raijaun does."

"I will have to speak to my husband and get him to spend more time with Daebian. There is no reason he cannot take an hour or two out of his day for his son."

"I wish you luck. Azerick needs something to take his mind off these preparations. He is obsessed and needs some healthy diversion."

Daebian would go to his room, but he had several stops to make on the way. It could take him hours to finally reach his room. By then, the day would be almost gone and his punishment little more than an inconvenience. Hopefully Mother would not catch on to her poorly worded disciplinary action and be more explicit about how long it should take him to reach his room in the future.

Daebian watched Simon enter the old tower and silently followed him down the stairs. The little accountant was as predictable as a clock when it came to doing his duties. Daebian had to wait only a few minutes for him to do the morning inventory of his father's vault.

He waited around the corner of the open door until Simon became totally engrossed in his counting. Daebian slipped into the room and scanned the shelves holding an assortment of items. His eyes fell upon a small brass chest resting at his eye level, just as Klaraxis had shown him in his dream. He opened the lid of the box and saw four gems, each the size of a human eye. Daebian had no interest in any of the jewels except the black one.

It had been fairly easy to find a nearly black piece of costume jewelry with which to replace the soul stone. Without hesitating, Daebian swapped the pieces, deftly palming the soul stone and slipping it into his pocket.

"What are you doing in here, Daebian?" Simon demanded.

Daebian did not so much as flinch and gave Simon an innocent smile. "Just looking at Father's shiny things."

Simon looked at the gems resting in their padded box before snapping the lid shut. "This is not a place to play. There are some very dangerous things in here. Go along and play elsewhere."

"Okay, Simon."

Daebian waggled his fingers at Simon over his shoulder as he skipped out of the room and back up the stairs. His fake gem would not pass scrutiny, but Simon was no wizard to detect the lack of magic and Father was unlikely to ever use such an artifact. Daebian was not sure he would use it either. He did not trust the demon, but he did like the idea of power. He figured it was best to have the gem on hand in case he decided to use it.

He had also best check on Mother's whereabouts in case she decided to look in on him before she left for the city. Daebian snuck out of the old tower and skirted the nearest buildings. He was about to dart across the open ground between one of the classrooms and the new tower when Mother and Father appeared in the doorway and descended the steps.

"Must you leave right away?" Miranda asked.

"I do. Peck will have been several days on the road, and I want to engage the assembly before they have too much time to develop a proper strategy to resist me."

"I suppose you are right, but promise me that when you return you will spend some time with Daebian. He longs for a father and is acting out to get your attention."

"All right, when I get back, I will take some time for him. Alex says he is an amazing swordsman. I would like to see him at practice."

Miranda embraced and kissed Azerick. "Good, and I will take Raijaun to the city and show him around the castle. Hopefully, your attention will alleviate some of Daebian's jealousy."

Jealous? Hardly. However, he did not like to share. If boring old Father wanted to spend time with him, which he offered with great reluctance, he would allow it, but he was not about to share his mother with that freak.

"I will make time when I get back," Azerick promised, then returned her kiss.

Azerick crossed the compound and paused atop the wall. To the south, over a thousand warriors engaged in fierce training. Some groups practiced with weapons and performed movement drills while others ran in teams with logs on their shoulders and maneuvered past a series of obstacles. Younger students not physically ready for front-line combat trained with weapons inside the walls and were drilled in support duties.

In the open field to the east, Ellyssa and the other cadre drilled students of all ages. The field was awash with fire, lightning, and brilliant orbs of arcane power as they smashed the illusionary enemy conjured by the instructors. Younger students wove wards around the older, learning how to draw power from the Source and maintain invisible barriers to slow and stop the enemy long enough for the stronger students to cut them down.

The training was intense and Azerick saw more than one student falter under the relentless assault. Students waiting in reserve rushed forward, ushered the fatigued mage back, and took his or her place in the line, never allowing a break in the wall. As the mock battle intensified, the line began to waver. More students collapsed and the reserve was not filling in fast enough. The illusionary ravagers broke through the shields and vanished just before tearing into the beleaguered wizards. Azerick could not hear from this distance, but from Ellyssa's furious gesticulations he surmised they were getting an earful.

Azerick jumped down from the wall, easily managing the substantial drop. He set a course between the two training groups and walked briskly for the distant tree line. He made a brief study of the two sides as he walked. He hoped they would be ready for joint training within the year. He *would* have them ready for combined training within a year.

Azerick enjoyed the peacefulness and solitude of the forest. It was the first real peace he had had in years. The kiss of the wind against his face and the smell of the pine trees made him feel almost human, but the lonely tranquility did not last long.

"If you are going to follow me, you may as well come out and help me find her."

Wolf appeared from behind a tree a few dozen yards away, and Ghost crept out of the shadows nearby. Azerick was still surprised by the appearance of the nearly grown young man. In his mind, Wolf was still the wildling he met and seemingly adopted all those years ago. Or, perhaps it was Wolf who had adopted him.

"Ghost still doesn't like the way you smell."

"If he could get used to your stink, then he will get used to mine."

Wolf flashed his signature broad smile. "Where are you going?"

"I need to find Sandy. I could use the help if you want to tag along."

"Why don't you just make your face appear in the water like last time?" Wolf asked as he fell into step next to Azerick.

"She told you about that?"

"Of course; she tells me everything."

"I need to ask a favor and would rather do it in person. The two-way scrying feels a little obtrusive."

Wolf bobbed his head in understanding. "So, Raijaun is what exactly?"

"He is my son," Azerick replied flatly.

Wolf mulled over his next words for almost a minute before asking, "What was his mother?"

"She was complicated."

"I imagine so."

"She was a Guardian, a creature crafted by the elves by combining the essence of an elf and a dragon to help fight the Scions."

"I see. And you two…?"

Azerick grinned and shook his head. "No. She created Raijaun much the same way the elves created her."

"Oh, okay." Wolf paused and thought a moment. "And the elf and dragon never…?"

Azerick laughed so hard he had to stop walking and catch his breath. "Wolf, I think you need a girlfriend."

Wolf crossed his arms and looked defensive. "Maybe I already have one! I might have several. In a year or two, your school could be overrun with pointy-eared little wildlings."

"The gods help us if there is ever more than one of you."

"It would be the greatest blessing the gods ever bestowed upon mankind."

"The kitchens would never survive such an infestation."

"Infestation?" Wolf protested loudly. "My offspring will be like the rain following a devastating drought!"

"Which eventually drowns everyone."

Wolf scoffed. "Drown the rats maybe."

"Unfortunately, it is always the rats who find a way to cling to safety and survive."

"Ain't that the truth. That's why there's people like you and me to kick them back into the water."

"Wolf, when the Scions come, they are going to swarm this valley. I have a plan to evacuate everyone to Brelland. You need to stay close when the fighting stops so you can join us."

Wolf's boy-like humor vanished and Azerick saw the young man he had become emerge. "This is my home, Azerick. I spent a couple years wandering with Ghost, not having a home or a place I felt accepted and loved. I have fought invaders in these woods before, and I will fight them again."

"I do not think you understand the magnitude of what is coming. This is not some band of mercenaries or even undead monsters crawling from the earth. Their numbers will fill this valley for as far as the eye can see."

"That just means there will be more to kill."

"I have no doubt as to your courage or strength, but neither of those things can hope to defeat them. Only by fighting together can we hope to survive."

"I guess surviving isn't enough for me. You know I have some rather lofty standards."

Azerick squeezed the half-elf's shoulder. "Coming from you, they are not so lofty."

"I don't need you to affirm my greatness—but thanks."

"So, do you know where Sandy is?"

"Of course. She's been sticking closer to the school since you came back. We can probably reach her before nightfall."

Wolf was true to his word. Just before nightfall, they found Sandy relaxing in a clearing largely devoid of the destruction caused by her training.

"Sandy, guess who's here," Wolf called out as they entered her grove.

"Azerick."

"It was rhetorical," Wolf said, cross at her ruining his surprise.

"Hello, Azerick. What brings you walking all the way out here?"

"I need to ask a favor."

"Why not put your face in the water again and save yourself the time?"

"That's what I asked!" Wolf exclaimed. "He said it was rude or something."

"I said it was obtrusive."

The sand dragon snorted with a blast of heated air. "More obtrusive than walking into someone's home without notice?"

"Right? Who can understand humans? They're all weird," Wolf agreed.

"I certainly gave up trying," she replied. "What did you come to see me about?"

"I need to ask a favor."

"Of course you do. Only Wolf comes to visit for purely social reasons. Although, I do always end up feeding him, so his motivation may not be entirely altruistic either."

"Hey, I pay for my meals with the pleasure of my company," Wolf protested.

Sandy ignored him. "What do you need?"

"I need to get to Brelland as fast as possible. I was hoping you would suffer taking me."

"Of course. Anytime anyone around here is in a hurry they think they can just strap a saddle on Sandy as if she were some old riding horse," Sandy said bitterly. "Their convenience is far more important than my dignity."

"Sandy, I am very sorry and I would not ask if it were not important. Will you take me?"

"Of course, but you don't think I am going to make it easy on you, do you?"

Azerick could only smile and shake his head. Some things never changed, and for that he was grateful.

Wolf scratched his head, either in thought or due to fleas. "Ellyssa said you could turn into some big demon thing with wings. Why not fly there yourself?"

"I do not want to take the demon's form. It makes it harder for me to contain him, and it is uncomfortable."

"Uncomfortable? Try strapping a saddle to your back and flying someone halfway, or all the way in Wolf's case, across the kingdom sometime," Sandy complained halfheartedly.

"I am not unaccustomed to flight and can spare you the discomfort of a saddle."

"You're all heart, always thinking of others' comfort."

Azerick sighed as Wolf burst out laughing, enjoying the taunting.

"Are you ready to go now?" Sandy asked.

"Sooner is much better than later."

Sandy crouched low and Azerick climbed onto her broad back. "You're a lot heavier than you look!"

"Can you manage it?"

Sandy snorted. "Of course I can. Sand dragons can do anything they put their mind to."

"Except diet!" Wolf said, slapping his knee and laughing uproariously.

Sandy glared and flicked her tail, catching Wolf in his rump as he bent over laughing, and sent him tumbling. "Ow! I think I broke my funny bone. Sandy, what does that feel like? You must have broken yours at one time, if you ever had one."

Sandy thrust up with her legs with all her might and began beating her huge wings. The force of the wind she created knocked Wolf down once more just as he was getting back to his feet. Sandy released a fierce roar as she strained to break gravity's hold. Every beat of her wings lifted her and Azerick a few feet higher until they cleared the towering treetops.

Once Sandy gained some appreciable altitude, her struggles lessened and she fell into a comfortable rhythm. Azerick knew the feeling of flight and was not as awed as Ellyssa and Wolf had been by the experience, but feeling the awesome power of the dragon beneath him was impressive. Despite Azerick's formidable weight, Sandy made the week-long journey to the capital before sunrise. Azerick pointed to a patch of open ground amidst a huge tract of maple trees perhaps an hour's walk from the city.

"Will you need me to ferry you back as well?"

"If you are at all amenable, I would greatly appreciate it."

"I will stay in the area a few days."

Azerick stroked the brilliant scales on her foreleg. "Thank you. You are a very good friend. More than that, you are family."

"Do not thank me just yet. You may be getting a rather large bill from local ranchers depending upon how long I must wait and the availability of local game."

Azerick chuckled, patted her side, and began walking toward what would likely be the toughest meeting he would face. So much depended on Jarvin. He hoped the king still had a tight leash on his nobles and had not lost any of the resolve he gained after his return to the throne. He would need every bit of it to help Azerick badger the nobles into supporting his cause, or rather their cause. Azerick gave a humorless laugh as he thought of how hard he would have to work to convince the fools to save their own lives.

CHAPTER 10

Azerick stood surrounded by nobles and people of influence like the recently appointed head of the Church, Archbishop Howarth, and Headmaster Florent from the Academy. King Jarvin sat at floor level with everyone else instead of seated on his throne upon the dais. Almost everyone had expected to have several days to prepare their arguments before Azerick arrived, and they spent the first hour complaining about the suddenness of the meeting.

"Lord Giles, this tale of gods before gods comes off even more spectacular than your apparent return from the dead," Lord Malcolm of Brightridge said. "You say you want us to open our coffers to fund a massive preparation for war against these alleged gods who wish to destroy us."

"That is precisely what I am saying," Azerick responded.

Lord Watkins of Argoth stood. "Why are we entertaining this fairytale when there are real issues to discuss? This man threatened Duchess Paullina, sprang a convicted criminal from the Hall of Inquisition, and absconded with a major artifact! I demand he be tried and dealt with!"

"After reviewing the charges against Miss Jensen and seeing that she only killed those whose crimes warranted execution, I have pardoned her. Therefore, Lord Giles was within his right to request her release even if the order of actions was a bit out of sorts. As far as the artifact is concerned, I find that the Codex Arcana was the property of Lord Giles and he was within his rights to request its return," Jarvin calmly explained.

"But the duchess…"

"Is lucky to retain her head, much less her crown, and would do best to remain quiet."

"Your Majesty," Headmaster Florent interjected, "I must argue your position regarding the codex. By kingdom law, it is illegal for an individual to possess a major magical artifact. The Academy was within its rights to confiscate and secure it. Lord Giles is even now violating the king's law by possessing it, much less forcing its return."

"I named Lord Giles Defender of the Crown, and as such, his possession of the codex is by way of office not individual. So long as I feel he is using it to protect the kingdom, he is violating no laws of mine."

"He and his apprentice murdered over a dozen inquisitors! Surely that is still a crime in this kingdom regardless of position?"

"Lord Giles and Miss Jensen defended themselves from an unjustified attack. Who gave the order for them to recover the book? Did you, Headmaster?"

"No, Your Majesty."

"That's right. Duchess Paullina exceeded her authority by ordering it, and the inquisitors violated the separation of power by following those orders. Were I so inclined, I would be quite justified in ordering an inquisition of their actions for possible charges of treason. Let this matter of Lord Giles and Miss Jensen rest, and let us focus on the matter at hand. What has the Academy to say on the matter of these Scions?"

"My people have spent the past two weeks scouring our archives and have found no mention of any gods before our gods. Our history clearly recounts the dragons as oppressing and enslaving the races for millennia until we rose up as one and cast them off. I have no doubt Lord Giles believes his tale, but the evidence clearly shows it as a falsehood, perhaps created by the trauma of his experiences."

"Is Bruneford's Mill also a falsehood?" Azerick asked. "More than two thousand people died that night. Are their deaths also part of my insanity?"

"I understand you and Miss Jensen just happened to be there as well. Am I right?" Headmaster Florent asked.

"We were, and a good thing too, or the town may well have been completely lost."

"Does anyone else find it difficult to believe this was a coincidence? So, in answer to your question, yes, the destruction at Bruneford's Mill may very well be part of your insanity. Should my people verify your hand in the destruction, you can be sure there will be a reckoning, with or without the king's support."

"Headmaster, there were bodies of the creatures responsible for the atrocity. If you truly believed I murdered those people, then you would not be sitting idly by," Azerick said tiredly.

"We found the bodies of demons. You yourself proclaim you spent these last five years in the abyss as the master of the Fifth Circle. How do we know you did not summon them there?"

"Because you know summoning demons on that scale is impossible. You should also know those were not demons. Any Chosen of the Church should be able to verify that."

"After reading the reports of your actions, and the fact you are in possession of the Codex Arcana, I have no idea of what you are capable. Perhaps you summoned them from some other world."

"Lord Giles brings up an interesting point," King Jarvin said. "What has the Church to say on this matter?"

Archbishop Howarth, newly appointed head of the Church of Solarian at Jarvin's urging, stood. "Your Majesty, I ordered a contingent of Solarian's Light to Bruneford's Mill. Their report does indicate the creatures were not demonic in origin, but they could not discern from whence they came. Lord Giles's assertion of being informed of these Scions by the goddess Sharrellan does beg the question. If the gods know of these beings, are fearful of their return, and require us mortals to defend against them, why did they reveal all this to him? Why would they not speak to those of us who hold true faith in them?"

"Perhaps because the gods do not hold faith in you," Azerick answered. "The kingdom was nearly torn asunder by the arrogance of the Church and many of its most esteemed members. You claim to hold the gods in faith, but you elevated your own desires of power and importance above the teachings of Solarian. That is why he abandoned

Bishop Caalendor. The fact you are so arrogant to think the gods should take the time to speak to each of you, or any of you, shows you have not learned your lesson well. You have before you a messenger of one of the gods, yet you choose to ignore him. You, in your hubris, expect, perhaps even demand, the gods come speak to you personally in order to act upon their wishes. You speaking of faith is like a whore speaking of virtue."

"Heresy!" the archbishop shouted, his face coloring in rage.

"Heresy is speaking out against the will of the gods, not a member of their church. I call you a heretic for placing yourself on a level with the gods by claiming heresy and for denying their messenger!"

"You see how he is! He defies the Church, he defies his order, and if you do not agree with him, Jarvin, he will defy you too!"

The room erupted into a cacophony of voices, mostly shouting down Azerick but some defending his position. Jarvin allowed the esteemed members of his kingdom to voice their opinions and concerns for several minutes before standing and demanding order.

"It is apparent we will make no real headway today. Let us adjourn and digest what Lord Giles has said and resume a more civilized discourse in the morning. Lord Giles, if you will follow me, I will show you where you can stay during your visit."

Everyone stood as Jarvin led Azerick from the room before resuming their noisy debate. Such was their choice, but they could carry on without him until dawn as far as he was concerned. Jarvin's more immediate interest was in Azerick.

"When your messenger brought me your letter requesting a meeting and portending our doom, I had assumed something more...mortal. This talk of returning gods with an unbelievably vast army is difficult to comprehend. I sympathize with those having an equally hard time with it."

"The archbishop is right, you know. If you resist me, I will defy you. Do you believe what I say?"

Jarvin stared at the ceiling for a moment as they walked. "When I first heard of your return, I suspected it was for something as significant as it would be unpleasant. Ill-tidings seem to follow you like a shadow."

"That they do. Will you command the nobles to fall in line if they refuse to come of their own accord?"

"Only as a last resort. We must make them believe our position and come to our side on their own, or at least let them think they did. Politics is a difficult and aggravating game."

"I am afraid we do not have a great deal of time to play. Even if I can delay the Scions' escape for a few years, we will need every day we get and a few thousand more to be even remotely prepared."

"I looked over the training suggestions you sent as well. They are quite grueling. You are trying to create an entire army with the fighting prowess of my Blackguard."

"I understand that, and I know it is unrealistic to expect that kind of mastery on such a scale, but I know we can make our entire army an elite force. We have to, Jarvin. You must believe how crucial it is that we reach that kind of preparedness."

The king answered with a weary nod. "Even if I cannot comprehend what you say, I believe your sincerity. Your battle plans show a greater defensive network at the east side of the city with the least amount of defenses at the west where you say they will strike. Should we not fortify more greatly in the direction of the attack?"

Azerick stopped and locked eyes with Jarvin. "I do not think we can save Brelland, nor Brightridge. Southport and North Haven are lost already. Their fall waits only for the battle to begin. I plan on creating stable gateways between our cities to evacuate all the citizens and the bulk of our fighting forces. Once the Scions attack our combined forces in Brelland and Brightridge, we will battle them in tactical retreat to the east where another set of gateways will see us all to a large valley near the Witchcrag and Great Barrier Mountains. It is there we will make our final stand. With any luck, that is where the elves, dwarves, and other races will join us."

Jarvin stood with his mouth hanging agape. His lips moved in silent protest as he tried to form the words flying chaotically about in his mind. "Your plan is to allow these gods and their creatures to destroy our land and cities? It is insane! The council will never agree to such a thing."

"That is why we will not tell them. It has nothing to do with allowing them anything. It is an acceptance of the inevitable and creating a plan to make it survivable."

"These Scions wish to destroy all civilizations, not just ours, so why are we to take the brunt of it? Why can the elves and dwarves not lend their support before the valley?"

"You must understand this is not like any war we have ever fought or even conceived of. Dragons will swoop from the skies, spewing fire and unleashing destructive magic. The Scions have ships capable of flying through the air. Ravagers move more like cavalry than infantry, but with more destructive power. This is not some slow army, forced to move at a crawl to keep pace with their supply trains. These fights are going to be swift and fierce. Only moving our people through these portals will allow us to keep from being washed away like a piece of flotsam in a tempest.

"We do not know when they will strike. We will have little or no warning and, once they do attack, they will engage us in battle within days or even hours. How long would the people tolerate several foreign hosts squatting on their land waiting for an enemy to come? Do not forget, the Scions will enslave all the races, not just those we deem tolerable. I do not know what the gods have in store for the goblins, ogres, orcs, and other races, but it is unlikely they would be pleasant guests if invited."

"I would have to agree with you. Even if we win, my kingdom will be in ruins."

"There is no winning this war, Jarvin, only surviving. Cities can be rebuilt and populations restored, but only if we survive."

"You paint a truly bleak portrait. Hopefully, we can make the lords see the picture beyond the canvas." Jarvin stopped before a door. "I thought you might like this room. It is simple, but away from most of the castle traffic."

"There is still time left in the day and I would rather not squander it. Are those adventurers you hired to recover Dundalor's armor still around?"

Jarvin scratched his beard. "I believe so. I have not had anything official for them to do since I sent them after the necromancer. I will send some runners and have them located if they are still about."

"Thank you."

"Someone told me you were looking for me?"

Azerick looked up from the small desk and saw Maude leaning casually against the doorframe of his room. She looked much the same as she did the last time he had seen her, except for perhaps a few more lines etching her face. She was wearing a set of leathers in place of her usual full plate armor, but still carried her huge sword strapped across her back.

Azerick stood, eager to get this finished. "Actually, I need to speak with Tarth, but since he is prone to wandering off and can be difficult to find, they sent for you in hopes you might know where to locate him."

"Still the flatterer, I see." Maude grinned, not the least bit insulted. "Yeah, I probably know where he is."

She turned and walked out, not bothering to see if Azerick followed. Azerick jogged out of his room to catch up.

"I see you've moved up in the world, *Lord Giles*."

"I suppose so. I am surprised to find you still living here in the castle. I guess Jarvin was not too upset you failed to bring back Dundalor's armor?"

Maude smirked. "To be honest, I think most everyone simply forgot about us or didn't care enough to ask us to leave."

"I heard you were instrumental in ending the undead scourge."

"We had a lot of help. Since then, we really haven't done much. There just aren't many undiscovered tombs and treasures anymore, if there ever were. I feel kind of foolish for believing all those stories my grandfather told me and for devoting my whole life to myth and folklore."

"You found a fabled artifact, destroyed a lich, live in the king's castle, and probably saw more of the world than almost anyone you'll meet. It sounds to me like you found enough adventure to kill a hundred lesser men."

Maude mentally tallied up all the adventures and near disastrous situations they had been in over the past several years. "Yeah, I guess you're right. All this comfortable living made me forget how much we really went through."

Azerick's voice took on a more serious tone. "I am afraid you, and the rest of us, will be going through much more soon."

Before she could ask the sorcerer to clarify, Malek came hopping through an open door as he pulled on his boot and began stuffing his shirttails into his trousers.

"Oh, Maude, there you are. Someone said you were looking for us. I just had to finish off some, uh..."

The handsome cleric's excuse was cut short by a woman's voice. "Hurry back, Malek. I think I still have some sins in need of absolving."

Malek blushed. "Right, never mind. So what did you need?"

"Azerick asked for us. Have you seen Borik?"

"I think I saw him headed toward the kitchens." Malek studied Azerick for a moment. "Oh, right, you're the one who helped us find Dundalor's armor then destroyed it. So what did you need us for?"

"It is rather complicated, and I would prefer explaining when we are all together. I have already had to repeat it more than I like."

"Fair enough," Malek replied. "I suppose you are why there are so many nobles and suchlike buzzing around like angry hornets."

"I have certainly kicked the nest a bit."

Maude led the way to the kitchen nearest their living quarters. None of them were much for small talk, so they walked largely in silence. Maude was not the curious type, and Malek felt oddly uncomfortable around the sorcerer. The priest wrote it off as having to do with his unexpected return from the dead.

Their rooms were not far from the kitchen, mostly upon Borik's insistence, and it was only a couple of minutes later they ran into the dwarf just as he was exiting. In his arms was a loaf of bread the length of Maude's sword, stuffed to overflowing with meat and cheese. He stopped short upon seeing Maude approach and smiled widely when he recognized Azerick.

"Ice beer man! Let me find a mug!"

"We don't have time for that, Borik," Maude snapped. "What are you carrying?"

"Food. Every time you ask us to come to you, you have some moronic adventure in mind that is either a huge waste of time or nearly kills us, and I ain't doin' either one on an empty stomach!"

"Your stomach hasn't been empty from the day your mother squeezed you out and left you for dead on a cave floor! I thought you liked adventuring?"

"I like squashing a few goblins or skeletons and filling my pockets with treasure. You always drag us into vampires and liches and a whole bunch of stuff that kills us and don't make us a single copper!"

"If we were dead, you wouldn't be complaining so much, and I wouldn't be hearing it all the time," Maude countered.

Borik pointed his sandwich at Malek. "You killed the priest! It was just dumb luck he got better." He turned to Azerick. "I heard you got killed too. I guess you can't keep nobody in the ground these days."

"Malek was killed?" Azerick asked.

"Yep, by a lich. He was deader than dead."

"Actually, I was able to shift my soul into my holy symbol and Solarian was able to move it back into my body," Malek explained. "I can't describe the feeling of having my god so close to me like that. Were you touched by one of the gods as well?"

Azerick nodded. "I was."

"What was it like?"

"Painful. Sharrellan knocked me all the way through the Fifth Circle of the abyss from her throne room."

"You got struck by a god and lived?" Malek asked.

"To be fair, I hit her first. I prefer not to talk about it, and I really need to find Tarth."

Borik scoffed. "What for?"

"I need to talk to him."

"Good luck. Talking to him is like talking to a chicken…with brain damage…born simpleminded."

"Nevertheless, it is important."

"Fine, but I'm taking my sandwich."

Maude looked crossly at Borik. "Borik, that thing is ridiculous."

Borik looked at his sandwich and sighed. "You're right. There's no way I can hold a beer and eat this at the same time. It's a good thing I'm not thirsty right now."

Maude gave up and stalked into the kitchen. "Tarth has been spending a lot of time in a meadow inside the park. We can reach it fastest by cutting through here."

Maude led Azerick and her oddball crew through the kitchen and onto the palace grounds. After passing through a small gate set in a low garden wall, Azerick found himself at the edge of an enormous park of manicured lawns, bushes, and flowers. The sculpted grounds stretched for acres until they reached the edge of a forest of maple and fruit trees.

It took several minutes to cross the perfectly cut grass and step into the rows of trees. The orchard opened up a few hundred yards in to display an enchanting meadow. Next to a small pond, Tarth sat looking at his reflection in the water and braiding small blue wildflowers into his long black hair.

"Tarth, look who's come to visit," Maude called out as they stepped into the glen.

Tarth looked up and all the color drained from his face. Azerick had never seen fear so profound in his life. The elf leapt to his feet and pointed a shaking finger at Azerick.

"I see you, demon!" Tarth shouted, then began a horrific keening.

Black clouds rolled across the previously clear blue sky with the sound of an avalanche. Powerful winds tore through the glade, stripping leaves from the trees and setting the placid pond roiling. Azerick barely had enough time to erect a ward as he saw Tarth pull an awesome amount of power into his thin body and hurl it directly at him.

The force bolt struck harder than anything Azerick had felt before with the exception of the one with which Sharrellan had hit him. The power of it shoved him back and his feet plowed deep furrows in the soft soil as he braced himself against it. Again and again Tarth struck at him, driving him farther away with each hit.

Lightning flashed across the sky and began striking the ground all around him, splitting trees and setting them on fire. Tarth continued to howl his shrill cry as the ground began trembling and then heaving upward. The quaking earth and stone split apart, opening deep chasms that swallowed the pond and nearby trees like a sea of hungry mouths.

Maude and the others leapt about, desperately trying to avoid falling into the fissures while barely able to stand against the awful shaking. Lightning cracked against Azerick's ward with the rhythm of a hailstorm while Tarth continued to batter against it. Azerick knew there was little time before he would have to do something, but he was unsure what. Tarth's attack was relentless and nearly as powerful as anything Azerick could unleash without losing control of Klaraxis.

Azerick looked upon the searing aura surrounding the elf and saw he was unconcerned with control. Tarth's terror at seeing Azerick washed away any regard for himself or his friends as he pulled in more power than could possibly be safe.

"Cleric!" Azerick shouted desperately. "You have to do something before he destroys us all!" *What did you do to him, demon?*

I just played with him, Klaraxis replied laughingly.

Malek looked at Tarth standing on a small island surrounded by a bottomless chasm. He waved to Borik to get his attention, made a running motion with his fingers, and pointed at Tarth. Borik looked at the fifteen or twenty feet of open air between him and Tarth, tapped on his chest, and wagged his head with an incredulous look on his face.

Malek shook his head and jabbed at himself. Borik smiled and nodded vigorously, knelt down on one knee, and slapped his shoulder. Malek got his feet under him and broke into a sprint. When he reached Borik, he planted one foot onto the dwarf's shoulder as Borik heaved upward at the same instant. The stubby but powerful legs launched Malek into the air and over the chasm.

The priest landed just behind Tarth and nearly rolled off the far end. Digging his fingers into the dirt, he stopped himself from going over, sprang to his feet, and slapped a hand over the top of Tarth's head. His amulet glowed on his chest as he beseeched Solarian to instill peace in the heart and mind of his friend. Malek eased the elf to the ground as he collapsed in his arms. The ground went still, the lightning stopped, and the roiling black clouds calmed and cast a grey pall over the land.

CHAPTER II

Maude got to her feet and staggered toward Malek and Tarth. "Malek, what's wrong with Tarth?" she cried out.

"Maude, Borik, watch him!" Malek shouted as he kept a hand pressed firmly to Tarth's forehead. "He is not what he seems! I see what Tarth saw, creature! Take one step and I will let him up even if it means he destroys us!"

Maude did not understand what Malek was saying, but she trusted her fellows and drew her sword, pointing it at Azerick. Borik pulled a hand axe from his belt and circled warily around to Azerick's left side.

Azerick did not try to stand. He sat on his knees with his hands held out before him. Malek knelt next to Tarth with one hand still on the elf's head and his holy symbol outstretched in the other.

"Please stay calm and let me explain," Azerick said. "When I destroyed the armor, I thought I could finally live in peace, but I was wrong. An assassin came for me, the same one I am certain murdered my father. I went searching for whoever sent him and it took me to the Black Tower in Sumara. I was beaten and taken captive. A wizard sought to use my body as a vessel for the demon lord Klaraxis. He failed to force out my spirit and I remained in control, but with him as a parasite."

Hey! This is my body. You are the parasite.

Azerick ignored him. "When I died, our two souls were so entwined I was taken into Klaraxis's body along with him but was still able to keep control. Tarth's grandmother was a Guardian, a creature created by the elves during the Great Revolution to battle the old gods, and she pulled me from the abyss. The old gods are returning and Tarth is the only elf I know. I need him to tell the elves the Scions are returning. We will all have to fight together or the Scions will destroy us."

Maude looked to Malek. "Is what he says possible?"

"I don't know. Demonology is not my area of expertise."

Borik grumbled, "Yeah, if only he had been possessed by a prostitute."

Malek ignored him. "It does sound plausible, though. As far as these old gods or Scions go, I have never heard of them."

"Few if anyone amongst the humans remember them. Even the dwarves have forgotten, but I am counting on Tarth, or at least his people, to still remember." Azerick looked at Tarth lying peacefully on the ruined ground. "Can you wake him now?"

"His spirit is still in turmoil. It is likely he will attack you again if I do," Malek answered.

"Can you do something similar to me and send me to him?"

"If you cooperate I can, but Tarth could attack you inside his mind, and he could be even more powerful there. Given his mental state, I cannot even guess as to what you will find inside that head of his."

"I have to take the risk. Tarth is probably the most important piece in the defense of our realm and continued existence."

Malek hated the idea of letting this creature near Tarth, but if what he said was true then Tarth and the elves were going to be desperately needed. "All right, but if I sense you are going to harm Tarth, I will pull you out and do whatever is in my power to protect him and everyone else."

"Fair enough. What must I do?"

"Lay down next to Tarth."

Azerick stood, channeled a measure of the Source, and erected a bridge of stone. He stepped across the void separating him and the island upon which Tarth and the cleric resided and lay down opposite Tarth's recumbent form.

"Just relax and let your mind go on the trip. It is merely your consciousness I am moving into Tarth, not your soul. It will be like a shared dream, only more real."

Azerick nodded and Malek laid his palm on the sorcerer's brow. The cleric began chanting softly and Azerick felt a relaxing warmth spread through his body. He felt himself floating a moment before darkness overtook him. He knew the elf was out of sorts at the best of times and had no idea what to expect inside his mind in such an agitated state. Azerick spotted a flickering light and willed his body toward it. What he discovered upon reaching the light surprised him.

He stood near the far wall of a quaint bedroom. The walls of the room were made of what looked to be live tree limbs grown so close together they sealed the room from any draft or rain. It was like being on the inside of an enormous closed tulip. Tarth sat at a small desk brushing his hair. Flickering candles framed his reflected image in a halo of yellow light. An elfin woman of impossible beauty sat on the bed near the center of the room.

"Tarthanalis, I swear you are the vainest creature I ever met," the woman said, yet smiled lovingly at the back of Tarth's head.

Tarth returned her smile in his mirror. "It is not vanity, Lahilonah. It calms me. My foster mother used to brush my hair every night to help put me to sleep."

"It worries you," Lahilonah said, her smile slipping.

"It is a foolish thing to attempt, but the people have chosen and I will not deny them. I am certain they would try even without my help, and that would guarantee disaster. At least I can give them a chance."

"You are the most brilliant elf I have ever known. You will not fail."

"I wish I was as certain as you," Tarth replied as he set down his brush and stood with obvious reluctance.

Lahilonah stood with him and crossed to his side. Plucking a small, blue wildflower from her long golden hair, she deftly wove it into Tarth's ebony locks. "Here, for luck."

Tarth embraced Lahilonah and kissed her passionately. "I wish I could stay in this room with you forever."

"That would be incredibly boring, and I rather enjoy our walks in the Grove of Heroes. Our people await their savior. Now go."

Tarth kissed her once more and left the room. Azerick found himself overlooking a large plaza. Unknown sigils inscribed in silver, or possibly arcanum, decorated the polished stones of the courtyard.

Elves, wizards given the look of them, surrounded a large circular area near the center. Tarth took his place upon a raised plinth and stood behind a pedestal. Azerick gasped as he recognized the object open before Tarth. It was the Codex Arcana.

Tarth looked at each of the score of mages forming the circle. "Are you still certain you wish to attempt this?"

An elf wearing the robes of an elder spoke. "We must, Tarthanalis. The humans continue to expand and we must protect our way of life from their encroachment." He looked pointedly at the codex. "Even if they do not expand this far north, they or someone else will eventually learn of your possessing the codex and seek it for themselves. The humans' Academy of wizards in particular would stop at nothing to claim it, and we dare not let such power get into their hands. They are a rash and irresponsible people, and the damage they could inflict if they had the codex is too great. This is our only option."

Tarth inclined his head once. "As you wish. Let us begin."

Tarth began chanting in elvish, and soon the assembled wizards took up the songlike incantation as well. The runes within the circle glowed until they became too intense to look upon. The blue sky of mid-morning went dark and the stars began shining down. Then the stars blurred and the black sky turned grey and dull as the tiny elven nation slowly phased out of its home dimension.

The ground started to tremble. Several wizards, as well as those in the crowd watching the spectacle from the edges of the plaza, looked concerned. Tarth stood locked in concentration, but nodded to signal that the event was not unexpected. The ritual went on until one of the sigils flared up and left a black imprint in the stones. Tarth now looked worried.

Azerick shifted his vision to capture the astral energies of the wizards and the incredibly powerful spell they were enacting. All of the wizards' auras glowed with power equal to any mage he had ever met, rivaling and even surpassing Allister and Aggie. Tarth's level of power vastly exceeded even those, but he was losing control of the incredible forces at work.

"We are losing it!" Tarth shouted over the crackling energy and nervous conversations of the gathered elves. "We have to shut it down!"

But still the power of the spell continued to build and more silver runes flared and turned black. Cracks began forming in the polished stones of the courtyard and a small tear opened in the air.

"Tarth, we are losing control!" an elder wizard shouted. "What is happening?"

Although Tarth spoke only in a whisper, Azerick was able to hear him clearly. "Something has taken control from the other side."

The rift between dimensions tore open at that moment and began disgorging demons into the crowd of elves. Pandemonium erupted as the demons hewed into the defenseless bystanders. Lesser mages, not tasked with controlling the spell, leapt to defend their people and began beating back the demonic minions, but the rift continued to grow and more demons leapt forth.

Elves in shining chain and plate armor shoved through the fleeing masses of civilians and engaged the monsters with steel and bow. The demons spewing forth began overwhelming the elven defenders and were now rampaging through the pristine streets of the city, killing and destroying with glee.

Several demons began concentrating their attacks on the wizards desperately trying to close the rift. Half a dozen grackin and belphor demons launched themselves at Tarth, but he was too focused on preventing the rift from opening any further to do anything about it. Lahilonah interposed her body between Tarth and the demons, hurling curses, fire, and lightning with equal fury. Her strength was not remarkable, but she compensated with sheer ferociousness.

The elf maiden pushed a host of creatures back toward the rift with her magic, but she was tiring quickly. Lahilonah looked around as she realized she was too close to the rift and needed to get back to Tarth, but she could not give up her assault or the demons would leap upon her and tear her to pieces.

Lahilonah unleashed a final wave of force, shoving the demons back, and made to race toward the minor refuge of her fellows. Just as she turned, a black, spectral hand slithered out of the rift and wrapped around her slender waist. Her eyes met Tarth's for just a moment before it pulled her into the gaping transdimensional maw.

Tarth's focus broke as he watched his beloved pulled into the rift. He looked at the gash in the air oozing demons and made a decision. Grabbing the codex, he strode purposefully toward the rift.

"Tarthanalis, what are you doing?" one of his fellow wizards called out.

Tarth cut several demons down with a slashing beam of power. "We cannot close it from here. I must go through and close it from the other side."

"No! We cannot lose you!"

Tarth looked at the rift. "I am already lost."

The elf sent a pair of enormous blasts into the rift, clearing away the demons clawing to get out. Tarth then floated up into the rent in the air and vanished. Azerick's world disintegrated, and he found himself looking over a very familiar landscape.

Not far away, Azerick spotted a score of demons toying with Lahilonah like cats playing with a mouse before devouring it. The elf struck out with her magic, but she was weak and her spells feeble. Tarth stepped through the rift and choked back a cry as he saw the demons mocking and taunting his love. A bluish-white curtain of arcane energy surrounded Lahilonah and burst outward, destroying her tormentors.

"Lahilonah, run through the rift!" Tarth shouted.

"Come with me! There is something else here, something terrible!" Lahilonah pleaded.

"I will be right behind you, but first I must break whatever has a hold of this."

Tears poured down Lahilonah's face as she saw Tarth's lie for what it was. "I love you!"

"And I you. Please, get away from this place. Our people need you."

Lahilonah ran for the rift. From a cleft in the ground, the shadowy arm streaked after her, unwilling to relinquish its plaything. Tarth severed the spectral appendage with a lance of power and breathed a sigh of relief when Lahilonah leapt through the rift. He turned his eyes back to the dark fissure as a pair of black hands sprouted from a cleft in the ground and heaved a huge demonic form into the open.

"You took away my toy, elf. No matter; I shall play with you for an eternity," Klaraxis taunted sadistically.

Tarth did not hesitate. He struck out with a bolt of power laced with Guardian magic. Azerick detected the strange power in the spell, although it was significantly diluted compared to what Lissandra, or even Raijaun, had produced.

The attack and its power took Klaraxis by surprise. The demon lord howled in pain and outrage as he tumbled across the barren landscape, kicking up large clouds of dust in his wake. Tarth turned to the codex and spoke to it. The book flipped open and he studied the pages intensely.

Klaraxis roared to his feet and charged like a bull, horns down even as he summoned his abyssal power to crush the impudent elf. Tarth opened a gate and stepped through just as Klaraxis unleashed his spell and charged through the space in which he had been standing a moment before. The demon spun around in search of the elf. A massive crack opened under his feet, and he pumped his wings to avoid falling in. Before he was able to get more than a few feet in the air, a pair of gigantic stone hands reached up, grabbed him by the ankles, and pulled him into the open ground.

The cleft slammed shut with finality and Tarth began working magic to close the rift. With Klaraxis distracted and no longer working to keep it open, Tarth was able to mend the tear between realities. He found relief in knowing his people were safe despite having just doomed himself. Just as Tarth closed the rift, the ground exploded like a volcano, sending rock and dust high into the air. Klaraxis stepped from the cloud as a rain of stone pelted the ground.

"You surprised me, elf, but no more. You will pay for your effrontery in the most horrible manner of my devising."

Azerick watched the epic battle unfold, but now familiar with the elf's power, Klaraxis gained the upper hand. Here in his home realm, Tarth was outmatched and fell to the powerful demon lord. Azerick looked on as time flew past, witnessing the tortures Klaraxis inflicted upon the captive elf for what must have been decades. Just as Azerick thought he could not bear to witness any more, the abyssal landscape vanished and he found himself back in Tarth's quaint bedroom.

Azerick jumped as Tarth's voice sounded from behind him. "Now you understand what your demon did to me. She loved me with all her heart. Not because of my power or influence, but because I was me. When I came back, shattered and lost, I was no longer that person. She still loved me, or tried to, but I could not bear to be near my people, and I was ashamed of it. I was ashamed for being a coward. I should have refused them when they posed this insane solution, but I could not. I was afraid they would resent me for not trying. My vanity and desire to be loved by all nearly destroyed my people."

Tears shimmered in Tarth's haunted eyes. "Do you know the worst torment? It was not the abuses inflicted upon my body, but the fear remaining in my heart and mind. For decades after I returned, I was certain I was still Klaraxis's prisoner and, at any moment, he would tear away the illusion of my freedom and renew my torture. When I saw you, all those fears returned. I thought you were here to take me back."

"I am sorry, Tarth; I had no idea, but Klaraxis is not in control of me."

Tarth crossed the room, sat at the small desk, and began brushing his hair in the mirror. "I understand that now. Now that you are here, I see you for what you are and understand the nature of your shared existence, although not how it came to be. I suppose it is not important."

"Tarth, what is this place?" Azerick asked as he looked around the room.

"It is the last bastion of my sanity. Sad, is it not? A mind once capable of delving into the farthest reaches of the cosmos now relegated to this paltry speck of an existence. Something weighs heavy on your mind. What is it you came here for?"

"Do you know of the Scions?"

Tarth stopped brushing his hair and looked grim. "I do."

"They are returning. I am trying to maintain the barrier trapping them in their prison, but it is only a matter of time before it falls."

"The Guardians?"

"They are all gone. The last one gave her life to pull me from the abyss and used the last of her strength to reinforce the barrier. She was the same one who eventually saved you. She was your grandmother, Tarth."

"My grandmother," the elf whispered. "I never knew from where I came or who my parents were. It explains many things. Thank you. You have been in possession of the Codex Arcana. I can sense its influence upon you. I wondered if it would ever leave the abyss after Klaraxis took hold of it."

"A creature of the Scions' creation was able to enter the abyss and somehow took it away. I was a slave to it, but I escaped with the codex."

I was distracted when that vile creature snuck into my citadel and stole my property. His minions I captured suffered greatly for his audacity.

"The codex speaks to you?"

"My apprentice as well."

Tarth smiled and looked into the distance. "Things must be truly desperate if the gods and codex have selected two masters of the book. What is it you need of an insane old elf?"

"We need you and your people if we are to have a chance of defeating the Scions. Can you tell your people of their return and ask them to stand with us?"

"It is hard for me to return. There are so many memories and so much pain, but you are right. The elves and races must fight together again."

"I need one other thing from you if you will indulge me."

"What is it?"

"My people have forgotten about the Scions. You remember. Can you speak to them and try to help me convince them of the danger they pose?"

"I will speak, but I cannot make them listen."

Azerick looked around the room, at the tiny sanctuary in Tarth's mind. "Will you remember what we talked about here? Will you be able to deliver my message to your people?"

Tarth cast him a mischievous grin. "You refer to my...instability? I can manage. There is a slight exaggeration on my part in that regard. I find people do not ask much and expect even less from me that way.

Besides, it aggravates the dwarf no end, and that is one of my greatest amusements in life. His face turns so many hues and his invectives are quite creative. I suppose we should be going. It sounds as though you have more important matters to attend to than sitting within the mad mind of a broken elf."

"It has been interesting and informative."

Azerick felt a gentle push and the tiny room receded until he could no longer see it. His eyes fluttered open and he was once again lying in the shattered orchard. He turned his head and saw Tarth waking as well. Tarth stood and looked at the devastation his magic had wrought.

"Tarth, are you all right?" Maude asked.

"I am fine, dear, but the gardeners are going to be terribly upset."

Borik looked almost on the point of tears. "This is terrible."

"Borik, I did not think you appreciated the garden that much," Tarth said.

"To the abyss with the garden! I dropped my sandwich in one of these cursed crevasses you made, you moron! You killed my lunch and almost killed us!"

"Your lunch needed killed, you rotund ruffian," Tarth snapped back. "You are getting fat."

Borik's face turned scarlet and his nostrils flared. "I am not fat! I just…" Borik held his belly in his hands. "You're right; I have really let myself go. Too much high living in the castle, I guess."

"You should have no trouble walking it off on our way to my homeland."

"Your homeland?" Borik exclaimed. "That's like a million miles through the coldest, most beer freezingest place on the planet!" Borik sighed heavily. "I'm going to need to make another sandwich before we go."

"I'm sure your hot breath will keep your disgusting beer in a liquid form," Tarth retorted.

"It better!" Borik snapped, crossing his arms.

CHAPTER 12

Azerick decided today he would start off using tact. There was always time to be a thug later. "Lords and Ladies, I understand the difficulty you have believing the things I have told you and your reluctance in supporting my recommendations," he told the assembly. "Since I cannot convince you of the veracity of my news, I have brought to you a representative of the elven nation. The elves were directly involved with the battle against the Scions, and they are a much longer-lived race than us. Tarthanalis Moonglow is venerable even by their standards. The elves have not forgotten the Scions. Tarth, would you please tell them what you know?"

Tarth stood and smiled at the crowd. "Hello. I know black should not be worn with brown, nor should you mix plaid with stripes. Your shoes should match your belt and dwarves do not go with anything, except maybe rocks."

Azerick rolled his eyes at the elf's antics. "Tarth, tell them what you know of the Scions."

"Oh, of course. The dwarves worked with the human wizards to create the five suits of armor that enabled the races to fight the dragons and other mundane minions while the Guardians and new gods battled the Scions. They fought to a standstill, and the Scions eventually agreed to banishment, where they have been for the past two thousand years. Now they are coming back, and I have to go tell my people so we can prepare. I would suggest you do the same."

The representative from Argoth stood. "Lord Giles, I have seen this elf and his cohorts around the castle these last few years. They were tried for assault and burglary and pressed into service by the king. Tarthanalis has routinely displayed odd behavior, and their conduct flies in the face of credibility."

"Your shirt flies in the face of credibility," Tarth replied with a sniff of disdain.

Azerick laid a hand on Tarth's shoulder and gently pushed him back into his chair. "Thank you for being entirely unhelpful, Tarth."

Clarity shone in the elf's eyes as he responded, "Nothing I was going to say would convince them, so why not mock them for the fools they are?"

Azerick nodded to Tarth and took over the debate. "I am beginning to think you would argue with the gods themselves if they came. It is not a case of credibility, but of your refusal to believe no matter the evidence at hand."

"What evidence? A strange attack on a faraway town and the word of a disturbed elf?"

Klaraxis gently stoked the anger burning in Azerick's gut. "How deep can your greed go? You all spent fortunes continuing the war with Sumara for nothing more than the chance at reclaiming your losses with the wealth of copper and silver within their hills, but you cinch your purses tightly closed when asked to save your own miserable lives! What good is your gold when you and your heirs and everyone else are dead?"

"You answer your own question, Lord Giles. The war with Sumara was an investment that would have reaped profit had Jarvin not ended it prematurely."

"Are your lives not an investment? Is there no profit in life? If it were just you, I would agree and say no, but it is not just your lives but the lives of everyone in our kingdom and beyond." Azerick turned to Jarvin. "Your Majesty, you named me Defender of the Crown. You said it was more than a ceremonial title, that it came with duties."

The king nodded. "It does."

"Then I demand you allow me to do what I must to fulfill that duty since your nobles are fools and too stupid to save their own lives."

Lord Preston of Brightridge shot to his feet, his voice trembling with indignation. "You dare make demands of the king? You overstep yourself, sir!"

"I have not yet begun to overreach myself, and will reach as far as I must to protect the people of this kingdom."

"You would defy the king?"

"I would fulfill my duty to the kingdom, even if it means defying every lord in the land, even the king."

"You speak the words of a traitor!"

"I speak the words of a patriot! You who would ignore impending doom on the chance you would lose coin are the traitors."

"We are loyal to the king!"

"What good is a king if we lose the kingdom? What is a kingdom without its people? You put yourselves at the top of the pedestal and forget that it is the people who make up the base. Without the base, the entire thing tumbles down, and you with it."

"Perhaps we need more time to consider this," the mayor of Groveswood suggested. "Should an invasion occur, we can send our soldiers and wizards to intercept it."

Azerick shook his head. "You, like nearly everyone else, do not understand the enemy we face. If we wait for them to come, it will be too late. When they break free, they will flood our coastal cities within days. Brelland and Brightridge will be under siege within a week and fall soon afterward."

"Brelland's walls are fifty feet high!" someone exclaimed.

"And the Scions will pile the bodies of their troops up sixty feet and leap down upon your heads!" Azerick shouted back.

"I still say we should take time to consider the reality of the threat and what measures to take in the interim, as well as how to respond to an invasion if it should occur."

"There is no time," Azerick stressed through his clamped jaw.

"There is even less evidence," the nobleman countered.

"What manner of evidence must you have before you will heed what I say? Must your coins and manors be covered in the blood of your people and families before you act? If that is the case, it can be arranged!"

"He threatens us all with murder!" someone shouted above the renewed din.

"I threaten nothing, but promise everything!"

Jarvin stood and banged his mug on the table. "We have all heard what Lord Giles has come here to say, and we have all said our piece. It is time to end all this barking and decide a course of action. Whatever we decide will affect us all, especially if Lord Giles is right and we choose to ignore his warning. I created this council because I do not believe in the ultimate wisdom of one man, even if he is king. As Azerick said, the kingdom is more than just the king. Let each representative for their duchy speak their decision."

Lord Preston was eager and the first to speak. "Argoth finds the claims of Lord Giles to be preposterous and votes to avoid taking unnecessary and costly actions."

Lord Blackburn stood and sniffed contemptuously toward Lord Preston. "North Haven places its trust in her first son and elects for full militarization and conscription."

"Southport agrees with Argoth," Lady Palmer voted. "Such an expense and massive disruption in trade and production is unwarranted. We should wait and see what comes to allow us to make an intelligent and measured decision."

"If it pleases Your Majesty, Brightridge abstains," Lord Fowler said, eliciting a few insulting murmurs.

"It would appear the duchies vote to stay our present course," Lord Preston announced.

The doors to the meeting hall opened and a shrill voice sounded clearly over the muttering assembly. "Brightridge does not abstain!"

Jarvin smiled at the handsome young man who would one day be the duke of Brightridge. "Thomas, what an unexpected surprise."

Thomas strode toward the king and leaned upon bended knee. "Forgive me, Your Majesty, but I thought this decision too important to be left to a proxy." Thomas Everingham stood and looked boldly at the crowd of adults. "Brightridge will arm and defend itself and the kingdom with every ounce of its gold, breath, and blood!"

Lord Preston laughed loudly. "The boy gets his first black and curly betwixt his legs and thinks he's ready to make a man's decision!"

Thomas's eyes locked with those of Lord Preston, silencing the nobleman and the entire room. "You have offended me, Lord Preston. Mark your calendar three years, nine months, and eleven days from today. On that day I claim my throne and my manhood, and you will answer for your insult with steel."

No one laughed at the boy now. Thomas had taken to his sword studies with a fervor the likes of which few had ever seen after the assassination of his father. He could probably take Lord Preston in a duel now if it were not against kingdom law for a boy to demand satisfaction by blade.

"Thomas—Lord Everingham—I misspoke," Lord Preston said nervously. "I simply wished to alleviate the tension of the room."

"And I intend to alleviate the tension your oversized head places upon your fat neck."

"Your Majesty, surely you will not allow young Thomas to make such a reckless declaration. I am certain that when he matures, he will see how inappropriate such a reaction was."

Jarvin looked at the angry boy. "Thomas, I look forward to your birthday and coronation."

Headmaster Florent stood. "If we are through with the entertainment, may we return to the issue at hand? Let the Academy break the stalemate by voting for reason and not rash militarization."

"Let the Magus Academy speak for themselves," Commandant Reese boomed over the crowd. "The Martial Academy will not turn a blind eye to a possible threat, no matter how improbable. I have read Lord Giles's ideas on training and have already begun to enact them. My cadets will be ready to teach these new standards on a wide scale to the common army within a year."

"Then we are at an impasse once more!" Magus Florent shouted.

"We are not," Jarvin spoke calmly. "As the lord of Brelland, I vote we support Lord Giles and his plan fully. As king, I demand it of you all as well. Expect visits from my auditors within the month to all major noble houses so that they may be assessed their war tax. Let me be perfectly clear. If my auditors discover anyone withholding information regarding their financial assets, I will view it as treason and you will swing in the plaza."

Several amongst the assembly looked as though they wished to speak out, but the king's voice left no doubt that he would entertain no more argument on the matter. Jarvin ordered the room vacated and the nobles and representatives filed out.

"Thank you for backing me, Jarvin," Azerick said when the room finally emptied.

"I was afraid not to," the king replied dryly. "Besides, I believe what you say, and I cannot allow us to fall into complacency. You do understand this is going to place an enormous strain on the kingdom's resources?"

"I do, and I plan to use my wealth and resources to the fullest."

"Do not expect too many others to follow your example. The people are not going to welcome the idea of mass conscription either. To be honest, that is a greater fear than keeping my nobles in line."

"Send criers out with news of Bruneford's Mill. Employ some artists to paint accurate pictures of the attack and post them around the towns. I find fear one of the more powerful motivators," Azerick said.

Jarvin gave a slight nod. "My spies tell me Sumara is conscripting and arming on a large scale. My advisors tell me that could only mean they plan on invading."

"My former master was Devlin Sabaht, brother to King Sabaht. I gave him the same information and suggestions I gave here. I asked him to convince his brother to prepare and come to our aid when the Scions invade. Whether they will come or stay to defend their homeland I cannot say."

"The war was not so long ago, Azerick. Sumarans on Valerian soil could result in a war on two fronts. You say they may come to help, but many would see it as an invasion of opportunity."

"It seems to me that would only strengthen my argument for military preparedness."

"Or as an unnecessary distraction. Preparing for the wrong war could be as bad, or worse, than not preparing at all."

"I do not care what they think as long as they act. Sumara does not want a war with Valeria, and we will all be too busy fighting for our existence to worry about politics or expansion. When the time comes, even the stupidest, most self-serving of your people will understand that. I just hope the realization does not come too late."

CHAPTER 13

Seated at Daebian's chessboard, Raijaun and Daebian squared off across from each other. Although Daebian had just begun teaching his little brother how to play, it was their fifth game that day, and Raijaun already played at a respectable level.

Raijaun watched Daebian move his rook to put pressure on his king. "Father is home."

"How do you know?"

"I can feel his presence when he is close."

"Then we should go welcome him back," Daebian said, standing up.

Raijaun smiled. "You just want to go because I was going to beat you this time."

"You were going to lose in three moves."

"You are bluffing. I was about to take your rook and put your king into check."

"Yes, you were. You were going to take my rook with your knight. That would clear a path for my bishop. You were then going to put your bishop in my path, but that left an opening for my other bishop to move and trap your king between it and my other rook. Had you left your knight in place, you could have delayed your loss by four more moves, but you were too focused on the quick kill. You see, little brother, these eyes of mine may be weird, but they see ten steps ahead of everything you are going to do."

"They are not that weird, certainly not as weird as me." Raijaun sighed. "At least you look human. I do not fit in anywhere."

"Nonsense. You have all kinds of magical power. With that, you fit in here more than I do, especially with Father."

"No I don't. I'm elf, demon, and dragon. What does that make me?" Raijaun asked plaintively.

"Three different kinds of ugly?" Daebian replied with a smile. "Stop moping. Father is back, and you and he can disappear under the tower just like before."

Daebian listened intently as they neared the top of the stairs and heard his parents speaking as they entered the big living room.

"I think you need to take the time to get to know Daebian," Miranda was saying. "He is desperate for your attention. I know I need to spend time with Raijaun so I can get to know him better. Technically, I am only his stepmother and he is very…different. It would be easier for me if I spent more time with him."

"All right, Miranda, but Raijaun and I both have things we must do. I will do my best to make him available to you."

"Thank you."

"Raijaun, catch me," Daebian said as he turned his back to the top of the stairs and leaned away.

Raijaun's eyes flew wide, and he reached out with surprising speed and strength and caught the front of Daebian's shirt. Although he was much smaller than his brother, Raijaun had no problem arresting Daebian's fall.

"What are you doing?" Raijaun demanded frightenedly.

"Solving a problem," Daebian replied as he stabbed Raijaun's wrist with one of Miranda's knitting needles.

Caught by the suddenness of his brother's attack, Raijaun let slip his grip and watched helplessly as Daebian teetered backward.

"Raijaun, no, don't!" Daebian cried out as he fell.

Azerick and Miranda looked up just in time to see Raijaun release his grip. Daebian toppled over and tumbled down the long flight of stairs. Azerick and Miranda raced over and reached him just as he rolled to a stop, holding his left arm and wincing.

"What is going on?" Miranda demanded as she knelt and held her son.

"Raijaun pushed me down the stairs!" Daebian cried out. "I think my arm is broken!"

"Raijaun, come down here," Azerick ordered.

Raijaun broke out of his spell of bewilderment and slowly descended the stairs. He stopped a few steps up from where his brother sat cradling his arm.

"Father, I did not push him."

"Yes, he did, Mother!"

"Daebian, why would he push you down the stairs?" Miranda asked.

"He asked what being a dragon, elf, and demon made him, and I said that made him three kinds of ugly. He got mad and pushed me. I was just joking!"

Miranda glared up at Raijaun. "Raijaun, you cannot do this over words! What Daebian said was not right, but you could have seriously hurt him."

"But I did not push him. He calls me ugly all the time. It does not bother me much."

"I saw you with your hand on him, Raijaun. Do not lie to me."

"I was trying to stop him from falling. He stabbed me with a needle," Raijaun tried to explain.

"Are you telling me he made himself fall? For what reason? Who would do that?"

"I do not know why he did it."

"I have a healing potion in my lab. I will go get it," Azerick said.

Miranda turned her angry eyes on Azerick. "Do not bother. Just take Raijaun with you. I will have Brother Thomas tend to Daebian."

Miranda helped her son to his feet and walked toward the door. Azerick laid a hand on Raijaun's shoulder and guided him toward the basement stairs. Raijaun paused and watched his departing brother. Daebian looked over his shoulder at him and smiled.

"Father, I did not push him, I swear," Raijaun said as they reached the lab.

"I know."

"We were playing chess all morning and getting along fine. Why would he do that?"

"There is something off about your brother, Raijaun. I think it best if you stay clear of him as much as possible."

"Miranda does not like me. Especially now."

"She does not understand you, is all. She saw her son hurt by you and is doing as a mother does."

"She saw him hurt by a monster," Raijaun said softly.

Azerick knelt next to Raijaun and gripped his shoulder tightly. "If there are any monsters around here, it is not you. There is a kindness and gentleness about you I envy. No matter what anyone says or does, never let their stupidities make you feel less about yourself."

"Not even Miranda?"

"Not even me. I have a lot to do here. Why don't you go find Ellyssa and practice with her and the other students?"

"Okay, Father."

Raijaun pulled his hood over his head as he stepped out of the tower, hiding his face within its deep pocket. His looks made people uncomfortable, which made him uncomfortable. Ellyssa should be at the eastern training field with most of the arcane students. Only the novices continued to study and practice in the classrooms. Everyone else was on the mock battlefield raining down destruction and erecting shields day in and day out.

Today was full action day. The students formed battle lines and fought hordes of illusory ravagers until they broke. Tomorrow would be a rest day to allow the mages to recuperate. It was not a day off, however. They came to the training ground and studied different scenarios, practiced movement formations, and listened to lectures on how best to use the least amount of magic to effect the greatest return for defensive and offensive actions. Older students helped the younger ones improve their weaves so they did not waste power on inefficient castings.

It was just after lunch, and a stream of students was filing through the eastern sally gate on their way back to the training ground. Raijaun hung back as the mages began piling up at the gate. Only when the last one passed through did he fall in behind them and follow the mass onto the field.

Ellyssa, Roger, Joshua, Rusty, and three other full wizards waited patiently as their students formed into six platoons of fifty. Compared to the precision of the martial students, their ranks left much to be desired, but they were learning. Ellyssa spotted Raijaun trailing behind the rest and called him over.

"Raijaun, how are you doing?"

"I am okay. Father wanted me to practice with the others today."

"Okay. You are probably the strongest caster here, so I will put you in the center. Do you know what we are doing here?"

"I do. I have watched you from the walls."

"Good. The platoon leaders and I will be conjuring illusions of ravagers. There are going to be a lot of them, but just remember, they are only illusions. You aren't meant to win, only to fight until they break through. Then we talk about how to do better next time."

"Okay."

"Fall in to third platoon's first rank. Remember, these are just illusions," Ellyssa reminded him, concerned about how he had reacted in Bruneford's Mill.

Raijaun nodded and shuffled over to the third platoon. The closest students to him shied away, making him an island in a sea of people.

"Who told you to break ranks?" Ellyssa shouted. "Roger, control your platoon!"

Roger flicked a glance at Ellyssa. "Form back up, people. Raijaun is no different than any other student here."

The ranks closed back up marginally but still with a noticeable gap. Unkind whispers and a few scoffed mutterings passed between ranks until Roger ordered them to silence.

"Swords to the fore," Ellyssa shouted, her voice magically amplified for all to hear. "Shields form to the rear."

The strongest students marched forward to provide the offensive magic used to slay the invaders while the less adept mages stayed several yards back to create wards against any enemy who made it through the hail of destruction. The training field already displayed the abuse the mages had wrought upon it. Acres of churned-up and scorched ground lay fallow and would take years to recover before anything would likely grow upon it.

Ellyssa and her fellow instructors spread out to the far corners and began conjuring their enemy. It took them almost a week of practice to create illusory ravagers who moved with the speed and power of what Ellyssa had seen in Bruneford's Mill. Few would mistake them for anything except an illusion, however. They had to sacrifice visual quality to create the numbers they needed to challenge so many students. As the mages got better, they would need more wizards to create enough illusions to continue challenging the students.

A thousand ravagers materialized a quarter-mile away from the leading ranks of mages and ate up the ground between them. The students designated as shields were the first to act, erecting wards and barriers of raised earth and stone to slow the charging ravagers and to stop any who might get through the sword's spells long enough to strike them down.

Raijaun watched as the first spells began to fly and decimate the onrushing ravagers. Most students hurled fireballs, lightning, and bright balls or rays of arcane magic, which Raijaun emulated as well. As the number of ravagers increased, Raijaun saw their spells were becoming less effective. The horde spread out and even the large blasts of fire struck only a few at a time. More and more were getting through the onslaught to crash against the wards created by the shields.

Raijaun shifted his focus to the ground and raised a wall of earth ten feet high and a hundred yards long. Several students cried out as it blocked their view of the battlefield. Raijaun ignored them and sent power into the wall, breaking it apart into thousands of earthen spears hovering for a moment in the air before launching as swiftly as arrows into the tide of enemies. Although the spell was devastating to the illusions, he realized that this spell would be far less effective against creatures with real mass.

Diaphanous bubbles floated from the ground and into the air by the dozen. When the sun struck the orbs, intense beams of concentrated sunlight lanced down into the ranks of ravagers. Raijaun saw his spell was insufficient to deal with the overwhelming threat, but instead of conjuring more bubbles, he shaped them into prisms. The prisms split the beams of light into multiple rays, rotating and dancing across the battlefield, destroying scores of enemy.

"That is a very interesting spell," Rusty said to Ellyssa.

"It certainly is. We will have to see if we can adapt it for the wizards to use. What is more impressive is his aura. Look, he is not coming close to using his full potential."

Rusty shifted his sight and saw Ellyssa was correct. Although the power Raijaun channeled was remarkable, especially considering he looked the equivalent of a six-year-old, both wizards could tell he was not straining himself.

"Let's see if we can push him a bit."

Ellyssa signaled the other instructors and increased the tide of invaders. More ravagers slammed against the shields' wards as the swords fought desperately to slay them. Raijaun sensed their impending defeat and sent his arcane senses out into the ether. A massive well of power lay just beyond his "fingertips," but he could not make himself grab hold of it. The energy loomed like a giant, a giant that would break his bones and crush them all flat if he dared disturb it. He withdrew his grasping tendrils of magic, quaking inside from fear of the pain he knew would come and the uncontrolled destruction it could cause.

It did not take long before wards began to fail and ravagers descended on the humans. Just before the creatures would have cut into the wizards, they vanished. Raijaun stared at the ground, ashamed of himself for knowing he could have destroyed the ravagers but chose not to out of fear.

"Fall in!" Ellyssa shouted over the tumult of voices. "You are all dead. Why?"

"Raijaun let the center fail!" a young man shouted from third platoon's rear rank.

"You all failed! Why do you cast blame on him? His spells were far more effective than yours."

"He wasn't trying. I saw."

"You are telling me you had the luxury to focus on what Raijaun was doing? It sounds to me like you were the one slacking."

The young wizard looked at the ground. "I'm just saying we could have done better if our supposedly secret weapon would have tried harder."

"It sounds to me like you are trying to shift blame on someone else for your failures."

The vocal wizard leaned to his left and whispered, "It looks to me like we have a demon too scared to fight and a leader who is a crazy bit—"

He did not whisper quietly enough. A force grabbed him in an invisible grip, lifted him over the heads of his fellows, and crushed him to the ground at Ellyssa's feet. He stared up helplessly into Ellyssa's furious face.

"Do I look crazy to you?" she demanded.

Unable to draw breath, he swallowed hard and nodded anxiously.

"You're right. I suggest you watch your tongue and tread lightly. Crazy people can be very unpredictable."

"Ellyssa, enough!" Rusty shouted. "What do you think you are doing?"

Ellyssa released the frightened mage and shifted her angry gaze to Rusty. "I am instilling discipline. Had he been a martial student, the arms master would have beaten him bloody with a training sword."

"These are not martial students!"

"No, they are not, and it is my job to correct that deficiency." Ellyssa stepped toward Rusty and raised an invisible sphere around them to prevent anyone else from hearing her words. "Azerick put me in charge with a full understanding of what we all need to do to ensure this lot is ready to fight. If you ever chastise me in front of our war mages again, I will put you down just like I did Ben. Do you understand me?"

Rusty's face grew dark and his voice trembled with anger. "Do you think you can?—"

"I know I can, and you had best know I will. Maybe you do not fully believe what Azerick says, or maybe you simply cannot understand it. But I saw what the ravagers did in Bruneford's Mill, and I will do everything in my power to make sure it does not happen here." Ellyssa softened her tone. "I know I do not have a fraction of your experience, and it must be hard for you and the others to accept my position. I reacted the same way when Azerick told me he planned on putting me in charge. But what you just saw is exactly why he did it. I am willing to be feared, hated even, if it means some of these people will survive this war."

Rusty took several deep breaths before answering. "We will be lucky if they survive this training!" he hissed, then stalked away.

Ellyssa looked to where two of Brother Thomas's Chosen were treating several wizards who had been injured or overreached themselves. Angela nodded that they were fine, so Ellyssa pulled Raijaun aside as the others dispersed.

"Ben was right. You were holding back."

Raijaun studied the ground at his feet. "I'm sorry. I will try harder next time."

"Is everything all right?"

Raijaun nodded. "I'm fine."

Ellyssa knew his answer to be false but let him go. He had been through a lot and probably just needed time to adjust. She walked back to the school once the training grounds were cleared. A voice called to her just as she passed through the small postern gate.

"Hi, Ellyssa," Daebian hailed her, then fell into step next to her.

"Daebian. I heard you had an accident."

"Nope."

"You didn't fall down the stairs?"

"It wasn't an accident."

Ellyssa stopped and faced the boy. "I don't believe Raijaun pushed you. He is too nice a person to have done it no matter what you said or did to him."

"Don't be so sure of that."

"Are you saying he isn't kind?"

"No, about his being a person. He is too nice, but that is the least important part of that incident. I saw him out there today. He looked pretty pathetic."

"He did very well," Ellyssa defended Raijaun. "His spells were more effective than anyone else's."

"I guess, but the way Father treats him you would think he could have scoured the field clean all by himself."

"He isn't used to being around people, is all. He will come around. You used to be kind as well. What has changed you?"

"Who says I changed? Anyway, I'm glad you're back. You were the only person I ever found interesting around here. See you later."

Daebian deviated toward the new tower while Ellyssa sought her room in the old. He poked his head in the door and made sure no one was around before jogging up the stairs to his room. He found Raijaun sitting morosely in a chair in his section of the tower landing.

"Hey, short, dark, and ugly."

Raijaun looked up, his displeasure evident in his expression. "How is your arm?"

Daebian raised his arm, waggled his fingers, and flipped his brother a rude gesture. "Right as rain. Brother Thomas does good work. Are you mad?"

"You made me look like a monster!"

"No, your thrice-damned parentage made you look like a monster. I made you look like a jerk."

Raijaun looked away. "Yes, I am mad. Wouldn't you be?"

Daebian pursed his lips in thought. "I don't think so. I don't really know. I've never been mad before."

"You have never been angry?"

"Nope.

"You are a sociopath."

Daebian considered his brother's accusation. "Do you think so? Wouldn't that be interesting? Can you imagine, being free of social angst no matter what you did? It sounds liberating."

"It sounds insane."

"This world needs some insanity to combat the rampant stupidity, like cats to take care of a rat infestation."

"What happens when there are no more rats and a city full of cats?"

"The cats destroy each other until the strongest ones reach some sort of balance of power. That is the beauty of my system, it's self-correcting."

Raijaun shook his head, unable to grasp his brother's insane ideas. "Why do you hate me?"

Daebian looked startled at the question. "Hate you? I don't hate you."

"Then why do you act like this? Why would you do what you did if you do not hate me?"

"Because I don't like to share. It had nothing to do with you other than the fact Mother is mine. Until you came, she was all I had. She was the only one who didn't look at me like I was a freak."

"I still think you are an ass."

"Whoa, potty mouth. That kind of language is unbecoming from someone your age. What are you, six months old? Anyway, it had nothing to do with you, not directly. I suppose I desired some attention from Father, but not at the expense of sharing Mother. My little trip down the stairs satisfied both. It was a total win-win."

"You got negative attention from Father. Why not do something good and get positive attention?"

"You are too young to understand. It's like in business; you want to reap the greatest reward with the smallest investment possible. I don't really care how I get what I want just as long as I get it."

"I still do not see how anyone can act like you do without hating the person they are doing it to."

"You're going to make me say it, aren't you? You are my brother, even if you are as ugly as a troll's ass. No matter what I do or how horrible I behave, you are my brother. Don't try to understand it; it will just give you a headache."

Raijaun thought about his brother's words after he left and realized he was right. He would never understand and trying was going to bring nothing but confusion and frustration. Father said to steer clear of him, and he would as best he could, but Daebian said they were brothers and he was fairly certain he meant it. Raijaun also felt their bond, or at least he thought he did. Whether it was the true bond of siblings or just his desperate desire to belong, he could not be sure.

Every night, Klaraxis invaded Daebian's dreams with vivid images. Some showed him the glories of victory, others the pain and humiliation of defeat. Oftentimes, Azerick or Raijaun would save him and remind him how weak he was.

This night, Daebian sat astride a powerful warhorse surrounded by corpses. Some were allies and many were foes, but that fact was unimportant. The only thing that mattered was he was the one still standing at the end of the battle.

You like what you see. This can only happen if you let me help you. You have your blade. Why do you not take your father's blood so I may bring you power?

Daebian looked down and saw the dagger Ken had made him, riding on his hip, the black soul stone prominently affixed to the hilt. "I do not trust you, demon. I do what I want when I wish to do it. Your continual badgering is not going to make me act any sooner. In fact, it will only serve to make me trust you less."

As you wish, young master. I only desire to see you where you belong.

Klaraxis was indeed getting impatient, but Daebian was as intractable as his father, and he knew he could not push the boy. He needed subtlety to influence the boy and create an optimal situation to turn him against his father. Klaraxis reminded himself to remain patient. There would be opportunities to widen the rift between father and son, but if he moved too quickly, he could ruin his own plans.

CHAPTER 14

Azerick toiled away in his laboratory, prying every bit of knowledge he could out of the Codex Arcana. The Scions pounded mercilessly against the barrier and he had to maintain a constant vigilance to shore up the weaknesses they created.

His people were putting everything they had into their training. He was certain that within a year he could pit both martial and magical students against nearly any equal force in the kingdom with a strong likelihood of victory. But that was not enough. His people, all of the people, would soon face an enemy capable of crushing them at their current level of military preparedness.

Someone cleared their throat near the doorway to the lab. Azerick turned and saw it was one of the former Academy wizards. Morgan was young, barely accepted into the ranks of full wizard, but he was very intelligent and creative.

"Yes, Morgan?"

"Lord Giles, I received a letter from a friend still at the Academy. She told me they have increased their applied magic lessons and combative training but only marginally. It is still short of what the Hall of Inquisition trains for to protect the border," Morgan reported nervously. "The Martial Academy has implemented much of your training doctrine, however. They are focusing far more on large group tactics and defending against swift and powerful assaults from a much larger force."

Azerick frowned but nodded as Morgan reported the martial students' training. He had expected much of this. The Martial Academy people were soldiers and recognized the value of what Azerick showed them. They would take advantage of a superior training doctrine regardless of whether or not they believed Azerick's story. The Magus Academy, on the other hand, was a bunch of bureaucrats set in their ways who looked at any change as a challenge to their authority and general sense of superiority.

"Thank you, Morgan. Please have Ellyssa call her people together. I will be out momentarily to address them after I pen a quick letter to the Academy."

Headmaster Florent led the procession of councilmembers and two score of wizards down the vast halls of the Academy in preparation for their meeting with Lord Giles. The headmaster had received the request, actually little more than a notice of his impending arrival, just two days ago.

"I still do not understand why you agreed to meet with him," Magus Louis Douglas stated bitterly once again.

"He informed us of his inevitable arrival, and I do not like the thought of having to replace any doors by refusing him an audience with the council."

"You do not think he will attempt a repeat performance, do you? The Hall was unprepared. He would never get away with that here. Not now," Louis scoffed.

"Quite frankly, I do not know what he will do, but I would rather not create any more tension than necessary. My reports from his school indicate they are becoming exceptionally militant, and I would prefer to avoid any sort of conflict. I imagine he is here to complain about our not dancing to his tune. It will do no harm to listen to him before showing him the door."

Louis snorted. "The man is a renegade. Who knows how he will react to our not bending the knee. As you said, we cannot know what he will do."

"If he acts foolishly, we will be ready for him," the headmaster said confidently. She stopped and looked around quizzically. "Louis, did you feel that?"

"Feel what?"

Maureen shook her head. "Nothing. All this talk must be making me agitated."

The procession turned down another hallway and made its way to the council chambers. The group paused a moment as they stepped into the chamber and saw Azerick already waiting for them. The headmaster led her fellow councilmembers to their elevated seats while the other wizards formed a half-circle around the dangerous sorcerer, keeping as much distance from him as possible.

"Lord Giles, it is customary for those seeking an audience to wait in the antechamber until summoned," Headmaster Florent informed him.

"My apologies, but I detest waiting on others and must profess a certain amount of claustrophobia."

"I liked you as a boy, Lord Giles. It is a shame your rise to power appears to have equally elevated your arrogance, if not exceeded it."

Azerick grinned. "If arrogance were oil, we could light this entire academy as bright as the sun for all eternity." Azerick spotted a familiar face amongst the surrounding wizards. "I see you have recovered, Magus Harvey. I was concerned after you took that nasty fall."

"It was no fall, you monster!" Harvey shouted, his voice quavering with indignation and more than a little fear.

"And my sentiment was more out of politeness than any real concern." Azerick turned back to face the council. "My only concern here is the fact you have all chosen to ignore my repeated warnings and are not properly preparing to deal with the looming threat to us all. I had hoped the king's acceptance of my proposal would have spurred you into action."

"The king does not dictate to the Academy. I assure you, Lord Giles, this academy is prepared to handle any threat against it and, right now, the only threat we see is you," the headmaster said.

"I am not the threat to your academy, Headmaster. The real threat is to us all, and you chose to ignore my warning. You think you are prepared? I could bring two score of my students in here and destroy the core of this academy. They would not even need my help because they are prepared, and they continue to push themselves to their limits every day."

"That is where you are wrong," Headmaster Florent retorted. "Our wizards have reinforced every ward in the Academy. No one can sneak onto the grounds without our knowing. Anyone attempting such a thing would then face the might of the most powerful establishment in Valeria."

"Really?" Azerick smiled devilishly.

The illusion vanished and the entire enclave of wizards found themselves surrounded by Azerick's people. The councilmembers, seated upon nothing more than a raised section of earth within the Martial Academy parade grounds, looked around in fright to find daggers and swords pricking against their backs. Sandy hovered over Headmaster Florent, breathing hotly upon her neck and showing off her sharp teeth.

Wolf aimed an arrow straight at Magus Douglas's chest with Ghost standing at his hip ready to pounce. Fifty of Azerick's students surrounded the Academy Wizards, already prepared to unleash their summoned arcane energy.

"I can feel several of you reaching for the Source. I recommend you not force us to defend ourselves. You have been caught with your proverbial robes down," Azerick said coldly. "Half a company of students could have just gutted the core of your academy if they had the mind to. Who would be left? Your students and a few lower-class mages? Prepared? Hardly. You are not prepared to fight a cold."

"How did you...?" Headmaster Florent began. "You breached our wards and placed illusions and disorienting spells within the halls to direct us out here. Very clever, Lord Giles, but neither I nor the Academy will bend to your bullying! Strike us down now if you wish. Prove to the world you are nothing more than a petty tyrant who wishes everyone to dance on his strings. We will not! I have had my most learned wizards working with the heads of the Scholars' Academy, and not one of them has uncovered more than an old wives' tale about these Scions you keep spouting off about. If you wish to send your students off to hunt for bogeymen, so be it. You have shown us we cannot stop you without more bloodshed than we are willing to spill, but we will not play a part in your grand delusions!"

Azerick shook his head slowly. "Delusions?"

Azerick held out his hands palms down, and the ground near his feet began churning as an object broke through the earth. Azerick laid his hands upon the crystal resting on a plinth of stone before him. The sky and parade grounds vanished, and the assembled wizards found themselves gathered near a shimmering screen stretching to all horizons of a grey and barren world. Several astonished gasps and mutterings broke the eerie silence as they looked upon the flying ships and floating crystal castle hovering above an army of creatures whose numbers were impossible to gauge.

"Azerick, what is this place?" Headmaster Florent asked, desperately trying to keep the fear from her voice.

"It is my delusion."

The image of five emaciated, faceless figures appeared on the other side of the screen, towering over the group of mages. Despite their lack of facial features, their scorn and disdain for the intruders was felt by all. A wave of loathing and animosity washed over the wizards with such intensity it crushed them to the ground, making them beg for mercy as invisible needles stabbed deep into their brains.

"What is this, false Guardian? Have you brought us a sacrifice in hopes of appeasing us? Very well, for your tribute we shall grant you a mercifully swift death. Your time draws near. The barrier weakens with every passing moment, and when we are free, the pain of your demise shall be felt throughout the universe."

Azerick broke the connection and the wizards found themselves on the parade grounds once more. Many wept openly, while others lay on the ground vomiting. It took several minutes for the most stalwart men and women to compose themselves enough to speak.

Headmaster Florent and three other councilmembers stood, still visibly shaking. "Lord Giles, you have shown us we are indeed ill-prepared, but we shall not be caught so again, especially by you and your ilk. I do not know what foul demonic magic you used, but we will not yield no matter your tricks, threats, or actions."

Azerick sighed in resignation. "Very well, Headmaster. Let the blood be on your hands and upon your soul. I have done what I can."

"You speak so readily of spilling blood. You will attack us?"

Azerick shook his head ever so slightly. "No, Headmaster, I will not have to."

He drew in the Source and created a portal to take him and his people almost the entire way to the docks where Azerick's swiftest ship awaited. Azerick and his people stepped through the shimmering soap bubble-like screen and vanished. The gate snapped shut as the last of the orphans' academy stepped through.

The Academy mages worked to compose themselves. Several were still too shaken to speak. Those who could spoke nervously of their experience and argued about what it all meant.

"I must say, that was probably one of the most unpleasant experiences of my life," Magus Douglas said.

Maureen nodded. "Very much so."

"What are we to do now?" Magus Sorenson asked.

"We shall redouble our wards and extend them to the near outer grounds," the headmaster said. "Let us re-evaluate our training curriculum, particularly amongst the staff. We are obviously vulnerable and must better prepare to defend ourselves and our students."

"The doctrine Lord Giles sent with Magus Harvey, although extreme, is impressive," another councilman said.

"It is too extreme. I will not put our students under so much pressure. His training is wrought with danger. I will not have the prestige of the Academy lowered to the barbarity of the Black Tower," the headmaster replied.

"What about what he showed us?" Louis asked.

"What of it?" Headmaster Florent snapped. "He is obviously adept at weaving illusions."

"What we experienced was not a simple illusion, or even a complex one. We all felt the overwhelming evil, and I am certain I am not the only one unable to recognize the type of magic being employed."

"He is a foul spawn of the abyss! Who knows what kind of magic he is able to weave? We shall increase our security and step up the training for our staff, but I will not begin a militant indoctrination of our students based on the threats of an obvious megalomaniac whose demonic inhabitant has made him mentally unstable. No, the only threat to the kingdom is Lord Giles and those who believe his ridiculous story. The man is going to bring a great deal of suffering, and it will be up to us to clean up his mess," she declared firmly.

Once Azerick was certain his people were safely underway, he gated several times until he stood in the forest northeast of Southport. Sandy waited in the clearing with a look of annoyed impatience.

"You using me as a mode of transportation is becoming a habit."

"I do apologize and greatly appreciate your assistance. I will be sure to tell Peck to rub you down and give you an extra helping of oats."

"Do you want to walk back to North Haven?"

Azerick patted her affectionately on her side. "I apologize. I'm just trying to relieve some of the tension those idiots at the Academy put in me."

"They would not listen?"

"Of course not."

Sandy tensed her muscles and prepared to launch into the air. "I will take that rubdown when we get back."

Azerick returned home physically and mentally exhausted. His theatrical assault upon the Academy had taken a toll on him and he needed to rest. It was a rare occasion he expended so much energy that he felt the need to rest, but when he walked into his bedroom, he knew right away he was not going to get it. The look upon Miranda's face clearly hinted he would not enjoy this conversation.

"How did it go at the Academy?" she asked.

"Not as well as I had hoped and about as poorly as I expected."

"No one was hurt?"

"No, there was no violence."

Miranda took a deep breath to steady herself. "You promised to spend more time with Daebian."

"I did and I am sorry, but there has been too much to do. This confrontation with the Academy was too important to put off."

"There is always something to do!" Miranda exclaimed in frustration. "What good is winning this war if you abandon your family in the process?"

"I am not abandoning my family. I am trying to ensure there is a world left for our family, ours and everyone else's! This is about more than any individual, but you, like everyone else, refuse to understand that."

"I understand you spend a lot of time with Raijaun! Why can't you spend some of that time with Daebian?"

"When was the last time you spoke to Raijaun? Did you ever go into the city like you said?"

"He pushed my son down the stairs and broke his arm! He could have been killed, so I am sorry if I needed some time to get past that little fact."

"Is it a fact?" Azerick asked. "Would you be so quick to condemn Raijaun if he looked different?"

"What are you saying, that Daebian threw himself down the steps himself? What kind of person would do that?"

"What kind indeed."

Miranda took a deep breath and fought to regain a sensible tone. "Maybe it was an accident. Maybe Daebian mistook Raijaun's attempt to catch him as a push. I am doing the best I can, given the fact I am in a marital and parental situation unlike any in the entire world. Why do you spend all of your time with Raijaun and none with Daebian? Maybe it is you who has a problem with their looks."

"I need Raijaun to help me with many of my projects," Azerick defended himself.

"Why not let Daebian help you as well?"

"Because Daebian is useless!" Azerick shouted in a sudden and unexpected burst of anger.

Miranda's hand flew to her mouth as she gasped and took a step away. Tears flooded her eyes as she looked at Azerick and shook her head.

"How can you say that about your son? Daebian is the most brilliant boy I have ever seen. He is not useless!"

Azerick stood mouth agape at the shock of what he just heard himself say. "Miranda, I did not mean it like that…"

Daebian heard all he needed to hear. He knew his father detested him and looked down on him for his inability to use magic, but hearing him admit it struck him a harder blow than he had anticipated. He could never learn to use magic, but there were other sources of power out there, and he knew where to find one of them.

"Daebian is extraordinarily bright and a master of just about anything he puts his mind to," Azerick continued. "I am proud of his abilities beyond words, but the things I do he simply cannot help with. It does not mean I think any less of him than Raijaun, just that his skills are not what I need to accomplish my tasks."

"I am just asking for a little time, Azerick. Show him you care about the things he can do and enjoys."

Azerick nodded and embraced his wife. "All right, I will make time. I will go and watch him practice tomorrow and take the time to do so a few times a week. It has been a while since I practiced my staff work; maybe we can do a little sparring."

Miranda returned Azerick's embrace and wiped her tears on his robe. "That is all I ask. Thank you."

Klaraxis chortled as he took pleasure in his accomplishment. It had been so easy to tweak the human's pathetic emotions and twist his words. He had felt the boy's presence outside the room and leapt at the opportunity to take advantage. It had been perfect. The rift between father and son was now great, and Klaraxis would ensure nothing could ever bridge the span. Daebian was in his grasp, and he would never let him go.

Unlike most nights, Daebian was eager to speak with Klaraxis in his dreams. Daebian laid his head down onto his pillow and willed himself to sleep. He tossed and turned until he finally surrendered and let his body take control of the endeavor. Once he allowed his body to relax, Daebian slept and found himself alone upon a barren sea of stone and sand. He first thought he was somewhere in the deserts of Sumara, but the sand and rock were the wrong color. They were more red than orange. That was when he realized this must be Klaraxis's abyssal realm.

You recognize your home.

"It is your home, not mine, demon."

You are mine, and as mine, this is yours. You are the son of the lord of this realm. It is your inheritance.

"One day, perhaps, but not anytime soon. I have decided."

I know.

"How do I get my Father's blood?"

Carefully. If he thinks for a moment you are purposefully taking his blood, it could upset everything. He could question me, and I would be powerless to withhold my knowledge for long. You are clever. You will know your moment when it presents itself.

"What happens when I get his blood?"

The stone will do everything. I will urge a tiny portion of my essence into the blood. The stone will absorb it and me into itself. We will then be able to link through the stone.

"And I will have your power?"

Klaraxis laughed. *Not by even the smallest of fractions. You will possess a sliver of my being and therefore a sliver of my power. However, that sliver is a seedling and, with the right care, can grow into a plant that will bear fruit. I will be able to then transfer a portion of my power through you in a variety of ways. I can make you faster, stronger, and give you other abilities beyond that of these pathetic mortals.*

"You said I could be like a god."

One day perhaps. A sapling must grow before it can be a mighty tree, towering above the pathetic creatures scurrying about in the dirt.

Daebian liked the sound of that. One day, he would be a towering figure, looking down on the world. The lesser creatures would kneel before him, seeking refuge beneath his powerful boughs and paying homage to his greatness. He would give life in his beneficence or take it away as his desires demanded.

Daebian awoke the next morning, strapped on his dagger, and sought out the dining room, feeling much better than he had last night. His timing was perfect as always, arriving just as the cooks served the morning meal, because he detested waiting on anyone for anything.

"Good morning, darling," Miranda welcomed him as he practically skipped into the room. "Will you be sparring today?"

"Good morning, Mother. Probably. I have been training for a few days without a problem, and it's not as though I had broken my sword arm."

"I have a surprise for you. Your father is going to come watch you. I have been telling him how good you are, and he is eager to see you."

Just as Klaraxis had said, an opportunity arose and Daebian's swift mind instantly formulated a plan. "Wonderful, I am eager to see him there as well. I had best choose a challenging opponent."

The martial students started their day early and Daebian had to hurry to avoid being late. Today was a sparring and tactics day, which meant they spent only the first hour of the morning enduring brutal calisthenics and strength-building exercises. Daebian sought out Alex while everyone was suiting up for sparring practice.

"Weapons Master, my father is coming to observe my training. I would like to wait until he arrives to start my bout."

"All right. Have you chosen an opponent?"

"Yes, sir. Brent."

Alex considered Daebian's choice. "Brent is in a higher level than you and quite a bit bigger. Are you sure you want him as your opponent?"

Daebian nodded enthusiastically. "Yes, sir! I have been practicing a lot, and you know no one my size is much of a challenge. Even if I lose, I think I can make a very good showing of it. I want to put on the best display I can for Father."

"All right. I know Azerick is busy, so queue up and we'll start your match as soon as he arrives."

The matches had been going on for forty-five minutes, and Daebian had begun to think his father was not coming when Azerick finally took a seat next to Miranda on the wooden bleachers set up for the other students and the occasional spectator.

"I was beginning to think you had forgotten," Miranda said as he sat down.

"Of course not. I just got tied up and could not break away without wasting an entire night's work. Has he fought yet?"

"No, he has been waiting for you to come. He should be next when this match is over."

The match soon ended when one of the young men trapped the other's sword arm and bashed his head a few times with the hilt of his training sword after a poorly executed lunge. The blows rang like a gong against the steel helm, but the heavily padded armor protected him from getting more than a headache and a bit of dizziness.

"Oh, the other boy is so big," Miranda said when Brent and Daebian took the field.

Azerick understood Miranda's concern. Daebian was the size of an average twelve-year-old, while Brent was seventeen and nearly a grown man, and not a small man at that. Their increased training was already adding muscle to all the martial students, and Azerick ensured they were well fed.

Alex shouted for the match to begin and Daebian went on the defensive as Brent launched into an aggressive assault. Although Daebian continually retreated before the much bigger boy, Azerick was impressed with his son's swordwork. Daebian fought with a master's conservation of energy, never expending any more than necessary to block or dodge a stroke.

Daebian continued to let Brent push him around the yard until the older boy had had enough and used his greater size to bull Daebian over. Brent lunged with a powerful thrust and Daebian flicked his sword just enough to make it slip harmlessly past. But instead of drawing back for another strike, Brent pushed forward, grabbed the collar of Daebian's armor, and jerked him forward. Daebian's feet beat a rapid pace and his arms windmilled to try to maintain his balance, but Brent twisted and landed a hard strike against Daebian's back and sent him crashing to the ground.

Alex ordered a stop to the fight to allow Daebian to recover. Most matches were set for either three or five decisive blows or falls. Daebian climbed back to his feet, dusted himself off, and nodded that he was ready.

"This is hardly a fair fight," Miranda said. "He is so much bigger than Daebian."

"War is rarely fair, and never civilized despite what some of the ballads would have us believe," Azerick responded. "I am sure Alex would not have placed them together if Daebian had a problem with it. I am proud of him for being willing to challenge himself even if it means losing. Better to lose and learn here than lose on a battlefield."

"We are not on a battlefield!"

"Life is a battlefield, now more than ever."

Brent pushed Daebian around the yard for several minutes, but his fatigue was starting to show. Both young men landed a few soft hits, but none were strong enough to score points. Brent was beginning to tire and his frustration at not being able to defeat someone so much smaller was beginning to show. He intentionally left himself open and, when Daebian thrust at his midriff, he grabbed the dulled training sword by the blade, held it tight, and struck a clanging blow against his helm.

"Break!" Alex shouted, then helped Daebian back to his feet. "Are you okay?"

"I am. Just let me catch my bearings."

Alex turned to Brent. "Try a move like that in real combat and you will likely lose some fingers at the very least."

"Yes, sir."

"All right. Daebian, can you continue?"

"I am ready, sir."

Daebian and Brent squared off once more. Brent knew his fatigue was greater than Daebian's and sought to end the fight quickly. Brent's attack was strong but not the wild, hectic swings of a man concerned with losing. He was one of the top students in his ranking and fought with the mental discipline Alex, Jansen, and the other instructors instilled in all the students.

Daebian was now showing signs of tiring, and his last block took his sword low and left him open. Brent lunged to deliver a powerful thrust that would end the match. Daebian smiled when he saw Brent fall for his feint, turned the incoming sword aside with his gauntlet, and thrust his blade up under his opponent's helm.

Brent dropped his sword and clutched his throat as it swelled closed and choked off his air. That should have been the end of the bout, but Daebian launched a fury of blows, his blade ringing off Brent's armor in a rapid staccato of abuse. Alex shouted for Daebian to break but he kept attacking, unable to hear over the noise of his attack or too lost in battlelust to obey the command.

Daebian drove Brent to his knees then onto his back. Still Daebian hammered away, pounding his sword mercilessly at Brent's upraised arm. Azerick, being closer to the pair, launched himself from his seat and grabbed his son by the wrist as he reached back to strike again.

"Daebian, stop! What are you doing?" Azerick shouted as he practically lifted Daebian from the ground by his arm.

Wild-eyed, Daebian came across in a blindingly fast slash with his other hand, the blade parting the sleeve of Azerick's robe and deeply cutting the flesh beneath. Azerick flung Daebian several feet with a curse. Daebian rolled in the dirt and looked at his knife, his father's bleeding arm, and at Brent lying in the dirt with one of the Chosen tending to his injury.

"Father...I don't know..." Daebian stammered. "I'm sorry!"

Daebian got to his feet and ran for all he was worth, carefully holding his dagger so the blood ran down the blade and into the channel down its center. Unlike most blades with a blood groove, his ran the length of the shank so the blood could reach the soul stone affixed to the hilt. When the blood reached the black gem, it drank it up like a sponge, leaving no trace of it behind.

Miranda cried out after her son, "Daebian!"

Azerick laid a restraining hand on her shoulder. "Let him go."

"But he's upset and just a boy!"

"He is not just a boy, Miranda, and you need to come to terms with that just as he needs to come to terms with himself. I know how hard this is for you. I want to treat Raijaun like the child he appears to be, but I know his mind and abilities go far beyond his physical appearance as do Daebian's."

"But what if he gets himself into trouble?"

"He is smart and strong. I am sure he can handle any trouble he might find. I was about his age when I had to make it in this world on my own, and I did not have half the skills he does."

"He's only six!"

"And almost a man despite that. You must look beyond his exterior, Miranda, and see what is inside of him. Even if what you find is unpleasant."

Miranda took a step away. "What do you mean? Daebian is a wonderful, sweet child."

"Is he? Are you so certain of that?"

"Of course I am! I am his mother! What makes you say such a thing?"

Azerick raised his arm to display his cleanly slit sleeve. His flesh had already knitted back together so the bleeding had stopped, but traces of it still stained the ruined garment.

"He was upset and not himself."

"What about the stairs?"

"You know what I think about the stairs."

"Nothing else has ever sounded any warning bells in your head? You are as smart and intuitive a woman as I have ever known, Miranda. Are you saying you were never troubled by events surrounding him?"

Miranda thought back to the young man who had fallen from the school wall. He, and many students, had walked that wall on their guard duties without ever having an incident. The fact it was the same boy who had beaten and insulted Daebian earlier in the day had left her uneasy. Grick had also found a few dead rats in the sublevel that looked to have been tortured. Miranda had dismissed it as an animal.

"What are you saying?"

"I am saying there may be a darkness within him that he does a very good job of hiding."

Miranda knew Azerick's accusation was not groundless, and the truth made her angry. Daebian was her son, and logic fled in the face of her mother's love and protectiveness.

"If there is darkness within him then you put it there!" she said in an angry, hushed voice. "You put it there and you had better fix it! You spend all day and night figuring out how to save the world. You had better spend some of that time figuring out how to save our son!" she hissed, jabbing him in the chest with her finger.

Azerick had never felt so helpless as he watched Miranda storm away, her body shaking from the effort of holding back a flood of tears. What she was asking was impossible. Whoever, or whatever, Daebian was, it was part of his character, and only by experiencing the events life placed him in could change that.

CHAPTER 15

Daebian ran out of the gates and down the road toward North Haven. It was not until he had covered half the distance that he realized he was not yet winded. He looked at the dagger still gripped in his hand, its blade completely devoid of the blood once staining it.

What you are experiencing is a taste of what I can give you.

"You can talk to me now, outside of my dreams?"

As long as you possess the soul stone, yes. You are now realizing your increased strength. It is just the beginning. As I grow stronger within the gem, I can share more of my strength with you.

"How do I make you stronger?"

The same way you make anything grow. You feed it.

"Feed it what?" Daebian asked although he already knew the answer.

The life of another, Klaraxis confirmed.

Daebian did not want to think about that right now. What he needed now was to keep his father from thinking too much about his actions. The best way to do that was to give him something else to worry about. Running away would definitely worry his mother, and she should do a good job of keeping Azerick distracted. He also needed time to think about this new relationship he had with the demon. Daebian was no one's fool, and he would not let Klaraxis play him for one.

Azerick looked up from the Codex Arcana when Raijaun entered the room. "How was your training today?"

"It was fine."

"Ellyssa says you are not exerting yourself."

"I do as well as any of the others."

Azerick crossed the room and knelt next to Raijaun. "Raijaun, it is not enough for you to do as well. You must be better and stronger than the others. The things I need you to do cannot be done by anyone except you."

Raijaun shuffled his feet and twitched his wings beneath his heavy cloak. "I am trying, Father. I just…it scares me. I am afraid I will lose control like I did in that town. I do not want to hurt anyone again—or myself."

"Was the pain that bad?"

Raijaun shuddered. "It was horrible. It felt as if it were tearing me apart."

Azerick laid a comforting hand on his son's shoulder. "I know it must be hard for you, being different, but you cannot let your fear or the other students hinder your ability. I think as long as you do not combine abyssal magic with your Guardian magic you will be fine. The rest is up to you. I need you to be strong, Raijaun. There will come a time when you will have to use all of your power, and you cannot let fear, pain, or even the thought of hurting someone else stop you."

"I will try, Father."

"Have you seen your brother?"

"No. I heard he went crazy or something and stabbed you."

Azerick chortled at the typical exaggeration. "No, but he did cut me when I pulled him off another student. He is probably in town tormenting someone by now, having completely gotten over his episode on the sparring field. Come, I want to show you how to travel to the Scions' prison and repair the wall on your own in case I am ever not here. Keep in mind, I do not want you going there alone unless I tell you to, or it is absolutely crucial. The Scions will torment you endlessly, and it is easy to let them get to you if you are not strong. Remember what I taught you."

Azerick guided Raijaun to the crystal standing in the center of the room. "Place your hands on it and create your weave like the runes on the wall show you."

Raijaun studied the runes for a minute even though he had committed them to memory already, and began drawing in the Source. He fed the arcane power into the crystal and watched as the room slowly dissolved and was replaced by the Scions' prison world.

Have you come to sacrifice your ill-begotten progeny, false Guardian?

"Push them out of your mind, Raijaun," Azerick instructed. "You have the ability to resist them."

For now, but soon we shall be free, and we will crush you, little abomination.

"I do not like them, Father. They frighten me."

"Ignore them. Come, I will show you what I do and teach you how to do it when I am gone or otherwise occupied." Azerick laid a hand on the translucent screen and bent his mind into its substance. "You must feel all along the barrier with your mind. It should feel smooth and solid beneath your mind's touch. Try it."

Raijaun touched the screen and focused much like he did on the crystal. He felt the oily solidity of the wall and let his consciousness slide along the barrier's expansive surface. His mind was a vehicle with no limitation on speed. He circled the entire world in minutes and explored the vastness like an eagle looking down upon it from the heavens.

"I think I feel something amiss, Father. This spot here feels rough and brittle."

Azerick "flew" to his son's side. "Very good. Now draw in your power and use it to strengthen the weakening."

Raijaun focused and began infusing the barrier with his magic, sealing cracks and reinforcing the thinning area. Azerick studied the way his son drew in the Source and expertly wielded its power. He was like a fish swimming in the sea, whereas the humans were but guests in the alien environment.

"Pull in more power and add a bit of your Guardian magic to the weave," Azerick said.

Raijaun grimaced but did as he was told. Arcane energy flowed into him as he bent his will to the task. Azerick was amazed at the amount of power his son could wield, especially at such a young age. He was unsure if his ability would scale with his physical growth, but it was apparent his performance in training was based on emotion, not ability.

Raijaun's Guardian magic did more to repair the weakness than anything Azerick could manage without significant time and expending a great deal more energy. However, Raijaun's ability to make the repair needed practice. Azerick helped him shape his magic to effect the best results for the task. Working together, Azerick and Raijaun were able to complete his work in half the time. Eventually, he expected Raijaun to be able to find and repair any weaknesses on his own but, for now, he could not leave him alone in this terrible place.

Even now, the Scions pushed their thoughts through the barrier. Azerick helped shield his son's mind from the words and awful images of the tortures the Scions would inflict upon them all when they broke free. Raijaun needed to learn how to protect his thoughts and avoid the Scions so they did not distract him while he worked. Their job complete, Azerick pulled them out of the prison world and back home.

"You did very well." Azerick could see Raijaun visibly shaking from the experience. "Are you all right?"

"It hurt when I used my Guardian magic. Not as bad as in the town, but it was uncomfortable."

Azerick pondered this unexpected revelation. "It must have to do with the strong link to the abyss in both body and spirit. Even when you are not actively channeling abyssal power, your body and essence conflict with your Guardian nature. How bad is it?"

Raijaun's shoulders slumped and he sighed. "It's not that bad. I can do it if I have to."

Azerick squeezed his shoulder. "We'll take our time with it. Maybe with practice it will come easier. Why don't you go and rest up."

Raijaun nodded, exited the door, and met Miranda waiting anxiously on the other side. He ducked his head and hurriedly skirted around her. Miranda forced a smile and took a few cautious steps into the lab, worriedly wringing her hands.

"Miranda, is something wrong?" Azerick asked, knowing Miranda disliked coming down here.

"Have you seen Daebian? It is getting late, and he did not show for dinner."

"I have been down here all day, I'm afraid."

"Could you look for him, with your magic I mean? Aggie is trying, but she said he is very hard to locate for some reason. She thought maybe you would have better luck since you share a connection through blood."

"Her reasoning is sound. I will see what I can do."

"Azerick, I want to apologize for what I said earlier. I know it is not your fault."

"Your concerns are not without merit. It is something that has worried me since I found out you were pregnant."

"It was still cruel. I know you did not choose any of this, and I cannot blame you for what has happened. At least I try not to, but sometimes I get so scared it is hard not to. I think it is how I try to understand all of it. I know it's not fair, but I need something to focus on to cope. Just know I always love you."

"I know, and if me being the focus of your frustration is what you need, then I gladly offer it. It may be the only thing I have to give you right now."

Miranda wrapped her arms around Azerick and squeezed. "Thank you for allowing me my craziness."

Azerick smiled. "Being crazy might be the only thing keeping us all from going insane."

"You will find him, won't you?"

"Of course, assuming he does not come back on his own before I do," Azerick promised.

Given his link with his son, finding Daebian should have been relatively easy, but Aggie was right, something within his son made him very hard to magically track down. After more than a fruitless hour of scrying, Azerick prepared to have a long night ahead of him.

Zeb turned the ship's wheel a touch more to starboard to catch a little more wind. It was a favorable blow, and it put them significantly ahead of schedule. The ship had a hold full of fish on ice and other food stores, as well as furs from the frozen north. Many of these they would trade in Southport for grain out of the Habberback Plains. They would then load up some cattle and take the grain and remaining furs to Bakhtaran to trade for copper, tin, and spices.

"Will, come grab the wheel!" Zeb called out into the darkness.

Will bounded nimbly across the gently rolling deck and took the steps to the wheelhouse two at a time. Will was younger than almost everyone except the greenest crew members, but his mind was nearly as sharp as his renowned eyesight, which is why Zeb had made him first mate last year.

"Looks like we caught a good wind, Cap'n."

"Aye, I think it's the best I'm gonna pull out of her. Hold her steady while I catch some shut-eye."

"Aye, aye, Cap'n. Best you say thanks to Serron so you don't blame me if we lose it on my watch," Will joked.

"I'll do that, and I'll say a prayer to keep it the whole way. I think we'll have us a record if we manage to hold it more than a few days."

Zeb retired to his cabin and kept his promise by whispering a quick prayer of thanks to Serron for the calm sea and favorable wind. He was glad to be under sail once again. The militarization raging through North Haven and much of the kingdom made him long for the open ocean, where the only doomsday scenarios he had to face were sinking or pirates. An anxious rapping at his cabin door woke him from his troubled sleep. Looking out of the large window in the aft of his stateroom revealed the dull grey of the coming morning.

Zeb crossed the room and tore the door open. "We better be sinking for you to raise all this fuss!"

"Sorry, Cap'n," Will said with a knuckled salute, "but we got us a stowaway."

Zeb craned his neck and saw Daebian pinned between two of his sailors. Will stepped aside and the two sailors gave Daebian a push. The boy took a couple of steps forward and smiled at Zeb.

"Hi, Zeb!"

"We caught him trying to sneak some food from the galley."

Zeb took several deep breaths and rubbed his forehead with a calloused hand. "Damn it, boy! Do ya have any idea what ya done?"

"I hitched a ride on one of my father's ships," Daebian answered easily.

"Does your father know you're aboard?"

Daebian shrugged. "He might, if he even bothered to look for me."

"Are you telling me you ran away?"

"It sounds so cowardly when you put it that way. I prefer to say I anonymously chose to no longer be in the same vicinity as my father."

"I'll lose at least three days if I have to turn this ship around, all on account of a spoiled boy who got his feelings hurt!"

"Then don't turn around. It is not as though my father will be overly concerned for my whereabouts."

"Even if that were true, which it ain't, your mother would skin me alive. This trip is scheduled to take a month, and she'd have my hide for sure if I kept her fretting about you that long."

"Yes, Mother always did have a soft spot for me."

Will asked, "So what are you going to do, Cap'n?"

Zeb sighed and scratched the stubble on his neck. "I'm gonna go shave. I'll let you know what I decide."

Zeb figured he had two choices. He could turn the ship around and march Daebian back to Azerick, in shackles if needs be, or he could kick him off in Southport and pay someone to escort him home. The latter would cause the least disruption to his schedule, but it would also require placing the boy into someone else's care. If anything happened to him, Zeb would be responsible.

A good shave and beard trim always set his mind at ease and let him think clearer, so Zeb wet his shaving brush in a basin of water, worked up a good lather, and liberally covered his neck with the foam. After giving his razor a few quick swipes on a leather strap, he touched the fine blade to his neck and leaned toward the mirror nailed to the wall.

Azerick's face appeared in the reflection. "Zeb."

Zeb dropped the razor to the floor and leapt back. "Curse your wizard ways, boy! Ya damn near made me slit my own throat!"

"My apologies, Zeb," Azerick said, trying to force his sincerity past the smile tugging at his mouth. "Have you seen Daebian? Miranda mentioned he had a fascination with pirates and may have stowed away on one of my ships. Yours was the only one to leave port around the time he ran off, and I got the feeling he was out at sea."

Zeb picked up his fallen razor and wiped the foam from his neck. His hands were shaking too badly to attempt a shave now. "Yeah, he's aboard. Will just dragged him to my quarters a couple minutes ago. It's your ship. I can turn her around if ya order me to, or I can dump him off on someone in Southport if ya know anyone who'll take him."

Azerick pondered the situation a moment. "I have a third option. Take him with you. Perhaps being away from here and doing some honest work will be good for him. Treat him like one of the crew."

"You know me; no one gets a free ride on my boat. I'll still put you to work if'n ya come aboard."

"Thank you, Zeb. Keep him safe."

"Aye, ya know I will. I'll treat him like one of my own. Just know I wouldn't hesitate to take a strap to any kid who was mine."

Azerick grinned. "I doubt that would have any positive effect on him."

"Couldn't hurt to try."

Azerick doubted that very much.

Zeb found Daebian sitting on an overturned bucket next to Balor, tying knots in a length of rope.

"What else do you do?" Daebian asked. "There has got to be something more interesting to do than tying knots all day."

"Half this ship is held together with knots. You tie a bad knot, and the whole thing can come unraveled. Rechecking your knots is a big part of every sailor's duty. Sails are constantly in need of trimming to catch the best wind. That requires you to tie a knot. Adding more canvas requires tying more knots. If a storm blows and you gotta take down the sheets in a hurry, you have to know how to untie those knots with quickness. You also better have a good knot on your lanyard, or you'll be swept overboard and sent straight to Serron. Nope, there ain't too many things more important than knowing how to tie a proper knot."

"How's he doing?" Zeb asked as he approached.

"Really good. I only have to show him once and he has it down."

"Sailing runs in his blood. I guess there's something of his father in him after all."

Daebian looked up from the knot he was tying. "Yes, poor Daebian is the magically ungifted son. I'm practically a cripple in our household. A boy to be pitied."

"I was referring to your lack of common sense and overdeveloped foolishness. I don't give half a spit if you can or can't use magic. As far as I'm concerned, the whole world would be better off without it."

"So what are you going to do with me?"

"If it were up to me, I'd put you in a longboat and let you row back to North Haven. But your father thought you might want to stay aboard and do this run with us."

"You spoke to my father?"

"I talked to his face in my mirror, if that counts."

"And he told you to keep me aboard?"

"Aye, he said you showed an interest in sailing."

"More likely he just wants to keep me out of his hair."

Zeb frowned and wagged his head. "I said I don't care if a man can't use magic, but one who can't even be happy when he gets what he wants? Now there's someone to pity."

Daebian accepted the rebuke with a nod. "What am I to do, Zeb?"

"First off, you call me Captain when we're on the deck. Second, I'll tell you the same thing I told your father the first day he hopped aboard. There are no free rides on my ship. You'll work like any man aboard."

Daebian leapt to his feet and saluted. "Aye, aye, Captain!"

"Balor, you show him the ropes and put him to work."

"Aye, Cap'n. Come on, kid."

Daebian dutifully followed along, looking in wonder at the vast array of ropes and pulleys used to make the ship function. Men scrambled through the rigging, checking knots, tightening ropes, and performing various duties. A few men, mostly younger, scrubbed and mopped the deck.

"The most important thing to know on a ship is what everything is and where it's at."

"I thought the most important thing was tying knots?"

"The best knot in the world ain't worth a damn if you don't know where to tie it. A man's life may depend on you knowing exactly where to go. Failure to secure a lower yardarm properly can mean someone's life if you waste seconds trying to remember where it is."

Balor stopped at the stern and began pointing out various parts of the ship. Daebian listened with a rare show of attentiveness. Only in his weapons training did he show such a level of interest.

"We're standing on the aft deck, or aft castle. The back of the ship is the stern. This is the mizzenmast. We don't have it up right now, but the sail coming off the lower mizzen is called the spanker sail. When the spar is in place, it's only a few feet above the deck. It is easily the most dangerous piece of wood on the ship. If the line securing it in place snaps, that spar will sweep every man right off the deck. The other sails are the mizzen moonsail, skysail, mizzen royal, topgallant, topsail, and the spanker when it's up.

"The deck just below us is the quarterdeck, and that's the mainmast. The sails are much the same on each mast: moon, sky, royal, topgallant, topsail, and the lowest one on the mainmast is mainsail. On the forecastle, you have the foremast with the same sails with the lower being the foresail. It's all pretty self-explanatory. We try to keep it as simple as possible. Hanging off the bowsprit, you have the flying jib, outer jib, and fore topmast staysail. Those help catch the wind coming at us from an angle and allow us to tack into it so we don't sit dead in the water until a blow shows up to push us in the right direction. Before some bright seaman came up with the jibs, a ship could sit for days waiting for a wind coming from the proper direction."

Balor spent much of the remainder of the day explaining the finer details of running a ship. Daebian had no trouble repeating everything Balor taught him whenever he stopped to quiz him. No matter how hard he tried to trick the boy, Daebian was able to recall everything he was told even to the minutest detail.

"I tell you, your father is one of the smartest men I ever met, but not even he picked up all this as quick as you."

Daebian beamed under Balor's praise. "Was Father a good sailor?"

"He could'a been. He was a quick study too, but even though sailing was in his blood, it weren't in his heart. I got a feeling you got sailing in your heart. Am I right?"

"I never gave it much thought. I mean, I always thought I'd like to sail, but I don't know if it's what I want to do."

"Well, maybe you'll have your answer by the end of this voyage. It don't take most folks more than their first haul to know if'n they want to be sailors or not. Let's see if I can help make your decision any easier." Balor led Daebian to a group of men scrubbing and swabbing the deck. "Lewis, I got you another greenhorn. Daebian, Lewis is going to show you what your duties are. Every sailor starts here until they become an able seaman. Swabbing ain't glorious, but it's an important duty. This salt will eat the deck and everything else it touches."

Lewis looked Daebian up and down and smiled as Balor left the boy in his charge. "Hmm, you don't look like much."

"Looks can be quite deceiving," Daebian replied.

Lewis sneered. "It also looks like you showed up several hours late for your shift. Since we've been working all day and you've been lollygagging, you can finish the last two hours yourself."

"That hardly seems fair, especially considering I was doing as I was ordered."

Lewis leaned down to get eye level with Daebian. "Fair is what I say is fair. I run this crew, and you best watch that smart mouth of yours, if you know what's good for you. I can put you on the foulest duty this ship has to offer. You best remember that next time you think to smart off, boy."

Daebian matched Lewis's glare. "You had best remember that my father owns this and a fair number of ships besides, if you think to mistreat me and shirk your own duties."

The hostility instantly vanished from Lewis's face. "You're Lord Giles's kid?"

"Daebian Giles at your service," he answered with a sweeping bow. "You said there was still two hours left on your shift, so I suggest we get busy."

"We, you say?"

"Yes, we, a word denoting oneself and others. Usually ascribed to a particular group. In this case, our group."

Lewis nervously licked his lips. "Right, we. Uh, what do you want to do?"

"I simply wish to do my fair share of the detail. Instruct me and I shall obey."

"Okay. Um, take Bill's brush and scrub while he swabs."

"Aye, aye, taskmaster Lewis," Daebian quipped with a sharp salute.

Daebian knelt next to the bucket of fresh water and began scrubbing while the man called Bill mopped it up. The work was back-breaking and, although he did not complain, Daebian decided being an ordinary seaman was not for him. If he was going to crew a boat for long, he was destined for a leadership role. Captain rang pleasantly in his head.

"All right, boys, shift's up," Lewis announced. "Stow your gear and get ready for mess."

Daebian got to his feet, stretched, and followed his fellow deck scrubbers to put away his tools. One of the men whispered he had a jug of rum stashed away, and the others followed him with a smile to whatever dark nook below decks he had it stashed. Daebian had no interest in the drink even if they would have shared it with a boy of an apparent age of twelve. He made for the bow and climbed out onto the bowsprit. He clambered out onto the rope webbing as easily as a spider and rode the gently rising and plummeting bow as the sea spray peppered his face and the wind blew through his hair. Daebian did not need an entire voyage to know sailing was something he enjoyed.

"Enter," Zeb gruffly answered the rapping on his door.

Lewis stepped into the captain's quarters twisting a knit hat in his hands. "Pardon my interrupting your meal, Captain."

"I assume you think it important. What's on your mind, Lewis?"

"It's about the new boy, sir. He says his father is Lord Giles. Is that the truth, sir?"

"Aye, he is. Is he causing you grief?"

"No, sir, not really. He worked well enough today. It's just I'm unsure how to deal with him. I'm a bit nervous about offending him and losing my job, sir. I like to think I'm up for able seaman soon, and I don't want to jeopardize that by ticking off the owner's kid."

"I plan on putting you up in the rigging after this voyage. I know Azerick as well as any man, I like to think. He never asked for special treatment of anyone, and I don't expect he'd ask it for his boy either. I ain't gonna treat him much different than I would any man on my ship and you shouldn't either. If he throws a tantrum, I'll deal with it," Zeb replied gruffly.

Lewis bobbed his head as he backed out of Zeb's cabin. "Thank you, Captain."

Daebian tied himself to the bowsprit and slept beneath the stars, cradled in the web of supporting ropes. It took him back to the times his mother held him in her arms and smiled at him with limitless love and acceptance. Even when she discovered how different he was, she never treated him as anything other than her beloved son. Nibbling at the very edges of his heart, the emotion was as close as Daebian would ever come to feeling remorse, for he knew he was destined to betray her unrequited love.

CHAPTER 16

A gruff voice roused Daebian from his sleep. "Wake up, boy."
Daebian opened his eyes and looked up at Lewis standing near his feet.

"Shift's starting soon, so if you want to eat, you best hit the crew's mess right quick."

Daebian undid his tether, sprinted across the deck, and raced down to the mess hall as fast as the narrow passageway and low doorframes allowed. Lewis was correct; the galley workers were already packing up and Daebian was the last to arrive. Being late was a gamble. If you were lucky, the galley workers scooped the last of the food from the pots so they could clean them and you ended up with more than a normal ration. If you were unlucky, you could be quite hungry by the time lunch rolled around. Luck was with him today.

He had barely had time to wolf down his meal when a shrill whistle sounded the call for all hands to report to their shift. Daebian ran back to the deck, not wanting to give Lewis any reason to berate him. He should have taken his time.

"You louts grab your mops and brushes. Daebian, you stand fast. I have a special task for you. I spoke with the captain, and he told me he don't care whose son you are. He says you get treated like any other sailor, and if you give me lip, he'll toss you off the ship."

"I see. So what is my task?"

"You're gonna clean the bilges."

"By myself? It sounds like an unpleasant job. Is this something any of the other sailors would do by themselves?"

"Don't matter. It's what you're gonna do," Lewis said with a sneer.

"You're sure this is the route you want to take with me?"

For a moment, Lewis was anything but sure. But Daebian had embarrassed him in front of his crew, and ego overrode his mind's urgent warning.

"If you don't like it, go cry to the captain."

Daebian smiled and saluted. "Aye, aye, Mister Lewis."

He would do as he was told, but this would not be the end of it. Daebian did not cry to anyone about anything. If he had a problem, he solved it, and Lewis had made himself a problem. Although Daebian's solutions to problems seemed perfectly logical and reasonable to him, few others would see them that way. Lewis certainly would not.

Daebian did not work entirely by himself. Others worked the pumps to force most of the stagnant water from the bilge, but he was alone in the fetid water and disgusting muck. He was sure Zeb did not say Lewis could single him out for details that went beyond the normal scope of duties. This work should have an entire detail assigned to it, not just him scooping sludge, climbing back above decks, and tossing it overboard. Lewis was punishing him for what he perceived as backtalk, and obviously had a desire to flex his limited authority.

For three days, Daebian spent his entire shift hauling bucket after back-breaking bucket of putrid sludge up from the hull. It was easily the worst detail on the ship. The air was foul and the water downright toxic. It was a miserable task even with a proper crew, but Lewis's desire to punish him for whatever slight he perceived made it torturous. Still Daebian persevered.

You should kill him. I hunger, and his blood would give us both power.

"Lewis will pay for his insult, Klaraxis, but I cannot do something as overt as killing him in his sleep. I will seize the moment when it appears. Forcing it to come will only create more problems."

You have a great deal more patience than either of your fathers.

"I have more of a lot of things, things I will show the world when I am grown."

You are a son to make your father proud—one of us anyway.

It was three days of scrubbing the bilge before the ship finally arrived in Southport. After clearing customs, all hands began unloading the cargo destined for sale or caravans in Southport and bringing aboard the stuff for export to Bakhtaran, with exception of the cattle, which they would load in the morning just before setting sail.

The crew was given a night of shore leave, and most of the men headed for one of the more popular inns near the harbor. What little Daebian saw of Southport impressed him. It was much larger and busier than North Haven. It was raw, and all the sights, sounds, and smells gave the place a chaotic feel he liked.

The inn was equally impressive and occupied the bulk of the entire block. It sported at least a hundred tables and three bars. It bustled with hundreds of patrons shouting for more beer, ale, liquor, and food, while a continuous stream of prostitutes led men upstairs. Zeb and the bulk of his crew found a space where they could sit mostly together.

"Stay close to me, Daebian," Zeb ordered. "If you get lost in here, it's more likely trouble will find ya than any of us."

Daebian nodded and continued to watch the crowd, always keeping one eye on Lewis who sat two tables to his left.

"How do you like working on the ship?" Zeb asked as they ate their meal.

"I am more tired than I have been in my life, but I like it."

"Lewis says you been a good worker. He was worried you would raise a fuss doing the labor of a lowly seaman."

"I think of it like my weapons training. We spend hours practicing the most routine exercises. Thrust, return, guard, over and over. It is tedious and exhausting, but it is necessary to learn before jumping in the ring and sparring. I look at it like that."

"That's a real mature attitude you have," Zeb commended. "I told Lewis I wouldn't treat you any different than any other sailor, but the truth is, you are the heir to this operation, and there's not much to learn doing swabby duty. I wanted to test your attitude more than anything. When we set sail tomorrow, I'm putting you and Lewis up in the rigging. You especially should learn everything there is to a ship since one day you will be giving your captains orders, and you should know what you're talking about when you do. Had you been a whiner, you'd be scrubbing decks and cleaning bilges the whole trip."

"Thank you, Captain. Captain, how many men should be in the bilge when it's being cleaned out?"

"That's a job for the entire shift. It takes everyone to form the bucket chain to toss the gunk overboard and return the buckets. Any less and it's not efficient. Why, how many did ya have?"

Daebian smiled. "All we needed. I was just curious."

He turned his eyes back to Lewis, glad Zeb was not aware of his mistreatment. It could have complicated things had he condoned such treatment. Daebian watched Lewis make for the nearest bar. He had to squeeze through the press of people and drew several displeased looks as he did. One rough sailor in particular looked up from his drink and glared, firing off an expletive at Lewis's back.

"Captain, I need to use the privy. I will be right back."

"You want someone to go with you? I'm not keen on letting you out of my sight in this place."

Daebian stroked the black jewel set in the hilt of his blade with his thumb. "I'm a proficient fighter. I'll be fine. I'm small enough most people probably won't notice me anyway."

Zeb looked unconvinced but nodded, torn between not wanting to be a mother hen to the boy and reluctance about letting him wander off in a place like this. He wished now he had picked a calmer tavern.

I sense intent in your movement. Your moment has arisen?

"It has. Can you help me?"

Minimally, but it should be enough. You feel the thrum of power within me. Reach for it with your mind and shape it to your will. I will show you how.

Daebian focused on the images and feelings Klaraxis fed him. The demon was a link to his abyssal power and, through him, Daebian could channel and shape the dark energy to his will. The thread he was able to draw upon was a thin and feeble thing, but there was power in subtlety if properly used.

Daebian stepped behind the sailor who had shown himself to be especially unforgiving of Lewis's jostling and slipped his hand to the small purse at the man's belt. He untied the strings securing it in place with unnatural dexterity while using Klaraxis's infernal power to make himself less noticeable to those around him.

With purse in hand, Daebian watched for Lewis's return. As he expected, Lewis threaded his way back to his table using nearly the same path he had cut just minutes before. Daebian slid through the crowd with the ease of a schooner using its sharp prow to slice through the water. Tacking an intercept course with Lewis, Daebian dropped the purse into his pocket as he passed. Lewis never saw Daebian as he disappeared back into the masses like a ghost ship in heavy fog.

Daebian tapped the grizzled sailor on the shoulder. "Excuse me, sir."

The man jerked his head around, one hand flying to the knife at his hip. "What do ya want, boy?"

Daebian took half a step back and gave the man his most frightened look. "I just saw a man pilfer your purse, sir. I thought I should tell you."

The sailor's other hand slapped against his now vacant hip. He leaned forward and grabbed the front of Daebian's shirt. "What man stole my coin?"

Daebian pointed a shaking finger at Lewis just as he was sitting back down at his table. "That man there. I saw him slip it off your belt and into his right coat pocket."

Several of the men sitting nearby stood with the sailor and motioned for others of their crew to follow the angry man to Lewis's table. Sensing impending violence, patrons began sliding away as the crew barged forward.

"You stole my coin, you scurvy-ridden rat!" the sailor shouted as he glared down at Lewis.

Lewis had to scoot his chair away to stand and face the man. "I didn't steal no purse!"

Zeb's crew stood as well and the two sides squared off. Daebian spotted Zeb trying to push through the hostile mass of bodies to prevent bloodshed, but everyone's attention was focused on the two men facing each other down and they impeded his progress.

"What's that in your coat pocket, then?" the sailor asked, gesturing to the slight bulge.

Lewis looked at his pocket, and then at the coin purse he drew out of it in confusion. It was a simple matter for Daebian to feed a tendril of Klaraxis's black power into his victim and stoke the fires of his anger. The sailor snaked a hand forward and closed it around the pouch and Lewis's fist. He then pulled Lewis forward and buried his knife into his guts. Lewis spotted Daebian smiling near his side just before darkness overtook him, and had a brief understanding of the source of his demise.

There was a slight pause as Lewis's body crumpled to the ground before all hell broke loose. Blades and bottles appeared in the hands of the two sides and a massive melee broke out. Daebian felt a hand grab his shoulder and pull him back just as a chair went flying near his head. He released his grip on his dagger when he saw it was Zeb.

"Stay with me, boy, and keep your head down!"

Zeb towed him in his wake as the crew beat a fighting retreat to the door. Masses of people spilled out onto the street from the inn's entrance. The aggressors, figuring the matter largely resolved with Lewis's death and not wanting to add themselves to the list of the dead, did not press far beyond the inn.

Several of Zeb's crew sported wounds and three men had to be carried through the streets and back to the ship. Zeb ordered the gangplank drawn in and posted a watch in case the other crew decided to continue hostilities. After seeing his wounded to the ship's infirmary, Zeb went topside to join those on watch.

He spotted Daebian near the rail and stood next to him. "You all right?"

"I'm fine."

"I never took Lewis for the thieving type," Zeb said with a sigh.

"Looks can be deceiving."

Zeb clapped Daebian on the shoulder. "I guess you'd know that better than just about anyone. That fool Lewis's deception just cost him his life."

"My weapons master always told us that nothing will kill a man faster than his own foolishness."

"Aye, that is so."

CHAPTER 17

Zeb ordered the cattle loaded aboard before first light so they could ship out at the earliest possible moment. Just because no one from the city watch had come to question them about the tavern brawl yet did not mean no one would. Zeb had no fear of the legal ramifications, but such an inquisition could hold them in port for days if not weeks.

The ship pushed out to sea the moment the tides allowed the hull to clear the shallowest reef. With Southport and any angry sailors or inquisitive law behind them, the crew soon fell into a relaxed routine. Balor was once again tasked with Daebian's seafaring education and was busy teaching him the importance of splicing line.

"Like I told you before, line is what holds a ship together, and those lines can snap at any time. When a line snaps, you have to splice it back together. This is called an eye splice."

"Why do we have so many people in the rigging?" Daebian asked as Balor wove the loose strands of line back into the rope to create the eye.

"We're leaving Valerian waters now, which means the navy isn't patrolling out here. Sumara never increased their navy size much after our buildup. They probably didn't want to look like they were preparing for war. Politics, you know. That means a lot of the pirates who used to hunt our ships up north moved down here."

"Do you think we will see any pirates?" Daebian asked excitedly.

"Doubtful. Even without a strong naval deterrent, pirates prefer to hit ships farther out to sea where there's less chance of a merchant getting away or running into another ship that might come to their prey's aid." Balor handed the line to Daebian. "Look that over and see what I done."

Just as Daebian grabbed the line, the ship bucked wildly, tilting the tall masts steeply to the side. Daebian tightened his legs around the yardarm, gripped the rigging over his head, and unconsciously drew upon Klaraxis's power to increase his strength and balance.

Balor was less fortunate. He was off his center of gravity when the rogue swell hit the ship. His arms flailed as he tried to grab a line. His hands brushed a rope but grasped only empty air as he fell. His leg caught a line ten feet below and arrested his fall, but his perch was a precarious one.

Daebian looked at the eye splice in his hand, pulled the rope through it to make a lasso, and threw it at Balor's other leg as he hung upside down. Balor lost his feeble grip on the line as the ship righted itself and swung back in the other direction. Daebian leapt off the yardarm into empty air just as Balor resumed his plummeting. Although he was much lighter than Balor, the yardarm acted as a fulcrum, and he was able to arrest his fall.

Daebian shinnied down the rope until he was eye level with the upside down Balor. "So, did you have something else you wanted to show me, or are we just going to hang around up here a while?"

Balor laughed deeply as he swayed on the end of the rope. "I don't know how you made that throw, but I owe you my life!"

"That and a few pieces of silver ought to get me a decent meal at a good inn."

A shout from the crow's nest cut off Balor's renewed laughter. "Sails, three points ahead of the starboard beam!"

"Give me a push toward that rigging," Balor ordered.

Daebian braced his feet against Balor's shoulder blades and pushed off. Balor arched his back and swung his body toward the lines crisscrossing nearby. As soon as he had a firm hold, Daebian slid down his end of the rope and climbed out onto another set of lines. Swinging almost apelike through the intersecting ropes, Daebian dropped onto the deck near Captain Zeb.

"Captain, is it pirates?"

"It's too early to say." Zeb called up to the crow's nest. "What are ya seeing?"

"Looks like a schooner, Cap'n, and headed right at us at a fast clip."

"Pirates?" Daebian asked again.

"I don't know for sure, but not many ships go out of their way to sidle up to another just to wave and say hello." Zeb turned and shouted toward the lower deck. "Put up every piece of canvas we can string up! Helmsman, find us some more wind and tack us ten degrees to port."

"Ship's tacking to maintain intercept and closing, Captain."

"Unless they got that schooner piled to the rafters with men, they can't expect to take us with a ship that small, much less make off with our cargo," Zeb mused aloud.

The lookout gave him his answer an hour later. "Another set of sails beyond the schooner! Looks like a frigate!"

"Looks like we found your pirates, boy. Our bad luck they're a smart bunch too."

"What do you mean, Captain?"

"They're using the schooner to run us down like dogs. They'll probably hurl chain and shot into our sail to slow us down so the frigate can catch up with us. Then they'll both board and take the ship. If *Majestic* is badly damaged in the fight, they can load most the cargo onto the frigate."

"Do you think they can take us, sir?"

"Not without one hell of a fight. We aren't just some merchant taking his goods to market. This is a fighting crew with as much, and probably more, combat training as most of the ships in the king's navy. It's gonna be a bloody affair, I can tell you that. That frigate and schooner may be smaller than us, but I bet they each pack a crew as large as ours. Probably half again as many on the frigate alone."

"What do we do?"

"We fight. You stay in my cabin."

"Captain, I am not a child, and I can fight as well as any man on this ship!" Daebian argued heatedly.

Zeb narrowed his eyes and furrowed his brow. "Meaning no insult, boy, I don't rightly know what you are. Are you six, or are you twelve or thirteen? What I do know is your father asked me to make sure you stayed safe, and that's what I'm gonna do. If those ships close and board, I want you in my cabin out of the way. There's a crawl space between decks you can access through a hatch beneath the trunk near the window."

"And what if they find me?"

"You tell them who you are. They're certain to ransom you back to your father rather than toss you overboard. Truth be, you're probably the most valuable thing on this ship."

Daebian furrowed his brow and his anger spiked. He was tired of people judging his worth by who his father was. "I would rather show them who I am than tell them."

Do not argue with me about this. I'm the captain, you're the crew, and you'll follow orders!"

"Aye, aye, sir," Daebian answered in a low voice. "May I make a suggestion?"

"I'll listen to advice from any man if it has a chance of saving my ship."

"From what I understand, the greatest threat is their superior numbers if they board us. If we can slow their boarding party, we can pick them off with crossbows and thin their numbers some."

"It's a sound idea. You have a plan on how to do that?"

"When Balor fell, the only thing keeping him from splattering onto the deck was the crisscrossing lines that arrested his fall. We could run line and netting above the railing to create an additional obstacle for the pirates. Our ship sits higher in the water than the schooner and frigate, so they will have to climb over or breach it to gain the decks. The time it takes to do so gives our men an opportunity to put a bolt or blade through them before they do."

"Balor, you understand what he's saying?" Zeb asked.

"Aye, Cap'n. It sounds like a good idea."

"See to it, and we'll talk about your fall later."

It would take hours for the pirates to catch *Majestic*, so the crew put the time they had to good use erecting barricades and obstacles like Daebian's nets and ropes. They set buckets of caltrops on the forecastle and quarterdecks where the crew would make their final stand. These they would hurl onto the main deck below to cripple the mostly barefoot invaders.

Majestic tacked a wild course in hopes of catching a better wind and keeping as much distance between them and their pursuers as they could, but the schooner closed rapidly. Within a few hours, the schooner crew could be seen with the naked eye, manning catapults mounted at the bow and stern. The frigate was also visible against the horizon from the deck as it closed on *Majestic*.

"Crew the heavy weapons. I want everyone else below. No sense in standing on the decks to catch whatever they start flinging at us," Zeb ordered.

The sun was setting rapidly and Zeb felt a glimmer of hope. If they could slow the schooner enough, they had a chance of escaping into the night. Unfortunately, the schooner extinguished that hope as it came within range to hurl shot and chain into the sails and rigging near dusk. The crew remaining on decks hid behind the bulwarks and the simple shields made of wood banded with iron attached to the railing.

Stones and chain tore through sails and line and rained onto the deck. Zeb shoved Daebian through the door to his quarters then ran to help Will at the wheel. *Majestic* returned the assault with heavier stone. The pirates' attack was hindered by their desire to avoid sinking their target, but Zeb had no such impediment.

The schooner's lighter shot gave it an advantage on range, and the crew did their best to maintain their distance. Within an hour, *Majestic*'s sails were severely shredded and they lost speed. As the schooner closed, crossbow bolts began hissing through the air, burying their heads into timbers and any crewman who failed to keep his head down.

Zeb ordered his full crew to the decks to repel the boarders as the schooner's catapults hurled a dozen grapnels attached to stout ropes. Zeb had to remark on the pirates' cleverness even as they drew their ships together.

The value of Daebian's anti-boarding nets became apparent as the pirates struggled to climb over or cut through them. It gave Zeb's crew time to aim and bury crossbow quarrels, spears, or cutlasses into their exposed bodies. Several pirates tried to swing across by throwing hooked lines from the upper yardarms, but this provided *Majestic*'s crew with exposed targets. Those who did achieve the deck fell quickly.

The two sides exchanged crossbow shots, but few found anything more than wood or the open sea beyond the ships. Pirates used long-handled axes and hatchets to hack at the ropes and nets denying them access to their prey, but it was a slow and often painful assault. Zeb's crew pushed the pirates back time and again, but their numbers were greater and the damage they inflicted on the barriers and crew was taking its toll.

Even so, Zeb was feeling confident in his defense until the frigate drew near. Her crew added their own crossbow volleys to the fight and scoured the deck with heavy shot, making it even harder for the defenders to repel boarders as the assault forced them to hunker behind their barriers. Then the real nightmare began. A bolt of lightning arced from the frigate, shattering crates and scorching the defensive netting.

"Damn it all to the abyss," Zeb shouted. "They have a wizard!"

Pirates began forcing their way through the barriers and swarmed onto the ship. The ringing of steel on steel created an awful din as swords clashed and men fought for their lives. The pirate mage sent orbs of arcane power streaking into the defenders with pinpoint accuracy and lethality. Within minutes, Zeb's crew was fighting a retreat to the reinforced forecastle and stern.

"That sounded like lightning," Daebian remarked as he listened to the ensuing battle outside.

I sense magic at play. It is difficult for me to gauge it with my current limitations, but I think it is a hedge wizard of some sort. He lacks the structure and control of an Academy-trained wizard.

"Zeb does not stand a chance if the pirates have a wizard on board."

The blood of a mage would greatly increase the power I can share with you.

"Zeb told me to stay here."

When have you done what you are told? Zeb wants to keep you from harm. I can keep you safe, and Zeb is going to lose this ship and you along with it if the mage is not neutralized quickly. You wanted to meet some pirates. Let us go say hello.

Daebian opened the cabin door and found himself staring into the filthy face of a pirate. The man flashed a gap-toothed grin as he saw the boy barring his way inside. Now was a good time to find some loot while the battle still raged, and he would be damned if a boy was going to stop him. His smile vanished when Daebian thrust his dagger into his gut.

The pirate dropped to his knees, looking at Daebian in confusion as Klaraxis absorbed his dwindling life force through the blood washing over the boy's hand and onto the black gem. Daebian felt his bond with the demon grow as Klaraxis fed off the dying man's soul.

Zeb looked at the cabin door past the pirates battering against his defenses and watched Daebian stab the pirate. He tried desperately to fight his way through, but there were too many men between him and the boy.

"Daebian, get back inside and bar the door!" Zeb shouted above the raucous tumult.

Daebian smiled at Zeb, scooped up the pirate's fallen cutlass, and vanished into the press of bodies. He used Klaraxis's abyssal power to help him go unnoticed just as he had at the inn. Klaraxis showed him how to bend the shadows to his will and use them to help cloak his form when the simple deception was insufficient to avoid notice. Daebian struck from those shadows with lethal efficiency, killing and critically wounding pirates as he slipped his way across the deck in search of the mage.

The demon's power, and Daebian's ability to wield it, was limited. Several times a pirate took notice of him, but Daebian's skill with the blade and demonically enhanced speed and strength allowed him to dispatch his attacker.

Climbing up the mainmast, Daebian grabbed a line connected to the far end of the yardarm and swung across over the heads of those engaged in the melee and the short expanse of water separating the two ships. Every hair on his body stood on end as a lightning bolt went sizzling past his head just as he dropped to the deck.

"Find the infiltrator!" Daebian heard the mage shout as he crouched behind a wooden crate.

Daebian cloaked his body in shadow and darted around the mainmast as three men ran to the crate with cutlasses and dirks held at the ready. The men cursed as they searched and were unable to find the intruder. Daebian scampered around the deck, ducking behind coils of rope, crates, and masts, striking from the darkness and leaving bodies in his wake.

The mage conjured a bright orb of light and set it floating over his head. While it did illuminate the darkness-shrouded deck, it also created even deeper shadows in which to hide. The pirates still aboard the frigate scoured the ship in groups of three after seeing several of their fellows fall to Daebian's guerilla tactics.

Daebian crouched in the dark space between two crates and watched as a group of pirates searched for him just a few feet away. Shaping the shadows to his will, he created a man-shaped silhouette jutting out from the base of the foremast. When the pirates raced to encircle what they thought was their prey, Daebian leapt out and sank his dagger in the back of one man and his borrowed cutlass in the second. The third pirate caught an arcane bolt in his chest when Daebian leapt aside as his preternatural senses warned him of the attack. Daebian's eyes teared from the acrid smoke wafting up from the man's ruined flesh.

"Where are you, you little rat?" the hedge wizard shouted furiously. "Crawl out of your hiding place and face me like a man!"

"As you wish," Daebian whispered as he plunged his blade into the man's back.

Daebian heard Klaraxis sigh in pleasure as the demon drank in the mage's life force. The gem hummed like a pleased cat, purring as it lapped up the dying man's energy. He felt the shadows grow stronger and more substantial. What once felt like shaping and directing smoke became more liquid and easier to grasp and manipulate.

"Your wizard is dead, Captain," Daebian said, his voice echoing from the shadows all around.

The pirate captain stood next to the ship's wheel surrounded by half a dozen of his most stalwart crew.

"Where are ya? Show yerself!" the captain demanded as he turned in a circle in search of the voice.

"I am all around you, Captain." Human-shaped shadows leapt out from every crack and corner, dancing around the men and taunting them in a chorus of musical voices.

"Fiddle dee dee,
Fiddle dee doe,
What can a pirate do Against shadows?
With blades made of the dark,
They'll stab you through the heart,
And hang your soul from the gallows.
Of gold and riches you were dreamin',
Of plunder and mayhem you were schemin',
But your luck ran dry,
As your crewmen die,
Because this boat is crewed by a demon."

"What are you?" the captain screamed into the night.

"I am a creature full of power and bereft of conscience. I am your nightmare come alive. Do you wish to live, Captain? Recall your men and set sail. Flee while it amuses me to allow you to do so."

"W-who are you?"

"I am the Prince of Shadows. I lurk in the hearts of evil men, feeding upon the putrescence of their souls. Now take your men and go!"

Beads of sweat ran down the pirate's face as he raised a whistle to his lips with a trembling hand and blew it shrilly. He blew until his face purpled from the effort and he nearly passed out. His crew finally obeyed and began fighting their way back to their ships. Zeb and his crew did little to prevent them from doing so.

Not wanting to be seen, Daebian slipped over the side and swam back to *Majestic*. Grabbing a boarding line chopped free by one of the retreating pirates, he easily made the climb back to the deck. Balor nearly clubbed him with a belaying pin when he poked his head over the rail.

"Damn it, boy! Where ya been? I almost brained ya!"

Daebian grabbed Balor's hand and let himself be helped aboard. "I went for a swim," he replied with a grin.

Zeb stormed over and gripped Daebian's upper arm in a vice-like hold. "What in the blazes do you think you were doing?"

Daebian jerked his arm free. "I killed the wizard and made the captain call off his pirates."

"I gave you an order to stay in my cabin!"

"An order, which had I followed, would have had those of us still alive rowing a longboat to the nearest shore, assuming the pirates didn't just slit our throats and be done with us!"

"Just because you got lucky and it turned out your way don't mean disobeying my order was right. Ships run on discipline, and when a sailor doesn't follow orders, especially one as green as you because you think you're so dang blasted much smarter than everyone else, people die and ships sink!"

"The big difference in thinking something and knowing it are in the results."

"Boy, you best be glad you aren't mine, or I'd put you over my knee right here in front of the entire crew."

"Let us both be glad I'm not so you don't foolishly try."

Zeb clenched his fists as if he were trying to squeeze juice from rocks. "Get to your rack, sailor, and don't let me see you until we get to Bakhtaran."

Daebian turned and headed for the crewmen's berth. He stretched out on his rack and stared at the ceiling. There would be a lot of empty bunks tonight.

You should kill him for belittling you.

"I am not going to kill Zeb."

Why not? You have punished others for less.

"Because it would cause problems. Besides, in any other situation he would be correct. Crew must obey the captain without hesitation. It is not his fault he cannot know or appreciate what I am or can do."

You are too forgiving.

"You are too shortsighted."

CHAPTER 18

"How is Raijaun progressing in his training?" Azerick asked Ellyssa.

"He is extremely talented, and the way he weaves his magic is almost an art form, but he is still holding back. I have tried everything to get him to push himself, but he just won't do it."

"It has been nearly a year since Bruneford's Mill, but I think it still frightens him. He has little trouble with tasks within the laboratory, and many of those require expending enormous power, so it is not as though he lacks the ability."

"What do you want me to do?"

"Just keep training him as you have. I will talk with him more, but ultimately, I think he will have to overcome it on his own. I do need you to go get Aggie for me before you go back to the field."

"Okay."

Ellyssa disappeared and Azerick delved back into the Codex Arcana in an attempt to unlock its mysteries. The amount of knowledge recorded in its pages was mind-blowing, but the true challenge was asking it the right questions. Azerick had been studying the creation of permanent, stable gateways for months, but his attempts to create one had met with mixed success.

"The Little General said you wanted to see me," Aggie said from the doorway.

Azerick looked up and smiled at the old wizard's use of Ellyssa's nickname. "I do. I am struggling with something with which I hope you can help."

"So the mighty Lord Giles and his magically savant son found a problem they can't solve, and now they call upon the old crone to bail them out," Aggie taunted.

"Pretty much, yes."

"How long you been wrestling with it?"

"Aggressively? About three months."

"It took you three months to overcome your pride and ask for help?"

"Something like that," Azerick said sheepishly.

Aggie responded with a knowing grunt. "Typical man. Although I have seen some take half their lives to set aside their pride, so I guess you didn't do too badly. What has you stymied?"

"When I was captured by the psylings, I saw a gate in the middle of the sea. It transported the entire ship and crew to their city. I want to duplicate it here so we can evacuate the populations of Southport and North Haven to Brightridge and Brelland."

"You haven't found anything in the codex?" Aggie asked, surprised that the god-sent book did not have the answer.

"I found plenty, but the best-explained theory can prove to be an insurmountable task without practical experience. I'm sure Ken could tell me how to forge a sword, but the resulting product would likely be a disaster."

"Your increased wisdom continues to astound me. Transdimensional magic is one of the toughest and most dangerous studies a wizard can delve into. Gates like you are talking about require a multitude of points to perfectly fall in sync, and the farther apart the points, the greater the difficulty."

Azerick nodded. "It is akin to threading a needle with an arrow from hundreds of miles away."

"No, it is akin to threading a thousand needles and every shot having to be perfect. There are no retries. One point not in perfect alignment can result in disaster."

"That is what I have observed with my experiments. The fact Ellyssa was able to make one to take her a few miles to North Haven is incredible."

"Lucky would be a better term. She was foolish and had no idea how dangerous and close to disaster she was. She was a hair's breadth from doing the Academy's job of executing her for them."

"Do you think we can pull it off? Aggie, my entire plan hinges on these gates. Without them, I do not think we can survive this."

Aggie sighed and looked at the ceiling as if silently beseeching the gods for guidance. "We're really in a mess, aren't we?"

"We are. One which even my most ardent supporters probably do not fully appreciate."

"If it were anyone else, I'd say we were all well and truly screwed. But I have seen Raijaun at practice, and his ability to manipulate the subtlest strands of magic is nothing less than astounding. With the two of you, I think we have a shot."

Azerick and Aggie sat down with Raijaun the next morning and explained what they wanted to attempt. Raijaun nodded along as Azerick laid out what he had learned from the Codex Arcana, and Aggie filled in some of the finer details of creating such a gate.

"Do you think you can join the strands of magic between the two gates?" Azerick asked his son.

"It is possible, but it will not be easy. How big and how far apart will these gates be?"

"I want to create a small one between here and Southport. There are things happening that will soon require my ability to travel there quickly."

"That is a very long distance to attempt a stable gateway. The strands cannot bend, which means we will have to take into account the curvature of the world and align the gates almost perfectly on their x and y axes."

Aggie smiled at the young creature. "Such a brilliant young man."

"Can you do it?"

"I understand the math involved. We will need help from one or more of your best engineers to align the stones."

"It is more than just the alignment that has to be perfect," Aggie said. "Each of the runes must be a perfect match on each of the gate pillars as well. This will require the work of a master stone carver and possibly an artist to draw and chisel the sigils."

The physical work took several painstaking days of drawing out and carving the identical structures. Azerick ordered the stone pillars destined for Southport to be loaded on one of his swifter ships while he, Raijaun, and a crew of engineers carted the other two pieces into the woods to the south.

Wolf and Ghost emerged from the trees as Raijaun and the engineers studied the complex mathematics written across several pieces of parchment. A team of workers using a series of levers and ropes positioned the stones as surveyors and engineers called out instructions to make minute shifts in the heavy pillars.

"What are you doing?" Wolf asked as he watched the humans placing the pillars.

"Creating a gate," Azerick answered.

"I won't pretend to understand wizards, but what use is a gate without a fence?"

"Not that kind of gate, Wolf. It is a magical gate that will allow me to travel to Southport."

"I see. Why is it in my woods?"

Azerick gave the wildling a look but let his possessiveness go. "It works both ways, and I would rather not have unexpected guests showing up in the school."

"Why do I have to deal with unexpected guests?" Wolf demanded.

"Because I know no one is going to sneak into your woods without you knowing. Besides, you do not have people who want you dead."

"That's true. You should probably take a good look at your people skills."

"I will take your criticism under advisement."

Raijaun interrupted the banter. "Father, we have the stones placed as best we can. You should let me go to Southport instead. It would make aligning them much easier."

"It is too dangerous. I prefer you to stay here. We have the equations and the speaking stones. You can guide us in their alignment from here."

Azerick thought about Daebian as the ship carried him and the gate pillars toward Southport. He once again considered contacting Zeb to check up on him, but Azerick doubted Daebian would appreciate it.

The boy was fiercely independent despite Miranda's insistence about his desire for his attention. Zeb should be nearing his return run, and Daebian would be back in a couple of weeks anyway.

That is what he kept telling Miranda every time she asked him to look in on their son. He kept making excuses, most of them involving not having the time and assuring her Daebian was fine and in good hands with Zeb. He wondered how badly he was botching his job as a husband and father and if he could ever repair the damage. There would be a great deal of rebuilding when this war was over, his marriage and the relationship with his family amongst them.

Azerick fed arcane power into the wind and willed it to speed him to Southport. It was a subtle type of magic; one he could maintain for hours with little concentration. It was just enough to distract him from his morose thoughts.

The schooner carried no other cargo, so clearing Southport's customs was a swift affair. The crew loaded the heavy pillars onto a wagon drawn by a team of sturdy draft horses. Azerick's group had barely cleared the docks when a contingent of wizards led by Headmaster Florent barred their path.

"Lord Giles, I would know what business you have in Southport," the headmaster said without preamble.

Azerick looked at the dozen wizards accompanying Headmaster Florent and assumed there were several more hiding nearby. "I own the largest shipping company in the kingdom. It occasionally requires my attention. What business is it of yours?"

"You represent an arcane threat to the Academy and the kingdom. That makes it my business."

"I am trying to protect the kingdom. The only threat to it is your stubborn refusal to prepare for its defense," Azerick countered.

"I refuse to kowtow to the likes of you and your grand delusions. The Academy is prepared to deal with whatever threat arises. If you step foot on Academy grounds, we will consider it a hostile act and act accordingly."

"I have no intention of visiting the Academy. My business lies elsewhere. Now, unless you wish to strain our relationship any further,

I request that you remove yourselves from my path and let me go about it."

Maureen turned her eyes to the canvas-covered cargo on the wagon. Azerick knew she was examining it for traces of magic, but she would not find any. He would not imbue them with power until they were in place.

"I warn you, Lord Giles, do not approach the Academy."

"Of course, Headmaster, you know how much I appreciate a good warning."

The headmaster glared at Azerick for several moments before turning and walking away with her contingent. Azerick waited a few minutes before ordering his men to move out. He knew Maureen was having him watched, so he chose a route that would take him through some narrow streets with little traffic. It would force anyone watching him to follow or risk losing them in the city.

The two wizards waited until Azerick and his group turned the corner before entering the street and following. It was not an easy feat to disappear with a laden wagon, so there was no need to shadow them closely. As the wizards cautiously made their way down the narrow street, a pair of large men entered the confining passageway and blocked their egress.

"Well now, it looks like we found us a couple fancy lads," one of the men said. "Are you two out for a nice walk together then?"

"We are on official Academy business. You had best not interfere and be on your way if you know what's good for you," one of the wizards warned.

The thug raised his hands. "Oh, we don't want no trouble with the Academy."

"Good, you're smarter than you look."

"Aye, but they might."

The two mages slapped at the back of their necks as something stung them just before they dropped to the ground.

"Well now, let's see what goodies they got under them fancy clothes," the speaker chuckled. The four men lifted everything of value with practiced hands. "Come to think of it, I bet them clothes would fetch a nice price."

Azerick and his crew reached a lesser gate at the outer northeast wall. A man in fine clothing and sporting a fancy hat large enough to look ridiculous on anyone else pushed off the wall and fell in step next to Azerick.

"Andrill," Azerick greeted him.

"Azerick Sir."

"I have not seen anyone from the Academy pathetically trying to follow me for some time. I assume you got my message?"

"Indeed I did. Still flouting authority, I see."

"There are occasions on which authority requires flouting."

Andrill chuckled. "It's a shame you followed such a disreputable path. You would have made a fine thief."

"We cannot all find a virtuous life like yourself."

"How is your apprentice these days?"

"She went through an ordeal, but I think she came out better for it. She is quite resilient."

"I trust she found some appreciation in my gift? I had hoped it would assuage some of the hard feelings between us."

"I think she understands. She has achieved a measure of wisdom through her trials."

"And what about you?"

"I understand. If I did not, you would be dead now."

Andrill responded with a nod. During the course of his life, he had been threatened by some of the most dangerous men and women from the highest and lowest elements of society, but none had ever filled him with such certainty of being able to fulfill that threat. It was in that moment Andrill truly understood that this was no longer the angry boy he had met all those years ago, but a man who knew precisely who and what he was.

"Well, I'm glad we're friends." Andrill extended his hand. "I wish you luck in all your endeavors."

Azerick shook the man's hand. "I am glad we are friends as well. There is a terrible storm coming, Andrill. Be prepared for it."

"I have received some weather reports. We are ready to move when it blows in."

Azerick's troop did not travel far beyond the outermost walls of Southport. The site Azerick had chosen for the gate was only a short distance beyond the Martial Academy's parade ground. He cast several wards to prevent any magical or mundane spying before ordering the engineers to erect the stones. It took two hours of constant, minute adjustments before Raijaun declared them in alignment and several more hours for him to connect the strands of magic joining them.

Azerick stood back and studied his son's work from afar while the engineers and surveyors played dice or found other ways to pass the time. There were thousands of web-thin strands of arcane energy connecting the pair of gates, each one crucial to perfectly sync them to warp time and space. Anything out of alignment could cause part of anyone using it to arrive at the far gate at a different time or location than the rest of them.

"It is as perfect as I can make it, Father," Raijaun said through the speaking stone.

"I can detect no flaws. I have faith in you."

Azerick fed power into the stones and brought them to life. Tiny arcs of stray energy sparkled along the pillars' surface and the space between them. A shimmering veil appeared between the pillars and resolved into an image of a changed landscape. To the casual eye, it looked as though a slice of distant forest had been cut out and dropped in the clearing.

Azerick turned to his men. "Would you like to follow me home?"

"I think we'll take the boat, if it's all the same to you."

Azerick smiled, gave the men a wave, and stepped through the gate. The familiar feeling of disorientation washed over him as two hundred miles flew by in the blink of an eye. His demonic form minimized the discomfort, but it was going to cause mayhem on the cities' populations when they used the enormous gates he planned to construct.

He emerged from the gate in North Haven and stood before Raijaun. His son's face was etched with concern.

"I would call that an unparalleled success," Azerick said.

"What now, Father?"

"Now comes the hard part. We must take what we have learned, make it bigger with an even greater distance between gates, and create instructions for a team of wizards to duplicate it. Neither of us has the time to devote to making these gates ourselves."

"Do you think the Academy will listen to you this time?"

"They will soon have no choice."

"Azerick, Zeb's ship has returned!" Miranda exclaimed excitedly.

Azerick looked up from his desk and put down his quill. "Is Daebian with him?"

"Of course he is. They should be almost here by now."

Azerick stood and allowed Miranda to pull him up the stairs and out of the tower. Zeb and Daebian were just inside the gates and approaching the tower when Azerick and Miranda emerged. The instant Daebian appeared Miranda dropped Azerick's hand, rushed forward, and wrapped her arms around her son.

"Are you all right? Don't you ever run off like that again!"

"I'm fine, Mother. I got to go to Bakhtaran and we were attacked by pirates!"

"Pirates! You could have been killed!"

"I'm fine, Mother!" Daebian insisted again.

"Well, you're home now. Come inside and get something to eat. You also need a bath. You stink."

"I'm a sailor! Sailors are supposed to stink."

"When you are not on a ship, you are the grandson of the duchess and no longer allowed to stink."

Miranda hustled Daebian toward the tower. Daebian smiled and gave Azerick a cheerful wave.

"Pirates?" Azerick asked as Zeb stepped next to him.

"We gotta talk."

"All right. How did Daebian do on the ship?" Azerick asked as he led Zeb to his study.

"He's a fine sailor. He'd have made your father proud. He worked hard and never once complained, even when my swabby foreman set him on cleaning the bilge by himself."

"That's a crew task."

"Aye, but I guess he had something to prove, or maybe the boy said something he didn't care for. I don't know. He got himself knifed in Southport for lifting a purse. Funny thing is I never took him for a thief, and I like to think I'm a pretty good judge of character."

"You think Daebian may have set him up?"

"I don't know. I didn't even think about it until after the pirates attacked us."

"Tell me about that. What happened?"

"We were about a day into Sumaran waters when two pirate ships ran us down. We were already outnumbered, but they had a wizard of some kind on board as well. If your son hadn't come up with the idea to string nets and line above the bulwarks, they would'a swarmed over even faster. Even so, it wasn't looking good for us, I can tell you. I ordered your boy to lock himself in my cabin and stay there. He didn't listen. He came out and stabbed a man."

Azerick nodded sympathetically. "I was near his apparent age when I first killed a man, and Daebian's mental maturity is even greater than his appearance. It is a hard thing to understand."

"How did ya feel when you killed him?"

"It was just after my mother had been murdered. He grabbed me in an alley. I was scared, angry, and I did what I had to do. I did not regret it, but I wished I had not been in that alley."

"Aye, that's how a man should feel when he takes a life. It's an unpleasant necessity on occasion, but you don't take no joy in it. He smiled, Azerick. A man shouldn't have that look in his eyes unless he's with a woman. He stuck the man in the gut and smiled as he watched the life go out in his eyes. Then he disappeared. He got onto the pirate ship and raised all kinds of havoc over there. I don't know what he did or how he did it, but that captain called his crew back even though they had us done for."

"What do you think happened?"

"I don't know, but that captain raised sails and made for the horizon as if Sharrellan herself was on his heels."

"Daebian never said what happened?"

"He never said a word other than he killed the wizard and made the captain call back his men. He just went about his business with a smile like nothing ever happened. I don't want to speak ill of your boy, but there is something not right in him. There's darkness in his heart, and I don't see anything good coming from him. I won't ever sail him on my ship again. I'll retire first."

Azerick sighed heavily and clapped Zeb on the shoulder. "If he ever sneaks into your ship again, put him off at the nearest port. He can find his way from there. I'm sorry about that, Zeb. I know there is something off with him, but I just don't know what it is or what to do about it."

"Well, he comes from good stock. Maybe he'll straighten out when he's older."

They were kind words, but neither man really believed it. Daebian was an enigma and far from a passive one. Azerick was certain he had a large role to play in their destiny, but what part he could not begin to fathom.

CHAPTER 19

Weeks passed without any more trouble from Daebian. Apparently, his adventure on the high seas had cooled whatever fire burned within him. Raijaun walked briskly from the small summoning room and went in search of his father. As usual, he found Azerick in his main laboratory poring over the Codex Arcana. Azerick did not look up from his studies as his son entered.

"Father, I discovered a weakening in the barrier."

"I told you I did not want you to go there alone. Any mistake in making repairs could weaken it further. Besides, it is more important that you focus on your training for now."

"I know, Father, but training is finished for the day and I thought to study the Scions and the barrier in more detail. The flaw is rather substantial and could soon become a breach."

"I am aware of it. I found it several days ago," Azerick replied nonchalantly.

Raijaun did not understand his father's seemingly disinterested attitude. Weaknesses in the barrier were almost common now, but Azerick had always been quick to repair them, often asking Raijaun for his help in doing so.

"What are we going to do about it?"

"Nothing."

"Father, I do not understand. The weakness is large, and many of the Scions minions could get through; far more than in Bruneford's Mill."

"I have warned against as much, yet people still fight me. People vital in our defense ignore my warnings and withhold their full support. If they continue to do so, we stand no chance at victory. Do you understand?"

"Where will it open?" Raijaun asked quietly.

"Somewhere near the Academy grounds."

"A lot of people will die. A lot of children."

Azerick nodded. "This is true, but a lot more children will die if the Academy and the nobles continue to resist my efforts to prepare. They ignored what happened at Bruneford's Mill because they are far from that place and the people there have little voice in the heart of the kingdom. They ignored my warnings even when I showed them the face of our enemy. Due to their arrogance, they refuse to acknowledge them as the threat they are. Commoners will rally and take up arms if they perceive a threat, because they are accustomed to bearing the brunt of the harm. The powerful and privileged feel secure in their strength and often ignore a threat until it draws the blood of their own. Do you now understand?"

"I do, Father, but I do not like it."

Azerick finally looked up from his book and smiled at his son. "It pleases me to hear you say that. One of us must keep a warm heart, and I am afraid mine has frozen to the core."

"It is time to exploit the weakening," Xar told his fellows.

"I sense the false Guardian's presence upon it. I find it suspect he did not repair it like so many others," Zyn said.

"Obviously he wishes us to use it, but for what end?" Arhal asked.

Kaz asked, *"Where does it lead?"*

"I sense a powerful conglomeration at its exit point. I suspect it leads to either their precious Academy or Hall of Inquisition. It is certainly in the kingdom the humans call Valeria."

"Why leave it to allow us to exploit it? What is his gain?"

"*Knowing the arrogance of humans, many resist him, and he wishes to make a point or punish them. Their wizards in particular are far too confident in their power, and he wishes to create some much-needed insecurity.*"

"*What should we do?*"

"*Oblige him, of course.*"

"*You want to help the humans unite against us? I fail to see the logic in that,*" Doaz said.

"*That is because you were never one for understanding the mentality of the humans. We want them to be at their absolute strongest when we crush them. The few we allow to live will know their pathetic kind was at its strongest point in history. This will sap the will of our supplicants to ever attempt to overthrow us in the future for we will never allow them to attain any such strength again. It is not enough to defeat them; we must crush their spirit and any hope of ever resisting us again.*"

"*Wise as always. Let us then make the breach.*"

The five Scions gathered around the crystal and placed their hands upon its smooth surface. The searing beam of light lanced out from the floating fortress and stabbed the barrier with its awesome intensity. The barrier warped and wavered for a mile in every direction until the incredible power of the Scions overcame its resolve to keep the horrible masses at bay.

Headmaster Florent sat bolt upright in her bed as she sensed the destruction of several of the Academy wards. She had barely gotten her robes wrapped around her when there came a furious knocking on her door. Maureen grabbed her staff, cast a series of protective wards upon her person, and opened the door from a distance with a simple spell.

A fellow mage burst into the room, blood evident on his robes. "Headmaster, creatures are breaching our wards and swarming the grounds!"

"Where?" the headmaster demanded.

"Everywhere! There are thousands of them!"

Fear warred with rage at knowing her school was under siege. Never in the history of man had the Academy been attacked, much less infiltrated and its populace threatened.

"Rouse the cadre, tell them to arm themselves as quickly as they can, and make for the nearest student dorms. We must protect the children."

"Should they go to the artifact vault first, Headmaster?"

"There is no time. It takes three councilmembers and the vault master to open it. They will have to go as they are and do their best. Once we gather the students together, perhaps then we can detach a group to the vault."

The two wizards were running down the steps of the headmaster's tower when a hellish chorus of terrified cries resounded up the spiraling stone staircase. Maureen's blood turned to ice at what those screams portended.

"Dear gods above, the novice quarters," she whispered, breaking into a sprint, heedless of moving so quickly down the treacherous stairs.

The headmaster's tower residence was the closest to the novice quarters with the exception of that of the master of novices. There were only a few hundred feet of hallways to traverse once she and the junior wizard reached the bottom floor. Just as they reached the ground level, explosions and the crackling of unleashed magic helped drown out the cries of the young children.

The pair sprinted around the corner and nearly ran into the rear ranks of ravagers as they piled through an adjoining hallway, bent on reaching the novice quarters and the young mages inside. Wilfred, the young wizard, looked to the headmaster for instruction, but Maureen was already channeling the Source. The headmaster lowered the tip of her staff, using the power it contained to focus and amplify her magic, and unleashed a great ball of fire that nearly filled the hall from wall to wall. The fiery orb rolled away from her and picked up speed, leaving the passageway filled with the ravagers' blackened corpses. When the miniature sun nearly reached the entranceway of the novices' quarters, it exploded back in the direction from which it came, catching any ravagers not killed in the initial attack as well as the new ones already filling the corridor in its fiery blast.

"Wilfred, shield us please," Maureen said calmly as the wall of fire raced toward them both.

Wilfred was a young wizard with lackluster talent, but self-protective wards were minor magic for the most part, and even the least amongst them could effect a reasonable amount of protection. Wilfred hastily raised a ward just before Headmaster Florent's fiery blast washed over them.

"Keep these creatures from reaching us, Wilfred, so I may deal with them."

Her devastating assault did not end the fight, but at least the ravagers were now more focused on her than trying to get at the children. Maureen sent more fire, lightning, and pure arcane power scything through the ranks of murderous creatures. Even her awesome magic was unable to destroy them faster than they piled into the hallway, completely heedless of the death around them. Several broke through Maureen's assault and struck Wilfred's ward, their blades casting blue sparks as they tried to stab through.

Headmaster Florent adjusted her attacks to deal with those who got close before they could break through Wilfred's ward. The two wizards continued to fight their way to the novices' quarters under the constant harrying of ravagers. Another heavy knot of hellish creatures threw themselves into Maureen's cleansing mage fire, some striking against the invisible shield. A smaller, blue-skinned creature pressed through the ranks of ravagers, but the headmaster dismissed it as a lesser threat and chose to deal with the bigger, stronger ravagers first.

It was a fatal mistake. The bone blade gripped in the creature's hand cut through Wilfred's ward as if it were tissue paper. The ravager leapt onto his chest and sank its knife into the young man's neck several times before Maureen could even register the breach. She conjured a sphere of force around herself before exploding it outward, flinging back the host of attackers.

Whatever ability the blue-skinned creature had to destroy wards, it did nothing to protect it from her mage fire. She incinerated it before it could regain its feet and turn that blackened bone knife on her. Still the ravagers poured into the hall, and Maureen realized she was not going to be able to kill them all before they overwhelmed her. The senior archmage pointed her staff at the ceiling of the hallway leading outside and brought down the entire length of stone overhead, effectively sealing the passage.

She had no time to waste. It would likely not take long for the creatures to find another way through, and the sounds of resistance emanating from the novice quarters had ceased moments ago. Maureen ran down the passageway, destroying the few remaining ravagers with her magic. She burst into the first dorm room and nearly collapsed. The chamber housing a dozen children was a charnel house, its walls awash in blood.

Maureen could not afford to allow grief to weigh her down as more screams reached her ears, children crying out for help from the rooms farthest down the hall. There would be time for mourning later, if they survived. She did not pause to look into the dorms as she ran past them. They were as silent as a midnight graveyard, and the cries of the living called out louder than the silent pleadings of the ghosts.

The headmaster found a knot of ravagers trying to claw and cut their way through a thick mass of sticky, web-like strands crisscrossing the length of the hallway. The magically slicked floor made it even more difficult for the monsters to breach the webs and reach the rooms where terrified survivors huddled together for support.

Maureen used her magic to take control of the novices' spell, turning the webs into living things that reached out and wrapped around the ravagers. The creatures writhed like insects caught in a spider's trap until the headmaster transmuted the strands into razor-sharp glass. With the clenching of her shaking fist, the glass contracted and cut the ravagers to pieces. She did not see or hear any more of the bestial men and dispelled the minor defensive magics. She found several of the doorways leading into the dorm rooms barricaded with what was probably every piece of furniture in the rooms. Not a sound emanated from behind the barriers.

"Children?" Maureen called out.

"Headmaster Florent?" a young voice answered.

Tears of joy sprang to her eyes at hearing the voices of her students as they began whispering excitedly to each other. "Yes, children. Help me tear down these barriers. We must be away from here and find the others."

The sound of shifting furniture broke the quiet of the death-shrouded hall. It took several minutes to move the barricades and for the first few young mages to step warily into the hall. The oldest were the first to peek around the doorway before daring to step fully out of their rooms, but the younger students followed as the older ones passed back the all-clear.

"I am so proud of all of you!" Headmaster Florent gushed as she hugged several of her students. "Come, let us find the others."

"Are they all gone, Headmaster?" one young girl asked.

Maureen felt a slight tremble in the stone beneath her feet and could hear the faint sounds of battle echoing from somewhere within the Academy. "No, I am afraid they are not. We must find the others and fight together. I want you all to stay very close to me. Those of you who can, focus on slowing the creatures. Defensive magic only unless there is no other choice."

Maureen did a quick head count and tallied seventy-three novices. Seventy-three out of a roster of two hundred forty-seven. Had she not had the lives of those seventy-three counting on her, she might well have crumpled to the floor and wept until the ravagers found their way back and tore her to pieces.

She paused only briefly to call into the devastated rooms she had passed over to reach the survivors. Her heart leapt when a voice called out from beneath a bed or from inside an overturned wardrobe. One young girl stepped out of the corner of her room, breaking the perfect illusion she had cast to hide. Thirteen more novices clung to their headmaster as they left the dead behind but not forgotten.

The group, led by the headmaster, ran into the first ravagers soon after leaving the novice dorms. They were thankfully few, and Maureen dispatched them. As they grew nearer to the journeyman wing of the Academy, the sounds of conflict grew louder. Headmaster Florent called out into the dorms and received a few replies after several heartrending moments.

The dorm farthest from the hall was sealed much like she had found at the novices' dorm. Seventeen terrified young boys and girls, most of them barely into their teens, stepped into the hall and looked upon their headmaster and the gaggle of younger novices.

"What happened here? Where are the rest of the journeymen?" Maureen asked softly.

A young man spoke up. "Magus Morgarum and Magus Sorenson came just as those creatures attacked. They were able to hold them back long enough to get most of us out, but not all. Headmaster, they killed us! They killed us like animals!"

"I know, but we must all be strong. What is your name?"

"Eric, Headmaster."

"What happened next, Eric?"

Eric swallowed hard and continued in a quavering voice. "Magus Morgarum and Sorenson were leading us toward the apprentice dorms. A group of those monsters came from one of the side passages and split our group. They tried to get to us, but there were too many and we were dying so fast. We ran back here. Those of us who made it barricaded ourselves in our room and warded it as best we could. Marian thought they might be able to smell us, and Jonah thought they might be sensing our magic ability, so we sealed the room from smell and scrying as best we could. I don't know if it worked, but the ones that chased us finally left. Maybe there were others easier to get to, I don't know."

"You did well, Eric. You all did well," Headmaster Florent said, encompassing the group with her eyes. "I know you are all frightened, but we must control our fear and fight."

"But they'll kill us!" a girl cried out.

"Yes, child, they will kill some of us. I will not lie to you. More of us will die tonight, but I for one will pull as many of these creatures into my grave with me as I can. Now buck up and act like wizards! We are the pride of the kingdom, and we will act as such. If we die, it will be with our hands around the throats of our enemies, not cowering in fear as they slaughter us like sheep! Are you sheep, or are you wolves?"

"Wolves!" the children cried out.

"Then let us find the rest of our pack, cast these interlopers out of our den, and drive them from our territory!"

Headmaster Florent led her pack of pups toward the apprentice quarters and soon faced the first sign of real resistance since fighting her way to the novices. Swarms of the creatures piled in through side passages as lightning and fire scythed through their ranks. It was apparent there was an organized resistance beyond the mass of ravagers, and by full wizards, not just students.

Maureen broiled the tightest mass of ravagers alive with a powerful ball of fire while her strongest students used their lesser magic to slow and force the creatures into tighter groups where large area spells like her fireball could kill more of them at once. Desperate to reach the others, Headmaster Florent brought down the roof of the hallway giving the ravagers the greatest access to their position. Their flow of reinforcements momentarily squeezed off, it took only minutes for her to get her small band of children pressed into the larger ranks of those battling within the apprentice dorms' small, open courtyard.

"Headmaster, the gods be praised you made it!" the chubby alchemy instructor, Magus Morgarum, exclaimed. "You brought the novices! But where are the rest?"

Maureen shook her head sadly. "This is all of them now."

Magus Morgarum's hand flew to his mouth. "Dear gods. We tried to go to them, but the creatures had us completely cut off. There was no way for us to go that direction and survive. Magus Sorenson and I thought it more prudent to reach the apprentices."

The headmaster nodded her agreement. "You did well. I see many adepts here also."

"Yes. Magus Douglas and several other members of the staff brought them this way when they detected the outer wards fail. We have been defending the inner courtyard, since it is the only area large enough to accommodate us all and rotate out our defenders. The problem is that courtyard has too many entrances and the beasts are unrelenting in trying to reach us."

"It was wise, but we cannot stay here. The position cannot hold forever. We need to reach the outer courtyard between the adept and journeyman wings. That leaves us surrounded on three sides by buildings and gives us a larger front where we can destroy greater numbers with our more powerful spells. I fear we will exhaust ourselves before the enemy exhausts their numbers if we continue to fight smaller, pitched battles. We will collapse the halls behind us to prevent the creatures from coming at our rear."

"Collapse the halls! But the Academy?"

Headmaster Florent pointed at the children. "This is the Academy." She stabbed at the high walls of the courtyard. "This is just a building, and I will bury these monsters beneath its last stone if I must! Wards are insufficient. The little blue men seem to be capable of piercing them with ease."

The alchemy teacher nodded. "Yes, we learned that the hard way. Magus Clayton thought he could block one of the hallways leading into the courtyard while we defended the others. He was successful until one of the blue ones leapt right through and cut him down. We lost a dozen fighters pushing the monsters back out before we could control that egress once more."

"Has anyone attempted to scry where these things came from? I cannot imagine they marched through the city on their way here."

"Magus Pugh!" Magus Morgarum called out. "Megan, what have you discovered of the creatures' arrival?"

"Headmaster!" Magus Megan Pugh called out as she jogged over. "I discovered a temporal disturbance out on the far maneuver training grounds. I believe it is closed now."

"How many of these creatures do you guess could have made it through?"

"It was not open long, but it was substantial. Given what Sorcerer Giles showed us of their army, I would guess at least two thousand could have made it through, if not more."

The headmaster looked doubtful. "We are assuming what he showed us was not a contrived image of his own delusions."

"These are hardly delusions, Headmaster," Magus Morgarum stressed.

"Are we sure they are not his creations?" Maureen countered. "Megan, were you able to ascertain the nature of magic involved?"

"The only thing I can say is...otherworldly. It was completely alien to me. It was neither Source generated nor abyssal in origin, both of which we all detected on the sorcerer."

"I suppose it is irrelevant at the moment. Right now, we need to get out of this box before they smash it flat with us in it. We shall collapse all the passages leading in and make our way to the outer courtyard where we can establish a proper front. Instruct apprentices and below to focus on defending the adepts and wizards while they crush these creatures. Kill any of those little blue buggers immediately."

The wizards relayed the headmaster's orders, collapsing the hallways behind them as they fought through the only open passageway to the outer courtyard. Ravagers still came at them from the front, striking with fearsome speed and ferocity at every side passage they passed. Those halls, the mages simply collapsed as they reached them, burying the invaders and preventing them from harassing their rear as they fought to reach the grounds of their final stand.

When they achieved the outer courtyard, the host of ravagers seemed to be waiting. Headmaster Florent and the four remaining councilmembers created a beachhead, clearing the courtyard and driving the monsters back onto the open maneuver grounds. The buildings provided forty-foot walls on three sides, leaving a hundred and fifty-foot opening to the maneuver field in which to defend. Maureen called her senior wizards forward to hold the front, supported by the junior mages who created wards to slow the ravagers' charge and shield their fellows as they exacted a terrible death toll upon the invaders.

"The hallway behind us should be secure. That is where we shall treat our wounded. I want the adepts evenly distributed between the full wizards. I want no weak points," the headmaster ordered. "Magus Morgarum, were you able to bring any healing potions with you?"

The alchemy teacher held up a small wooden chest. "I had the foresight to grab these from my chambers before I ran out. I am afraid I have already used half of them."

"We will do the best we can with what we have. You know best how to use them, so stay back at our makeshift infirmary and see to the wounded."

"Yes, Headmaster."

"Gods, I would sell my soul to Sharrellan for a couple of Chosen right now," Maureen said to no one in particular.

Magus King hustled to her side. "Headmaster, the creatures appear to be massing. There are at least a thousand of them!"

"Bring up our strongest forces and prepare to repel them. Have those unable to reach the front focus on defensive wards to…"

Her words were cut short as a dark figure dropped from the sky, plunging its black blade into the councilman's neck. Maureen stabbed out with her magic, searing a hole through the creature's chest. She looked up and scanned the high walls.

"'Ware the roofs! They are jumping from the roofs!"

A dozen more ravagers dropped from the roofs and lower ledges of the surrounding buildings, bringing chaos to the center and rear of her battered army. The main host of ravagers struck the front and Headmaster Florent watched her people being pushed back. They were dying. As the battle raged around her, she closed her eyes and spared a moment to pray.

"Dear gods, forgive this fool and preserve us."

A sharp clarion call split the air, and the courtyard thrummed with the rapid staccato of charging horses.

Commandant James Reese had read the report from Bruneford's Mill and even traveled there to see the destruction for himself. He interviewed dozens of survivors. He knew peasants were prone to exaggeration, but weighing their recounting with the evidence he saw, he knew the attack for what it was; an initial sortie to gauge the strength of the enemy and cause widespread fear before an invasion. It was an effective tactic when one was certain they had the advantage of strength.

He had gotten a copy of Lord Giles's training doctrine and found it impressive, if a bit extreme. After his return from Bruneford's Mill, he requested copies made for his cadre, but the fools at the Magus Academy had refused to entertain the sorcerer's ideas. Fortunately, the

Scholars' Academy loved nothing more than reading and penning and provided him with a dozen manuals within weeks.

His cadre enforced standards only put into effect during times of war. That meant sleeping with arms and armor under bunks instead of locked in the armory, static and roving patrols guarding the grounds at all times during the day and night, and frequent readiness drills. When he ordered a muster, his troops had ten minutes to don armor, grab weapons, and form ranks before the main building. After more than a year of intense drilling, his soldiers grumbled of the hardships placed upon them. But that intensity was going to pay off this night in lives saved.

"Lancers, at the ready!" the commandant ordered, then paused as his officers relayed his command. "Charge!"

Five hundred mounted lancers charged the fearsome creatures laying siege to the Magus Academy. It pained him to know his response was slow, but none of his sentries survived to sound the alarm, and only the hellish sound of wizards doing battle had roused his men. Whether it was sheer luck or design that caused the invaders to largely ignore his sleeping troops and go straight for the mages, he did not know. Regardless of the reason, he counted it a blessing. Had these monsters caught him flat-footed, there would be no reinforcements and little chance of anyone surviving.

His lancers crashed into the massed ranks of ravagers with a resounding clash of steel, flesh, and snapping lance hafts. The cavalry did not pause to draw steel. Instead, the riders wheeled their mounts and raced back to their lines. The attack had taken the ravagers by surprise, but their swiftness allowed them to pull many of the riders from their mounts before they could be safely away.

The commandant watched the ravagers give chase, and although they were not faster than his horses as the townsfolk had said, they were incredibly swift.

"Auxiliary lancers, ready! Charge!"

Three hundred more cavalry charged toward the onrushing horde, passing so close between their own retreating fellows they could feel the air rushing through their visors. Seconds later, they struck and greatly slowed the bulk of the charging ravagers. The cavalry pressed through and did not slow their charge until well clear of the creatures.

Knowing they could not catch the horses, the ravagers continued to charge the formed ranks of humans in front of them. Fearlessly, they threw themselves against the shields and spears of the weak and hated humans despite their decreased numbers.

This was where Commandant Reese would see how well this new battle doctrine worked against these monsters. Instead of men carrying swords and shields, the bulwark of his footmen wielded spears with large, rectangular shields capable of locking together at their edges. A fist-sized hole set in the right side of the shield allowed the spear to thrust into their enemies' bodies without creating an opening and making them vulnerable.

The two armies clashed and the greater strength of the ravagers pushed his first, then second and third ranks back, but the fourth rank held as the fifth rank braced their shields against their fellows' backs. Spears stabbed out of the holes in the shields, finding any bit of exposed red flesh presenting itself.

Against a human army, the assault would have ended there, but ravagers farther back leapt over the heads of their brethren and landed within the deeper ranks of soldiers, slashing and clawing. A lesser army may have succumbed to panic against such an alien attack, but these were not conscripts or even common soldiers. The Academy produced officers and knights, men whose training made them elite amongst any army in the known world. The rear ranks wielded swords and smaller shields and did not waver. They laid steel into their enemy without balking even as their friends died around them.

Headmaster Florent breathed a sigh of relief and whispered thanks to the gods and to Commandant Reese as his men drew the bulk of ravagers away from her people. But now was not the time to lick their wounds. Despite numerical superiority, the martial students were hard-pressed and dying.

"Wizards and adepts, forward! Apprentices and dorm masters, stay with the others and guard yourselves," the headmaster ordered.

It was a long run to reach the soldiers, especially after such an exhausting ordeal, but the mages used the Source to feed their weary muscles. The wizards reached out with their magic, sending huge balls of fire exploding into the nearest ranks of ravagers brought to a halt by the unyielding shield wall.

The rear mass of ravagers ceased pushing and leaping over those in front of them and sprinted at the mages who were destroying them from behind. Before they could drown the fires of their hatred in the wizards' blood, the two groups of cavalry thundered into both flanks in perfect formation, seemingly passing through each other like phantoms as they wheeled about for another charge.

Without the bulk of ravagers pressing against them, the footmen pushed forward and began driving the creatures back. Swordsmen ran to the outside flanks of shield bearers and closed the three-sided box upon their enemy, gaining momentum as they hacked their way into them.

Their numbers nearly exhausted, many of the remaining ravagers broke away and fled into the darkness in the direction of the city proper to wreak as much havoc as they could. Commandant Reese ordered a large detachment of cavalry to give chase, rouse the city guard if they were so oblivious to have slept through such chaos, and hunt down every last monster.

The battle was over and Headmaster Florent could not imagine a more bittersweet victory. Large sections of the Academy had been destroyed. The losses at the Scholars' Academy were too horrible to contemplate. With no way of defending themselves, the scholars had been decimated by a small group of ravagers. Once numbering just over a thousand students and faculty, fewer than four hundred had managed to reach and lock themselves within the expansive vaults protecting the most cherished archives in the kingdom.

Tears flowed freely down Headmaster Florent's face as she stood at the entrance to the novice dorms, absorbing the horror that had occurred there. Although all of the student houses suffered terrible losses, the bulk of them had occurred here. The ravagers struck the hardest at those least able to defend themselves.

She continued to stare down the hall as an icy chill crept up her spine. "Did you do this?"

"No," the voice behind her answered.

She stroked the Source, prepared to tear at it with every ounce of her being and unleash it upon the sorcerer. "On your mother's soul!"

"I did not cause this," Azerick said.

Maureen choked on a sob and faced the emotionless sorcerer. "Could you have prevented it?"

Azerick inclined his head ever so slightly.

"Was it easy? Was it easy to make the choice of letting these children die to teach us a lesson?"

"When I compare it to the number who will die if you continue to ignore my warnings and choose not to prepare, yes, it was easy. My people are prepared, the Martial Academy is prepared, or at least preparing, and armies throughout the kingdom and beyond are preparing, but it is not enough. Without the Magus Academy, we will all die."

Maureen shuddered. He was right. Never in their history had the Academy been attacked. She and her people had been confident, arrogantly so, that such a thing could never happen. Despite Lord Giles practically begging them, in his way, to prepare, they chose to ignore his warnings and suffered for their hubris.

"Damn you to the abyss!"

"I have been damned once. I would be surprised if it was the last time."

"Does it at least hurt? Are you even capable of feeling pain or remorse for your choice?"

"Giving in to sentimentality and guilt will kill as surely as the ravagers and the host of other creatures clawing to get at our throats. But yes, it hurts. It was as painful a lesson to teach as to learn, but one none of us can ignore."

"Good, I am glad it hurts. I hope you take the pain to your next grave and, this time, you stay in it! If you were not part of this, how is it you are here already? Did you fly in on your dragon?"

Azerick handed her a thin, leather-bound book. "This is something I have been working on. It explains how to create a stable gateway capable of transporting people hundreds, even thousands, of miles. I saw one when I was taken captive by psylings. It transported the entire ship and crew to their city. I made a small one just outside the walls.

When I sensed the breach in the barrier, I used it to carry me to Southport. You will erect one at each of the city's main gates. My people are already constructing similar gates in North Haven. Yours will take the people to Brightridge, mine to Brelland so we can evacuate the cities."

"You believe Southport and North Haven might fall?"

"There is no might; they will fall. You saw what just a couple thousand ravagers did to the most concentrated and powerful forces in Valeria. Imagine a thousand times that number assaulting our cities. I believe they will come from the sea, ferrying the initial assault force in their flying ships. Once they have secured a beachhead, they will erect gates similar to these to bring the rest through."

Headmaster Florent looked at the book in her hand and to Magus Armand and Magus Sorenson. "Have the vault unsealed. I want every artifact we can use to defend ourselves put into the hands of the staff and every wizard-level mage available to us."

"Headmaster, the council must discuss all of this before we act rashly," Magus Armand replied.

"Look around you! We are the council! The rest are dead along with hundreds of our students! I am declaring martial law and taking command of the Academy."

"Martial Law? Headmaster, such a declaration is reserved for the most desperate times of war!"

"We are at war, Magus," Headmaster Florent stressed. "We have squandered a year of preparation, and I will not let another minute pass. Coordinate with Commandant Reese to begin combined training exercises. I want a copy of Lord Giles's training doctrine in the hands of every staff member by tomorrow. I want two dozen adepts from the most influential families to scour the cities in search of anyone with the propensity for wielding magic. If we can construct these gates quickly, we should be able to find most of them within a few months."

"Headmaster," Magus Armand said, "if you insist upon this overzealous, overreaching demand for power without first gaining the consensus of the staff, I must oppose you on this."

"If you oppose her, you oppose me, Magus," Azerick said simply, but the threat was evident in his voice.

Magus Armand looked to Magus Sorenson but found no support there. "Very well, Headmaster. But when this is through, there will be an inquiry, I promise you."

"If we are alive when this is over, I will welcome it."

"It appears you have things in hand, Headmaster,' Azerick said. "I shall leave you to your creation."

As Azerick walked away, Maureen wondered if his last comment was directed at her efforts to prepare or a final barb for the massacre her failures created this night.

Azerick stumbled through the gate, dropped to his knees, and emptied the contents of his stomach. His entire body shuddered as he tried to wall off the pain of what he allowed to happen this night. It had all been so much worse than he had expected. Whether he underestimated the Academy's ability and strength or the ravagers' resolve and numbers he would never know. In the end, none of it really mattered. Their blood would forever stain his soul. He gulped in several deep breaths before getting to his feet and making his way home.

Wolf watched Azerick from the inky recesses of a tree. He did not know what terrible thing Azerick had done or witnessed, but he was grateful not to have the responsibilities placed upon Azerick's shoulders.

Azerick climbed the stairs, which may as well have been a mountain, to his room. He had not been in his bedroom for weeks since he felt little of the effects of physical fatigue, but this pain was emotional, and it was crushing him beneath its weight. He feared he would collapse at any moment.

He stood for several minutes and watched Miranda as she slept. Her lone form was a testament to one of the many sacrifices he and his family had made, and one of his greatest failures. He needed to reach out to Daebian before he became so lost he might never find his way, but there never seemed to be the time. Both his sons were growing so fast. It was all out of control. Daebian was a man in mind and rapidly approaching adulthood in body as well, Raijaun even more so. His rapid growth, due to his demonic and draconic natures, had him standing a few inches taller than his brother and almost as mature in appearance. How could he possibly manage the defense of an entire kingdom when he had no control over his own family?

Miranda stirred as Azerick conjured a light. "Azerick, what's wrong?" she asked as she blinked against the soft light and saw the remorse carved on his face.

"I murdered a thousand people today, hundreds of them children."

"What?" Miranda exclaimed as she threw her legs over the side of the bed and rushed to Azerick's side.

"Ravagers attacked the Academy tonight. They penetrated the wards around it and caught them unprepared."

"Azerick, you cannot blame yourself."

"Yes, I can. I let it happen. I saw the weakening. I knew where it was going. I chose to ignore it and repaired others of lesser threat instead. I told myself it had to be done."

"Could you not have warned them?"

"No. They would not have believed me, or worse, accused me of masterminding the attack. Even if I had warned them and they prepared for the attack, they would have made excuses afterward, taken half steps, not thinking beyond what they saw tonight. They had to experience the full horror of what we face."

"Then this is what needed to happen. I trust you."

Azerick shuddered. "I wish I could trust myself. I kept telling myself this was the only way, but part of me wanted to punish them, wanted to make them hurt for not listening to me. I am the man who returned from the dead, who spoke to the gods. I am a hero many times over. Who are they to ignore me? I fear there is a tyrant in me, Miranda. There is a tyrant who preaches benevolence until he does not get his due, and I hate him. I am terrified at becoming what I most abhor."

Miranda held him tightly. "I do not think you ever have to fear becoming a tyrant. A true tyrant never doubts himself, never questions his actions or rights. You will always question yourself and do what you know is proper no matter how hard the choices you face. It is why the gods chose you above all others to save us. The gods could have given power to anyone. It is your morality and conviction that cannot be duplicated."

For the first time in months, Azerick lay beside his wife and took comfort in her arms.

CHAPTER 20

Daebian defeated his fourth opponent today, each of them the best the school had to offer. He could even beat Alex two out of five times without using Klaraxis's power. Only Jansen remained as an insurmountable opponent. Even when heightening his physical and mental acuity with the demon's dark power, he barely held his own for the majority of a match.

The day of sparring was over and it was time to feed his demon. Klaraxis whined incessantly if he went long without consuming the life of another creature. He still complained since Daebian would feed him nothing other than the life force of animals he caught in the woods despite the demon's constant insistence of going into the city and relieving the occasional vagrant of their wasted life.

That was something neither of his fathers understood about him. Everything he did had a purpose. Azerick droned on and on about choosing the right path, considering the welfare of others. Not putting himself first seemed like the shortest path to failure. Killing people in the streets who had not offended him would draw too much attention, especially when the task could be accomplished just as easily with animals.

Carl the blacksmith watched Daebian depart the sparring field and head toward the gates to go run around in the woods as he often did. The boy was a natural with the blade; it was about the only thing natural about him. He had spent the past several months memorizing the moves and routines of the major players on this gigantic chessboard. The mundane days of playing the blacksmith were nearly at an end. Finally, the king would soon depart the field. That would be when the Rook made his move, taking first the prince, followed by the queen, and when the king reached the apex of his grief and failure…checkmate.

"Carl!" Ken shouted at the man's back. "We have too much work in here for you to be taking extended breaks."

The Rook turned toward the source of the castigation. "Yes, sir."

The Rook looked back for a moment and found himself locking eyes with Daebian. The boy stood near a postern gate staring right at him. Daebian smiled, waved, and exited through the gate. The Rook stood a moment, dumbfounded. Could the boy know what he was, what he intended? No, that was impossible. He had probably just spotted him watching the sparring matches as he often did and waved to a familiar face.

"Carl, let's go!"

It was a good thing this charade would soon be at an end. If he had to take orders from Ken much longer, he might let slip his character and feed the man's body to one of his forges. After consuming his soul, of course.

Daebian jogged across the open field and into the forest. He had several traps and snares set within the woods. The live animals he caught he fed to Klaraxis to shut him up for a time. The first trap was not far into the training field and was set along a rabbit trail running from the field into the forest. Something had tripped the spring snare, but no animal was present.

He followed the path another quarter-mile into the forest and located his second trap. It too was sprung but empty. When his third snare showed the same results, he began searching the area and found what he expected, a large wolf print. Wolf never left a sign of his presence unless he wanted to, but Ghost was not as concerned apparently. Wolf was obviously aware of his predation and was not pleased with it. Daebian could not care less what the wildling thought. Everything needed to eat, including demons.

Daebian had set some new snares farther from his usual hunting grounds the last time he came out. With any luck, Wolf had not found those yet. It added an hour to his circuit, but his investment paid off when he found the rabbit struggling against the cord cinched tight around its rear leg. He grabbed a fistful of fur and skin behind the rabbit's shoulders and neck. The unfortunate creature made an awful keening as Daebian slid his blade beneath the animal's skin without touching any of the vital organs. Klaraxis grudgingly accepted his tribute and drank in the rabbit's life essence. Klaraxis whispered a warning through the gem.

"You know, it's rude to spy on people," Daebian said without looking up.

Wolf and Ghost separated from the shadows of the dense shrubbery. "It is more detestable to needlessly torture an animal. If you think yourself a hunter, then have the decency to kill it swiftly and eat it."

Daebian threw the carcass at Wolf's feet. "You eat it if you are so concerned about it. I eat from a plate prepared by cooks like a civilized being."

Ghost stepped back from the rabbit and growled. Wolf gripped his bow tighter and fought back his mounting anger. "You are far from civilized. There is something very wrong with you."

Daebian shrugged. "I prefer to think there is something wrong with everyone else."

"You're insane."

"Probably, but can you blame me? My father is a demon and only the gods know what my little brother is. They both think some ancient gods are coming to wipe us all out, including your precious rabbits probably, and spend all their time turning my home into a huge military camp where they indoctrinate everyone into training so fiercely, they practically kill themselves. Hell, some have already died, and you're worried about a few rabbits and squirrels."

"Stay out of my woods," Wolf warned.

"Your woods? My father owns all of this. He might entertain your insistence on squatters' rights, but I do not. I will go where I wish and do what I please. Now, unless you truly want to try and stop me," Daebian said as he shifted his grip on his dagger, "I have more traps to check."

"I won't let you keep torturing these animals!"

"Then go tell my father on me and see if he cares any more than I do. He probably will, but don't expect him to take the time from his busy schedule to actually do anything about it. He has too many other concerns to worry about what his son is doing to a few vermin out in the forest."

Daebian turned his back on Wolf but used Klaraxis's presence to keep a wary eye on him. He doubted the half-elf would attack him, but he was not foolish enough to leave himself unguarded to anyone. Daebian was many things, but a fool was not one of them.

You should kill them. The animal in particular has a powerful spirit and will satiate me for a long while. Far better than the rodents you feed me.

"I told you before; I kill only when doing so furthers my own goals. Wolf and his dog play no part in those goals, at least not yet. Should they begin to interfere beyond being inconvenient to you, then I will revisit my options."

Wolf and Ghost shadowed him through the forest as he went in search of his other trap. Daebian wondered if he could use Klaraxis's power to lose his spy, but he doubted it. The two forest dwellers were acutely aware of just about everything in these woods. Let him enjoy his pathetic voyeurism. It would not deter him from doing what he needed to do.

The thrashing of wings and cawing alerted Daebian to another successful trapping. He pushed through the thick foliage and found a large crow beating at the brush with its free wing and noisily vocalizing its displeasure. It looked at Daebian with those intelligent black eyes that were so much like his own. It ceased its squawking and thrashing and studied the human with more curiosity than fear.

"Hello there," Daebian called out to the crow as he approached. "You are not what I was looking for."

He bent down and saw that the crow's wing had been damaged by the snare. The bird squawked a loud accusation for its plight and demanded to be freed. Daebian slipped a finger beneath the wire noose and worked enough slack in it to slide it over the bird's wing.

"There we go. We'll have to splint that wing, but I'm sure you will be right as rain soon enough."

"You slaughter rabbits and other animals without remorse," Wolf said from the cover of the brush. "Why is the crow's life more valuable to you than that of the other animals?"

"Because I find myself fond of the crow. I could not care one whit about the other animals. Their deaths served my purpose. The crow shall serve another purpose."

"I cannot understand what purpose the sadistic slaughter of those animals could serve."

"Of course you can't. No one understands. It is beyond the limit of their feeble minds, their inability to see beyond their reach. They will understand one day, and they will all regret their shortsightedness."

"You really are insane."

"You are redundant, and I find redundancy tedious." Daebian looked at the crow sitting quietly in his hands. "I shall call you Gloom. Let me take you to your new home and patch up that wing of yours."

"Have you seen Daebian with that bird of his?" Miranda asked while she and Azerick ate their breakfast together.

"I have. I think it is good he found something to care for. Perhaps it will help him build a little more empathy for others."

"Perhaps, but the thing gives me the creeps. How long will you be gone?"

"It will take a week and a half to reach Brelland. I cannot say how long it will take to align and join the stones. It could take another week, or even two, to get the three gates working."

"Why so long? Did you not make one to Southport in a night?"

"Although the distance is only a little farther, these gates are vastly more complex. The one we made here was designed to accommodate a handful of people. These must unerringly move the population of the entire city. The slightest flaw could result in disaster for hundreds, maybe thousands, of people."

Miranda entwined her arm with Azerick's and leaned against his shoulder. "I will miss you."

"I do not see why. I have not been pleasantly social since I returned."

"I am the daughter of the duke and duchess of North Haven. I understand the difficulties of leadership. This is a challenging time, and you must consider the welfare of a nation, not just your wife. But know this, mister," Miranda warned as she poked a finger into Azerick's shoulder, "your pass expires when this is all over."

Azerick smiled at his wife. "That certainly sounds ominous."

"I have made a list of the things you are going to do to return to my good graces. I must warn you, it is extensive and growing daily, so I do not recommend you dawdle in defeating these false gods."

"With encouragement like that, I shall go strike them down before lunch."

The Rook watched the sparring matches from the shadows of a distant building. The sorcerer's abominable son was making short work of a slightly older boy, a boy Daebian would exceed in apparent age in a matter of months. In the several months the Rook had been working in the guise of a lowly blacksmith, the boy had aged nearly two years.

The task tested the limits of his patience, but the sorcerer was too powerful to risk a direct confrontation. Killing a man was easy and rarely took a great deal of imagination, but to destroy someone without shedding a drop of blood was a true art form. His contract was to kill the sorcerer, but the Rook figured his employer would not object to a more painful end. Now that Lord Giles had left the school with his other monstrous child, he would kill the boy. It was none too soon. Already people were inquiring about his rapidly deteriorating health as he consumed this shell.

The Rook considered killing the wife too. Would it cause the sorcerer more pain to lose them both at the same time, or would experiencing the woman's grief over her son cause a greater amount of pain? To delay her death could cause undue risk to himself. No, let them both suffer in their shared sorrow. Once the sorcerer experienced the full impact of his loss and failure, the Rook could move against him directly. Even if the sorcerer managed to destroy him, the Rook's soul would be at peace knowing he had succeeded in destroying his target.

He watched the sun's slow decline with the attentiveness and patience any enemy required. The Rook counted his heartbeats, tens of thousands in number, before stealing out of the bunkhouse he shared with a dozen other men. No one sensed his departure, just as no one would detect his return.

The Rook approached the tower under the cover of darkness, carefully noting the roving guards' positions. He was not too concerned with them. Even without his abyssal skill in manipulating shadows, his lifetime of being a preeminent assassin ensured he would go undetected. The wards protecting the tower were a greater problem, but only marginally.

His skill in disabling wards allowed him to breach the foyer of the new tower with a moderate amount of exertion. Subtle magic like illusions and unraveling the spells of other wizards had always been his strongest magical ability. Hurling balls of fire and turning his enemies to ash with powerful strokes of lightning were never his forte.

He had spent months learning the routines of everyone who went in or out of the tower or patrolled the grounds. His humiliation at being brought down by a pathetic goblin would not be repeated. The creature called Grick had been an unexpected variable, one that his overconfidence had allowed to become a critical factor. He might still decide to kill the creature after this was done. But doing so would acknowledge the goblin as being worthy of his attention. It was a choice made difficult by his overdeveloped pride and ego.

The Rook reached the landing to the woman's suite of rooms. It would be a simple matter to creep in and slit her throat, but he decided to leave her for now. Let her tears rain down upon the sorcerer and drown him in her anguish. Only then would the Rook finish dissecting the sorcerer's world and take away everything he held dear.

He crept up the stairs to the floor above. Daebian's rooms were to his left, the abomination's to the right. He was with his father and would pose no unexpected variables this night. The Rook had watched the creature on the practice field. He knew Raijaun wielded powerful magic and would be an insurmountable foe if not taken completely by surprise.

Both rooms had supremely well-made wards upon the doors. There was a foreign element to them that made him think the demonic freak had crafted them, or at least modified those placed there by the sorcerer. It was a challenge, but not an insurmountable one. All magic had its roots buried within the same Source, no matter how divergent the path from which it came. A lock, no matter how masterfully crafted, was still a lock and could be picked given enough patience and skill.

Unraveling the wards protecting the rooms beyond was an arduous task, but the Rook was emboldened by the Sorcerer and his progeny's absence. It took far longer to breach the room than he had initially planned, but it was within the allowable time frame. It was still dark out and at least two hours before anyone would begin stirring within the tower.

The Rook scanned the first room for a full minute before stepping inside. He cast a strong but simple spell to prevent any noise from traveling beyond this or the next chamber's walls instead of silencing himself. The Rook seldom made mistakes, but on the rare occasion he did, like with the sorcerer's assassination, he never repeated them. His spell allowed him to hear everything within the room yet would not alert anyone outside no matter how much noise he made.

The assassin had reached the center of the room when he felt a slight shift in the air currents. He spun, blade at the ready as the door clicked shut. A deeper shade of black separated from the shadows against the wall.

"Did you think I would not recognize you, assassin? I spent a decade tracking you, crossing blades with you and barely surviving. I would know you no matter what face you wore."

The Rook smiled and stood up straight from his half-crouched position. "Well, well, if it isn't my old friend Jansen. How long have you known?"

"I suspected something off about you the day you showed up. I was all but certain of who you were weeks ago and have been waiting for you to make your move ever since. I just needed you to reveal yourself so I could finally kill you once and for all."

"You are getting a little long in the tooth, Jansen. I am far more than what I once was, and you are past your prime."

"That's where you're wrong."

"I guess we will have to see."

Deep within Jansen's heart, he knew the Rook would one day return. When Lord Giles seemingly rose from the dead, he was certain the assassin would eventually follow. The few people who truly knew the former Blackguard said he was obsessed with the Rook, and he admitted they were probably right. But obsession did not always mean a person was wrong. Three times he had faced the Rook, and three times he barely escaped with his life. This time would be different. He knew how the assassin fought, and he no longer concerned himself with surviving the encounter. The Rook would die tonight even if it cost him his life to achieve it.

Jansen moved first, leaping at the assassin with both his blades twirling in a dance of death. The Rook moved like a snake, leaning, ducking, and darting away from the lethal swipes with uncanny speed and agility. The assassin's weapon of choice was a large knife, ill-suited for a duel against an opponent wielding heavier blades with a greater reach. This made for an eerily quiet battle. Only the men's breathing, the slap of a hand blocking the forearm, or the grunt resulting from a punch or kick broke the silence of the room.

Borrowing from a painful lesson the Rook had taught him, Jansen swept his foot around in a swift arc, the small blade attached to the toe of his boot cutting open the Rook's shirt and several layers of flesh beneath. The assassin leapt backward, narrowly avoiding a more debilitating strike, and nodded his approval.

The Rook burst into a flurry of activity, slashing and stabbing at the former Blackguard captain and forcing him to back across the room as he desperately fended off the attacks. Jansen broke his retreat by lunging forward and blocking the next strike with his forearm. He tried to bring his other blade around, but the Rook grabbed his wrist in a vise-like grip.

Jansen tried to kick at the Rook's groin with his toe blade, but the Rook used their clasped arms as leverage and flipped over the weapon master's head. The assassin twisted in midair, breaking the grip on each other's wrists, and landed a kick to Jansen's back. Jansen rolled with the strike to absorb as much of the blow as he could and to put some distance between them.

In the split second it took him to roll to his feet, the Rook was on him, stabbing for his neck then heart as he stood. Jansen once more found himself on the defensive and in a poor position to counterattack. He knew then what he would have to do. Deep down, he had always known how their final battle would end.

Jansen swept his sword in a powerful, horizontal arc. The Rook nearly folded himself in half as the blade swished past his stomach, and he buried his knife into Jansen's chest before the fighter could bring it back in to block. Jansen did not attempt to block the thrust. He dropped his sword the moment the Rook lunged in and grabbed his arm with his now free hand, pulling them together as he thrust his other sword deep into the assassin's stomach.

"I got you now, you son of a bitch," Jansen hissed out with a spattering of blood. "Now I can follow you to the abyss and make sure you stay there!"

"You stupid fool. There was once a time where your sacrifice may have meant something, but that time is gone. You managed to destroy this shell, but I can simply take another. Perhaps I will take the mother or the boy."

"Or perhaps I will take you," Daebian said as he buried his knife into the Rook's back.

The Rook felt his panic surge as he tried to escape the dying mortal body, but he could not as an unseen force seemed to grab hold of his spectral form and began drawing it into some dark oblivion. Klaraxis rejoiced in the assassin's silent screams as he devoured the creature that had caused so many problems of late.

The one called Jansen still clings to life. If you hurry, I can consume his soul as well.

Daebian looked into Jansen's dying eyes as he sat crumpled against the wall. "No. I liked Jansen. He deserves to rest well."

You weaken yourself with your pointless sentimentality! You will never achieve your desires if you limit me to the pathetic life forces of lowly animals.

"You know nothing of my desires, demon. No one does. I gave you the assassin. Be content with that."

You know people like you and I can never be content. To settle for contentedness is to limit yourself and deny your own desires.

"Perhaps, but I will not allow anything to control me, including my own desires." Daebian left his warning to the demon hanging in the air as he stepped out of his room and shouted down the stairs. "Mother, there are dead people in my room! Mother!"

Miranda appeared at the top of the stairs in moments, holding her robe closed with one hand and gripping a light sword in the other. "What is it? What happened?"

"Someone came in my room. Jansen killed him but he got stabbed too," Daebian explained without emotion.

"Dear gods, are you all right?" Miranda asked, searching her son for any injuries.

Daebian stepped away and slapped at her probing hands. "I'm fine, Mother."

Miranda grasped his shoulder and ushered him down the stairs. "Come, we need to get Allister and Rusty."

"We need to get a maid to clean up my room," Daebian muttered under his breath.

CHAPTER 21

It was a somber mood around the breakfast table that morning. No one had returned to sleep after learning of the foiled attack and Jansen's death.

"Have we learned anything about this assassin?" Miranda asked.

"We know he was adept at using magic," Rusty answered. "He disassembled the wards in the tower and was able to raise a barrier of silence inside Daebian's room."

"The fact he was able to match Jansen in a fight shows he was a master of the blade as well," Alex added.

"Thank the gods Jansen was there and able to kill him before he reached Daebian. Why would someone want to kill my son? He is just a boy!"

Allister spoke up. "He is Azerick's son. My guess is our enemies wished to cause grief in hopes of distracting him from his preparations. A better question is what was Jansen doing in Daebian's rooms?"

"What are you saying? I don't care what he was doing. He saved my son's life!"

"I am saying Jansen either saw the man sneaking into the tower or he suspected the man had ill intent and had been watching him. Either way, I do not understand why he did not raise an alarm."

"Unfortunately, that answer died with Jansen," Alex said. "He is a hero many times over, and we will send him to the gods as such."

All heads turned as Brother Thomas entered the dining room and sat at the table. He had taken charge of both the bodies for final rites.

"Thomas, we were just discussing last night's events. Do you bring us any news?" Allister asked the cleric.

"Ken identified the man as Carl Rothschild. Simon hired him on as a general blacksmith about eight months ago. He said the man was competent enough in his duties making nails, horseshoes, and such, but he often watched the sparring matches on his breaks. Ken said he felt uneasy around the man."

"An assassin, a mage, and a master swordsman. The man certainly had many talents," Allister grumbled.

"They may not have all been naturally acquired."

"What do you mean?"

"The man showed signs of significant premature aging. I found some residual dark energy tainting the man's flesh. I believe he was possessed by some abyssal entity."

Miranda slammed the table with her fist. "I live in an armed camp preparing to battle ancient gods, and demon-possessed assassins try to kill my son! What else must we endure?"

Rusty grabbed at Miranda's anguish-driven question. "That brings us to another issue I strongly believe needs addressing. Our students have been sustaining these brutal training exercises for more than a year now. In that time, seven have died and dozens have been seriously injured. How much longer are we going to continue this? How many more students are going to have to die before we take a stand against this brutality?"

"I have broached the topic several times, and each time Azerick has been unbending," Allister said.

"He has become fanatical; he is obsessed with these Scions that no one else seems to know anything about."

"We are all aware of the attacks on Bruneford's Mill and the Academy. Do you doubt their veracity?"

"I acknowledge the fact there have been deadly attacks by these monsters, but both times they were defeated by a population totally unprepared for them. We are no longer unprepared. People around the kingdom are training and on guard for more incursions. Last month, several hundred of these things struck Brightridge. The army crushed them before they could breach the walls."

"Azerick says what we see is but a trickle from a sea of invaders that manage to slip through the cracks he works diligently to stem. Do you doubt his word?"

"I do not doubt his word, but I must question his assessment of the situation. I am not suggesting we lower our guard, only that we readjust our curriculum to a more moderate level to prevent more injuries."

"Azerick is adamant about his training and preparations," Allister argued. "He is not going to budge on this."

"Then we have to try harder to convince him."

Miranda interrupted their debate. "Has anyone seen Daebian?"

"I think he said he wanted to go for a ride today," Alex answered.

"After what just happened? I told him I did not want him out of my sight!"

Daebian knew everyone was going to make a huge fuss about what happened in his room last night, so he took his breakfast from the kitchen and ate it on the way to the stables. Mother wanted to watch him like a hen on an egg. He would have none of that. Klaraxis explained who, or what, the assassin was, and it was very unlikely there was another. It was not as though he was defenseless. He had known the man was up to no good for weeks. His entire countenance and behavior spoke of ill intent. He marveled at how oblivious everyone was—except Jansen. He almost felt some regret for not having intervened sooner. Oh well, it was Jansen's problem, not his.

It was still early, but the grounds were abuzz with activity thanks to the failed assassination. Twice as many martial students were making roving patrols, each with at least one adept or full mage amongst them. Peck was up feeding the horses, which was not unusual at all. He was often one of the earliest risers. Daebian failed to comprehend his dedication to such a mundane existence.

"Peck, I need a horse," Daebian loudly announced as he entered the enormous stable.

Peck emerged from one of the stalls with a bucket of oats. "Um, okay. Pick one, I suppose."

"I want that black stallion I see you on all the time."

Peck shifted his feet nervously as he stammered, "Um, you should probably take another one. Newmoon is pretty fiery and can be downright mean with people he is not used to."

Daebian stepped close to the stableman and rose up on his toes just a bit so he could look down on Peck. "I want the black stallion. Is that a problem, Peck?"

"It's just that I wish you would choose another."

"And I wish I did not have to stand here and ask more than once for the stableboy to saddle and bring me my horse." Gloom flew into the stable, lit upon Daebian's shoulder, and let out a loud caw. "You're right, Gloom; he does have very shiny eyes."

Peck stood and glared for a moment before spinning on his heel and fetching Newmoon. He hated to give anyone, especially Daebian, his horse, but with Azerick gone, it was not a battle he was going to win. He strapped on the saddle and fitted the bridle onto Newmoon's head before reluctantly handing the reins over to Daebian.

Daebian grabbed the cinch strap and pulled sharply upward. "Looks like the saddle was a little loose. You wouldn't be trying to kill me, would you, Peck? There does seem to be a bit of that going around."

"I can't imagine why," Peck replied.

"It is one of life's many mysteries."

Daebian spurred his mount and raced across the grounds, kicking up clods of dirt as he sped through the gates and raced across the open field. He chose a wide path and used the leather reins to mercilessly drive Newmoon at a reckless pace. Newmoon's nostrils flared as the big stallion fought to feed his lungs with air while Gloom did his best to keep pace overhead.

Daebian was not in the mood for a confrontation with Wolf, so he did his hunting far away, which necessitated the use of a horse. Peck appeared to be genuinely fond of this one in particular and had been petulant. Such familiarity from the help could not go unpunished. He had learned early on that it was often easier to punish people who possessed a conscience by hurting those they cared about instead of the offender. Once again, he was grateful not to be burdened with such a thing.

When Daebian finally returned to the stables, Newmoon was worked into a froth and favoring his right foreleg. Peck ran across the stable and knelt down to inspect the hoof.

"You're right, Peck; he does have a poor attitude, but I was able to work it out of him."

"What have you done? You've lamed my horse!" Peck shouted, barely able to keep himself from grabbing a pitchfork and attacking Daebian.

Daebian looked down at Peck as the young man examined Newmoon. "Your horse? Did you pay for him? No, you did not. My father owns all of these horses and, in his absence, as his eldest son, they fall to me to do with as I choose. That is what this little lesson was all about. Father's problem is his kindness breeds too much familiarity with the help."

"You won't get away with this!"

"Do you think not? I suppose you could go tattle on me to my father whenever he comes home, but it is my experience he has far more important issues to worry about than his son, much less a horse."

"It must be so hard to be you," Peck said, his voice dripping with sarcasm.

"On the contrary, it is supremely simple. Life is amazingly easy when you are not poor, stupid, and constrained by the hypocrisy of morality." Daebian began to leave but turned back as he neared the stable entrance. "I see why you like that horse. I hope you get him well soon. I look forward to riding him again."

Daebian was still a hundred feet from the tower when Miranda came rushing out the doors and practically leapt the steps as she ran to him.

"Daebian, where have you been?" she demanded fretfully.

Daebian wriggled from her embrace. "I just went for a ride, Mother."

"What are you thinking? A man tried to kill you last night!"

"And now he is dead. Dead men rarely pose much danger to others. Father is obviously an exception."

"Do not be glib with me! Jansen is dead, and we do not know if there are more assassins around. Go get washed up for supper, and you will stay close to the tower."

Daebian reluctantly obeyed, not wanting to increase his mother's agitation since it would only make her more impossible to deal with.

Peck liberally applied a liniment to Newmoon's leg and wrapped it tight. The tendons in his knee were stressed but thankfully not torn. Newmoon would need rest and some light exercise, but he would recover with proper attention…this time. Peck knew he had somehow offended Daebian. There were rumors floating around about bad things happening to people who did.

Peck did not consider himself a coward, but he knew facing Daebian directly would get him nothing except possibly an inexplicable accident. He needed to show Daebian he was not easy prey, but he would need help. Tangling with Daebian was a dangerous endeavor, but he would not let anyone abuse his horses.

He saddled a mare and headed for the forest. He did not usually ride through the woods, preferring the open fields and pastures closer to the school. Peck chose a path at random, calling out into the trees and counting on Wolf to find him since he would never find the half-elf. Just as he thought they would, Wolf and Ghost emerged seemingly from the ground as if the forest had suddenly given birth to them.

"Hi, Peck, I don't see you out here much. Must be about your stallion," Wolf said as he stroked the mare's neck and fed her a handful of pine nuts.

"You saw what he did to Newmoon?"

"Of course."

"I can't let him kill my horse."

"What do you want to do?"

"I have a plan for when Azerick returns, but Daebian has to be taught a lesson. He won't do something just because Azerick tells him to. In fact, he would probably do the opposite just to be spiteful. I won't pretend to know how Daebian thinks, but I do know animals. If I show weakness, he'll just keep coming at me."

"You can't fight him," Wolf said definitively. "I've seen him fight and he's really good."

"I know. I'll have to outsmart him."

"No offense, but you're probably better off fighting him."

Peck grinned. "It seems some guys get all the breaks, doesn't it? If he has one weakness, it's his ego. I can use that against him, and he could get hurt, really hurt, but I don't care. I know he's Azerick's son, but he is a horrible person, and I cannot let him keep hurting my horses."

Wolf nodded. "I understand how you feel. What he did to Newmoon today was nothing compared to what I have seen him do to other animals. I'm in. What do you need me to do?"

"How are your birdcalls?"

Peck spent three days icing, steaming, and massaging Newmoon's injury before Daebian reappeared. He was almost relieved when Daebian came strolling into the stables. The anxiety of waiting for him was unbearable.

"Peck, is my horse ready?"

Peck finished applying a new wrap soaked in liniment. "No, it will be at least a week before anyone can ride him."

"What if I insisted on riding him now?"

"I would do everything in my power to stop you. If you ride him too soon, you will create an injury that will never heal."

"Lucky for you I plan on riding him a great deal, so I will heed your professional recommendation and not force you to tax your limited abilities. I will return in four days to ride him whether he is ready or not. My tolerance for weakness is one of the few limits I possess."

Peck did not bother to respond, and Daebian did not wait around to hear it. Peck went back to working with Newmoon in the corral. He needed to slowly work more strength back into the limb as well as teach him a new command. It was a short amount of time to teach such a thing, but no one was better at getting a horse to listen than he was. He hoped Azerick returned soon.

As always, Daebian was true to his word and returned on the day promised. Peck tried to convince him Newmoon was not ready, but

Daebian insisted and would brook no argument. Peck wrapped the horse's knee with a fresh bandage to stabilize it as best he could.

"That should hold as long as you take it easy."

"If I wanted to take it easy, I would have grabbed one of these other nags," Daebian retorted.

"If you push him too hard you could permanently lame him!"

"If that is the case then the horse is weak and deserves to be put down. This is an academy preparing for battle, not some school of etiquette with a stable full of leisure horses. He will either come back whole or be fed to the dogs."

Peck bored holes through Daebian's back with his eyes as he galloped away. "With any luck, Newmoon will be the only one who comes back."

Daebian put his heels into Newmoon's flanks, urging him to greater speeds. The open fields vanished in an instant as he plunged into the forest and raced down the narrow trail. Almost any rider would have slowed down significantly, but Daebian was confident in his balance and reflexes. Even without touching the soul stone, he could feel Klaraxis's influence on his body.

Trees flew by in a blur of green and brown. Only the wind whistling past his head could compete with the sound of Newmoon's labored breathing and thundering hoofbeats. The next stretch was tricky. A fallen tree created a nice jump, but the trail curved sharply left just beyond the obstacle. He had to brace for the jump and shift his weight into the curve.

Newmoon flew over the log like a dolphin breaching next to the prow of a ship. So smooth was the horse's gait that Daebian could not discern the exact moment his hooves left the ground. Daebian began to lean in preparation of making the turn, but Newmoon kicked up the instant he touched down and twisted.

Daebian experienced the joy of flight for seconds that dragged on for an eternity. He looked back and saw Newmoon kicking and bucking wildly before galloping away. He turned in the direction of his trajectory and watched the ground rising to meet him with agonizing slowness. He never felt the impact, only the sensation of floating in a pitch-black sea as waves roared in his ears. And then he knew nothing.

CHAPTER 22

Miranda looked around the dining table. "Has anyone seen Daebian?"

"Riding again, I think," Alex answered.

"I swear that boy tries to worry me to death."

"I'm sure he's out doing whatever it is he does when not doing drills," Allister said.

Gloom flew through the door to the kitchen, nearly causing the serving woman to drop her tray of food as she entered the dining room. He landed in the middle of the table and began cawing noisily and fluttering his feathers in agitation.

"Ugh, it's that bird of his," Miranda said disgustedly. "Daebian must be nearby. Shoo, go away, you vile thing!"

Gloom only began squawking louder and started flinging food from plates with his big onyx beak.

Allister watched the bird's antics a moment. "Has anyone checked with Peck so see if Daebian returned from his ride?"

"Do you think something has happened to him? Did he take a fall?" Miranda asked worriedly, then stood.

"I don't know if anything has happened to him, but perhaps we should make some inquiries."

Rusty, Allister, Miranda, and Alex hurried from the dining room and crossed the grounds. Only a few lanterns remained lit as Peck and his team of groomsmen finished feeding and stabling the horses for the night.

"Peck, did Daebian take a horse out today?" Allister asked as they entered the stable.

Peck started at the sudden question and his eyes shifted nervously. "Um, yes, late this morning."

"Are all the horses accounted for, particularly the one Daebian took?"

Peck looked at the stalls behind him. "Yes, they are all here."

"So you saw Daebian come back?" Miranda asked.

"No, not exactly."

"What do you mean, not exactly?"

"I found Newmoon in his stall."

"A horse came back without a rider and you did not bother to tell anyone?" Allister barked.

"I—I thought Daebian just put him in there and did not bother with his equipment. He does that, saying it is our job."

Allister gave Peck a stern look that promised more questions later. "We need to find him. Does anyone know what direction he went?"

"I think I saw him ride out of the east gate and enter the woods near the southeast area of the training grounds," Alex supplied.

"There are thousands of square miles of woods out there, and it's dark. How are we going to find him?" Miranda asked.

Gloom flew into the stable, roosted on a rafter, and squawked. He flew back out of the stable and landed on the roof of the smithing shop, cawing loudly.

"I guess we follow the bird," Allister grumbled.

"Gods, if that bird takes us to Daebian, I'm going to have to start liking it," Miranda said under her breath.

"Peck, saddle us some horses," Rusty ordered. "Time may be of the essence."

It took less than five minutes to have the horses saddled and the search party underway. It was impossible to pick Gloom out from the darkness, but his constant squawking kept them all on track. They began calling out Daebian's name but there was never an answer.

"Wolf!" Allister shouted into the trees. "Where is that blasted boy? Any other time you couldn't stop to relieve yourself without him throwing pinecones at you. The one time we need him, he's decided to keep to himself!"

The party continued to follow Gloom's insistent calls as the two wizards illuminated the surrounding forest with bright orbs of light. Fortunately, they did not need Wolf's excellent tracking skills or Ghost's powerful nose to follow the trail churned up by Newmoon's hooves. They continued to follow the path until Gloom landed on a downed log lying across the trail, and began hopping up and down, cawing madly.

"He must be near. Daebian!" Miranda called out.

The riders listened for a moment before deciding to dismount. Miranda and Allister peered into the woods while Rusty and Alex climbed over the log and searched beyond it. A tiny reflection of light twinkled several yards off the trail and down a small ravine.

"I think I see something," Alex called out, then began picking his way down the slope. "I found him! Rusty, bring that light closer."

Daebian lay in a pool of blood long dried and soaked into the ground. His face was deathly pale and a large gash split the top of his head where it had struck a rock when he fell.

"My son! Is he alive?" Miranda begged to know, her tears flowing freely.

Allister climbed down to him and knelt. "Aye, but he's in a bad way. We need to get him to Brother Thomas as quickly as we can."

Wolf sprinted through the forest as quiet and invisible as a shadow with Ghost easily padding along beside him. The soldiers guarding the gate instantly recognized him and did not bother to challenge the half-elf before letting him pass. It took only a frantic moment for Wolf to find Peck nervously brushing Newmoon's black coat.

"Peck, they found Daebian," Wolf said, only slightly winded from his miles-long dash.

"Is he alive?"

"Yes, but he cracked his head pretty hard on a rock when he fell." Wolf recognized Peck's unease and the doubt clouding his face. "That's what you wanted, wasn't it?"

"I guess so. I don't know. It all sounded a lot better when it was just words."

"Well, I for one am only sorry he didn't die. Now we have to deal with what happens if he wakes up."

"You think he'll wake up?" Peck asked nervously.

"They're bringing him to Brother Thomas, so it's likely unless Sharrellan calls him home before he reaches him. I'm pretty sure they have to be related."

"I have to talk to Brother Thomas!"

Wolf did not wait around as Peck darted out of the stables. He figured it was a good idea to stay away from the school for a while. Peck ran across the compound to the church, leapt the steps leading to the front doors, and raced inside. He found Brother Thomas blowing out the candles and tidying up after the evening prayers.

"Peck, is everything all right?" he asked as Peck burst into the room and almost went sprawling across the carpet.

Peck shook his head vigorously. "Daebian fell from his horse and hit his head!"

"Is he in the infirmary now?" Thomas asked urgently, then made to hasten away.

Peck grabbed his arm and stopped him. "No, they're bringing him in now. Thomas, it's my fault he fell! I made the horse buck and throw him."

"What do you mean? Explain that."

Peck told the priest how Daebian was abusing his horses and the animals in the woods. He told him of how he was afraid of what Daebian would do if he did not stop him.

"Peck, I have known you a long time, and I do not think there is a mean bone in your body. I understand how you may have felt that what you did was your only choice, but there were other ways. What you did was wrong."

"Do you think Daebian will recover?"

"I cannot say for certain until I see him, but I would say it is likely."

Peck looked plaintively into Brother Thomas's eyes. "If he finds out I did this, he will kill me."

"Peck, as angry as he may be, I doubt he is going to kill you. Daebian is a bit intense, but he has always seemed to me to be a friendly young man."

"You don't understand. You don't know what he is like. That is why his evil is so insidious! He smiles at everyone and sings and pretends to be nice, but bad things happen to anyone who angers him."

Thomas quirked a doubtful eyebrow at Peck. "That sounds like a lot of conspiracy talk to me."

"What about that boy who just happened to fall off the wall and just happened to get his sword arm crushed the same night he beat Daebian senseless and insulted him?"

Thomas remembered that night well. It was rather suspicious. Daniel had been walking the wall for at least two years, as well as hundreds of others, all without an incident. Daebian had been so young Thomas had dismissed any thoughts of foul play, but he was a very unusual boy in many ways. There was something troubling about Daebian, but Thomas was afraid he was feeling some sort of subconscious prejudice against his demonic heritage and tried to ignore it.

"Even if what you say has any truth to it, what would you have me do? I cannot refuse to aid him."

Peck's shoulders slumped and his face fell. "I know. Maybe you could just make him rest a while, just until Azerick gets back. I can't keep him from hurting me, but I have a plan to protect my horses. I just need time for Azerick to come home."

"I don't know when Azerick is going to be back. I don't think even he knows when he will be back." Thomas sighed. "I won't force him to rest, and I won't abuse the tenets of my faith or conscience, but I can give you time. How much will depend on Daebian's own powers of recovery."

"Thank you, Thomas."

"All right, let's get to the infirmary."

Peck had no intention of being around when they brought Daebian in, and returned to his horses. Brother Thomas had just entered the infirmary and made sure there was a bed with fresh sheets and blankets ready when Miranda burst in a few steps ahead of Rusty and Alex who were carrying Daebian between them.

"Thomas, thank the gods you are here!" Miranda exclaimed as she ushered the men to lay her son on the bed.

"Thank the gods, sure, why not?" Thomas muttered.

"He took a fall from his horse today," Rusty explained. "He's been lying unconscious for several hours."

Thomas held his hands palms down with his fingers extended above Daebian's body and began chanting a soft prayer. He guided his hands up and down the boy's form, paying particular attention to his head. Thomas dropped his hands to his sides and spoke to Miranda.

"He broke three ribs and his left arm. The greatest concern is obviously his head injury. It is very severe."

"Can you help him?" Miranda begged.

"Of course, but head injuries like this can be problematic. It is not a good idea to try and heal it all at once. Trying to heal it too rapidly can cause damage to the brain, so it is best to do it slowly and let him wake up on his own."

"How long will it take?"

"It's impossible to say. Much will depend on his natural rate of recovery. Even without his unique physiology, it is not possible to make a realistic estimate."

"Please, do what you can."

Thomas raised his hands and began chanting once more. Healing energies radiated from his hands like static electricity and gave off a faint white nimbus of light. The bones knitted almost instantly, but the injury to Daebian's brain was far from simple. The gods rarely made things easy for their followers, even their cherished Chosen. Thomas sensed the bruising and bleeding inside Daebian's head and used his mystical energy to revive the damaged tissue and stitch the tiny veins and capillaries back together.

"I have done as much as I think should be done for now. I will tend to him each day until he is better. With any luck, he will wake and be on his feet again in a week or so."

Miranda embraced the priest. "Thank you, Thomas."

Daebian floated in a black sea of nothingness, slowly bobbing on gentle waves of oblivion. It was soothing and warm like the soft hands of a loving mother cradling her baby. That must be it. He was back in the womb, protected from the painful outside world. A pale light glowed far away in the starless sky and he became aware.

"Where am I?"

Trapped within the confines of your mind, much like I am with your father.

"Why aren't you trying to dominate me, take control of my body?"

Because I cannot. I still exist within your father. A fragment of my essence exists within the gem set in your blade. Neither of them exists within you. I speak to you now only through our shared connection with the soul stone.

"How did I get here? What happened?"

The answer lies within you.

Daebian began fitting the shattered pieces of his memory together. Bit by bit they began to create a mosaic inside his mind. The mosaic animated and he saw the forest, Newmoon racing along the trail, leaping over the log. The horse bucked and twisted. Daebian was flying once more. The horse had startled and thrown him. On instinct, he closed his eyes and the mosaic vanished. Hoofbeats thundered in his ears. The gently rocking became stronger, no longer the slow rise and fall of a low swell but the hurried gait of a galloping horse. For a brief second, all was silent except for the wind rushing past his ears as Newmoon leapt.

A pine thrush called out. Newmoon bucked and twisted and Daebian went flying. No. He felt his body stop then rush backward. His legs tightened against the saddle again. Stop. Forward. Newmoon leapt, the bird tweeted loudly, and he was airborne. Back, leap, trill, fall. Back, trill, fall. Back, trill. Trill. The call was wrong. Near the end, the whistle rose in pitch and held, too high, too long.

"Gloom!" Daebian called out into the blackness. "I need your eyes!"

Daebian could not see Gloom, but he felt his presence. The forest appeared once more, now looking more like a fine painting than a tiled mosaic. He was higher and saw the world with amazingly sharp contrast even compared to his normal acute vision, displaying more shades of color than he thought existed. He saw himself below, hugging the horse's broad back as he galloped along the trail. Newmoon jumped, the pine thrush trilled off-key, Daebian flew from the horse's back and landed several yards away down the short ravine.

A shadow moved within the bushes. Daebian looked intently, but even Gloom's eyes failed to see what had moved. He swooped lower and studied the ground. There in a soft patch of soil was half of a print—a wolf print. Daebian had his culprit. No, culprits, and he did not mean Ghost. Wolf did not have the time, nor did he think the inclination, to train the horse to react to the modified bird call.

"It would seem Peck has more spine and wits than I gave him credit for."

You will recover from this. When you do, you must destroy him and the half-breed!

"I might do that. Or I might not."

Will you allow your foolish sentiments to keep you from retaliating against those who just tried to kill you? Klaraxis demanded, furious at the boy.

"It has nothing to do with sentiment, demon. It is about you understanding that you will not now, nor will you ever, dictate my actions. I do what I want, when I want, and why I want. Why I *might* choose to let them live is not for you to question. Their time is coming, but it must not be hastened. All things happen for a reason."

Bah, you sound like a priest!

"Or a god."

Klaraxis laughed. *You are certainly ambitious, but you are no god. However, I may know of a way to become one.*

"Become a god?"

Perhaps, or at least be godlike. I know of an item that can steal the soul from any creature, man or god. You could slay a god, even your father.

"The sweet words of a demon, the prince of lies."

I am being true to you. I will not tell you it will be easy. In fact, it will be quite perilous to attain the weapon. You also cannot do it on your own.

"What makes acquiring this weapon so dangerous? Is it guarded by a dragon or some such?"

Worse; by the most powerful demon lord in all of the abyss. The soul blade is in my citadel within the Fifth Circle.

"It sounds a bit out of reach to me."

For you, most definitely, but perhaps not for your brother.

"My brother would never help me, especially with something like that. He is too much his father's son, too kindhearted."

Perhaps you will find a way to use that softness to your advantage.

"Most definitely."

CHAPTER 23

Azerick spoke into the speaking gem. "Is the gate clear?"
Roger double-checked both sides of the gate and saw that the guards were doing a good job of blocking traffic. "It's all clear."

Azerick fed arcane power into the massive stone pillars now framing one of the primary gates in Brelland. A shimmering screen appeared within the massive portal and resolved to show a crowd of spectators being held in check by a squad of city watch. Azerick nodded to a shepherd who began herding two dozen sheep through the portal.

This was the last of three magical gates connecting Brelland and North Haven. On instinct, Azerick had decided at the last minute to pay a sheep rancher to move some of his herd through the portal. That decision had saved his life. These gates were much larger and more complex than the one he made outside Southport and had far less margin for error. The number of magical strands connecting the two gates were increased by a multitude of factors. The first results had been unpleasant for several unfortunate sheep.

"I count twenty-four, Azerick," Roger reported a moment later.

"Finally! Okay, send them back through."

Azerick was able to see the sheep milling about in North Haven until a couple of watchmen prodded them back through using the hafts of their spears. He counted sheep until their numbers reached twenty-four and breathed another sigh of relief. All three gates were up and functioning as best as was possible.

"Good job, son. I was starting to doubt my theory for a while there."

"I knew we could get it right; I was just not certain if it would be before the barrier fell and the Scions crushed us all," Raijaun replied.

"How do you feel?"

"Not well. I used some combined magic to make the connections. I am tired and sore now."

Azerick laid a hand on Raijaun's shoulder. "We are done now. Let's go home and get some rest."

Raijaun made sure his hood was pulled up and his face hidden as best he could before following Azerick through the gate. They discovered a crowd with mixed reactions waiting on the other side. A few people looked amazed and interested, but most wore looks of fear and distrust. Even for the uninitiated, this was obviously a major magical undertaking, and it was now set in the middle of the city.

Seeing that neither the sheep nor Azerick was blended into an unrecognizable mass, the engineers decided to put their faith in their work and passed through the portal as well. A two-week-long caravan back to North Haven was an unattractive proposition and helped to alleviate their fear. It was also important for the common folk to see non-wizards passing through the gates as well.

Eager to get home, Azerick made the trip in minutes by opening two subsequent portals. His second rift deposited him just in front of the gates of the school. As much as he wanted to go straight to his lab, gating inside a building was tricky business.

Azerick had barely made it through the gates when Miranda came running toward him. "Azerick, thank the gods you are home. Daebian has been hurt."

Azerick returned her embrace. "Hurt? Hurt how?"

"He fell from his horse and injured his head. He has been unconscious for nearly a week, and I am so worried."

"What has Brother Thomas said?" Azerick asked as Miranda pulled him toward the infirmary.

"Brother Thomas said it was best to take it slow. He has let him sleep and kept his healing sessions mild."

Azerick nodded. "That makes sense. Forcing the brain to heal too rapidly is like casting a broken arm without setting the bone."

Miranda and Azerick found Brother Thomas seated next to Daebian's bed. The priest stood as they entered. Azerick stepped next to the bed and laid a gentle hand on his son's cheek.

"How is he, Thomas?"

"He is doing very well. He will probably wake tomorrow if he is ready."

"Is there any permanent damage?"

"None I can detect. He should make a full recovery."

"That is good news. Please send someone for me before you wake him."

Miranda grabbed Azerick's elbow as he turned to leave. "Where are you going?"

"I have been gone nearly a month. I need to check the barrier. I have allowed the Scions free reign for too long."

"Your son is lying in a hospital bed! You can't spend some time with him even now?" Miranda demanded.

"Miranda, he is unconscious. He has no knowledge of my presence," Gloom squawked loudly from his perch on the windowsill, "unless the bird tells him," Azerick amended. "He does not know, nor could he care in his present state, if I were here for five minutes or five hours. The Scions, on the other hand, could create another breach any minute and kill hundreds, maybe thousands of sons and daughters."

"Maybe they will, but right now this is your son lying in this bed."

"Brother Thomas said he will be fine. He will wake up in the morning, and I will be here."

"Fine, just go. I will not argue with you anymore about the merits of parenting. If you decide you need me, I will be here with my son!"

"I am sure your continual vigilance has worked as great a miracle as Brother Thomas's healing," Azerick snapped back, then stormed out.

"*You seem troubled, false Guardian. Give yourself to us. We shall end your misery.*"

Azerick ignored the Scions' constant harassment and let his mind fly along the barrier. Several places showed signs of weakening, but only one was critical. It would likely have taken the Scions several more days to have breached it, but he could not have known that. It was just as likely that its fall was imminent.

Keep telling yourself that, human. You know the truth, Klaraxis said.

"You would not know truth if it bit off your big black arse," Azerick snapped at the demon. He was in no mood to listen to him.

I know more truth than your kind could ever admit. I know my lies for what they are. You and your kind are so adept at falsehood you even believe your own lies. Admit it, the reason you did not stay with your son is because you cannot stand to be around him.

"I love my son, but I do not expect you to understand such a concept."

I may not know love beyond myself, but I do know hate. You hate Daebian!

"I do not hate my son!"

Then why do you avoid him? Why do you feel so uncomfortable in his presence? You cannot hide your feelings from me, human. We are of the same mind and body. I see what you see, feel what you feel. We are one.

"I just don't have the time. Daebian's interests and abilities run counter to my responsibilities. It has nothing to do with me hating him."

I think you fear him. We hate that which we fear.

"I do not fear my son."

You should.

Azerick sat at his small desk inside his laboratory and raised his weary head from his hands when a soft knock sounded at the door. "Enter."

"Azerick, can I talk to you?" Peck asked.

Azerick smiled, always happy to see the guileless young stableman. "Of course you can, Peck. What can I do for you?"

Peck walked carefully across the room, his eyes shifting about as if he expected demons or dragons to leap from the shadows and devour him. He set a small bag on Azerick's desk with a metallic clink.

"What is this?"

"It is almost everything you have paid me over the years. I want to buy the horses," Peck said, setting his chin resolutely. "I know it is probably not enough, but you can keep taking whatever you want out of my pay until you feel the debt is paid or we're all dead and it won't matter anyway."

The amount in the purse was substantial. Peck had few desires and virtually no expenses. There was enough there to buy a decent home and live modestly for several years.

"Why do you want to buy the horses?"

"I just need to have more control over them. I have to be able to decide what is best for them and who does what with them."

"Has there been a problem? Is there something you need to tell me?"

"I just need to buy the horses. Will you sell them to me?"

Azerick looked at the sack of coins on the desk. "Peck, you understand I need those horses and why."

"I do. I understand their duty, and I will make sure they do it. That is why I need to have more control, so I know they are ready to perform at any time."

Azerick grabbed the bag and slid it closer to him. "All right, the horses are yours. Since the majority of their training and conditioning was done by you, I will sell them to you at a standard rate under the condition that they are available to the school to perform their role no matter how dangerous it may be."

Peck nodded his agreement. "Thank you."

"Peck, you know you can come to me if you have any kind of trouble," Azerick said softly as Peck turned to leave.

"I know. I got this."

Azerick sighed as yet another issue arose that he could apparently do nothing about. He flipped idly through the Codex Arcana, looking for nothing in particular. He could have found a much more productive use for his time like apologizing to Miranda or sitting next to his son's hospital bed, but his mind was too jumbled to put thought into action.

He kept thinking of his strange meeting with Peck. Something had obviously happened that upset him greatly and made him fear for the safety of his horses. It was not hard to deduce that it also had something to do with Daebian. He could ask Daebian about it when he awoke, but Azerick knew his son would not talk to him, and it was obvious Peck wanted to resolve this on his own. Peck was a man now, or close enough to it, and Azerick respected him enough to let him make his own decisions.

Writing out what he had learned with the creation of his gates was time-consuming, but it provided the distraction he needed. It was important to get this information to the Academy so they could begin working on their gates. A knock at his door pulled him away from his musings, and he wondered what new trouble it heralded this time. A young woman, one of Brother Thomas's acolytes, entered when he beckoned her inside.

"Lord Giles, Brother Thomas wished me to inform you he is ready to wake Daebian."

"Thank you. I will be there momentarily."

The acolyte bowed slightly and disappeared back up the stairs. Azerick sat at his desk pondering the best course of action. Miranda would be there, and he doubted her anger at him had diminished much, but that was unavoidable. Not going was not an option. Should he confront Daebian about Peck? Any intervention would likely only make it worse for Peck if they did have an issue and create one if they did not. Azerick did not really know his son, but he had a good idea of his type. Daebian was naturally defiant and would instinctively do the opposite of just about anything Azerick said.

With a heavy sigh of resignation, Azerick climbed the stairs out of his lab and headed for the infirmary. Miranda and Thomas were already there, as well as Rusty and Allister. He was glad to see his old friends. Their presence would stifle Miranda's desire to revisit their argument.

Rusty and Allister nodded a greeting when Azerick entered the room, Thomas smiled, and Miranda looked away pointedly. Her rejection felt like a knife plunging into his heart. He wanted to apologize, wanted to somehow bring them back together, but the words would not come to him. He nodded to Brother Thomas who then began working his divine magic.

"This should not take long. Most of the significant healing has already occurred," Thomas explained as he worked. "The long rest and natural healing has helped prevent any lasting damage and residual pain."

Daebian began to stir. Miranda pushed closer and laid a hand on his chest. When his eyes fluttered open, Miranda practically threw herself on top of him and hugged him tightly.

"Mother, what are you doing?"

Miranda straightened up and wiped the tears of relief from her eyes. "You took a fall and have been unconscious for nearly a week. I have been sitting next to your bed day and night, praying for you to wake."

"You have spent hours on end doing nothing but watch me sleep? Why?"

"Because I was worried. Because I thought it important to be with you. It is called love."

"I would call it a colossal waste of time. Did not Grandmother need your help during this past week organizing and preparing the people? In case you have not heard, war is approaching and there are more important matters to attend to than watching someone sleep."

Miranda's face flushed as a multitude of emotions assaulted her. "You sound like your father."

"I am surprised to find myself admit that even Father occasionally gets something right. I too have things to do. May I go now?"

Brother Thomas answered. "I would recommend you stay here for at least another day. You will likely have a bit of a headache for a few days and some slight disorientation. I do suggest you get up, stretch your muscles, and walk about the room, but I strongly recommend against any exertion. You are still injured, and any knock to the head could cause some serious harm."

"I do feel a bit out of sorts. I am also starving. Mother, would you bring me something to eat?"

"Of course." Miranda hesitated, not wanting to leave her son, but she forced herself to hurry to the kitchens.

"I am glad you are well, son," Azerick said.

"Are you really? There is no need for false platitudes. Mother cannot hear you now."

"Daebian, I know I have not been an attentive father to you, and I truly regret it. But I want you to know it is not because I do not love you. We walk different paths, you and I, and it can be hard to cut through the foliage and brambles separating us."

"Do you truly mean that?"

"I do."

"I understand, Father. I understand what you must do and the sacrifices we all have to make. I understand a great deal more than anyone gives me credit for."

Azerick nodded. "I believe you do. I have work to do now. I will check in on you again later."

Brother Thomas followed Azerick out of the room. "I think we can agree his injury has caused no lasting damage or change in his character."

"Yes, an unfortunate thing that—his character, I mean."

Your father has become an accomplished liar, almost as accomplished as you.

"Was he lying? Was I? Father believes most of what he said, at least he wants to. And I understand far more than people think I do, including you, demon. You had best remember that if you think to control me like you try to control my father."

I would not dream of it. Ours is a mutually beneficial arrangement, whereas the one I share with your father is not.

"I care far more about the beneficial than the mutual, demon."

Of course you do. You are my son, and I would expect nothing less.

Most of the horses were out with the martial students doing maneuvers. Only Newmoon and a few swift messenger mounts remained in the stables. It was the best time to muck out the stalls. Normally, Peck had assistants to do the menial labor of cleaning the stalls, but Daebian was awake and the simple work helped distract him from the anxiety of their inevitable confrontation. Peck was certain Daebian would want to punish Newmoon for throwing him, but now Peck had the authority to deny him that, or at least the legal authority. He wondered how long Daebian would wait before exacting his revenge. As fickle as the fates were, it was not long.

"There once was a stableboy named Peck,
Who lived his life shoveling drek.
He trained his horse to kill,
A true testament of his skill,
A feat worthy of my respect."

Peck gripped his shovel tightly with both hands, but Daebian continued to lean casually against the stall's doorframe.

"It seems I underestimated you, Peck. That is a dangerous habit to get into, and one I will certainly work hard to break. You are neither as spineless nor dull-witted as I thought you were. There may be some value to your life after all."

"What do you want?" Peck asked nervously as he futilely looked for a way out of the stall.

Daebian pushed off the doorframe. "I want you to saddle that mangy beast of a horse so I can properly break him once and for all. I may even feed him to…my blade."

"No, I will not let you take my horse."

"I thought we already had this conversation regarding ownership? Perhaps it was with someone else. Once things become redundant, I tend to lose interest and do not pay much attention."

"These are my horses. I bought them. I decide who takes them out and for what. Ask Azerick if you want; he'll tell you."

A wide grin split Daebian's face. "You surprise me once again, Peck. You truly are a clever little muck shoveler, aren't you? Well done, Peck. I will have to find a new game to play now." Daebian began to walk away then turned back. "I meant what I said earlier. You caused me grievous injury in our little game. You earned my respect for that—once. A second time will get you killed."

Daebian walked away, whistling an off-key trilling of a pine thrush.

CHAPTER 24

"Lord Giles, I have a message for you."

"Thank you, Marcus." Azerick took the sealed letter and closed the door to his laboratory.

He sat at his desk and read. Lines of consternation appeared on his forehead as if a tiny farmer were tilling a field across his face. He sighed, tossed the paper on his desk, and tried to rub the worry lines from his face with his hands.

"What is it, Father?" Raijaun asked.

"The Academy is having trouble connecting their gates with Brightridge and *humbly* requests my assistance."

"Humbly?"

A wry smile appeared on Azerick's face. "Hard to believe, isn't it? Yet, there it is."

"What will you do?"

"I do not know. I have yet to truly put our students, our warriors, through a proper test, and we still have to erect the gates in the valley where we must make our final stand." Azerick thumped the desk with his fist, holding back his anger so he did not shatter it into kindling. "An entire academy of this kingdom's greatest wizards, and they beg the help of one man and his son!"

"You could send me."

"What?"

"I am not needed here nearly as much as you are. Send me to help the Academy connect their gates. They must have a team of wizards in Brightridge. I should not even have to leave Southport."

"I do not like the idea of sending you into their clutches."

"Would you send me if I were human?" Azerick's answer was evident when he looked away. "We are allies now, tenuous at best, but we must place some trust in each other. If you cannot trust the Academy, at least trust in our mutual desire to survive. At the very least, trust in the fact you scare the ever-living crap out of them."

Azerick laughed and squeezed his son's shoulder. "How did you get so wise so fast?"

"The popular consensus is I got it from my mother."

Azerick laughed again at Raijaun's rare show of humor. "Who said that?"

Raijaun shrugged. "Miranda, Allister, Aggie, Rusty, pretty much everyone who has bothered to express an opinion."

"Far be it for me to refute the masses. All right, go to Southport and help these fools align their gates. It would be good if you could get a firsthand assessment of their preparations as well. Take one of the speaking stones with you. If you even suspect treachery, contact me immediately, and I will come and show them their previous fears were but a tiny goose bump compared to the terror I will unleash upon them if they harm you."

Despite his and Raijaun's confident words, Azerick could not help but worry for his son's safety. Standing taller than Azerick now, it was easy to forget he was still just a boy. No matter how fast he grew, how smart he was, or how powerful he had become, he had barely had three years of life to learn how treacherous and illogical the human race could be. And those three years had been rather sheltered ones. Raijaun was right, however; they had to start trusting one another or none of them had a chance.

Azerick found the core of his school's instructors waiting for him in the main hall. Today was the largest combined forces training they had yet attempted. It was time to see what almost three years of training had produced.

"Is everyone ready?" Azerick asked as he entered the room.

"I don't think anyone can possibly be ready for what you have in mind," Rusty replied, "but the field is prepared."

Rusty had long been a voice calling for an easing of Azerick's rigorous and injurious training. Injuries were common, and seven people had died during some of the more intense maneuvers. Rusty was like a brother to Azerick, but he was too kindhearted for this kind of thing.

"You are right; we cannot possibly be ready for what is to come," Azerick agreed. "However, we must work as hard as we can to get as close to ready as we are able."

There was little more discussion as Azerick led a procession across the grounds and out onto the periphery of the huge eastern training field. Alex, always the dutiful general, filled Azerick in on their troops' disposition and tactical plans. It was largely redundant since they had all spent the last several days fine-tuning and choreographing the event.

Thousands of men, women, boys, girls, and horses covered a large swath of open field. They stood in ranks a dozen deep and two hundred wide. The cavalry lined up behind and to each side of them in anticipation of striking the invaders at their flanks. Three hundred archers wielding powerful longbows stood only a few paces behind a double row of mages. The spellcasters aligned themselves behind the ranks of swordsmen and shield-bearing spearmen. It was their job to provide magical barriers to slow and shield the warriors while the stronger wizards used their power to thin the gruesome horde of ravagers enough so they would not be overwhelmed and crushed by sheer numbers.

Azerick felt his heart soar when he looked upon the perfect ranks of his people. They had all worked so hard to become a powerful force against those who wished them all dead. Then just as quickly his heart plummeted when he remembered the reality that many, probably most, of them would die.

He opened a gate and stepped in front of his army. "I am very proud of you all," he said, his voice booming over the masses. "You have shown the true spirit of humanity by standing against those who would oppress you and seek to destroy us all. You do so knowing that many of you will not live to see the freedom your sacrifices will bring. Some have already given their lives in this endeavor. You have endured the hardest, most bitter training I could devise and you did not bend. You stand taller and stronger than ever before. You will need that strength today and in the days to come. I want you to fight with all your heart and strength, but remember, today is a day of training. Stay steadfast, but stay safe."

Azerick gated back to the leaders and nodded. "Let us begin."

Alex stood upon a raised platform with flags in each hand. Horns sounded across the battlefield as he whipped them about in a series of commands. Rusty, Allister, and Aggie used speaking stones to issue orders to their battlefield leaders.

It took only moments for the army to fall into their defensive positions. The instructing wizards bent their magic and conjured the enemy they all awaited. Thousands of ravagers materialized out of the ether barely a mile away and raced toward the human army on legs almost as swift as a horse.

The massive catapults and trebuchets struck first, the largest of them flinging three-hundred-pound stones nearly a thousand feet. Mages unleashed their firestorms shortly after. They spread their arcane attacks wide to disperse the charging ravagers and prevent them from gaining too much mass at any one point that could cause a major breach in their infantry's line.

Allister reminded his mages to pace their magic. There was little in the way of reserves to rotate out wizards who became too fatigued. This was going to be a war of attrition, swift but bloody with neither side likely to rest until the other was obliterated. The winner would be the one with survivors at the end.

The ravagers struck the first rank of spearmen with what would have been a hellish clash of flesh on wood and steel. Alex signaled the first three ranks to fall back to simulate the effect such a massive impact would cause. The rear ranks pressed forward, stabbing their short spears between gaps and raising shields overhead as illusory ravagers leapt over their brethren and landed in the rear ranks. Despite the intensity of the attack, their people held well—too well.

"There are not enough attackers," Azerick stated as he watched the battle rage on.

"Not enough? They are so thick there is hardly any open space between them," Rusty argued.

"The fact I can see any ground between them shows there are not enough to pose a true test. Double the number of ravagers."

Rusty bit his lip to stifle further protests and passed the word to increase the number of illusions. Allister, Aggie, and the other instructors conjured more ravagers and threw them mercilessly at the defenders. It was a feat of amazing concentration to play puppet master to so many phantasms. Not only did they have to make them move, they had to react to the real people's actions.

It was convincing enough that the lines began to bend under the assault as the humans slowly fell back to keep their foes from trampling them. Soldiers pushed forward and stabbed with more vigor to try to win back the ground they lost, or at least keep from losing more. Mages shook the ground and set the very air on fire with their magic.

"They are holding!" Rusty shouted excitedly.

"Yes, they are," Azerick agreed. "Let us throw in a couple dragons."

Rusty's elation at his people's success vanished. "They cannot take more! Their lines are already bending!"

"And now we will see what it takes to break them."

"You can't do this! Why do you want to take this victory from them?"

"I am not taking anything from them. I am giving them a clear picture of what they will face and the opportunity to learn from defeat."

"Don't do this, Azerick! Show a little compassion."

"Our enemies will not show them any, and neither can I."

Azerick took charge of conjuring the dragons himself. Two enormous scaly monsters circled overhead for a few seconds before swooping and raining down chaos. They belched great gouts of flame over the massed army, immolating entire ranks with a single fiery breath. The giant wyrms raced skyward and began circling once again, but they were far from idle. A strong wind picked up and became a near hurricane-force gale in seconds. Lightning arced across the sky and struck the ground and the panicked army below.

The illusions were wrought with such mastery that the smell of burning grass and flesh made the simple act of breathing a caustic and painful endeavor. Fear, real fear, ran rampant through the ranks of defenders. The stalwart amongst them tried desperately to hold the line and form a cohesive defense, but they were fighting against their own people just as strongly as they were against the enemy.

"Stop this right now!" Rusty demanded, grabbing Azerick by the front of his shirt.

"They must fight through their fear and suppress their panic."

Fueled by rage, Rusty turned back to the illusionary slaughter, attacked the illusions, and began unraveling the strands of magic holding them together. Allister and the others did not try to stop him and banished the illusions they controlled. Admitting to himself that the battle was over, Azerick dismissed his dragons. Shouting rang out over the battlefield and several of Brother Thomas's Chosen ran to help the wounded.

Azerick stood resolutely as Brother Thomas and his acolytes tended to the injured. Allister and the other leaders huddled together, getting reports through their speaking stones, and leaving Azerick an island unto himself. Azerick glanced over and saw his instructors were engaged in an animated discussion. Rusty separated from the group and stalked toward Azerick, his face flushed with anger.

"Four more dead and more than a score injured! For what?"

"So the others will become stronger."

"You are killing them! These Scions of yours will not have to destroy us; you are doing it for them. What was the point of this?" Rusty demanded, encompassing the battlefield with a wave of his hand. "They were doing well, but you had to break them. Why? Why put on this farce knowing you never had any intent on allowing them a victory?"

"Allowing them a victory would have been the farce! Do you think the Scions are going to *allow* them a victory? They fought against illusions, and they knew they were illusions. They even knew the dragons I sent were illusions, but they were convincing enough to break the nerve of entire squads. How will their courage hold, how level-headed will their thoughts be when the enemy and the death they bring is real, when they are slogging through mud created by the blood of their fellows?" Azerick shouted back. "Had this been a real battle, everyone you see down there would be dead now. Our people will be a major bulwark against an implacable enemy. If we fail, we leave tens of thousands open for slaughter! We cannot break because of fear!"

"You push them too hard!"

"I cannot push them hard enough! Their bodies are too frail for me to push them as hard as I must! I can only push them as hard as I can and pray it is enough, pray that those I called upon for help come and have been preparing just as hard, or we are all lost."

"I will not do this anymore," Rusty seethed. "I will not let you do this anymore!"

"You will not *let* me?"

"I will not let you! I will not stand by and watch you kill my students for a cause or an enemy we don't even know exists outside your own head!"

"You deny their existence? After all these years, you doubt my integrity? Why would I make this up and put myself and everyone else through all of this if the threat were not every bit as real as I have said?"

"Azerick, I will never doubt your integrity, but I do doubt your perception. You literally went through hell, and I cannot imagine what an experience like that would do to someone, even someone as strong as you. I fear you have brought some of it back with you."

"Denying the threat the Scions pose is the same as siding with them. Denial and ignorance of their existence has been the most effective blade they wielded against us, and now you of all people gladly pick it up and hold it to our throats. You are right, I have made a grave mistake, and that mistake was sheltering all of you from the Scions." Azerick grabbed a wad of Rusty's shirt. "If you need to see the face of our enemy to believe, then I will show you!"

Azerick tore open a gate with all his fury and pulled Rusty toward it. Rusty struggled against Azerick's grip, but it was as useless as a fly struggling against the clutches of a spider.

"Azerick, let him go!" Allister demanded.

"No! He demands proof, and I will give it to him! If any of you feel the need to look upon our enemy in order to put some steel in your spine, then follow us."

Azerick pulled Rusty through the portal and emerged inside his laboratory. He stepped over the ruins of his desk, destroyed when his gate bisected it, and threw Rusty to the floor with a flick of his wrist. Allister and Aggie followed the pair through the gate as much to witness what was to happen as to try to protect Rusty from Azerick's mounting anger.

Azerick did not spare anyone a glance. He crossed to the black orb mounted on a pedestal in the center of the room. Slapping his hands upon its cool, smooth surface, Azerick channeled his power into it, casting the room into darkness. A shimmering glow appeared, stretching from horizon to horizon and into the sky as far as the eye could see. Beyond it lay an army so vast one could not identify the far ranks or the end files. Hovering above it like a tight cluster of icicles was a massive crystalline tower surrounded by flying ships teeming with monstrous crews.

"*Have you brought us tribute, false Guardian?*"

Lacking Azerick's ability to filter the Scions' oppressive thoughts, their words crushed Rusty, Allister, and Aggie to the floor and made them writhe in agony. It was like a horse stepping on their heads while someone blew a deafening horn into their ears with enough force to make them bleed.

"I want you to tell them exactly what you are; show them what you will do when you break free!"

"*You have brought us a treat. It would be our pleasure.*"

"*Behold your fate, humans, and know the face of terror.*"

The landscape changed in the eyes of the three wizards and became the smoking ruins of a city. The bodies of the inhabitants, young and old, lay scattered in the streets and were being picked over by carrion birds and other scavengers. The city changed but the scene did not. Everywhere was nothing but destruction and death. Rusty's eyes were drawn to the bodies of a woman cradling two young children. He barely recognized them as Colleen and his twins. It was obvious someone, or something, had paid special attention in their deaths.

"Yes, little wizard, those who delve into the realm of the gods, and their entire bloodline, shall not get a swift death."

"We sense your terror and pain. We see in your mind your futile attempts at resistance and it amuses us."

"Continue your training; continue your existence of suffrage. It will make your breaking that much more satisfying and complete. Those few we allow to serve us shall know that they failed at the height of their power and will never find the courage to resist us again. Never will they again seek to raise themselves from the muck where they belong."

Feeling his point made, Azerick shielded the minds of his friends as best he could. The wizards lay on the ground, lungs heaving as they desperately tried to take back control of their minds.

"Do you see now why I do what I do? Do you believe, or do you still think this is a construct of my own mind?"

Rusty pushed himself to his hands and knees and fell back down, his trembling limbs unable to support him. "I—I see. I believe. Please, take us from this hell!"

The prison world faded and they were back in the summoning chamber. Azerick hated to inflict that kind of torture on his friends, but their strength and leadership were more important than their relationship. He *wanted* their friendship and love, but *needed* their cooperation. There were no words to mend the damage, so he left them to recover their strength, wishing there was a way to recover their minds and relationship.

CHAPTER 25

Azerick saw little of Rusty over the next few weeks. In fact, most of his people seemed to be avoiding him. It could have been his imagination. It was hard to tell since he spent most of his time beneath the tower. On the occasions he did see Rusty, his friend looked drawn, exhausted, and almost always drunk, or close to it. Azerick had been poring over his training guidelines and the instructors' reports, desperate to resolve the recurring defeats caused by the dragons' involvement in any given battle. He finally conceded it was not something he could solve by himself.

"We keep running into the same problem," Azerick explained to his core of wizards and officers. "Our army can stand against several times their number in ravagers, at least until the mages become exhausted. When we fight as a cohesive team with the Academy, we should have more in the way of relief forces. Our immediate problem is the minute we throw dragons into the mix, and we can be almost certain they will make an appearance, they overwhelm our mages. The number of mages it takes to deal with the dragons leaves us vulnerable. We need to find a way to impede the ravagers' assault enough to keep the infantry from being overwhelmed while the bulk of the mages deals with the aerial threat. That includes those flying ships of theirs. The gods only know what kind of chaos those things bring to the table."

"What about pit traps, pickets, trenches, or other barriers?" Alex suggested.

Azerick shook his head. "The ravagers are too strong and agile. They could leap over anything we could reasonably field, and once past the obstacles they would provide little hindrance."

"Magical traps throughout the battlefield," Rusty supplied. "We can place a lot of offensive wards since we are pretty certain where they will come from. We could create hundreds of them in little time if we make them just powerful enough to maim instead of expending the time and energy to destroy them outright."

"That's an excellent idea, and we'll certainly do that, but once tripped, it is gone and does not solve the problem. What we need is a battalion of giants!" Azerick joked. "Unfortunately, I have only seen one giant in my life, and he was not exactly an impressive specimen."

Roger scratched his head vigorously as if to shake loose a stuck idea. "What if we made some giants?"

"Make a giant?"

"Yeah, like the golem you made a while back to protect Ellyssa when she got into trouble. Wolf told her and she told me that it had given several of those Sumaran wizards and soldiers quite a challenge. We have dozens of blacksmiths just here at the school, and who knows how many in the city."

"Those would be an enormous help and could solve our problem, except it would be impossible. It took me almost a year to construct that thing. Sure, making the metal body would not be that hard, particularly if we focus on function over form, but creating the weave to make an autonomous fighting machine is incredibly complex. I could never have done it without the Codex Arcana."

"Then don't make it autonomous."

"What good would a metal shell do?"

Rusty broke in. "You're talking about something like the constructs Azerick made at the Academy! They were pretty simple, to him anyway."

Azerick looked doubtful. "Those were simple machines designed to do nothing more than crawl around and dust cobwebs out of the corners. Creating them with the instructions to attack and defend is too complex."

"But that's what I'm saying, don't make them autonomous," Roger insisted.

"Am I the only one missing the point here?" Azerick asked in frustration.

"No, the boy's got me confused as well," Allister responded grumpily.

"Mechanical manipulation is a simple form of magic," Roger explained. "I have been studying the speaking stones, and I think the magic can be modified to allow someone to see through it as well. Nearly a third of our mage cadets do not have the magical acumen to provide even decent defensive magic, much less contribute offensively. We make as many of these…pseudo-golems as we can, similar to what Azerick made at the Academy, only a lot bigger, and enchant them with simple magic. The novices should be able to power the constructs even with their meager magic and move them like puppet masters."

Azerick and the others nodded along. "And turn the speaking stone into a seeing stone to give the operator a first-person view of the battle."

"Exactly! We can make a cheap golem army in a few months."

"It would be like the earth constructs I summoned in Bruneford's Mill, except we would not need to form and hold them together with our magic," Ellyssa said. "Controlling an already formed construct would require a lot less energy and skill."

Azerick looked to his instructors. "I want every mage who lacks the skill to be a sword or shield to start training with the soldiers. Alex, I need you to teach these mages how to fight. I won't tell you how to train a soldier, but we do not have a lot of time, and fighting skill is vastly more important than tactics for this group. Someone go get Ken, please. Roger, if this works, you will be the first person I recommend for the King's Honor. You may have saved thousands of lives if we can get these things functional."

"I think our reward will be being alive at the end of this," Roger replied morosely.

"Josh, Maira, Umair, see to pulling aside the mages who would better serve controlling these constructs. Allister and Aggie, have Simon open my vault and pick through my jewels. See if you can make seeing gems out of any of them. Ellyssa, start thinking about how our tactics might change if this works. Roger, I need you to bring me the plans for my golem. They are in a cubbyhole in my study. Alex, you know what to do. These are mages and not accustomed to your style of drills. Work them in gently but swiftly." Azerick looked at Rusty as they all started to depart. "Rusty, could you stay a minute?"

Rusty stopped in his tracks and hunched his shoulders. He knew what was coming.

"Rusty, are you all right?"

Azerick's friend turned and looked at him with eyes red from exhaustion. "No, Azerick, I am not all right. I have not been all right for a very long time, and that…emotional raping the Scions gave me pushed me even farther from all right."

"Is that why you have been drinking lately?"

Rusty wagged his head slowly. "I see them every time I close my eyes. I see the Scions torturing and killing my family. I can't sleep. I have no appetite. Whenever I try to force myself to eat, it's all I can do to keep from vomiting. I succeed as often as I fail. Can you imagine what that is like?"

Azerick stepped toward Rusty to lay a reassuring hand on his shoulder, but he stepped away. "I do know what it is like. When I was in the abyss, a devil named Krade took me to a place called the Valley of Lies. I watched Miranda and Delinda torn apart by demonic dogs. I killed Daebian with my own hands and, Rusty, it was not the flashing images of a nightmare. It was as real as you and me standing here right now."

"How do you get past it? How do you cope?"

"I cope because I have to. Whenever I start to doubt, start to let fear make me forget why I fight so hard, I think about my family. I look into the faces of my students and friends and find a thousand reasons to keep fighting, because if we stop fighting and give up, your nightmares will become reality. You have to find the strength to work past it so it does not come to pass, and that strength is not in a bottle. It is in your heart, and you have the biggest heart of anyone I have ever met. It is your strength. Use it."

Rusty let out a shuddering sigh and nodded. "Thank you. Az, I'm sorry."

"For what?"

"For hating you. I don't want to. I want to think of you like I used to, but I can't. Is it possible to hate someone who is still your best friend?"

"Rusty, anything is possible these days."

Ken came into the room just as Rusty was leaving. "You needed me?"

"I do. Ken, do you remember the golem you helped me forge?"

"A man don't forget smithing something like that."

Azerick beckoned Roger over as the young wizard entered the room holding several rolled-up pieces of paper, and had him spread them out on the table. "How long would it take you and your men to craft one of these?"

Ken ran a soot-blackened hand through his hair. "That was a lot of fine crafting. Your specifications left no room for error. If it were all I was doing, probably two or three months if I was really on my game."

Azerick shook his head. "No, that's far too slow. I want a thousand of these, and I'll probably need them within a year or less. That's assuming this works."

"It can't be done," Ken insisted. "Each part required a flawless forging. Those were your words, and you sent back enough pieces to make me believe you."

"That's because in order to create an autonomous golem the magic required perfection to make an enduring bond. Anything less than perfection allowed the magic to seep out like water in a bad bucket. What I want is very different. These do not need to permanently hold vast amounts of arcane power."

"I don't know anything about all that, but if you're saying I can make these like any other tool, then that's a different story altogether. What level of craftsmanship do you need? How well do the parts have to fit together and move?"

"I just need them to function. The legs and arms have to operate, and the swords need to be able to cut something."

Ken studied Azerick's plans. "There won't be anyone inside them?"

"No, my mages will control them from a distance."

"All right. I recommend we do away with most of the outer shell and use a more skeletal system since you don't need to protect anything inside. This will save time and a lot of material that we just don't have these days. If you let me cast some of the more basic pieces it will speed things up a lot as well. Cast metal isn't near as strong as steel, but if you're not looking to make these things last for decades, we can get away with it."

Ken tapped his lips with a finger as he thought. "If you don't need a perfect fit, I can set teams to focus on a single component and have it all assembled by another group. Since each arm and leg isn't specifically designed for a perfect match, the minor variance will make an almighty racket, but it'll function well enough. If my people can do that, we should be able to get near your number. That's assuming we get the smiths in North Haven too."

"Do you know how we and the city stand on weapons?" Azerick asked.

"Oh, we got weapons aplenty. We got enough swords and spears to put two or three into the hands of everyone strong enough to wield them without dropping them on their foot."

"Good, then it should not be difficult to pull them away from weapon crafting to this. How soon can you have me a prototype?"

The master smith made several calculations in his head. "I'll need to finalize the plans, but I can get you one in about a week."

"Let's get to work then."

CHAPTER 26

Turning the younger, weaker mages into warriors was not as difficult a task as he initially feared. Although the skill they learned was different, their training had run a parallel course in challenge and intensity.

It took Ken and his team six days to construct the first machine to Azerick's satisfaction. Allister and Aggie managed to make a jewel that, when coupled with a simple scrying spell, allowed a mage to see through it as if it were his or her own eyes. They found that polished, unfaceted tourmaline worked best, and even a person capable of only minor magic could see through it hundreds of yards away.

Moving the construct, particularly in the precise, controlled manner required in combat, was the greatest challenge. Despite a drastically simplified version of the magic used to create true golems, Azerick still needed to imbue them with a certain amount of residual energy and function so the mages who operated the constructs could connect to them with their magic.

After much trial and error, Azerick was able to perfect a method simple enough for most of his full wizards to recreate. It came as a great relief. He dreaded the possibility that he would be the only one able to instill that necessary spark to animate the constructs.

Azerick found Raijaun waiting for him when he returned from another examination and repair of the Scions' prison.

"How does it look, Father?" Raijaun asked when Azerick's mind fully returned to their world.

Azerick wore a grim frown. "Not good. There are more flaws than I can possibly repair. I am glad you are back. I will need your help from now on if we are to buy ourselves any time of consequence. How did it go with the Academy?" Azerick asked, despite having gotten several reports from Raijaun over the past weeks.

"Technically speaking, their gates were a mess. I had to direct artisans to totally reconstruct two of the three. Once that was done, I was able to guide them through their alignment. I made certain the craftsmen understood the required level of perfection for the next set of gates before I left. Now that they have a functioning set, I expect them to be able to make the next ones properly. I may still have to help connect them once they are in place."

"Did they treat you well?"

"They avoided me for the most part and kept any conversations to the matter of gating and making the gates functional. Other than a few hostile stares and whispers behind my back, they were accommodating enough. How go these constructs you told me of?"

"Actually, you are just in time for our first field test," Azerick said with a rare look of eager anticipation. "I was able to put our prototype through its paces; now we get to see if a novice can make it work. Alex and the others are waiting for me on the training field."

"This should be interesting."

A large crowd was already gathered atop and just beyond the walls, all wanting to witness Roger's iron soldier in action. Azerick and Raijaun headed for a cluster of people standing a score of yards from the construct. The thing looked more like an eight-foot-tall armor rack with several pieces missing than a golem. Most of its body was a skeletal framework. The exceptions were its head where a single, large tourmaline rested in the center of a featureless ovoid face. The creature's legs were solid pillars of steel to help keep a low center of gravity and maintain balance.

"All right, Roger, time to see if your metal man idea is going to work," Azerick said as he took his place.

Alex added, "You know if this does work, you may have just changed the face of the battlefield for all time."

"It's going to work," Roger said with as much hope as certainty.

"Alisha, you may begin."

Alisha was one of the more recent students discovered when Azerick sent his people out in search of anyone with magical talent. She possessed a fair level of arcane aptitude but was slow in developing it to a level to be of much use on the front lines. Her slightly less than middling skill made her a perfect baseline for determining what they could expect from this iron army.

Alisha rested the circlet with its polished tourmaline set in gold atop her brow. She took a step back to regain her balance when the sudden magical connection and shifting of her vision caused a moment of vertigo. The construct swayed with her body but righted as she caught her balance.

"I'm okay," she assured those observing. Alisha tried to make her construct take a step and its "toe" dug into the soil and promptly fell face-first onto the ground. "I'm not okay."

"That's fine, just focus on what you want it to do. Picture how you want to move in your mind and guide the strands of your magic like strings on a puppet," Azerick instructed her.

Alisha took Azerick's advice literally, imagining strings connected to the limbs and body. She directed her metal warrior to lift its torso up with its arms then guided the legs to lift it back to a standing position. The young mage took a moment to steady herself before taking a more cautious step forward. The ponderous metal puppet took one step and then another.

She found her pace and directed the construct toward several targets that were nothing more than thick posts set in the ground. The construct plodded toward the posts, slowly picking its steps as it moved. It stopped before one of the posts and swung the heavy blade mounted on its right arm. The thick steel sheared clean through the four-inch post.

"It sure makes an almighty racket," Azerick said as he watched it destroy three more of the targets.

Ken nodded. "Aye, that's for sure. I could quiet them down quite a bit if I took the time to make better parts and floating joints, but that would take time you say we don't have."

"We certainly do not. Alisha, are you ready to take on a real opponent?"

"I think so. I'm feeling better on my feet every minute. It just takes some getting used to."

"Alex, you want to signal your men?"

Alex nodded and waved to a small group of cavalry waiting downfield. One of the men waved back and the five men lowered their visors and charged. Alisha braced herself and her construct as the riders each struck in rapid succession. Her construct took a steadying step back but remained standing, even as lances shattered against its metal body. Had they been a real enemy, Alisha could have certainly cut down at least a couple of the riders as they charged past.

"Alisha, see how far you can go before you lose control."

Alisha guided her construct across the field, her steps coming a little faster and more certain with practice. The pseudo-golem was a ponderous thing and a swift man could outrun it with ease, but its purpose was not to chase an enemy. It was a mobile bulwark to prevent a vastly superior army from simply swarming through the defenders. The construct ground to a halt not far from where the squad of cavalry had launched their assault. Alisha tried to reconnect, but could do little more than make it shudder.

Azerick turned to Alex. "What would you call that, three hundred, three hundred fifty yards?"

"Almost four, I'd say."

Azerick looked at the master blacksmith with a broad smile. "Ken, you and your people have a lot of work to do."

Ken's delighted expression matched Azerick's. "Aye, we sure do."

"I will need a copy of your plans to send to the Academy. They will have students there who will serve better as construct operators than fodder for the ravagers."

A shudder passed through Azerick, and a pain profound enough to make him stumble twisted his gut as he thought about the attack he had allowed to happen at the Academy. Novices would make the perfect candidates to control the constructs... novices like those he allowed to die during that horrible night. Azerick steeled himself against the tormenting wave of emotion, telling himself that the

Academy would still be set against him had he not allowed the ravagers to attack. His logic provided little in the way of relief.

The show over, Wolf and Ghost ducked farther back into the trees. Wolf had watched the proceedings through the small spyglass he found in Azerick's study during one of his foraging expeditions. He could have watched from a closer vantage point, but there were far more people around than he felt comfortable with.

The pair tracked along a narrow trail in search of Daebian's traps. It was now a long-running routine for him and Ghost to track his movements and destroy his snares, freeing any live animals and making a meal of the dead ones.

Ghost soon picked up a fresh scent and darted ahead with Wolf jogging swiftly after. They came upon a small clearing amongst a stand of thick brush, an ideal place for rabbits to congregate. The snare was easy to spot and Wolf walked over to cut the cord. He stood abruptly when a pine thrush called out nearby, suspiciously off-key.

Distracted by the discordant trill, Wolf was too slow to avoid the large trap hidden beneath the detritus. The thin but strong cord cinched tightly around both his feet, flipped him upside down, and yanked him off the ground. Ghost splayed his legs and growled furiously as Daebian stepped into the clearing carrying a loaded crossbow pointed straight at the half-elf's chest.

"You had best heel your dog," Daebian said without a hint of fear. "I do not know if the poison on this bolt will kill his kind or not, but a single scratch will certainly end you."

"What do you know of his kind?" Wolf demanded.

Daebian shrugged. "I'm curious to know what you know of his kind. It doesn't matter. What is important now is whether or not I decide to kill you. Do you think I was ignorant or had forgotten about your role in my *accident*? The answer is no to both. I just needed you to relax a bit, drop your guard. It was quite a feat to make a trap you would not readily spot. Anyway, back to the topic of killing you. Here's the rub of it. I only have time to shoot one of you. If I shoot you, your dog will probably succeed in tearing me apart. If I shoot your dog first, you will probably have time to use that incredibly nice sword my stupid father gave you to cut the cord, scoop up your bow, and put an arrow in my heart. In this environment, you definitely have the advantage even hindered as you are now. Father is rather fond of you. Do not look relieved; it is not a factor in your favor.

"Normally, when both options have a strong possibility of ending in the killer's death, the answer is to not provoke that action. Unfortunately, I am of the mind where I am fully prepared to risk my life in attaining what I want, particularly in satisfying a debt." Daebian stepped toward Wolf. "We are all still alive, Wolf. Please ensure your dog does nothing to change that."

Wolf gritted his teeth. "Ghost, back off."

Daebian stepped next to Wolf when Ghost edged away. "Are you familiar with the Habberback Plains barbarians? No? I think it is an error to call them barbarians. Their society is quite sophisticated and noble. Much more so than ours. Most of the animals populating the plains travel in massive herds. There are many tribes on the plains, and having such a concentrated but limited hunting ground obviously results in some serious competitiveness. Now, our society, the truly barbaric one, would engage in a war until one side was destroyed to the point it could no longer fight and would then become a slave class or simply perish.

"The barbarians long ago decided it was in no one's best interest to engage in this sort of fighting, so they created another sort. They call it honor rights. Thousands of horsemen from competing tribes would square off on the plains and do battle, but not with lethal intent. They carried long sticks and struck each other, often taking a token like a bead or feather from a fallen enemy. The tribe with the most honor rights gained the right to first hunt of a particular herd."

Daebian pulled his knife from his sheath and traced a line along Wolf's face. Wolf shuddered at the icy touch of the steel against his cheek but refused to show fear. Daebian lowered his crossbow, grabbed one of Wolf's beaded braids, and cut it from his scalp.

He held the lock in front of Wolf's face. "Do you know what this is? This is a symbol of your life, and it now belongs to me. I am taking this symbol of your life and allowing you to keep yours. You are now indebted to me for your life."

"You sick bastard!" Wolf shouted, his resolve having reached its limit.

"Such ingratitude. You should be thankful I did not take your dog's tail."

Daebian left Wolf and Ghost in the clearing, whistling a jaunty tune as if he had just had a pleasant conversation with a friend. Wolf waited until he could no longer hear his whistling before cutting himself down. As much as he hated Daebian and wanted to kill him, he was right. Daebian had given him back his life. It was a bitter feeling that felt like poison in his veins.

"Let him go, Ghost. Someone will give him his due one day."

CHAPTER 27

Daebian was bored again. Even tormenting Raijaun had lost much of its entertainment value as his brother seemed to be getting thicker-skinned and difficult to aggravate. Peck was easily riled, but the stableboy was so far beneath him that it was an insult to himself giving Peck any consideration and outweighed whatever entertainment he gained by tormenting the peasant. Azerick was busier than ever with his company of golems, and Raijaun spent most of his time practicing with the other spellcasters when he was not attached to his father.

Klaraxis was constantly whining for more souls, but killing animals was equally boring. He supposed he could find some small amusement in feeding the demon the soul of one of these vagrants. There were certainly enough of them despite the conscription, but even killing one of those riffraff would cause an uproar, and he did not feel like listening to his father's reprimands. Killing the pirates two years ago had been thoroughly stimulating, but where was he going to find a pirate around here?

With the thought of pirates still on his mind, Daebian found himself wandering the docks district. He looked up at the sign hanging over a tavern and decided to see if any fun was to be found within. It was only midday and the clientele was rather sparse thanks to the mass employment of the war effort. Daebian took a seat next to the only other patron sitting at the bar.

The barkeep looked up at his newest customer. "What can I get ya, boy?"

"Your best rum," Daebian answered, thinking all good pirates drank rum.

The man gave Daebian a condescending grin. "You're a little young for that, ain't ya?"

The man next to him said, "Best do as he says, Lucky. That's Lord Giles's boy."

Daebian's mood flashed from insulted to murderous without even a minute shift in expression. He turned to the man and asked, "Why would my father be a factor in what I am served? Is it because he employs most of your ilk?"

"Partly, I suppose, but mostly he just scares the hell outta me!" the man brayed into his mug.

Daebian smiled in a way one might assume he was amused, but those who knew him would be stepping away.

"Two men, one strong, one weak.

Both prone to anger,

Neither one meek.

The strong man can kill with a word,

But rarely does he speak.

The lesser man has only his blade,

But will murder in a moment of pique!"

Daebian's dagger appeared under the man's chin in the blink of an eye, the tip disappearing into the soft flesh beneath. The man dared not twitch as he felt a rivulet of blood tracking down his neck and disappearing into the collar of his filthy shirt. He suppressed the shudder running up his spine caused by the unnatural coldness of the boy's blade.

"I may not wield the power of my father, but make no mistake; I am by far the more dangerous of the two." Daebian sheathed his dagger and turned back to the barkeep. "Now, get me my order, not because of who my father is, but for who I am."

Daebian slipped a piece of silver onto the counter as the barman placed a shot of rum before him. "My presence in your putrid little tavern should be compensation enough, but I suppose it would be difficult to purchase your swill with such currency." He shuddered as the powerful spirit burned a course down his throat and into his belly.

"First one's always a bit fiery," the barman said, trying to relieve some of the tension. "I spit out half my shot the first time I tried it."

Daebian slammed the shot glass onto the counter. "Shut up and pour me another. I do not need the affirmation of a peasant, and likely a degenerate as well from the looks of you."

The tavern owner did as the young man ordered, hoping fervently the boy would either soon pass out or leave his establishment.

Daebian slammed back the second shot, willing his body not to respond to the vile stuff. He looked around the tavern and spotted a woman he correctly guessed to be a prostitute. She was not what one would consider pretty, but she could probably ply her trade in a better establishment than this. Daebian figured she was probably the barman's daughter or some other relation.

"You, go find us a room."

The woman smiled demurely and climbed the stairs to one of the small rooms above the bar. Daebian pitched another silver sword onto the counter and followed a moment later.

Spent and feeling properly relaxed for once, Daebian lay next to the harlot, his right arm pinned between his head and pillow. "So how was I?"

The woman traced a pattern on his bare chest with a finger and smiled. "Do you want the truth?"

"Do you want to keep your tongue?"

"You were fantastic," she moaned.

Daebian smiled. "Smart girl." He rolled out of bed and began collecting his clothes. "I had best get home. Father does fret so when I am away too long. He is such a brooding old mother hen."

He tossed a few coins onto the bed and strode cockily out of the bar. He fingered the hilt of his dagger as eyes appraised his youth and fine clothes from within the shadowy confines of open doorways. Much to his dismay, none sought to trouble him.

More eyes tracked him as he walked the long road to the school. He tipped an imaginary hat toward Wolf and Ghost whose eyes he felt upon him as keenly as a dagger in his back. Daebian pictured Wolf inside the trees with his bow drawn to the corner of his mouth, the tip locked onto his neck, and Ghost hunkered at his feet waiting to lunge.

It was still early in the evening, but Daebian thought he would turn in and avoid his father on the off-chance he crawled out of his dungeon. After stopping at the kitchens for a quick snack, he climbed the stairs to his room, certain his father and brother were both locked up in their precious laboratory doing whatever it was freaks did all day and night.

He sighed loudly as he reached the landing to his parents' rooms and looked into Azerick's glaring face. Why did everyone feel the need to tell his father whenever he expressed himself? He was already forced to walk to the city because of that tattling runt, Peck.

"Hello, Father. Have you been here all this time to tell me how disappointed you are in me, or did you wait until one of your little toadies informed you of my return?"

Klaraxis subtly tweaked Azerick's flaring anger. "Your behavior in the city is unacceptable. You cannot go bullying everyone around just to get your way like a spoiled child."

"You mean like you bullied the Hall of Inquisition, the Academy, even your best friend?"

"That was different. Things needed to happen for the betterment of all."

"You needed to get your way. You bullied and got people to do what you wanted. I bullied and got what I wanted—respect."

Klaraxis stroked Azerick's anger once more. "You confuse fear with respect."

Daebian shrugged. "Possibly. They both elicit identical levels of satisfaction, so I see no reason to split hairs over it. Admit what the real problem is, Father. The great and powerful Lord Giles simply cannot stand to have a *useless* son. It is not me who disappoints you. You are disappointed in yourself for what you created. I am a reflection of you, and a poor one at that. That is what you cannot tolerate."

Azerick tried to force down his mounting anger, but his frustration was evident in his voice. "I do not expect you to be able to do what Raijaun and I do, but it would not hurt for you to act a little more like him. Raijaun is kind, selfless…"

"Ugly as a troll's ass."

Klaraxis stabbed sharply at Azerick's mounting fury, fueling its intensity. Azerick's hand struck out seemingly of its own accord, slapping Daebian hard across the face. Daebian ignored the stinging wound and glared into his father's startled face as he looked at his hand in confusion.

"How easily you succumb to your true nature, Father. Do not expect me to weep into my pillow like Mother does every night, praying for her true husband to come back to her." Daebian knew he had struck a chord as Azerick began to visibly tremble and his face flushed. "Does the truth pain you, Father? Will you now kill me in a fit of anger like you did in the Valley of Lies?"

Azerick took a step back and gasped as if struck a physical blow. "How can you know that?"

"I was there, Father. The creature told you I was not a simple illusion. Granted, my body never left this place, but I saw everything. I saw how you let mother and the other woman die, and then you killed me, your precious little boy. You dare judge me and my actions? I do not know if I can ever be like you. You set a rather high bar for horribleness."

Azerick stood stunned as Daebian stomped up the stairs to his room. His son's parting comments buried his anger in an avalanche of guilt. He desperately wanted to go to Miranda and tell her how sorry he was, that everything would go back to the way it used to be as soon as this was all over. But he knew it was a promise he could not conscionably make. To give her hope only to possibly crush it later was too much. Maybe he could return to what he was once they were all safe, but he would not pin her hopes on a maybe. Azerick hung his head as he descended the stairs to his laboratory, wondering when the walk had become so long as the steps continued to spiral ever further downward, much like his humanity.

I can sense your anger and humiliation. Klaraxis said as Daebian sat on the edge of his bed stroking the black soul stone.

"He would never hit Raijaun like that."

Raijaun is too much like him. Your father respects him. Not like you. I can help you get his respect.

"How?"

The sword I told you about in my citadel. It functions much like the soul stone in your hand, only it is monumentally more powerful. It was what made your father what he is, and it could unmake him as well. What I have shown you so far is but a tiny fraction of what I could do for you, were you to retrieve the sword.

"You mean I should kill my father?"

His power would be yours. You would save your people from the Scions and be hailed the greatest hero who ever lived. You would be immortal. You are smarter than he is, and you would be even stronger if you wielded his power. I know you want to make him pay for his abuse and neglect. We have no secrets between us.

"It does not matter. I cannot get to it in your citadel."

Your brother can find a way. You are both tied to my realm through me, and he can use the Codex Arcana. I am certain he could find a way.

"Do you really think I could kill my father with it?"

It can kill a god!

A dark smile played across Daebian's face. A trip to the abyss did not sound pleasant at all, but it would certainly be interesting. He would get his father's respect if it killed him—either of them. He just needed to get Raijaun to agree.

Raijaun sensed Azerick's distress when he returned to the lab. He had heard about Daebian's conduct in the city earlier that day. Apparently, Father's talk with him had not gone well, which did not surprise him at all. Daebian was difficult when he was not being intentionally hostile. When he applied some effort, he was beyond impossible.

"Are you all right, Father?"

"I'm fine. How are you coming along with your spell?"

"The only way I have found to cover a large area is with a fog I can then give the solidity of water. It would slow the ravagers considerably, but it would also conceal them from our army."

Azerick nodded. "There will be so many, our ability to see them is unimportant. Arrow volleys and large area spells will have no problem finding targets. Can you translate it into something the mages can learn?"

"I should be able to within a few days."

"Good. I am going to check the barrier."

Raijaun watched his father leave for the summoning chamber. He had already checked the barrier for weaknesses and knew Azerick was using it as an excuse to remove himself from this world. The fact his father could find any sort of solace in such a place worried him. He watched Azerick pour everything of himself into protecting this world. He wondered how much he had to give, and what would happen when there was nothing left.

Raijaun found Daebian sitting on his bed looking almost as morose as his father had. "You should not upset Father so much."

Daebian looked up from the floor. "*I* should not upset *Father*? What about me? Does no one care if I am upset? Do you have any idea what it is like to know your own father hates you? Of course you don't. You are his pride and joy."

"Father loves you. He is just very distracted and gets too engrossed in his work. He is doing his best."

"I just feel useless. I feel like I am nothing more than a disappointment to him. All I want is his respect and for him to spend a little time with me." He threw his arms up in frustration. "Jansen was more of a father to me. Warmer too, and he hardly ever talked!"

"You do not exactly make it easy for him with your behavior."

Daebian looked back at the floor. "I know, but it seems to be the only way I can get his attention. I know it's stupid, but what else do I have?"

"You are an excellent swordsman and smarter than anyone I know, Daebian."

"Father does not care about that. All he cares about is magic and the Scions. He's right, I am useless, at least in that regard. But maybe I don't have to be."

"What do you mean?"

"What if I could get something, an artifact that could help me fight the Scions with you?"

"I have been through Father's store of magical items and do not know of anything that would be of much use fighting the Scions. There are things that could help you fight their minions though."

Daebian shook his head. "No, that is not enough. Everyone will be fighting the Scions' horde. I was at the library today."

"*You* were at the library?"

"Yes, I'm the smartest person you know, remember? I went there after the drunk made me angry. Anyway, I was frustrated at not being able to help. That's why I threatened the man. I found a reference to an artifact called a soul blade. It is rumored to be capable of killing a god. The only problem is that it is in Father's old house."

"What do you mean, in Father's old house?" Raijaun asked suspiciously.

"It is in Klaraxis's citadel."

"Now I know you are insane. I had always had suspicions, but this proves it. You cannot get to the abyss, and even if you did the demons there would devour you."

"That is why I need your help."

"I do not know how to get to the abyss, and I would not go there if I did. The whole idea is ridiculous."

Daebian looked back at the floor. "You would not say that if Father had said you were useless."

"Father does not think you are useless," Raijaun said defensively.

"Yes he does! I heard him say it. He said it to Mother."

"I do not believe you."

"He did. I was outside the door when he and Mother were arguing. All she wanted was for him to spend a little time with me. He got mad and told her the reason he did not want to be around me was because I was useless. Can you imagine how that felt? Can you imagine having your father come home after being away your entire life and hearing him say you were worthless? I know I have been an ass at times, but maybe you understand why I am angry, bitter, and so desperate for his attention."

A tear rolled down his cheek. "You want me to come out and say it? Fine, I'm jealous of you. I am jealous of your power and the time you spend with Father. I am jealous of how he looks at you as if you are the sun and I am something he stepped in."

Raijaun could not believe what his brother was saying, but he could not deny this was how Daebian felt. He understood how those feelings could fester and affect his behavior. Maybe his terribleness was not entirely his fault.

"Even if that is true, I do not know if we could get to the abyss, if the sword actually exists, or if it can do what the book claims."

"Hold out that ugly paw you call a hand."

"What?"

"Do it. Hold it out in front of you."

Raijaun held his hand in front of his face at arm's length. "Okay, now what?"

"What do you see?"

Raijaun looked at his hand and then at his brother quizzically. "I see my hand."

Daebian held his hand out in the same manner. "Do you know what I see?"

Raijaun shook his head. "What do you see?"

"Everything, Raijaun; these eyes see everything. I know the sword is there, I know what it can do, and I know you can find a way to get us there."

Raijaun looked into the strange, dark eyes of his brother. "I need to get back to the lab."

"Sure, we would not want to keep Father waiting." Raijaun shot him a pleading look. "Sorry. Just think about it, will you?" Raijaun nodded slightly. "Thanks. I know I have been a jerk, but you are a pretty good brother, even if you are as ugly as a troll's ass."

Raijaun shook his head and returned his brother's grin. He returned to the laboratory to continue working on his newest spell. Try as he might, he was unable to focus as Daebian's words and grief weighed heavily on his conscience. He was as wrapped up in his work as his father was and never gave his brother's feelings much thought. He never really looked past his taunting and troublesome behavior to see the boy inside him crying out for his father's attention, love, and acceptance.

Azerick did not return from checking the Scions' prison until the next morning. He found Raijaun dutifully studying the codex, but at second glance saw that he was not writing anything down and his eyes had a far-off, vacant look to them.

"Is something amiss?" Azerick asked.

Raijaun looked up. "No, Father. How fares the barrier?"

"Not well. There are flaws throughout its length and height. I have mended the worst of them as best I can. Hopefully it is enough to prevent a major breach. I will need you with me from now on. I think it is more important than your training with the other mages."

"How much longer will it stand do you think?"

Azerick released a long breath. "A few months, perhaps a year at best if we are supremely vigilant. Pinpointing an exact time of failure is impossible. The Scions appear to be biding their time and not attempting to create lesser breaches like the ones in Southport and Bruneford's Mill. For all I know, they could cause a major failure tomorrow if they poured their full strength into it."

Raijaun shifted nervously as he tried to think of how to broach the difficult subject. "Father, I have been thinking that it may be good for you to spend some time with Daebian. I can watch the barrier and even make some repairs."

Azerick sighed and rubbed his temples with his thumb and forefinger. "Did he say something to you?"

"I have just been thinking about how I would feel if my brother got so much more attention than I did. Especially if I was the one who resembled my father and my brother looked like a monster."

"You are not a monster, Raijaun, and you are more like me than Daebian in every way. But that is irrelevant. Our work requires us to work together, and because of that it is only natural we spend more time in each other's company. It has nothing to do with how much I love either of you. I love both my sons, but I have a duty to perform, a duty that will destroy thousands of families if I fail."

Raijaun looked down at the floor. "Did you tell him he was useless?"

Azerick's face fell and he stumbled over his response. "Did he tell you that?"

"Did you say those words, Father?" Raijaun asked as he looked into Azerick's eyes.

"Raijaun, I did not mean it the way it sounded. I would never intentionally say something so cruel."

"What is intent to a child, Father? Does a dead man care whether or not you intended to kill him? Your words struck Daebian like an errant arrow and with the same lethal results. Your words killed something within him, and we all chastise him for his wounds. You are right on one count, Father. We must not forsake our duty."

Azerick slumped into a chair and cradled his head in his hands as Raijaun left the room. He had taken in and cared for hundreds of homeless children when he was barely a man. He had provided them with a home, food, clothing, education, and even a sort of loving family. How could he fail so terribly at being a father to his own son?

He needed to connect with Daebian before it was too late, if it was not already. Although having been birthed less than nine years ago, he was already a young man. He was fierce, strong, and independent. Could he still reach him? Could he yet be the father Daebian needed? Azerick sighed as conflicting duties collided like two runaway carriages. It was the Valley of Lies all over again. If he tried to save both, he would lose everything. It would doom them all.

Deep within Azerick's psyche where the sorcerer could not hear, Klaraxis cackled gleefully, relishing the torment he was able to inflict. The human's children provided the perfect vulnerability to allow his subtle influence to destroy him. Subtlety belonged to the devils of the abyss, but necessity provided Klaraxis with a powerful learning tool.

Never taken by surprise, Daebian lurched up from his bed the instant Raijaun entered his bedroom.

"I will help you," Raijaun said without preamble.

Daebian smiled. "Thank you. Do you think you can do it? How long will it take?"

"Going from our world to the abyss is much easier than the other way around. Since we are bound to both worlds and are stepping from here to the abyss, I should be able to do it. I will need to seek answers in the codex, but I have a good idea of how to accomplish it already from what I learned helping Father with the gates between the cities."

Daebian clapped his hands together loudly. "Then stop standing around! You aren't getting any prettier. The Giles brothers have an adventure to go on!"

He shared in his brother's laughter before heading for the kitchens. Despite Daebian's eager insistence, he was famished and needed to eat. He was not surprised to find his father gone when he returned.

CHAPTER 28

Raijaun saw little of Azerick over the next few days. He assumed his father's vigilance had as much to do with guarding the barrier as avoiding his emotions or facing the source of his pain. He felt a bit guilty for his relief at having his father avoid him. If he were being more attentive, he might start asking why Raijaun was studying transdimensional magic instead of developing spells for the mages to better fight the Scions.

He was surprised to find the spell was not overly complex given the nature of it, but this was only because of his and Daebian's link to the abyss. Dark priests and wizards had been using something similar to offer sacrifices in exchange for power. It took a couple of days to prepare the small room Raijaun chose as the ritual chamber. It was one of the storage rooms located under the old tower and was perfect for his plans.

"Everything is ready," he told Daebian.

Daebian smiled and took a steadying breath. Despite his previous eagerness, he now felt some trepidation as the reality of what he proposed came to fruition.

"Okay, what do I need to do?"

"Follow me." Raijaun took Daebian to the room he had prepared. "The spell requires a bit of our blood to help anchor us to this world and connect to the abyss."

Daebian pulled his knife from its sheath and smiled as he held it up. Raijaun presented his hand and Daebian made a neat cut in the meaty part of the palm. Daebian watched the dark red rivulet slowly run down the blade toward the soul stone as Raijaun dribbled his blood onto the sigil etched into the floor.

"Now you," Raijaun told his brother.

Daebian wiped the rivulet of blood from the blade with his thumb just before it disappeared into the handle and drew it across his own hand. His blood spattered the design like the first fleeting drops of red rain as he imitated his brother's actions.

Raijaun handed Daebian a chit of stone with a similar design to the one etched on the floor. "Wipe a bit of your blood onto that and keep it with you at all costs. It links you to the sigil here and is the only method of return you have if anything happens to me."

"We certainly would not want that to happen. Imagine how upset Father would be—and me, of course."

Raijaun gave his brother a sour look. "Of course."

"I'm serious! You are very important to me. You are like the cow pie from which this beautiful flower blooms."

"Remind me again of who is doing who a favor?"

"Stop being so serious; I'm just joking with you. You have an even worse sense of humor than Father. Now make with the magic, spell boy," Daebian ordered imperially.

Raijaun shook his head but could not dislodge the grin he shared with his brother as he began the incantation. The runes marking the floor beneath their feet thrummed with arcane power and glowed, emitting crackling blue sparks throughout the designs. The glow turned red as it crossed the many dimensions of time and space and found an anchor within the abyss. Raijaun shuddered as he tapped into his abyssal power, tying its strands into his arcane weave to connect the two worlds. The room went black for a moment before light slowly began to fill it once more. Like the rising of the sun, the darkness melted away to reveal a red, barren landscape. Only the great black citadel thrusting above the horizon provided any contrast to the scene around them.

"Wow, this place looks boring," Daebian said as he looked around. "It certainly suits Father."

Raijaun nodded, despite feeling a powerful kinship with the strange world. It felt more like home than the school likely ever would, and that was very unsettling.

"Let us hope it stays boring. Excitement here usually means someone is getting torn apart. We must return to this exact spot to leave this place, so study it well. I have hidden it as best I can in case any of the denizens of this realm should stumble upon it."

"Do you think they could cross over?" Daebian asked.

"No, that would be impossible, but if they have any affinity for magic, they could unravel the weave linking the portals and trap us here."

"I definitely do not like the idea of that. This place has the wrong kind of light for this flower to grow, no matter how much manure is spread around here."

"I am going to cast an illusion on you to make you look like you belong here. Otherwise the demons will tear you apart on sight."

Daebian nodded. "It's a good thing I have my little brother to protect weak little me from the big bad monsters."

"Yes, it is," Raijaun replied seriously as he cast his spell.

"So how do I look?"

"Well, you are definitely now the second most attractive son."

"You must love this."

"I am not displeased."

The brothers began their trek toward the black fortress, keeping a wary eye on the denizens of this realm. The easiest to spot were the succubi and grackin flying about in the distance. Fortunately, none ever flew near for a closer inspection. Raijaun felt other eyes upon them as well, peering out of the few clefts and shadows. He was certain some of the shadows themselves watched them as they approached the citadel.

The pair spotted the main entrance flanked by two hideous insectoid creatures as they drew near the enormous onyx citadel. The guards were encased in armor made of a formidable white carapace and gripped a pair of spears in two of their four arms. At ten feet tall, they even topped Raijaun by a respectable margin.

"Do you think there is another way in?" Daebian asked as they approached.

"Possibly, but guarded just as well, I would guess."

"What is our plan, kill them?"

"Violence would alert the entire place to our presence and certainly spell our doom. Act like you belong here, but stay quiet. Let me do the talking."

Daebian nodded but kept a tight grip on the dagger hidden within the folds of Raijaun's masterful illusion. As they drew closer, he sought out the weak points between those bony plates. He studied the way they moved as they approached, identifying limitations to their movement and field of vision.

The creatures stiffened and lowered their spears as the two outsiders approached. "State your business," one of the creatures demanded in a hissing and mandible-clacking voice.

Raijaun took a few more steps toward the guards. "I am Raijaun, lesser prince of the Third Circle, here to pay tribute to Prince Drak'kar and congratulate him on his ascension."

"Prince Drak'kar attained his covetous seat long ago. Why do you come so late to give homage?"

"My progenitor understands how tumultuous such a transition can be and did not wish to cause undue stress by approaching too soon. He also needed time to stabilize his realm after his ascension to the Third Circle following Drak'kar's glorious victory over the failed demon Klaraxis."

"Prince Drak'kar has no time to spare for lesser lords of a lesser realm," the demon said.

Raijaun looked to his brother, unsure of how to proceed. Deception and guile had never been his strong points. Daebian, however, was a master liar, and if anyone could talk their way past it was him. Daebian picked up his brother's cue and stepped to his side.

"Does he not have a moment to receive a gift worthy of his greatness?" Daebian asked.

"I see no gift worthy of the greatest abyssal lord."

"A thousand prime souls travel with surprising simplicity," Daebian responded.

"Where are these souls?"

"Trapped safely within a soul stone and hidden away so as not to tempt overly ambitious demons."

The two guards understood the jewel for what it was, and their antennae waved around in their excitement. Soul stones could hold the life essence of living creatures just as the strangers claimed, and assuming they actually possessed it, prime material souls were the most valuable commodity in the abyss. Still, who would dare insult Drak'kar with an unworthy gift and risk a fate far worse than death?

"I will get you an escort. Skulk!" A sulfurous stench filled the air as the little red demog apparated in front of the gates. "Stupid demog, use those ridiculous wings to come! Take these two to see Drak'kar."

"You call Skulk then you yell at him and expect him to do what you say?" Skulk snorted and made a rude gesture.

One of the guards grabbed Skulk with surprising swiftness. "Drak'kar is not the only one capable of tearing off one of your wings for his amusement."

"Okay, Skulk take them to Drak'kar, but he needs his wings!"

The guard released Skulk, and both stepped aside and opened the great doors. Daebian and Raijaun had to hurry to keep up with the demog as he fluttered through the massive gaping portal and down the enormous black passageway beyond.

"Stupid bug faces threaten to tear off Skulk's wing like four-armed blattazuu's butt of a demon lord. Still hurts when Skulk flaps, and they yell at him for not wanting to fly," the demog continued to grumble.

The brothers kept a close eye on Skulk as he noisily flew ahead of them. They both noticed that one wing did bear a shinier, fresher look than the other. They looked to each other for a chance to get away from the demog so they could locate the sword. They needed to shake their escort, and Daebian was prepared to create the opportunity.

Just before Daebian's knife cleared its sheath, the deep shadows along the massive hall's ceiling and floor disgorged a host of demons blacker than the darkness that spawned them. The demons launched themselves from the darkness in a terrifying surprise attack. Raijaun reacted with surprising speed, largely thanks to the intensive battle training he shared with the humans at the school.

A brilliant light obliterated the shadows for a hundred yards in both directions. The sudden, intense light caused the demons to falter and shield their eyes as they shrieked out the vilest of curses. Skulk released a fearful yelp and instantly vanished in a puff of sulfur. Having gained a moment to focus, Raijaun summoned a massive amount of raw energy in each hand.

"Get down," he ordered Daebian.

Daebian did not argue for once. The power continued to grow in Raijaun's hands until he flung it away from him. The gathered energy split into a hundred scarlet bolts and sped down the length of the passageway, piercing and burning the demons coming from both directions.

Not wanting to feel useless, Daebian began to stand and pull his blade.

Do not attack. I sense Drak'kar is fast approaching.

Daebian began to warn his brother. "Raijaun…"

Intense darkness snuffed out Raijaun's light and plunged the hall into blackness so profound it felt almost tangible. Even Raijaun's demonic eyes did not see the huge form leap at him until just before Drak'kar's powerful fist slammed into him and sent him flying.

"…watch out."

The overwhelming darkness lifted and the brothers could see the demon lord standing contemptuously in the middle of the passageway.

"Did you think you could simply walk into my citadel and sneak past my guards with your ridiculous tale? What is your true purpose here?"

Raijaun slowly stood, pressing a hand against the pain flaring through his chest. "We only wished to offer you tribute."

Drak'kar smiled humorlessly at Raijaun. "I am Prince Drak'kar, lord of the Fifth Circle, and a master of deceit. You cannot fool me with your pathetic lies. No matter; I shall get the truth from you soon enough."

More black demons slithered from the shadows, climbed down the walls, and grabbed hold of Daebian and Raijaun. Another dozen demonic brutes tramped into view from farther down the hall, thoroughly blocking any chance of escape even if they could have broken free from the hands of the oily, black demons.

The creatures dragged them down the gloomy halls and descended deeper into the bowels of the fortress. A terrible moaning began filling the corridor. The plaintive cries rose in volume and desperation the farther they traveled. The demons shoved Daebian and Raijaun into a large room where black chains sprouted from walls painted in blood. Demons, humans, and unidentifiable creatures hung from these chains in various states of death and decay. Cruel iron tools of torture filled racks and covered blood-soaked tables. In moments, the brothers were hanging from the chains next to the creatures whose fates had long ago been determined.

Drak'kar stood close to the interlopers, leaned in, and sniffed deeply. "I thought I sensed something familiar in your magic, boy. You both reek of Klaraxis and his human parasite. Can you possibly be the unholy offspring of that detestable bonding? The dark queen denied me my desire to kill them, but perhaps I can take my revenge through you."

"I would like to take this moment to point out the fact that he is Father's favorite," Daebian said with a nod toward Raijaun. "In fact, I do not think Azerick would be the least bit troubled by any amount of pain you might inflict upon me."

"Daebian, you vile little worm!"

"Is that right?" Drak'kar crooned. "Does your father play favorites? Are you the cherished one?"

Drak'kar made a long, shallow cut across Raijaun's chest with his claw, parting the flesh as easily as the threads of the shirt he wore. Raijaun screamed in agony. The superficial wound burned like fire and sent tendrils of pain far deeper into his body than such a scratch should have.

"Do not worry. Your brother shall experience every bit as much agony as you, despite any preference your fathers may have."

Raijaun let out another shout of pain as Drak'kar drew a second thin, bloody line across his chest. Another of the demon lord's black demons separated itself from the shadows and approached with its belly low to the ground like a submissive dog.

"Prince Drak'kar, I bring troubling news."

Drak'kar turned away from his torture victim and faced his spy. "What is it?"

"Morta'sha's demons are massing near the Elutia Gate."

"She has always been too ambitious for her own good. Has she made any movement toward the gate?"

"No, My Prince, but her actions are suspicious."

"I had best see what she is doing before she gets the foolish notion that ascending to the Fourth Circle is an insufficient rise in her status. If she believes I am not yet established enough in the Fifth Circle to leave me vulnerable, I will show her the pain of her mistake." The demon obediently followed Drak'kar out of the torture chamber, leaving the two prisoners alone.

Daebian looked at his brother hanging next to him. "So far, your plan sucks."

"My plan?" Raijaun exclaimed. "This entire idiotic quest was your idea!"

"The idea was mine, yes, but the execution was entirely up to you, therefore my statement stands."

Raijaun turned his head, looked at his hand, and mimicked Daebian's words. "I see everything with these eyes. You sure failed to see the demons crawl out of the wall like roaches. Do you see this?" Raijaun flashed his brother an offensive gesture.

"I saw you get punched in the chest and fold faster than a bad gambler."

"I'm Father's favorite?" Raijaun shouted. "What in the abyss do you call that?"

"I call it an act of mercy."

"In what way is directing the torture toward me anything but an act of selfish and wanton cowardice?"

"I know you. If you had to hang there and watch me tortured, it would cause you great emotional distress. I knew Drak'kar was going to torture and kill us both. By urging him to do you first, I saved you the additional pain of watching him hurt and kill me. I basically cut your suffering in half."

"But watching me be tortured to death would not affect you at all?"

Daebian shrugged. "Proof that being a sociopath has its benefits."

"I do not think you are a sociopath. I think you are just a terrible person."

"At least I'm a person. Why don't you stop complaining and use some of that awesome power of yours to get us out of here?"

"It's a little hard with my hands shackled to the wall. Besides, I have been trying. These chains and manacles are enchanted to prevent such a thing."

"Can you defeat it?"

"Perhaps, with enough time."

"I don't think Drak'kar is the type to give us a lot of time."

"Maybe you should get him to torture you first. With any luck, he will get bored, and that will give me enough time to figure a way out."

Daebian rolled his eyes and shook his head. "It is that kind of terrible planning that got us in this mess in the first place."

"You are impossible."

"Impossibly handsome?"

"Just impossible!"

Skulk apparated into the room with the cloying scent of brimstone to announce his presence. He looked hurriedly around the torture chamber before fluttering near the two prisoners.

Skulk leaned close to Raijaun and sniffed. "You do smell like glorious human master!"

Raijaun asked, "You liked the human master?"

Skulk bobbed up and down, waggling his whole body. "Oh yes! Human inside ugly Klaraxis treated Skulk good. He would never tear off Skulk's wings like smelly Drak'kar did."

"Skulk, would you be willing to help him if you could?"

Skulk ceased his excited fluttering, landed, and sank into himself. "Help human master? Help how?"

"Azerick is our father. He needs a sword Klaraxis keeps somewhere. It is not large and its blade is as black as night. With your help, we could get the sword and be gone before anyone knows we escaped. You would be a hero, Skulk."

The demog's eyes widened. "Skulk would be a hero?"

"Yes, Skulk."

"Drak'kar would pull off both Skulk's wings if he found out Skulk stole from him and freed his prisoners."

"It is not his sword, Skulk. It belongs to Klaraxis, and since Azerick is now Klaraxis, it belongs to him," Raijaun coaxed him. "We would be gone from here and no one would know you helped us escape."

Skulk thought for several moments before bobbing his body up and down. "Yes, Skulk will help! Skulk will be a hero!"

The demon flapped into the air once more and pressed an engraved piece of black metal against the shackles clasped around their wrists and ankles. Daebian and Raijaun rubbed their chafed wrists and looked to the demog.

"There are two guards outside. Skulk will distract them and strong one can kill them. Weak one should stay back."

Daebian looked insulted. "I am not weak! I can kill a demon too!"

"I think you should let me deal with them. I think there will be less chance of them raising an alarm," Raijaun suggested.

"Fine, you do it. You've been doing great so far."

Raijaun ignored his brother's acidic remark and waited for Skulk to do whatever it was he was going to do. The demog vanished from the room. Several curses from the hall followed a series of dull popping sounds just beyond the door. Raijaun pressed his hands against the black stone of the chamber and sent small tendrils of power into it. Something in the stone called to him, welcomed him into its ebony embrace. He shook off the uncomfortable sensation and melted the stone with his magic. Onyx spears burst from the other side of the wall and skewered the two demon guards, killing them with no more sound than the frothy gurgling of their dying breaths.

Daebian and Raijaun stepped into the hall and nearly choked on the overwhelming stench of brimstone. The caustic fog was so thick they could not see more than a few yards down the passage.

"Quickly, Skulk, lead us out of here," Raijaun begged as he covered his nose and mouth with the sleeve of his ruined shirt.

They had to jog to keep from losing sight of the little demog as he raced out of the bowels of the citadel. They came upon several demons, but none seemed interested in them beyond hissing or screeching an invective as they passed. The fortress was massive beyond imagining, a veritable city encapsulated in black stone, yet it was sparsely populated despite its vastness. Skulk finally slowed as they made their way down a particularly long passage with no branching rooms or corridors along its length.

"Here at the end is Klaraxis's vault," Skulk said. "Two tar'raun'atu guard the door. Skulk can get in but cannot leave with sword. You cannot get in at all, even with Skulk showing you the way."

"All right, Skulk, you have been very helpful. Daebian and I will figure out a way from here," Raijaun said.

"Skulk going to go hide far away so Drak'kar cannot tear off both Skulk's wings."

"How should we approach this?" Raijaun asked after Skulk flapped away.

"I think we should kill them swiftly before they have a chance to raise an alarm or tear us to pieces."

"Skulk said there were two. Tar'raun'atu are extremely tough. I do not know if I can kill them both without making a lot of noise."

Daebian stroked the stone set in the hilt of his dagger. "You kill one, and I will kill the other."

Raijaun looked doubtful. "A knife is a poor weapon against these creatures."

"It has some special properties. It will do the job."

"What kind of special properties?"

"The none-of-your-damn-business kind of special properties. Now, are we going to go get my sword or stand here talking all day?"

Raijaun looked at the dagger suspiciously. Deciding his brother was not going to elaborate, he led the way down the gloomy hall. The passage sloped downward and made a sharp turn to the left. The brothers practically ran into the hulking tar'raun'atu upon turning the corner. Although about the same height as Raijaun, the brutes sported a much greater mass.

"You stop," one of the demons commanded. "None may enter except Drak'kar."

Daebian continued walking toward the guards. "It is all right, we are depositing something within, not taking anything out."

"None may pass but Drak'kar," the demon repeated.

"I am certain Drak'kar did not mean to keep out those who wished to give him gifts," Daebian said as he stepped closer and presented the dagger across his palm.

The tar'raun'atu leaned down to take a closer look. With lightning-fast reflexes, Daebian spun the blade around and thrust it under the tar'raun'atu's chin. Klaraxis put all his meager will into pulling the demon's life force into the soul stone. Had he possessed more than a shadow of himself, the task would have been easy. But given his partial existence and the relative weakness of the soul stone, it was like trying to run through waist-deep mud. Sensing Klaraxis's struggle with the impaled demon, Daebian leapt and wrapped his arms and legs around the flailing demon's head and neck, holding tight as it thrashed about in fear and pain.

Raijaun shaped the Source and touched the wall. Half a dozen black spears erupted from the stone, but the tar'raun'atu was extremely tough and only two managed to pierce its thick hide. The demon roared in pain and outrage. Its thrashing body snapped the spears from the wall, and it charged Raijaun. Thinking fast, Raijaun raised a wall of stone from the floor directly in the tar'raun'atu's path. The demon crashed into it hard enough to rebound. Before it could recover its senses, Raijaun brought a massive pillar of stone down from the ceiling and crushed it into a bloody pulp.

Seeing his brother struggling with the other guard, Raijaun summoned a pair of massive hands to pin it to the floor. The stone hands trembled and cracked as they fought to control the hulking brute. The beast managed to tear one arm from the floor with its wild thrashing, but it began weakening as Klaraxis and Daebian drained the creature's soul from its body.

The tar'raun'atu finally ceased its struggles and Daebian stood. "Well, that was a bit more work than I expected," he panted. "See, I told you I could kill a demon."

Raijaun pressed a hand against the ebony wall of the citadel and felt the writhing energy trapped within. "I think we have been discovered. Grab your sword and let us be away."

The brothers stepped into the room and looked on in amazement. Affixed to the walls and resting upon stone plinths was a myriad of artifacts. Some were easily recognizable, in form at least, while others were completely alien.

"It is like Father's vault only—much more," Daebian said in awe. "We should take as much back as we can."

"There is no time! Besides, we do not know what any of these things do. Find your sword and let us be on our way."

Daebian scanned the walls for a moment simply for show as Klaraxis directed him to the sword. "There. Give me a boost. Klaraxis must be a tall brute to put it so high."

Raijaun extended his hand and reached out to the sword with the Source. The blade flew from the wall and slapped into his waiting palm. Daebian's eyes flared in jealous anger at the sight of his brother holding his sword.

"Give it to me," he said in a low voice.

Raijaun narrowed his eyes at his brother with suspicion and annoyance as he handed him the sword. Daebian snatched the blade and threaded the sheath onto his belt next to his dagger.

"We need to go—now," Raijaun insisted.

"No argument here," Daebian replied as he hastened for the doorway.

The pair broke into a jog, their footfalls echoing off the black stone all around them. Raijaun was not certain they had been discovered, only that there was a disturbance in the fortress's stones. That doubt lasted until they came upon a mass of demons blocking the end of the long passage leading out of the lower vault chamber.

"Did you truly think you could simply walk into my home and steal my property?" Drak'kar asked. His amusement in no way hid the lethal intent in his voice. "Kill them."

The mob of demons charged the intruders, practically frothing at the mouth in their desire to rend their bodies to shreds. Raijaun filled the corridor with fire, incinerating the charging demons and leaving their charred corpses twisted into malformed blackened husks.

When the flames cleared, Drak'kar stood alone at the end of the hall completely unscathed. "I was hoping you were worthy of my personal attention."

Raijaun conjured stone spikes from the walls, floor, and ceiling in hopes of impaling the demon as he had the guards. Drak'kar extended his arms and stopped the spears from touching his flesh.

"Fool, this citadel belongs to me."

We cannot fight him! Klaraxis insisted. *Take the soul stone from your dagger and affix it to the pommel of the soul blade.*

Daebian wrenched the black jewel from the hilt of his dagger and held it near the base of the black sword. Klaraxis focused his meager power through Daebian to twist the metal of the hilt around the stone. The demon let out a satisfied groan as he felt the power of the soul blade merge with his shadowy consciousness.

Open your mind to me, and I will show you how to use the shadow ways to escape.

Daebian cracked open the door to his consciousness and slowly allowed Klaraxis in, wary of the demon's treachery. Thoughts filled his mind as Klaraxis showed him how to wield his abyssal power and command the shadows to do his bidding.

"Daebian, I hope you are right about that sword being capable of killing a god," Raijaun said as Drak'kar approached, "because we may need it to kill a demon lord."

Drak'kar will never let you near enough to him to use the blade against him. If you try to fight him within his hall, he will kill you both. Use what I have shown you to flee.

"Sorry, brother, but I am afraid this is where we must part ways. I am sure you will be fine. After all, you are the powerful son and I the useless one."

Daebian stepped into the murky black shadow sheathing the base of the high wall and vanished.

CHAPTER 29

Inside the shadow was nothing but darkness all around. There was no sight, sound, or smell within its confines. Daebian was blind and fought to suppress the fear trying to force its way into his heart.

"What is this?"

It is the shadow ways. It is the place between places. By using the shadow ways, you can step into a shadow and emerge from another, but you must be intimately familiar with them or risk losing yourself between worlds forever. Only my perfect knowledge of my realm allows me to traverse the shadow ways without seeing the point of egress.

"How am I able to do this?"

You are my son. You are the Prince of Shadows. This is but a taste of the power you can wield once you free my soul from your father's prison.

Following Klaraxis's guidance, Daebian stepped out of the shadow ways into the wan light of the abyss. He looked behind him and saw the citadel towering over him.

"I could certainly get used to this," Daebian said, jogging toward the teleport site.

Drak'kar stalked toward Raijaun who stood mystified and furious at his brother's abandonment. "It appears the battle shall be just between us. A shame. It would have been far more entertaining had he stayed."

Drak'kar lurched forward and Raijaun struck once again, twisting the Source and abyssal magic together into a powerful black and silver ray. The beam struck Drak'kar in the chest as he leapt, arms outstretched to grapple and crush his foe. The force of the ray hurled him back down the hall and crushed him against the black wall.

The demon lord waved his long black tongue through the air. "I can taste Klaraxis and his human parasite in your magic, boy. Your father wielded such twisted magic and failed to defeat me and so shall you. I shall enjoy exacting the vengeance your fathers denied me upon you."

Raijaun lashed out with his magic once more, but Drak'kar summoned his own power and slapped it aside. The demon struck Raijaun at a full sprint and sent him careening down the passage. Raijaun rolled into an ignoble heap as pain radiated through his body. Drak'kar was on him before he could recover. The demon lord grabbed Raijaun with two of his strong hands and began bashing him against the wall.

Raijaun's teeth rattled in his skull as Drak'kar repeatedly brutalized him. Something finally yielded and he was relieved to realize it was the wall and not his body. Raijaun crashed through the stone and found himself in an empty space between walls. He struggled to his feet and launched another spell at Drak'kar through the gaping hole in the wall. Drak'kar deflected it with a conjured ward.

"I know your tricks, boy. You cannot surprise me with it."

You stand within the house of your father. Claim your inheritance.

Raijaun heard the soft voice inside his head and understood its intent if not its source. He had felt the power of the souls trapped within the black stones when he touched them. It was vile and evil, but they belonged to him and he would not die here. He had far more important things to deal with, starting with his brother.

Raijaun sank his claws into the stone, took a deep breath, and glared as rage filled his body. "You know my father's magic? Then let me show you something from my mother."

Raijaun tapped into the stored power of the citadel. Dark energy poured into his body and he merged it with his Guardian and sorcerous magic to create a spell of colossal power. Drak'kar gazed uncomprehendingly at the strange triad of magic the child demon wrought. He suffered only a moment of confusion before the world exploded in a supernova of light and sound.

Black and reddish dust hung in the air, the only sound being the stones of various sizes falling from the sky and thudding into the ground. Dim light seeped through the cloying haze from a single direction. Raijaun followed it with the hope of finding a way out—and his brother.

Sharrellan stepped from the black cloud of dust and smiled as Raijaun furiously sped through the massive hole in the fortress. "So much like his father."

Daebian paced the reddish landscape in search of the portal that would take him home. He gripped the chit his brother had given him in his hand as he searched, but if it knew the way, it was being obstinately silent.

"Where did he hide that damnable portal? I really should have paid more attention."

Daebian felt the ground tremble beneath his feet a moment before a concussive force reverberated through him. He turned just as the sound from a massive explosion reached his ears. A huge cloud of dust now obscured the entire citadel from view.

"Wahoo! Give 'em hell, little brother!" Daebian crowed, then danced a jig. "Uh-oh."

Daebian began running and leaping to avoid the rain of massive black stones streaking from the sky like meteors, throwing up clouds of dust and shaking the ground as they struck. The hail of rock continued for several seconds before ending as quickly as it started.

"Well, this is not going to make that blasted portal any easier to find," Daebian said, looking at the scattered boulders as he began walking in an ever-expanding spiral.

Daebian turned toward an odd flapping sound just before a large object struck him at great speed. He felt himself flying upward for a moment before plummeting back down and smashing into the ground. The force of the impact drove the air from his lungs and sent pain shooting throughout his body.

"You left me to die, you wretched, selfish bastard!" Raijaun screamed as he pressed down on his brother. "What have you to say to me before I kill you?"

Daebian opened his eyes and looked upon his brother's seething face. He slapped at Raijaun's wrist and felt the pressure ease enough for him to draw a shuddering breath.

"Um, you're welcome?"

"What?" Raijaun exclaimed, taking a step back at Daebian's totally unexpected response.

"You were weak and too afraid to use your power to its full potential. Until you stopped being such an incredible wimp, you were next to useless. I had faith in you. You just needed the proper motivation to embrace your inner monster."

"You consider death a motivator?"

"I cannot think of a better one. So, you're welcome. Now you say…"

Raijaun stood in stunned silence. He could not deny his brother's words, but he could not help but doubt his intent. Daebian was a selfish narcissist who did nothing that was not to his benefit. Still, what he said was true. If Raijaun continued to balk in the face of his own power, he would be little help when it came to helping Father battle the Scions.

"Thank you?"

"There you go. And people say I'm the one lacking in manners." Daebian extended his hand. "Now, help me up. I think you shattered my spine; you savage brute."

Unable to respond any other way, Raijaun pulled Daebian to his feet. As his anger ebbed, the agony of his conflicting magic began to take root. His blood felt as if it had turned to acid and every muscle in his body tried to peel away from the bone and jump through his skin.

Daebian looked at his brother. "You all right?"

"No. Let us be gone from this place."

Raijaun limped some distance away and gesticulated. Black flames flared up and outlined the hidden glyphs of the transport spell. Daebian followed and stepped into the circle.

"So that's where it was."

Raijaun fought through the overwhelming pain and fed power into the runic circle. The black flames erupted all around them but did not burn. Upward they grew until they reached the dreary sky and tore a hole through its encompassing veil. The brothers flew skyward, bursting through the breach between dimensions. Blackness surrounded them once more until a faint nimbus of light slowly formed around them and they once again stood within the summoning circle beneath the old tower.

"I must go and rest," Raijaun said as he staggered toward the door.

Daebian held his prize in his hand and looked at it longingly. "Yeah, you go do that."

Raijaun dreaded the walk to his room, and it took every ounce of his will to force his legs to navigate the stairs. He lacked the strength to pause when he saw Azerick waiting in his chambers. He walked past his father and dropped heavily onto his bed.

"You and Daebian have been gone for over a day. Where have you been?"

Raijaun stared at the ceiling through his closed eyelids. "Likely making an enormous mistake."

Azerick swallowed and forced calm into his voice. "What have you done?"

"Daebian wanted to help us. He told me he knew of a sword that would make him useful in battling the Scions. He said the sword could kill a god."

'With that sword I can trap the soul of any creature, even a god.' Azerick shuddered as Klaraxis's words echoed in his mind.

"I discovered a way to the abyss and got the sword."

"Raijaun, how could you be so foolish? You could have been killed! You are too important to risk on such idiotic adventures!"

Raijaun summoned the strength to turn his head and look at his father. "I am too important. What of Daebian, Father? Is he not too important to you for him to risk his life as well? You see, that is why I had to help him. You look at him the way everyone else looks at me. You are his father, and you should be better than that."

Azerick turned his eyes to the floor. "Perhaps that is true, but you trust him too much."

Raijaun nodded and closed his eyes. "You are probably right."

Azerick crossed the upper hallway connecting the two towers and ran down the stairs in hopes of catching Daebian. He did not know what his son intended to do with the sword, but he knew it could not be good. He loved his son, but he knew too well what he was. Daebian was crossing the parlor when Azerick reached the main floor of the old tower.

"Daebian, I know what you have done, and I cannot allow it."

Daebian stopped and turned toward his father. "Cannot allow what, Father?"

"I cannot allow you to possess that sword. It is too dangerous to let loose in this world, particularly in the hands of someone like you."

"Like me, Father? All I ever wanted was for you to be proud of me, but you only cared about Raijaun because he had the power to help you. Now I have the power to be of use to you, and you want me to give it up? Why, so I can go back to being as useless as you told Mother? Why would I do that?"

"Daebian, I never meant what I said in that way. You may not be able to help me the way Raijaun does, but you are far from useless. You are smarter and more skilled than hundreds of thousands of men who will soon be fighting this war, and who will all be making a difference. If you truly want me to be proud of you, then show me you can think beyond your own desires, and give me the sword."

Daebian stroked the black gem set in the handle of the sword and nodded. "You are right, Father." Calling upon Klaraxis's abyssal power, Daebian moved faster than Azerick thought possible and plunged the soul blade into Azerick's chest. "The sword is dangerous in the hands of someone like me. More dangerous than you can possibly comprehend."

Azerick's body went rigid. He could not even force a scream as the evil blade tore his soul apart. Klaraxis cried out in exultation as he felt his soul being freed of the sorcerer's damnable prison. It was a horribly painful endeavor, and he rejoiced in the agony.

I told you I would destroy you one day, human! I corrupted your son, and soon his body will be mine. I will devour his soul before stripping and dining upon yours bit by delicious bit!

Klaraxis laughed as he felt his spirit excised from that of Azerick's and slide into the blade where it would soon be pulled into the boy's body. His laughter ceased when he reached out with his consciousness and found himself locked within a prison even smaller and more desolate than the one within the sorcerer's mind.

What are you doing? You have no need of the soul stone any longer. Take me into your body and my full power will by yours, as well as that of your father's! You will be like a god!

"Take you into my body, so you could be a constant annoyance like you were to my father? I think not. I could never tolerate your constant yammering. Did you truly think I would be foolish enough to let you into my body so you could steal it for your own? You thought you were using me, but I had you outsmarted when I was just a child. You are pathetic, Klaraxis. Besides, if you found my father's will difficult to tolerate, you would find mine insurmountable. Would I be godlike if I absorbed you and Father? Perhaps, but I cannot imagine an eternity of listening to him remind me of how disappointing I am. Besides, I think I will be able to torment him far better by leaving his soul right where it is. Now, shut up and let me think."

Klaraxis's furious keening cut off abruptly when Daebian sheathed the blade and took his hand off the black jewel that now housed the demon's soul. A new source of anguish filled his ears as Miranda shrieked and ran to Azerick's side.

"What have you done?" she wailed as she cradled her husband's head in her lap.

"It appears I have stabbed him, Mother. Do you really need me to explain the obvious, or are you just being needlessly rhetorical?"

"Why? Why would you do this?"

Daebian shrugged. "It seemed the right thing to do at the time. I hate such emotional scenes, so I shall leave you to your grief."

"Daebian, wait. Where will you go?"

"I do not know for certain. I always wanted to be a pirate," he mused.

Miranda looked at her son as if seeing him for the first time. "I do not know where we failed you, Daebian, but I pray you come back to us some day."

Daebian smiled down at his mother. "The day I return, it will be at the head of an army the likes of which you cannot imagine to conquer this pathetic kingdom." He then turned and walked away.

EPILOGUE

Miranda walked into the room where Azerick lay upon his bed unmoving. Next to him, Brother Thomas maintained his vigil, praying and using his divine magic to soothe and heal his wounded soul.

"Has there been any change?" Miranda asked.

Brother Thomas shook his head. "None I can tell. His soul was badly injured by whatever wound Daebian inflicted upon him."

"It has been a week. How much longer will it take for him to mend? How long can he live without sustenance?"

"I am sorry. I do not know the answer to either of those questions, Miranda. Remember, this is not Azerick's body, but an imitation wrought by the demon's innate ability. He could languish like this for months or even years. I just do not know."

It was another somber breakfast as the school's leaders sat around the dining table. Everyone felt the stress and fear of Azerick's condition, desperately wondering when or if he would awaken. Their battle was now divided on two fronts: the physical exhaustion of their rigorous training and combating the overwhelming despondency crushing the spirits of everyone at the school. Azerick was the hope for their survival and without him, they had none.

"Has there been any change in his condition?" Allister asked Miranda.

Miranda took a sip of her juice, cut liberally with wine, to try to steady her voice when she spoke. "No. Thomas says he is certain Azerick is inside the body somewhere, but his spirit has suffered some kind of significant trauma. Even though the wound itself was largely superficial and Daebian missed striking any vital organs or arteries, he suffered some sort of traumatic assault to his soul. There is little else he can do."

"I think we need to discuss the future of the school and our preparations," Rusty said. "What do we do now with Azerick…convalescent?"

"We do the same thing we have been doing," Ellyssa insisted. "We keep training and devising new ways to kill our enemy."

"I think with Azerick's prognosis uncertain, we should revisit the way we conduct our training. I have some ideas—" Rusty started to say.

"And unless they are to increase our efforts, you will do well to keep them to yourself," Ellyssa snapped.

"I have a right to express my opinion!"

"What you call opinions I call whining."

"I saw my family brutally murdered by the Scions! I am not talking about lessening our defenses or preparations, but without Azerick, we need to adjust how we are going to fight this war!"

"We are not going to fight it without Azerick," Ellyssa insisted.

Allister cleared his throat and raised his hands, beseeching calm. "We are all upset at what has happened. Azerick will recover. The gods will not allow anything less, so let us not turn our fears and frustrations onto each other. Rusty is right; we need to prepare for any eventuality. How does our training progress?"

Ellyssa took a deep breath and replied, "We have fielded almost a hundred of the constructs and assigned operators to each of them. All of them have come from the weakest of our defensive mages. We have gone through several scaled-down exercises and found that their ability to slow the ravager advance greatly outweighs the loss of their employing defensive wards and spells. The swords have been able to defend against a dragon without the ravagers destroying our front lines. They work."

"That is good news. How many of these things do we think we can field without pulling too many mages from the ranks?"

"Using Azerick's gates to reach Brelland and the towns near the capitol, we have recruited one hundred forty-seven people with enough magical aptitude to control a construct," Maira reported. "Seventeen of them have the propensity for higher-level wizardry if we had the time to train them properly."

"That is heartening," Allister said. "How is Raijaun doing? Has anyone seen him lately?"

"He rarely comes out of the basement," Aggie answered. "I think he is determined to maintain the barrier in Azerick's absence."

"Understandable, but let us not allow him to become too withdrawn or obsessed. Aggie, were you able to contact the Academy in regards to them fielding these constructs as well?"

"I did. Headmaster Florent reluctantly agreed to entertain the concept. I think she would do almost anything short of making a pact with the abyss to prevent another tragedy like the one they suffered. We put two score of the constructs on a ship yesterday bound for Southport."

"Good. Without the Academy, we would have had a tough time fielding enough of the things. As much as I hated Azerick's decision to allow the ravagers to attack them, I doubt they would have considered the idea to…"

An acolyte burst into the room and shouted, "Azerick is waking up!"

There was but a moment of hurried glances around the table before everyone leapt to their feet and ran for the infirmary. Brother Thomas intercepted the small mob just inside the building.

"I cannot have all of you charging through my infirmary like a cattle stampede! Four of you can come in, but no more. I leave it to you to decide who."

Alex, Ellyssa, Allister, and Miranda rushed to Azerick's side. Three acolytes struggled to pin him down as he thrashed on the narrow bed. Sweat beaded his brow and soaked the sheets that now lay wadded on the floor.

"What's wrong with him?" Miranda asked fretfully.

"His soul is fighting to reconnect with his body," Thomas answered. "It appears to be a traumatic thing."

"Can't you do anything?"

Thomas shook his head. "With his strength, it is taking all our power just to keep him under control. Anyone trying to guide his soul home could get torn to shreds, physically and spiritually."

Azerick screamed and the bed jumped several inches off the floor despite all the weight and force pressing down on it. With a primal shout loud enough to cause pain, Azerick bolted upright and threw off two of the three Chosen trying to hold him down. He dropped back onto the bed breathing heavily and stared at the ceiling.

Miranda tentatively reached out to him with a shaking hand. "Azerick, are you all right?"

"Miranda, he's gone!" Azerick shouted hoarsely.

"I know, Azerick. Daebian left. I do not know where he is."

Azerick thrashed his head from side to side. "No, not Daebian."

"Who then, who is gone?"

"The demon! Klaraxis is gone!" Azerick shouted, then manically laughed into his hands.

Daebian sat in the rope netting strung along the prow of the ship and idly made the gold coin dance across his knuckles. He had taken the coin from his father after he stabbed him. He made it balance between two knuckles and studied the stamped image of the tower with its three lightning bolts. It was his father's personal seal, an image to identify who he was and what he did. To Daebian, it was a token of his father's life, a debt he would one day collect.

"Sails, two points off the port bow!" the lookout shouted down from the crow's nest.

"Finally, things are getting interesting."

Daebian rolled out of the net, scanned the horizon for what he hoped were pirates, and stroked the black jewel set in the hilt of the soul blade.

To be continued in:

THE SORCERER'S DESTINY
Book Eight of The Sorcerer's Path

FROM THE AUTHOR

I hope you enjoyed this tale and will try my other works. Feel free to look me up on Facebook! You can also check me out on my website **http://brockdeskins.com/** where I write serial fiction, free for your enjoyment, and answer questions!

Author page:
https://www.amazon.com/Brock-Deskins/e/B005M6VQ1O

Facebook:
https://www.facebook.com/brocksbooks/

Twitter:
@brockdeskins

PLEASE <u>REVIEW</u> MY BOOKS (Especially if you liked it). Customer reviews are the primary means of enticing others to purchase them. I am dependent upon the sales of my books to earn a living that will allow me to continue writing stories that I hope bring you some measure of entertainment. Thank you for your support.

OTHER BOOKS BY BROCK E. DESKINS

The Sorcerer's Path is an epic fantasy series.

The Sorcerer's Ascension: Torn from a life of comfort and luxury, his family destroyed by political intrigues and aspirations, a young boy must quickly grow into a man before the deadly streets of Southport devour him. Follow Azerick through a page-turning adventure that pits him against thieves, thugs, murderers, and men of power that will stop at nothing to achieve their goals.

Azerick must fight just to survive, but for him survival is not enough. A hunger to avenge the wrongs committed against him burns deep within. But that is not all that lies within the young man. There is a power waiting to be unleashed that may be the key to achieving the justice and security he seeks--if it does not destroy him first.

The Sorcerer's Torment: Azerick flees The Academy but quickly falls prey to powerful beings that use his skills and power for their own amusement. What these creatures do not understand is the power of the young sorcerer's will and the lengths he will go to for vengeance. Despite becoming a prisoner, Azerick finds his first true love, but can he keep it?

The Sorcerer's Legacy: Azerick has found himself a home and tries to settle down. He takes on an apprentice and tries to put all the death and desire for vengeance behind him. But when the Rook finds him, Azerick is once again pulled back into Ulric's schemes. Knowing that all he has worked toward and everyone close to him is in danger as long as these schemes are ongoing; Azerick decides to put an end to it, once and for all.

The Sorcerer's Vengeance: After narrowly avoiding being killed in his own bed by the land's most feared assassin, Azerick leaves his school behind to find out who sent him and to put an end to the threat once and for all. Azerick's search will take him to the very pits of the abyss and back to unleash hellish fury upon those that threaten him.

The Sorcerer's Scourge: With the siege broken and Ulric dead, Azerick can finally relax, study his magic, and run his school in peace. Unfortunately, Jarvin's reign is far from uncontested and the true usurper decides to make his move. Jarvin escapes with help from an unlikely source—a vampire named Landrin who still clings tenaciously to his own humanity. While Azerick and a large force from North Haven race to save the king in exile, evil forces are preparing to unleash a nightmare upon the kingdom that may well destroy them all.

The Sorcerer's Abyss: Now the master of the Fifth Circle of the abyss, Azerick is challenged by another demon lord for supremacy. Azerick must face this threat as well as his innermost demons, all the while searching for a way to escape his hellish prison.

Ellyssa fears she is going insane as she plagued by nightmares of her capture and enslavement. Deciding the key to saving herself lies in the total destruction of the object of her fears, she embarks on a crusade to find and kill the slaver, Captain Jake, and eradicate the slave trade.

Ellyssa's nightmares and battles spill out onto the streets of North Haven and gains the attention of The Academy. Fearing Azerick's school is turning out rogue wizards, The Academy decides to hunt down and destroy the rogue and place the school within their control.

The Sorcerer's Return: Azerick has come back from the abyss in order to try to unite all the races against the return of the old gods who seek to destroy them and subjugate the few they allow to survive a brutal purging. However, fighting ancient gods may be the least of his troubles as he battles to save a fractured kingdom, a brilliant son traveling a dark path, and the splintered soul of his own humanity.

The Sorcerer's Destiny: Brutally purged of his demonic influence, Azerick continues the struggle of uniting the kingdom to face the coming of the Scions, ancient gods banished by the mortal races during the Great Revolution two thousand years ago. The fallen gods' prison is crumbling, and Azerick is powerless to stop them from breaking free and enacting their cataclysmic vengeance upon the world.

The humans must ally with the other races in a final battle against impossible odds while their entire world crumbles to the ground and is trod beneath the feet of an unstoppable foe. How can they set aside their distrust of each other when they fear the very person trying to save them?

Rise of the Order: Banished to the abyss after helping defeat the Scions and saving the world from eternal darkness, Azerick languishes in perpetual misery as Lord of the Fifth Circle. The denizens of his hellish realm view him as a usurper and outsider. The chaotic creatures form an alliance with one goal in mind: destroy Azerick Giles, but Sharrellan stands in their way.

A powerful spell tears through the demonic planes, and when the dust settles, the dark goddess is nowhere to be found. It is up to Azerick to return her to her seat of power, but he has a price: return him to his mortal form and send him home.

Back home, a vast empire is on a crusade to conquer the world, and it has set its sights on Valeria. Their goal is to unite the world under a single banner, eradicate the spawn infestation unleashed by the Scions, and replace the gods who they feel have forsaken them with their mystical rulers.

Can Azerick save the dark goddess from the clutches of her demonic subjects and become mortal once again? Will he have the power to protect his people from The Order if he does?

Descent Into Chaos: The Order has arrived in force, and the fate of Valeria, and perhaps all the world, is poised to come under their iron-fisted control. Azerick and Daebian are forced to flee Southport and make a contentious alliance when King Miles capitulates to the invaders. Reduced to insurgent warfare, Azerick and his allies attempt to battle The Order's vastly superior forces in a series of hit and run strikes, but the enemy legions may not be his biggest threat.

Princess Sylvian Attar, daughter to The Order's godlike emperor and empress, has taken a personal interest in Azerick. Herself a powerful sorceress, Sylvian hunts Azerick in hopes of removing Valeria's legendary hero from the battlefield thus sapping her enemies' will to fight. Azerick decides there is but one course of action he can take against this unstoppable foe. It was time to inject a little chaos into The Order.

Brooklyn Shadows is a modern-day vampire tale. Full of action and snarky dialogue, Brooklyn Shadows is an enjoyable read for anyone who enjoys the supernatural underworld and butt-kicking vampires.

<u>**Shrouds of Darkness**</u> (Brooklyn Shadows Book 1) Leo Malone has been a vampire for the better part of the twentieth century. Once a prominent Sherriff (vampire cop), he now earns his living as a private eye and occasional bodyguard for anyone that requires some serious protection. Leo is hired by the daughter of a mob accountant who has gone missing.

The fact that her father is also a werewolf has Leo following a trail of grisly murders that will lead him through a web of intrigue and conspiracy involving his fellow vampires and the local werewolves that make New York their home, all the while trying to keep one particularly determined cop off his back and himself out of jail. Leo is not some pretty-boy vampire that all the girls ogle over, but a hard-eyed, remorseless killing machine who does not take crap from anyone.

<u>**Blood Conspiracy**</u> (Brooklyn Shadows Book 2): While dealing with the aftermath of the failed vampire council coup, Leo discovers that the modified Cure has fallen into the hands of a black ops government project designed to create vampiric super soldiers. When the inevitable happens, the off-book Homeland Security operation forcefully enlists Leo to help them resolve the situation. Worse yet, he has to work not

only with an antagonistic werewolf named Meat, he is reunited with his hated creator, Lesile.

Primacy of Darkness (Brooklyn Shadows Book 3): Jack the Ripper, sadistic madman of old London, once thought long dead, has returned to New York in an effort to quench his thirst for blood and mayhem. When the city's vampire enclave finds itself insufficient to deal with a madman of Jack's caliber, Vincent, the enclave head, enlists Leo Malone to put the maniac down before he reveals the existence of vampires as he throws the city into the throes of chaos and terror. Leo soon finds that Jack is not the only monster with which he must contend. A ghost from his past has also seemingly crawled from its grave and seeks to put an end to him and the rest of his kind.

The Transcended Chronicles is the story of an outlandish young man as he goes from being a troublesome youth to one of the kingdom's greatest secret agents. Blessed (or cursed) with an amazing ability to both fight and abuse his body with every conceivable vice known to man, Garran Holt is either the kingdom's greatest hero or its biggest embarrassment.

The Miscreant (The Transcended Chronicles Book 1): Garran Holt is a troubled young man. Unable to tolerate his self-destructive ways, his mother sells him into indentured servitude as part of a work crew building King Remiel's new trade road. When mercenaries sent to disrupt the road's construction attack his work camp, Garran discovers an inner power capable of turning him into a warrior of unparalleled ability. When the leader of his work crew recognizes Garran as being one of the transcended (a fighter able to slip into the swifter currents of time), he is trained as an agent, one of the kingdom's elite spies. Crude, abrasive, and deeply committed to destroying himself with drugs, alcohol, and debauchery, Garran might be the kingdom's only hope against falling to The Guild, the powerful trade cartel bent on becoming the true and undisputed power in the land.

The Agent (The Transcended Chronicles Book 2): The Guild rules the kingdom through their puppet monarch, and Garran must race to save the last living heir to the throne before the powerful syndicate's assassins complete their extermination of anyone who could oppose them. Garran and Prince Adam Altena struggle to find allies in hopes of rescuing Adam's sister, who was forced to marry the usurper in order to prevent even the thought of rebellion, and raise an army capable of defeating The Guild. With The Guild now in control of Anatolia's powerful army as well as their legion of mercenaries, their future is grim. How can a disreputable agent and a deposed prince convince their neighboring rulers to oppose The Guild, an organization that has had them cowed for decades?

Empire of Masks is an exciting and explosive new series that takes place in the world of Hedon and takes you across the land of Eidolan where ships sail through the skies and men and women wage war with magic, swords, muskets, and cannons.

Highlords of Phaer (Book one of Empire of Masks): Born a slave, descended of kings, Jareen Velarius just wants to provide the best life he can for his family, but Eidolan is a realm that challenges even the most stalwart of souls. Caught between his masters and those brave or foolish enough to strike against them, Jareen struggles to reconcile his role as a dutiful slave with that of a man who desires to be free. His goal: to return his people to a life stolen by the highlords more than a millennium ago.

Auberon Victore, sorcerer, alchemist, son of a powerful overlord, and Jareen's master, creates an alchemic compound he is certain will change the world; he just does not know how. Jareen sees it for the weapon that could break the sorcerers' iron grasp wrapped around the necks of every lowborn in the empire. It will change the world, but not in the way his master desires.

Across the Tempest Sea, a mighty storm has raged for a thousand years, keeping a terrible, long-forgotten enemy at bay, an enemy whose cruelty knows no bounds. Only the perpetual storm and their fear of the sorcerer highlords keep the Necrophages from returning to Eidolan and cloaking the empire in death and darkness. But the tempest is waning, and the dissidents' freedom may well come at the cost of their total destruction.

Nightbird: The Great Revolution ended the highlords' tyranny two hundred years ago, but the legacy of that epic war, and that of the principal architects' descendants, lives on. With the highlords' death and their taking magic, as it was once known, to their graves, Eidolan fell into a time of darkness and its cities lived in isolation. However, some people, dubbed arcanists, discovered a new form of magic and the airships returned to the skies, rejoining the cities in trade as well as conspiracy, but a new darkness, more dreadful and deadly than any they faced before, is coming.

Kiera is a fifteen-year-old nightbird, one of many who flit about after dark, stealing whatever they can find in order to survive. She lives on a derelict airship in the poorest part of the city with Wesley, a young man who plies his trade as an escort to wealthy older women, and his little brother Russel, an autistic savant who communicates only through sign but who could secretly be the most powerful techno-arcanist the empire has ever known. Deep in debt to the underlord Nimat, Kiera dives into evermore dangerous schemes that put her at the heart of a secret war that could spell the destruction of not just the city, but the very empire.

Kiera is caught in the center of several factions on the brink of war. When she can no longer tell friend from enemy, there is only one side she can trust—her own.

Mourningbird: A creature of darkness lurks in the shadows of Velaroth, wearing the skin of its victims, and grips the city in terror. Dorian, a Necrophage bent on sowing chaos and paving the way for his people's invasion, has declared war on the humans of Eidolan, and there appears to be no one capable of stopping him.

Kiera's world is shattered by those who hold power, and she is forced to seek an ally. The nightbird is coming into power of her own, but can she stay alive long enough to seize it? Russel's behavior has taken a turn for the worse, and his actions have drawn the attention of those who would use his amazing talents for their own gain...and everyone else's loss.

The battle for Velaroth, and perhaps the world, has begun. Who will win? Who will live to mourn the dead? Will there be anything left for the victor to claim as their prize?

Standalone books

<u>**The Portal**</u> is a fun and exciting story of some less than popular teenagers that accidentally open a portal to a mystical land during one of their role-playing games. Drew, a dour and anti-establishment teenager, is pulled through and captured by evil creatures lying in wait on the other side. Now it is up to his friends and older brother to rescue him, but who will rescue Drew's captors from him?

<u>**Amelia (Battle for Ardentia)**</u>: Amelia is a precocious, ten-year-old girl with a powerful imagination. In her alter-ego guise of a demi-goddess warrior princess, Amelia fights against a powerful demonic sorcerer named Romut and his horde of monsters in a never ending series of battles to protect the people of her imaginary world. However, the true battle strikes home when Amelia is diagnosed with a brain tumor. Now Amelia must fight not just the evil living in her imagination, but for her very life.

ABOUT THE AUTHOR

    Brock Deskins was born in a small town located in rural Oregon. At age twenty, he joined the army and served as an M1A1 tank crewman, dental specialist, and computer analyst. While in the military, he became an accomplished traveler, husband, and father of three wonderful children. His military career completed, attended college to brush up on his skills as a computer analyst and gain new skills as a writer. Brock received his degree in computer networking and is now devoting his full time and limited attention span to writing.

BIBLIOGRAPHY

THE SORCERER'S PATH
The Sorcerer's Ascension
The Sorcerer's Torment
The Sorcerer's Legacy
The Sorcerer's Vengeance
The Sorcerer's Scourge
The Sorcerer's Abyss
The Sorcerer's Return

The Sorcerer's Destiny
Rise of the Order
Descent Into Chaos

BROOKLYN SHADOWS
Shrouds of Darkness
Blood Conspiracy

THE TRANSCENDED CHRONICLES
The Miscreant
The Agent

EMPIRE OF MASKS
Highlords of Phaer
Nightbird
Mourningbird

OTHER BOOKS BY BROCK E. DESKINS
The Portal
Amelia: Battle for Ardentia

Curious about other Crossroad Press books? Stop by our website:
http://crossroadpress.com
We offer quality writing
in digital, audio, and print formats.

Subscribe to our newsletter on the website homepage and receive a
free eBook.

www.ingramcontent.com/pod-product-compliance
Lightning Source LLC
Chambersburg PA
CBHW021441240626
47153CB00001B/233